HALLESWELL . . . . .

HALLESWELL HALL

LISA FULLER
AND
DAVID POVAH

Matador
9 De Montfort Mews
Leicester LE1 7FW, UK
Tel: (+44) 116 255 9311 / 9312
Email: books@troubador.co.uk
Web: www.troubador.co.uk/matador

ISBN: 978-1905886-890

Muse and Views Publications
www.museandviewspublications.co.uk

Typeset in 11pt Stempel Garamond by Troubador Publishing Ltd, Leicester, UK
Printed in the UK by The Cromwell Press Ltd, Trowbridge, Wilts, UK

Matador is an imprint of Troubador Publishing Ltd

Dedicated to the memory of our late mothers,
Eileen Tanner and Joan Povah

And to our many Internet friends worldwide.
Those Pasta reviews were great practise!

Foreword

Communication via the Internet has changed many lives and brought together people who would never meet in different circumstances. It was the Internet that brought David and I together and in the same context we started to write together. Those early attempts were made on a review site and before long we had started to write stories together.

I had found my writing partner and soon knew that I would like to write a book together. Ideas were tossed around but proved to be difficult. How could we "marry" our joint ideas?

After much thought we decided on a historical novel where we could use our different writing styles to cover a certain period in time.

As authors we were experiencing something new and exciting. Every single part of the collaboration has resulted from e-mail only. Just as I have seen David's characters, so he saw mine and they became ours to share.

The characters are not based on anyone living although many parts of the narrative consist of real places and people. (See the Index.)

Apart from some minor details, all the research for the book has been through the Internet. These sites were free to use and I wholeheartedly commend them to any aspiring author. The journey was long but well worth it.

Lisa Fuller

Five years ago I would not have even dreamed about writing a novel. Five years ago I would not have thought I had a book in me. That was before I joined a review site on a whim and met Lisa.

From little seeds do mighty oaks grow and the same was true for us, we started small, doing joint reviews on that site, but we grew and our goals and ambitions grew with us until just over a year ago we decided to put together a book of short stories. Once again it grew and as we wrote so the stories slowly became a novel.

We each have our own individual style of writing but they are not so different at heart and both styles have joined together to bring Halleswell Hall and the Meverall family to life.

We have lived with the Meverall's for a year now and they have become part of our lives as we have melded each one into their part of the history of Halleswell hall, characters that grew until they took on lives of their own. We even ended up referring to them by name and knowing what facet of their character we were discussing purely by knowing the character.

It is amazing to think that we have achieved what we have purely by E mail. Would our writing have turned out any different if Lisa and I had known each other in the "real world?" Who knows but I do know that we are immensely proud of what we have achieved.

It hasn't been easy, in fact it has been much harder than perhaps either of us had expected but we have grown into it and learned huge amounts. I think we are now both much better writers than when we first began this project, especially me and I have Lisa to thank for encouraging and pushing me into fulfilling my half of our dream that I hope you will enjoy.

David Povah

Acknowledgements

When we first came up with the concept of *Halleswell Hall* as a joint novel both of us had only a rough idea how we wanted our fictitious house to look. It had to be of late Tudor design and be surrounded by an ancient Wood with long gardens extending to a lake. Neither of us thought of the difficulty posed by the jacket cover until our book was accepted for publication.

Therefore we were both delighted when we found our vision in the Springs Hotel and Golf Club, the owners of the hotel have kindly allowed us to use this wonderful old house for our jacket cover.

Who knows, we could even write a theme for one of the hotel's murder/mystery weekends?

Cover image adaptation by Lisa Fuller.

PROLOGUE

BRANNON'S WOOD

Flurries of snow drifted gently in the vales, but over the hill fort the wind whirled around, piling up in drifts as high as a man's thigh. Spring was a long time coming in this high region of the Devonian lands. In the gathering gloom of late afternoon, shepherds trudged through the icy landscape in search of the early born lambs. Snow was to be expected in March, but not as heavy or prolonged as this storm. Smoke rose in the freezing air where wood could still be found to burn. If not for the great forest many people would have frozen to death over the long hard winter. Already game was hard to find as the wolves grew more bold and folk feared to go abroad without the men of arms acting as escort.

On the ramparts Eric huddled into his wet cloak and wished he hadn't been chosen for this, the longest stretch of duty. Surely no raiders would dare the coastal currents on such a stormy day? He would not dare to argue with Kai though. Ever since the Romans had left the land, more and more raiders sought to wrestle land where they did not just loot and plunder the villages. Their garrison was undermanned already with losses from the summer and autumn raids. Many of his men had perished during and after the battles. The flocks had scant time to breed again and many a calf had been lost in the birthing. It was almost as if there was an evil spell cast on them. He made the sign against the evil eye without thinking about it. The old gods had failed them, along with the gods of the Romans and slowly the druid religion was beginning to creep back again.

Stamping his cold feet to dislodge the carpet of snow, he heard the welcome sound of a housecarl bringing warm bread and a flask of the strongest brew. He would need the warmth before the night was through. He was halfway through his meal when a shout went up from the other sentry. Even through the sheets of white, he could see a light nearing the shore. What ship would dare to sail near the rocky cliffs and how could they kindle a light in such high seas? He would have to report it to Kai though and pray that it wasn't just a witche's light near the shore. Other men made light of such superstitions, but Eric has seen things before, sights to chill the very blood in the veins.

Padraig hung over the side of the little boat emptying the last drain of water from his already empty stomach. 'We are going to die,' he gasped out from his parched throat and salt-burnt lips. Brannon stood at the front of the boat, calmly peering in the direction of the shore.

'God will provide my son,' he said with that same quiet calm. 'If 'tis our time to die then soon we will sit at God's right hand.'

Another huge wave washed over the tiny vessel, but it merely spun around and once again faced towards the rocky shoreline. Brannon raised the makeshift lamp and by luck or good making it stayed alight in his steady hands.

From the shore another such lamp guided their path through the towering cliffs and the rocks that jutted out in the small bay.

Padraig crossed himself, wet hands brushing his sea-soaked garments, 'Master take care, 'tis some witchery bound on leading us astray.'

'Nay, do not be affright; some of Arturo's folk still live in this land. If my eyes do not deceive me, then 'tis just a maid, great must be her faith to venture out in the night. But we should offer thanks to God for her presence here tonight.'

Padraig was still wary; he did not understand this craft of the Cwmry that should have long since sunk. Neither did he believe that such light that guided them was not the work of the devil himself, even though they carried such a light themselves.

They had set out two days ago with a fair wind behind them and a sea as still as a millpond. Old Gruffyd had warned them of a storm to come, but Brannon was eager to make the trip and trusted as always in God's power to see them safe.

The light from the shore held steady and with one last mighty wave they plunged into the shallows. Strong arms reached out, and with Brannon's help, the craft was pulled up from the pounding waves and beached in a small cave.

Half dragged, Padraig managed to stumble to his feet but was led to where a fire burned high in another cave. Coughing and spluttering, he had no strength to protest when female hands took off his wet clothing and bundled him into warm furs. Brannon was already disrobing as if the presence of two females mattered not to him. Not a word was spoken until both had drained a large goblet of mead.

'Thank you kindly, Megan,' Brannon said to the younger of the two, 'and you, fair Dana, although you should not risk your health for the sake of us.'

Megan laughed, a gay sound in the dim light. Dana merely bowed low, her grey hair escaping from her covered hood.

'Kai will be here soon,' she said simply, 'already his men have mustered arms.'

'I think he will find us poor sport,' Brannon said, 'but mayhap you know more of this man than I?'

'He is a goodly man,' she replied, 'but he has suffered much from loss of men and still the raiders harry him every chance they can.'

'Then 'tis time we bring the faith to him, though I fear he may not take kindly to two poor pilgrims?' he said, his smile lighting up the worn face.

'I think you should go now, my ladies, I would not wish to bring trouble on you.'

'I think you will find that we are not without protection,' Dana said, as the light from the little silver cross caught in the firelight glow.

*

Kai was none to pleased to find followers from the new religion, but being a fair man he bade them welcome and offered them food and lodging. He was less inclined to overlook the women, his men were already muttering about witches. But he knew these two, mother and daughter, although they claimed no kinship with the great Arturo of legends, still, they came from his land. The village women went to them for birthing and minor ailments, and once the elder woman had set some kind of magic on the broken leg of one of his men. The seal oil lamps had caused some confusion at the beginning, but when it became known that it was a natural source of light then he could see the benefits of such knowledge.

The Christian men soon settled down in a clearing in the forest. Seasons passed by and a small but thriving community grew around them. For twelve moons no raiders came to the shores and some of his men went to hear the Christians speak. Kai made no move to stop it; they would soon turn their faces away when the raiders returned. But fate was about to step in and change their lives forever.

It started with a simple request from the man Brannon, to dig a well where the village folk could draw water. The request was welcomed. Long had the women and children traced the course of the forest streams to gather water for daily use. It seemed this man knew where the stream would yield water quickly and simply, by means of a well. There were plenty of volunteers to work with the two men. The harvest had been good that year and the herds had thrived. Food was stored against winter's season and Kai's wife was soon to bear him a child, a boy, if the gods favoured him. Girls he had aplenty, but his old wife had died in childbirth and he had taken a new, younger wife, as was the custom.

Another season passed by without raiders, still Kai drilled his men in combat. He took to walking through the woods and stopping in pretence to see how the well was progressing. Something about the calm surrounding the two men touched something deep inside him. The well was deep and many men carried the local stone to shore up the sides. Here and there he noticed that footholds had been cut inside the well and also little stone niches. Calling one of the men to him, he asked the purpose of such things. 'The Holy brothers say it will needed in times to come.' The man replied, and with that Kai had to be content. The well would be completed when his wife was brought to birthing. Peace settled over the valley and his heart was at ease.

The raiders arrived without warning. They crept up the coast hugging near to the cliffs and by the time they were spotted some of the herds had already been slaughtered for meat. The men clashed in battle and the villagers ran into the forest with their families. Many knelt in prayer at the small church raised by the Christian men. Whether it was the prayers or the depths of the forest no one knew, but the raiders were beaten back with few losses of life.

It was Frieda, his wife's maid that ran to Dana, although she was sore afraid the raiders would pick her up. The birth was not going well and mother and babe were in great distress.

Brannon caught her in his arms as he heard her screams. Dana was binding the wound of a man who had lost his arm in the fighting. Calling Megan from dressing a minor wound, he spoke low to Padraig who was almost as afraid as the women.

'This you must do, my son, draw water from the well and bring it to the house of Kai.'

'Master, what good is water now, surely the women have water to boil already?'

Brannon looked at his friend, he could see the fear in his eyes but God had spoken to him, 'This you must do or all our work here will be in vain, 'he turned away and ran through the heat of battle with the loyal servant Frieda by his side.

'Come, master Padraig, I will help you carry the water,' it was a child of about ten, one who had listened to the Christian men and believed the words he had heard.

The great bucket was filled to the brim and Padraig passed his hands over it in blessing.

On they ran, careful not to spill a drop, but was it too late?

The house was silent except for Brannon speaking the words for a soul about to depart this life. Entering he saw the woman, spent by the efforts of birth. Megan was weeping softly over a tiny blue-tinged child.

'Draw a cup for me and another for Megan,' Brannon said, as the boy hid behind Padraig.

Each one drew forth a cup and passed it to Brannon and Megan. Drop by drop the water was dripped into the mouths of mother and son. Prayers were said and tears flowed and then….

The baby cried and his flesh was pink and new. The mother stirred and held out her arms for her son.

'God be praised,' said Brannon and it was echoed by all who were present in that dwelling.

Years passed by and the story of the Holy Well became a legend. Tales grow in the telling and soon Brannon's forest became linked with the well. It was said by the goodwives that the presence of the well turned away the invaders and a time of peace and prosperity reigned over the land. Centuries later the forest and the surrounding land became known as Halliswell, the Holy well. It was said by many that the well would never run dry as long as there was one true believer in the Christian religion.

The cup that drew the water to save Kai's wife and child became an heirloom of the family and in time it too passed into legend. The villagers continued to draw water from the well and it was rumoured that the Holy Grail itself was to be found in the depths of the well.

Maidens went to visit the well in the hope that they would see a vision of their future husbands. Water that had been blessed by the surviving Christian monks was used to heal wounds of battle and folly.

Miracles still happened on occasion, a blind man would bathe his sightless eyes in the water and find his sight restored to him.

But then came the years of trouble across the land. Catholic fought with protestant believers as King Henry V111 sacked the monasteries, turning the monks into little more than beggars. The Holy Well became choked with weeds and the great oak trees hid it from sight. It passed into the mists of obscurity, lost to the faithful for many centuries.

Eventually a church was built in the village and Brannon became Saint Brannon. People came back to the faith, but where there is light, darkness still has one last foothold. So the last of the Druids and their priestesses kept the old faith and with it the rage built for those forced into hiding.

HALLESWELL HALL

The house stood on a hill, early April sunset casting a glow on the dull brown bricks, momentarily painting them in a benign pink wash. For a brief time the many gabled windows caught the fiery glow, sending back prisms of light almost as if they were winking at the couple standing arm in arm outside the gatehouse. The evergreen trees surrounding the house seemed to retreat a little in the evening sky. They drew the eye away, towards the nearby forest where late daffodils vied with yellow primroses to cast off the daunting appearance of the great old trees. Anyone with a fanciful mind would think the house was putting on this display in order to appear more welcoming. But then the sun sank and once again it became an ugly and forbidding old house, a mish-mash of architectural styles worn down over the centuries into a decaying grandeur.

Vivien shivered and her husband Graham placed a protective arm around her waist.

'What d'you think Viv,' he said, 'have we taken on more than we should?'

His wife stood silent for a moment. The house had more faces than she'd expected. For a while she had been almost mesmerised by its appearance, now she wasn't sure what to think.

'I don't know love,' she finally replied, 'I imagine it could be quite spooky here in the night.'

Graham looked at his wife. She was by far the steadiest woman he had ever known. She wasn't given to flights of fancy, neither was she afraid of anything. In fact, it was him who was indecisive, afraid to go out on a limb. Maybe the children flying the family nest had made her more upset than she'd previously shown.

'We can always pull out,' he said, 'buy another place not so far from civilisation.'

'Let's go inside and have a glass of wine and something to eat,' she said,' things always look better in the morning light.'

A few hours later they were sitting by a warm fire, replete from their meal and sipping at the last of the Chianti. The lodge was far more comfortable than it looked from the outside. Originally it had been part of the estate, probably where the gamekeeper had lived with his family. Over the years it had been modernised, only this room being left with an open fireplace and what remained of the old Tudor beams. It was a squat building, the open hallway lead into a comfortable parlour with every modern convenience. This room had survived centuries of change and if it was a bit draughty, still it exuded the atmosphere of days gone by. There was something cosy about sitting in front of a big log fire, something that appealed to both of them.

Another, smaller passage led to a modern kitchen, big enough to cook a mini banquet. The scullery had been made into a luxurious bathroom with a separate shower and Jacuzzi. Upstairs there were four bedrooms, another, smaller bathroom and a tiny storage space. Central heating kept the rooms warm; most of the tiny lead paned windows had been replaced by bigger ones that let in far more light. The roof was newly tiled and there was ample room outside for three cars to park. The agent for the National Trust had told them about previous caretakers leaving them in the lurch due to the draughty rooms and uncertain plumbing.

That had prompted the National Trust to update the building. They needed a couple that would stay and watch over the house until it was made safe for visitors. The work could take maybe two years to complete and after that the property would still need caretakers. The big house was a listed building, not grand enough to pull in many visitors but still too big to sell as a proper house. The post had been advertised all over the country, few people would be willing to take on such a place, isolated as it was from the nearest large town of Barnstaple. There was a tiny village about two miles away. Coombe Stratton was a pretty little village with rows of thatched cottages, a few main shops and some smaller ones given over to the tourist trade. From the Hall itself, only minor roads lead to the village. The local council were willing to widen the road if the proposed renovation of Halleswell Hall proved to bring in more trade.

Out of the many couples interviewed, Graham and Vivien Edwards had fitted the bill perfectly. Graham had sold his building company as a going concern and at fifty he was the ideal age (the added bonus of having a master builder on the site had not been overlooked). Vivien had been working for her husband as a secretary, business advisor and accountant as well. They had one older, married daughter and a son in his final year at university. Both had been raised in small towns and were used to the hustle and bustle of a busy town, but they were equally at home in the countryside. In the eyes of the interview panel they were steady, responsible people, not to be put off by the gossip of country folk. They had been looking for a house in the country after Graham's back problems had led to him retiring early, but both had missed working and answering the advert had seemed an ideal solution to their problems. The board had allowed them a three-week stay at the lodge; time enough to see if it suited both parties. Their own house in the midlands was on the market so the trial period left both sides with their options open.

Vivien woke in the night, unsure what had awoken her, normally she slept easily right through the night. Graham snored in his sleep oblivious to the world. Reaching out for her dressing gown she padded silently to the window. Some noise had seeped into her dreams, something vague that eluded her for the moment. Born and brought up in the country, the daughter of the local vicar, she expected the silence of the countryside to give way to nocturnal noises. The hooting of an owl or the bark of a fox hunting in the woods, perhaps that was what had disturbed her sleep.

The bedroom they had chosen faced towards the hall. They had chosen it for the big four poster bed that invited a bout of tender love-making. The memory made her smile; her dear husband could still surprise her after nearly thirty years of marriage.

Now, looking through the window, she felt slightly uneasy, a three-quarter moon had arisen and was bathing the forest behind the hall in a ghostly light. The windows of the Hall remained blank and brooding in the night. She could see the dim outline of the Hall, sinister in the pale moon glow. A wail rose from nearby and her heart thudded for a moment.

'Silly old sod,' she thought to herself, 'it's nothing but a vixen calling to her cubs.'

Still, she kept watch for a while. The Hall retained its gloomy visage, the ugly old chimneys now stark against the sky. The turrets of the Edwardian era seemed like a growth clinging to the beauty of the earlier, Tudor, facade.

'Thank God there were no gargoyles,' she thought to herself, that would have really spooked her. Perhaps it was the building itself that made her shiver as she had done earlier. She hated to see old buildings mixed up over the years as this one had been.

She went to turn away, her feet getting cold without her slippers on. Out of the corner of her eye she thought there had been a glimpse of light in the woods. She stood stock still for a moment but there was nothing in sight.

'Get a grip of yourself,' she said to herself, 'moonlight and night noises are nothing to be afraid of.'

Climbing back into bed she warmed her cold feet on Graham's back. He snorted once and then resumed his snoring. Sleep gathered her up in a bundle and by the next morning she had put the night's scare completely out of her mind.

It was a beautiful spring morning, one that comes rarely in April. They had awoken at the same time; years of getting up early had conditioned them both to waking at seven am. The country air had made them ravenous, over a cup of coffee they decided to make a real breakfast. Rattling around in the enormous kitchen was fun. Graham was like a teenager again, rushing around and juggling a frying pan with saucepans of scrambled eggs and tinned tomatoes on the go. Viv set the pine table with two place settings and made loads of toast.

'Eeeh bah gum lass, that were a right feast fit for a king,' he joked.

'Give over you old bugger,' Viv laughed at him. 'Just because I was born in Yorkshire doesn't mean we all spoke like that.'

It was an old joke they had shared since college days. She felt light-hearted, this move was doing them both a power of good and she resolved that nothing was going to spoil it.

'What shall we do today?' she asked him.

'Stay in bed all day,' he leered jokingly.

4

'Be serious darling, we should find out more about this place, after all, it could be our home for years to come.'

Right then,' Graham said, 've shall go to zee woods, and look over our domain.'

Viv laughed but somehow she didn't feel up to trudging through the woods today.

'As the lord and lady of the manor, I suggest we should go and look over the peasants,' she said trying to get into the spirit of the day.

'What a brilliant idea,' he replied, 'there's a pub I rather fancy trying, some real ale and a ploughman's lunch, sheer heaven!'

'No,' Viv wailed, 'I'm not watching you get pickled while I drive.'

'No need for that', he said, 'it's a one mile walk over the fields. I looked at the map last night, there's a common right of way. I guess the lord of the manor had it made so he could go and sport with the local maids.'

'You and your sordid mind,' Viv said, 'there were always common foot paths in those days.'

'Since when did you become the expert?' Graham said, mopping up the last of the tomato juice with another slice of toast.

'Since we decided to give this a try,' she replied, serious for once. 'I thought it best to do a bit of background research. Did you know that the name of this place was originally called Halliswell?'

'What's that got to with this place?' he said in the same serious tone.

'I looked it up, it means on or by a Holy well.'

Graham sounded quite intrigued, 'I never knew an old place could be so interesting, we'll have to ask the locals.'

'I wonder how people lived in those days?' she said.

'I guess the old house could tell a tale or two, ' he replied.

Viv had a sudden memory of the previous night, 'I don't expect we'll ever find out. Now how about getting ready for a good walk and a few pints of the local ale.'

'Race you to the shower,' he laughed.

'Not if I get there first,' she said, running in the direction of the downstairs bathroom.

It was late afternoon when Viv and Graham returned along the ancient pathway. The sun was still quite warm for that time of year and the hedges were already showing signs of an early summer to come. Viv was still deep in thought as she idly picked the last of the daffodils, the vetch and other wild flowers.

'Well that was an eye-opener, wasn't it?' Graham said referring to the conversation he had started with the locals.

'Maybe they do that with all newcomers?' but Viv didn't sound that convinced.

'Come on love, haunted houses and noises in the woods, it's straight out of a country yarn. I bet they're laughing at us right now!'

Viv was feeling a bit tipsy from the strong local cider but a few things she had heard had set her on edge. She had thought she had seen something in the house and later in the woods. But try telling that to Graham and he would laugh at her. Now she attempted a light tone, 'Then we'll prove them wrong, won't we. Tomorrow we'll look over the house and then the woods, that's if you aren't scared of course?'

'What, me? Scared of old wives tales? Graham the dragon-slayer, Graham the brave?'

'Graham the pissed,' Viv laughed as he fell against the hedge.

'My shoelace came undone,' he said, trying to appear nonchalant as he strode away from her.

'We'll see,' thought Viv.

The evening had passed pleasantly enough with both of them making a steak dinner and sharing a bottle of red wine. Now Graham was sprawled in front of the television and Viv was writing a letter to their son, hoping as always that she didn't sound like an old mother hen.

Graham started to snore and Viv put aside her reading glasses, 'Come on, old man, up the stairs to Bedfordshire.'

Sleepily he followed her and was soon snoring gently again, 'so much for a night of passion!' Viv thought, but she was getting very tired and soon drifted into a deep sleep.

This time the shriek was loud enough to wake them both. Graham peered at the radio alarm as if it was at fault, but the green light held steady at two am. Viv was shivering already, although the night was not that cold. Wrapped in their dressing gowns, both peered out of the window in the direction of the Hall and the woods beyond.

'It's the damn villagers playing a joke on us,' Graham said.

'No, look over there,' Viv said, pointing to a gap in the overhanging trees. From here she could see a shape that looked remarkably like one of the big cats, a Lion or a Panther, she thought. Then the moon came out from behind a cloud and she gasped as the light reflected tawny fur from the shape.

'What the devil...?' Graham spluttered.

'It's too big to be a fox,' Viv replied, 'but I swear that's no panther or polecat.'

Graham was inclined to agree, but he didn't want to alarm his wife any more than necessary.

'Remember that piece in the paper a few years back?' he said, 'people reported sightings of a large animal, much like a panther on Exmoor?'

'But Exmoor is miles away and that's no panther.'

'Maybe it just looks bigger than it really is?' he said as the shape moved back into the trees.

Both watched for a while longer, but there was nothing to disturb the night. Eventually they turned away and Graham made them both a hot toddy liberally laced with whiskey.

'Tomorrow we go exploring,' he said, 'and if I find someone's playing a prank on us I'll get the authorities in.' Numbly Viv nodded, but something told her it wasn't a prank. She wouldn't leave without a fight though; already the old house was working its magic on her.

'The house first, the woods later,' she said and nothing could persuade her otherwise.

Despite the interrupted sleep, both felt ready to tackle anything the following day. Once more they ate a hearty breakfast before preparing for their outing. Wearing stout shoes and carrying a torch they walked towards the Hall, the sun now dodging in and out of the cloudy sky. Graham walked up the large steps and turned the key in the lock, surprisingly it opened quite easily.

'Come on Viv, looks like somebody has been here quite recently, maybe the builders?'

'They aren't due until next week,' she replied, 'remember we have to agree by then whether we'll stay or not?'

'Well maybe it was someone from the National Trust, but let's get on with it.'

Her first glimpse of the inside of the house took Viv completely by surprise. Although it was dusty, the great hall and the stairs leading above were a rich dark brown and the light poured in from the high windows. Then it was Graham's turn to look surprised as he saw the newel-post with its carving of Eve. Running his hands over the carving he looked at Viv with something near to awe.

'Look at this?' he said, holding out his hand to display only the lightest touch of dust.

'This has to be late Tudor, done by a master craftsman. It's completely untouched by graffiti as well; I thought soldiers were stationed here in WW2?'

'Maybe they were as fascinated by her as you?' Viv said, somewhat jealous of the beautiful woman. 'We have loads more to look at, so let's get going.'

After nearly an hour both were ready to take a break. The interior of the house was far more welcoming than the exterior, but they put that down to the fact that very little had been changed inside for centuries. A lot of the larger pieces of furniture were left intact, as were many of the paintings. Viv had not expected the paintings, so took her time looking over them. Apart from a few, she decided that the family had all been exceptionally good looking, even by today's standards. One had really caught her eye. It was a beautiful work of art but the subject matter was unusual to say the least. The artist had captured a rare moment, with the swan prominent in the foreground and the hint of the house and wood in the background, the early morning sunlight just peeking through the mist. Looking closer she gasped at the name of the famous artist and wondered briefly if it was truly the original. Somehow she felt as if they were both trespassing and needed to get some air.

'No more exploring today' she told her husband, 'we'll leave the woods to tomorrow.'

Graham was more than happy with that, trudging through muddy woods wasn't his idea of fun, besides; there was an afternoon of television to watch and a football game he was dying to see.

'Beer in the fridge and a pizza to defrost,' said Viv as she was about to leave.

'Going on another field trip?' Graham asked as he saw her with the car keys in hand.

'Just a bit of research on the house,' she said, planting a quick kiss on his cheek,

'I thought I'd have quick look around that old church, maybe dig up some Meveralls?'

'Better take the spade them,' he quipped.

'Right, that's it, no lobster for you tonight.

'Sorry honey. If it's lobster then dig up whatever you want to.'

The car coasted easily down the steep incline to Braughton, where Viv had been told was the church of Saint Brannon. Here she hoped to find answers that would decide whether they would stay or leave. Parking the car was easy and she set off on foot to the church, where she had arranged a meeting with the local vicar.

The church itself was quite old, she soon decided, but it had an aura of peace and calm. She had arrived a little early hoping to look over the old church and was surprised to find it was unlocked. Entering the church she stopped for a moment and dipped her fingers into the font, 'once a vicar's daughter, always a vicar's daughter,' she thought, but then she saw the window and for a while could see nothing else.

Sunlight dappled the figure, but this was no ordinary stained glass window, but a work of art. She saw the plain robed monk in his brown robe holding a cup of finely made silver design. Although plain as opposed to some great windows, she felt as if he would suddenly step out of the window and hold his hand out to her.

'I see our Saint has had a profound effect on you,' the voice came from behind her.

Turning slowly she saw the smiling face of the local vicar.

'He does tend to have that effect on some people,' he said, and holding out his hand introduced himself as Martin Boyd. She took the warm hand in hers and introduced herself.

'Ah, you are the new custodians of Halleswell Hall,' he said.

'I must apologise for the absence of my husband,' she replied, 'but this was my own idea.'

'And you are looking for answers? I can help a little, but what you make of it must be your decision,' he said.

'Come, my dear lady, my housekeeper can soon serve us tea and a scone, the vicarage is nearby.'

Gladly Viv followed him, something about the window and the silver cup had touched a vague memory, though for the life of her she couldn't bring it to mind.

Later Viv found herself back on the road to Barnstaple and heading for the nearest fishmongers, where she bought some fine lobster and a pint of prawns. The vicar had raised more questions than answers, but now she felt more determined than ever. Looking around for a good off-licence she bought a few bottles of white wine. Tonight she would tell Graham that she wanted to stay and if the future might be a little rocky, still she would see it through.

THE FOUNDING OF HALLESWELL HALL

Robert Smyth sat at his desk in the private chamber of the Black Boar Inn. Earlier he had partaken of a sumptuous meal of venison and local fare. His ill mood had been somewhat assuaged by the good meal and the contents of nearly a full bottle of a good Flemish wine. Now he faced the onerous duty of receiving Master Jordayne in his private quarters. He considered ordering a cask of the best brandy, but thought t'would be wasted on his unwanted guest. 'Master Jordayne, pah, more likely plain Jordan,' he thought to himself. Still, he had his own good name to consider so he reached out and pulled the bell to summon one of the maids. Ordering a cask of the inferior brandy and two clean glasses he prepared for the arrival of this unwanted guest.

As usual he felt his temper beginning to rise as soon as the merchant walked through the door without pause to consider announcing his presence by knocking. Standing to his full height he greeted his guest, 'good morrow, Master Jordan, I trust you are in good health?'

The man had the ill grace to seat himself with scant reply, ''Tis Jordayne, you fool, do I have to repeat myself constantly?' he said.

'My apologies Sir, I find the French tongue somewhat difficult to remember,' Robert laughed inwardly, he was proficient in five languages but this buffoon was unlikely to know of that.

The man helped himself to a large glass of brandy and Robert took his time regarding the man. Truly he was a fool, a large florid man with the complexion of one who supped his drink rather too often. Today he was dressed in the height of fashion, but on him it looked merely foppish. There was a suspicious stain on his shirt, possibly a spillage of best claret. His sparse hair was powdered heavily and the large beak of a nose jutted prominently.

Robert instinctively smoothed down his own thick hair, unpowdered as nature intended. Pouring a small glass of brandy he awaited the purpose of the visit. It was not long in coming,

'Master Smyth I must insist you peruse the plans again, those rabble you have hired to build my house are loath to obey my instructions.'

'Those rabble, as you call them, are the finest workmen in England, the carpenters alone have worked for the Queen herself and the masons are waiting on finishing this house of yours to work on a new cathedral. Pray how have they displeased you now?' Robert could not keep the anger out of his voice. How he longed to send this merchant away, but he was offering ready money and in a land where credit could stretch over many a year, it was not a commission he could turn down lightly.

'I have no complaints with the house, it is, as you said it would be, a fine construction, but the men will not complete the carving to my satisfaction.'

'Ah, twass the carving,' Robert thought, he had expected something of this nature.

'Allow me to go through the plans with you again,' he said, trying to keep the contempt out of his voice.

Smoothing the interior plans on the desk Robert mentally prepared for yet another battle.

'Here,' Jordayne stabbed his finger on the plans.

'I asked for fine carving on the great stairs rising from the hall. Your men refuse me the making of the Saints. Also they refuse more than the plain Tudor rose when I asked for a full coat of arms,' the merchant's face flushed in temper.

Taking a deep breath Robert prepared once again to defend the carpenters.

'Master Jordayne, we have discussed this before now. The queen has but lately come to the throne and although she is inclined to be lenient now, she could easily take offence at any form of popery. As to the matter of the Tudor Rose,' he went on quickly anticipating another outburst, 'such decorations are meant to be subtle. If the queen were to honour your house with a visit, then mayhap she would find such elaboration of design a trite vulgar?'

'Aye, of course I see it now,' the merchant had been swayed by the mention of the Queen's visit, as Robert had planned it so.

As if the queen would ever step foot in this ugly merchant's house, no matter how fine it would be.

'Are we in agreement then,' Robert said, 'a tasteful design of Eve being tempted by the snake, or mayhap a carving of a noble gentlemen as yourself?'

The design was agreed with no further ado, pompous though this merchant may be, he knew that his men were skilled in carving and what man could resist Eve draped tastefully as the final touch to the grand stairs?

Simon walked around the great house with his father, Robert. Dearly though Robert wanted this first son of his to follow in his footsteps as an architect, he could see that the boy was more at ease with the carpenter's trade. The house was indeed very beautiful, rising from the lower slopes of the hill; it still commanded excellent views over the countryside of Devon. Local stone had been used for the foundations and the finest masons had dressed the brick-work. The old forest had yielded up the great oaks, which were the mainstay of the building, and roofers had finished their work, the great chimneys reaching proud to the sky.

Sunlight glittered from the tall windows of the great hall and where the two sides of the building stretched out to bring the building into proportion, smaller, lead-paned windows added to the grand design.

While an army of gardeners laid out the formal gardens, father and son wandered through the house, remarking on the final touches needed to make this a tribute to their joint skills.

Although Robert prided himself in giving the same attention to a minor house as to a grand mansion, even he was taken aback by the sight of the great hall.

The original plan had been for a smaller hall, some thirty by twenty feet, but Simon had seen the lay of the land and using his instincts had suggested a grander hall, some fifty by thirty feet. The wood glowed in the light, a rich dark brown with the great stairs reaching to the gallery above. Already the finial had been craved by Simon, now awaiting the final touch. From the tree of the Garden of Eden, Eve stretched out her hand to grasp the forbidden fruit. Her own hair draped the carving of the body, suggesting the curves rather than the shapely form. But it was the face that drew attention. It was the face of an angel, innocent as the dawn yet proud without haughtiness.

13

'My son, where did you find such a model?' Robert asked, knowing that even the best of artisans needed a muse, 'she must in truth be a noble lady?'

'I would wish it so father, but she is just a maid to the merchant's fat daughter.'

Robert laughed, his son saw clear, but the face of this maid troubled him. This carving had been made with love and no mere maid however fair, could be a bride to his son. Craftsman though he was by trade, Simon came from a goodly family. They could trace their ancestors back to the ancient Saxon kings of Britain. 'It must be a whim,' he thought, and sought to change the subject.

'Are the butteries finished?' he asked Simon.

'Aye, father, and stocked as well, what say you to a drop of the best local ale?'

Only the locals and a few favoured people knew the little clearing in Brannon's Wood, but Simon had won the hearts and minds of the small community. When the merchant, Jordayne, had received permission from none other but the Queen herself, it was feared that the lands around Stratton would be levelled for the building. Simon's father had suggested the location of the house on an earlier building site that few now remembered. It was a goodly position, looking seawards in the distance on one side and facing the nearby lands of the Meverall family on the other. There had been a village and smallholdings on the level ground near the forest as long as folks could remember. It 'twass said that once a great lord held all the lands, mayhap Arthur himself. Others said 'twass the Christian brothers that first settled here. However that may be, the villagers tended the land and paid a small levy to the magister.

The evening light was touching the trees with fiery glow when Rebecca finally arrived. Simon drew her into his arms and they sank down onto his spread cloak.

'I feared for you, my dearest one,' he said, running his hands through her lustrous dark hair.

'Mistress Amelia kept me long,' she replied, 'tonight they dine with Lord Meverall and no matter how I tried I could not lace her corset to suit her.' She replied with a hint of laughter in her voice.

'Twould take half the Queen's entourage to do that,' he laughed back.

'Do not jest, my love, if it was known I had left the inn then all would be lost.'

Simon knew the truth of her words. Prentice though he may be to the best craftsman and father, the fat merchant could dispose of his slaves as he saw fit to do. Though Rebecca was a maid to the merchant's daughter, in truth he owned her body and soul. His dear Rebecca was not just a maid; she was also a Jew without family to speak for her. Master Jordayne had borrowed heavily from Rebecca's father to fund his ships for trade. When the debt was called in, Aaron had been set upon and beaten to death leaving his daughter without kin. The merchant claimed to take her in out of piety, but all knew he lusted for her body. Only the presence of his daughter, Amelia, kept him from her bed.

Simon fought his rising anger; Jordayne was in the Queen's favour now, bought by cargoes of rare spices and stolen Spanish gold. Jews were tolerated for their art of making money, but slaves they were and would always be.

'My love, I have a favour to ask of you.'

'Ask and it shall be granted,' he replied, loving her more than ever.

'Do not ask me to sit for the carving again, already the master hungers for me. You have merely added to his insatiable appetite for power and greed.'

'Rebecca, beloved, I want the whole world to see your beauty; I swear now that this carving will bring men to their feet for all time.'

'Simon, dear heart, I have no need of immortality as long as I have your love,' She replied simply.

'Ah dear God, what are we going to do,' he said, his heart aflame with love and fear.

'I will find a way, 'he promised, 'as God is my judge.'

Halleswell Hall was finished in the September of 1561 and within two months it was nearly furnished. Many disagreements ensued over the naming of the house, but Jordayne was swayed by the Meveralls' whose knowledge of the lands around was formidable. Halliswell had been the common name for the ancient hill

15

fort, but no holy well could be found, so Halleswell became its name. In his pursuit of further fortune and a noble name, Jordayne sought to marry his daughter Amelia to Edward, the older son of the Meverall family. In some ways it was advantageous, the Meverall family could trace their lineage back to Norman times. The family was prosperous but there was a stigma attached to their name. Staunch supporters of the Catholic faith, they had to be seen to conform to the Protestant faith, although it was said they still kept a family priest. Queen Elizabeth was known to be capricious although she outwardly tolerated both faiths. Edward was a handsome man but readily accepted his bride-to-be knowing that he could still keep his women, of which he had many.

Amelia was content with her lot; her father's health was poor, with frequent attacks of gout keeping him confined to the house. In the following months her father decorated the house richly. The plaster walls were draped with Chinese silk hangings; carpets from the Orient that had been held in storage adorned the polished floors of the great hall, while each bedroom had its own heavily draped bed. Only one thing marred the perfection, the carving of Eve was much admired and Amelia knew whence the model came. In vain she pleaded with her father to hire another maid, but on this he was adamant, Rebecca was to stay. It pleased her greatly to keep Rebecca as her own personal maid, dressed in plain clothes with her features hidden behind an old-fashioned bonnet; she delighted in taunting both Rebecca and her father.

To Rebecca life was a constant battle of wits. As the season of Yule drew near, a great ball was planned to announce the betrothal of Amelia and Edward. She yearned to see Simon again, but the gossip amongst the servants let her believe he was now working on a grand project with his father. In her few private moments, the master tried again to seduce her, but was held back by Amelia's demands. In her heart she felt betrayed by Simon and dreaded the day when her mistress married and went to live with her new husband and family. She would not be needed then; the tales of Edward's women had reached even her sheltered ears.

Fate was unkind to her on the days leading up to the ball. Her mistress was to be dressed by a new French maid and the master had ordered that she be dressed in a style befitting her status as the new housekeeper. She would become little more than a common whore.

'Simon, dear heart,' she cried into her pillow, 'Come soon or I must take my own life.'

The dress was beautiful, but when she tried it on she knew instantly the effect it was meant to make. The underskirt was pure white, while the mantle itself was white as well. Delicately beaded with small pearls, it glittered in the soft candlelight. The neckline was discreet, merely hinting at the mounds of her full breasts. With no other trace of colour she would look as virginal as the carving of Eve that Simon had modelled on her alone. The French maid fussed around her, now lifting her hair and looping it into coils with a few strands curling around her face. Unlike the court fashion, her neck was left bare and made her feel as if she was undressed. She heard the footsteps behind her and her heart quivered in fright.

'Ah you are beautiful,' the master said, lifting her face to see the slim line of her neck.

'Hold still my dear, I have something to compliment such beauty, 'he breathed hoarsely fixing a diamond necklace around her throat.

'It was my dear wife's favourite,' he added, and she drew back as the brandy fumes almost overpowered her senses.

'You will greet the guests,' he demanded, 'then later you shall come to me.'

Rebecca was trapped in a nightmare with no escape. She took her place at the foot of the grand stairs, all too aware of the carving behind her. Yet how could she fail to be proud when her dear Simon had made of it a thing of beauty? Proudly she held her head up high and there was no man there that night who was not swayed by her great dignity. Amelia was furious, beside Rebecca she looked like an overdressed high class whore, in her pink underskirt and her mantle of burgundy and gold. Her stiff collar made her neck ache and she swore to get even before the night was through.

Rebecca had her own plans though. Flirting with the Master was dangerous, but by making sure he ate little and topping up his drink he was soon in a drunken maudlin state. Daring to be bold, she danced with him, making sure it was energetic enough to make him thirstier. Soon he was in a state of near collapse and it was then that she made her move.

'My pardon mistress Amelia,' she said, 'but I should not be here, pray give me leave to go to my room?'

Amelia was delighted, she would have the girl beaten in the morning, but for now there was Edward waiting for her.

Rebecca ripped the dress from her body, hating the feel of it. She dressed quickly in an old grey skirt with a mantle in the same hideous colour. She had drunk little this night, but now her resolve was weakening. Quietly entering the Master's bedroom, she took the bottle of brandy and drank a full glass. It burnt her throat but gave her the courage she needed. Stowing it away in a wicker basket, she added a thick cloak and donning her sturdy boots, she let herself out of the servant's door.

It was dark in the woods but her feet took her without err to the clearing where she and Simon had shared their snatched moments of happiness. She would rest here awhile before moving on to the sea and blessed oblivion. She bent her head in prayer, what she was about to do was a mortal sin, but she could see no escape. As she prayed she felt a calm surrounding her and then…. A light, a golden light came from a thicket nearby.

Cautiously she moved forwards, aware of something greater than she could ever have imagined.

'My daughter, why do you despair when God's love is all around you?'

The voice was unexpected but there was no fear in her heart.

'Come this way child, there is something you should see.'

Gladly she followed the voice, so soft, so understanding. Her feet trod on the ground, but her spirit soared. The light was coming from a well, deep it looked yet nearer than she imagined.

The man stood in front of her, robed all in brown,

"Will you drink from the well?' he said, offering a plain goblet filled with clear water.

'Gladly I will,' and she took the cup from his hand, draining it in one long swallow.

'Go now in peace, daughter of God, walk to the shore and take up your life again.'

She walked in a dream, never stumbling until she reached the shore. There was a small ship and a man standing by.

'Rebecca, dear heart, I have come for you,' and she smiled at her beloved Simon as he took her hand and led her aboard.

The disappearance of Rebecca became another legend. It was said that she vanished in a puff of smoke, but the villagers knew better and wished her well. Master Jordayne died of the drink and Halleswell Hall became a part of the Meverall estate. Amelia bore five children, two boys and three girls. Henry, the elder inherited the Meverall estate, but it was Thomas, the second son, who took Halleswell Hall for his own. Long he looked at the figure of Eve and wondered what had become of the model woman. Great was her beauty, but it was the heart and soul of the mysterious woman that called to him. Somehow he knew she was still alive and hoped she was happy wherever she had gone. But that's another story.

BETRAYAL AND REVENGE

The roan stallion tossed his proud head, spraying droplets of sweat as he slowed to a canter, while Ned, the groom, pulled him up short at the entrance to the clearing. Through wind and rain they had covered many leagues but at last had reached their destination. Still the stallion whickered softly, for despite the aroma of calm in this most hallowed of places; he could sense danger in the area. Ned slid from the saddle and hurried to his destination, while the wind howled around and the rain beat down on his travelling cloak.

Inside the clearing it seemed calmer and he stopped to catch his breath. Drawing a waxed-lined bundle from his clothing, he surveyed the scene for a brief moment, before hastily drawing the bucket up from the well and perching on the side, he slipped silently inside. Drawing back the secret stone, he placed the bundle carefully inside, replacing it as he found it. The stallion whickered once again, Ned looked anxiously around but sensing no danger, he led the stallion away and considered what to do next. He could not go to the hall, but maybe he could find a place for the night in the village. First though he had to warm his bones and drew the flask of brandy from his cloak.

Swallowing a large draft, he never even heard the swish of the blade before it reached his throat, and then he was falling into darkness.

Margaret paced the floor uneasily, her thoughts on her husband and her two vulnerable young children. Charles had been gone a long time now and she feared for his safety in these volatile times. Charles was not a popular king and his namesake, her dear husband, was too embroiled already in the service of his King. Halleswell Hall seemed far enough away not to draw attention, but still she worried about the family connection with the last of the Meverall family at Winterbourne House. Henry's son James was nigh on his deathbed, and with Sir Matthew Rothford married into the female side of the family, only Charles and her son James stood before Rothford inheriting both estates.

Rothford swayed with the wind. Sometimes following the king, but his allegiance lay where the power was. Margaret both feared and loathed him. His lovely, but gentle wife Helen, could never stand up to him, and what could she herself do, married to a true Meverall son?

'How the wind howled tonight,' she had half expected some communication from her husband, but in this foul weather no message could come direct to her. She feared for him naturally, but also for James and Jessica, their two young children. Already Jessie was becoming a beauty and it had not gone unnoticed when some of Cromwell's troops had paid them a surprise visit.

Confiding then in Charles, she had voiced her worries, but this had fallen on deaf ears. Her husband was more concerned with Cromwell's gathering following, and all his mind was bent towards the salvation of his king.

'Milady?' Her old servant Daisy had slipped quietly into the room.

'Can you not sleep either?' she replied.

'It wor the lights as woked me,' Daisy always lapsed into the local dialect when she was flustered.

'I have seen no lights,' she answered, but why then was she still awake and pacing the floor?

''Tis Brannon's lights,' the servant whispered, 'sometimes 'tis a blessing, others a warning.' Margaret was mindful of the legends surrounding the well, and the way the country folk saw omens around it, though few knew where the old well was hidden.

'Come now, faithful friend, let's get you back to bed, your hands are trembling with the cold.'

'Nay, milady, it's through fear I tremble so. You know this as well as me.'

Margaret knew the truth of the words. Had not Charles shown her the holy well and the secret hiding place? Mayhap he had left some kind of message this night, but fear of the woods was keeping her away.

'We will look in the morning,' she replied decidedly, 'this is not a night to be abroad'

'Yet I fear that it's a clear warning mistress, can't we send someone to look?' Daisy looked troubled and with reason.

'There is no one to send, only stable lads and I will not have you venturing abroad on such a night as this,' Margaret was also deeply troubled but could not let it show.

'I'll take my leave then; milady, but I fear this night's work.' Daisy shuffled off, her back bent with worry and years of toil.

Margaret looked in on her sleeping children, brushing a lock away from Jessica's fair face. Next she cast her gaze over her only son, James, so nearly a man but still with that innocent look that said he was but a step away from childhood. Even in sleep his hands were clenched into fists. Denied the approval to follow his father, but yet untried and tested, his instructions had been to stay behind and protect the family at all costs. All her instincts told her that she should take them all to safety, but who could she now trust, with each neighbour looking to their own safety in these turbulent times?

Daisy sank into the chair; there would no sleep for her tonight. Evil was abroad and not even Brannon's blessings could help them now. If only she were young again, but she couldn't even remember her age. 'Long past three score years and ten,' she thought. Aye, they had allus thought her dim, but she knew more than she could ever say. A single tear trickled down her face and caught inside the wrinkles on her old face. She remembered the beatings she had taken as a child when she fell down and said things that branded her as a witch. Once she had nearly bitten off her tongue but still nobody cared, not until Master Thomas had come back from that awful battle at sea. Her old eyes softened as she remembered him then, limping still from the wound in his leg where he had fought those Spaniards and gained a knighthood from the Queen herself.

Gently he had lifted her from the dust and held her until the dark dreams had gone away.

'Who is this child's mother?' he had said, and her mother had come forth with head bowed, expecting to be beaten in turn.

'Sir she is nothing, a curse on her family and a burden to be born; yet she's a good girl, polite an' a good worker.' Even now her mother sought to turn disadvantage into gain.

'Of what age is this child?' he spoke curtly.

'Ten years old, Sir, an' as good as gold except when she has these yere fits.'

Daisy kept quiet, as far as she knew she was about seven or eight, but held tight in the master's arms it didn't seem to matter.

'So old enough to go into service?' he said and then wiped the blood from her face with his own kerchief.

'Long past the age Sir, but what can us poor folk do with such a blighted child, God should have taken 'er long ago.'

'Then I'll take the child now, if that be your wish?'

Daisy sighed, that were so long ago now and the Master long since dead. She had loved him so and just being near to him were enough for her. Even when he set his sights on that woman from the village, that Jayne, still she covered for him, knowing by the sight granted to her that he would never love another. Aye she had cared for them both, though it nigh on broke her heart. First when Jayne had given birth to a strong man child and later on with his weak wife Catherine, bought an paid for and her dying in childbirth with Master Charles.

Still she cared for the family, casting her eyes down, for much is spoken before one who is supposed to be touched in the head.

Margaret knew, of course, 'twere no use hiding from her keen eyes. The falling fits only happened now an then, but Margaret had heard things, and knew them to be true. Why could she not listen now, when everything screamed danger to her?

The sun had barely reached the horizon before Rothford appeared with a group of men and her husband's favourite stallion. Behind them another group of men held a bier, and for one moment Margaret's heart nearly stood still. Now she had to stay calm, as Daisy had warned her she must do.

'I am feared that we bring bad news to your door.' Rothford said with only the slightest touch of regret in his voice. 'May I come in?' he said, affecting a superior tone.

'I am shocked that such a gentleman as you should rouse a lady from her bed at such an ungodly hour,' she answered placidly.

'This is not an occasion to stand on ceremony,' he said curtly.

Margaret turned away, 'my old nurse will see you into the parlour, but you must wait on my dressing, cousin, for I have my reputation to think of.'

Daisy led him into the parlour, but offered neither food nor drink, 'let him stew in his own juices,' she thought.

'Come here old woman,' he commanded.

'I mun help the mistress to dress, sor,' and with that she scuttled away.

Rothford was angry; the house should be in uproar, especially since he had Charles' favourite horse in full view. Yet he was being treated as less than a tradesman. Banging his fist on the table he resolved to bring the house to its knees and then take the greatest prize of all, the lovely Jessica, so full-blooded, so spirited, when his own wife was such a milksop that he had soon tired of her.

Damn it all, he thought to catch them unawares, but here they were acting as if nothing had happened at all. Catching sight of a young maid he ordered that wine be brought to him.

Margaret entered the room and dismissing the maid poured wine for them both.

'Now cousin, what can I do for you? I trust dear Helen is in good health?'

'Stop acting like a fool, you saw your husband's horse, does that not worry you?'

'You have me at a disadvantage, sir, I hear hammering on my door and I recently risen from my bed, pray tell me if ought is amiss?'

Rothford was losing patience, 'my groom was abroad early this morning and he found the roan stallion wandering, dragging the reins behind him. Naturally he called for me knowing that this is one of Charles' prized stallions.'

Margaret folded her hands carefully to disguise the tremor of her hands, 'He is, but Ned was exercising him yesterday while Charles is away on matters of state business. Very likely Ned had too much ale and is sleeping it off, he will be reprimanded if such is the case.'

'Then cousin, it is my unlucky duty to inform you that the body of your former groom is outside with my men. It appears that his throat was cut.'

Margaret jumped up and spilled the contents of her wine glass down her gown. 'No, it cannot be so; he had no enemy in this world!'

Rothford was taken aback; her distress was clearly visible and could not have been feigned.

Now she was sobbing, but made no question that would have showed any duplicity.

'Mayhap he was robbed? He enquired.

'A groom robbed? Sir you obviously know how much a groom earns? Or do you pay gold to your men?'

He had no answer, he had hoped for further question, anything to show that she was aware the groom was carrying a message from her husband. Could it be that his spies were wrong. They had found no message on the body when they slit his throat and he had been told that the man was dripping wet at the time. No, he could never have got to the hall and back again in the time his men were watching the house.

'Then cousin, can I be of any aid to you in this time of trial?' he had to be seen to show the proper responses.

'Thank you cousin, but this man had a wife and children too; James will see he has a proper Christian burial.'

It was a dismissal, but he had to make one last try.

'These are troubled times, surely now you can see the sense in letting Jessica come to our home? Helen would welcome the company and we would take good care of her?'

'Jessica will stay here with James and I, Charles will be home soon and what should we fear?'

Damn, but he admired her even as he longed for her daughter. He knew that Charles was in league with the Royalists and soon he would get his just reward.

James stood before the coffin, his head bowed as if in prayer, but deep inside his pulse was racing and once again he longed to be doing something else, even as he felt for the widow and her children. He was nearly a man at seventeen years old and more than anything he wanted to be with his father fighting for the same cause that killed the groom. His duty was clear, he was the sole representative of the Meverall family, but he did not like leaving the women alone at this time. In his mind he could see them now. His mother, her chestnut hair falling around her shoulders as if she were still a lass such as Jessie. His father, so upright, but kindly, dealing out justice with a firm, but fair hand, no wonder the villagers adored him so much. And then there was his sister Jessie, so proud and wilful, with a fiery temper to match her reddish-golden hair.

The blow of what could only be danger took him completely by surprise. He had seen Daisy in one of her fits and he respected the gift and burden they bestowed on her. But now he knew his family were facing that same great danger and it shocked him to the depth of his soul. Making his excuses he leapt onto his horse's back and pushed the stallion as fast he dare on the uneven path.

Galloping through the trees, his clothes and hair torn by brambles, still he rode on, the sweat running in rivulets down his pale face. Drawing near to his home he saw the dust of many horses disappearing in the distance. All was still, not even the sound of a bird broke the silence. Leaving Fleetfoot to run wild, he raced towards the house, but then he felt his heart racing and for a moment could not move. Walking towards the grand entrance, his heart did a double thump in his chest and then he knew what he feared had come true.

The great hall caught the rays of the sun and glittered off the crimson splash of colour. He heard howling but for a moment did not realise it came from his own throat. The bodies were still twitching, granting a semblance of life, but he knew even before he knelt down on the bloodstained floor that they were both dead. His parents lay back to back, as in life, so in death they had fought to the end, he could see that by the other bodies left behind, but also by the marks on his mother. Not even Cromwell's men would slay a woman in cold blood, she had forced them to fight to the bitter end and his tears mingled with her blood leaving blotchy stains on his crisp white shirt. His father must have returned suddenly with his pursuers close behind. Heartbroken he fell across the bodies and lay in a stupor of grief.

This was the tableau that Jessie saw on her return from the woods, one that would haunt her to the end of her life. She had lost her entire family in an afternoon. But wait! A tiny movement revealed her brother, covered in the blood of their parents, but alive, or so she prayed. Dropping her basket of flowers, she threw herself into the arms of James and there they lay for what seemed like hours.

It was Daisy that finally roused them and made them both swallow the fiery brandy to counter the terrible shock they all felt. Like a ghost of a woman going through the motions she tried her best to sooth them although her own heart bled tears for them all.

'You knew,' James screamed at her, 'why didn't you warn us?'

A small voice spoke quietly from a corner of the great hall, 'She took us into Brannon's Wood, we thought it was a treat, your mother never allowed us...' the voice tailed off as fresh sobs echoed around the hall.

'Sarah?' through tear-stained eyes James had his third shock of the day, for the first time he saw her properly and knew that his sister's friend had the same hazel eyes they both shared. He was looking at his own kin, the bastard granddaughter of his own grandfather.

So strange a feeling on such a day as this, but he knew then there would never be another woman in his life if he couldn't have her.

'I could not do anything son,' Daisy spoke for the first time, 'if the message had reached here, mayhap we would have had time to escape but even then the fates had decided. The sight came too quick, I had but little time to choose. Your mother bade me take you to safety while she waited for your father, it were an order, master James, what could I do?'

'You let them die,' Jessie swore an unspeakable word, 'you took us into the woods and you knew what would happen?'

'No Jessie, she saved you,' James spoke up. 'Look at mother, see what she did, they would have cut you down the same way or had done something much worse.' (In his heart he also thought of another life spared that day). Later he would tell her of his own vision, but now was not the time.

The sound of horse's hooves broke through the argument and all cringed, was this some final devilry sent by Cromwell's men?

But Daisy welcomed the strangers, 'Thank you for coming in this our hour of need, Lord Stafford.'

'How,' he stuttered, 'how do you know my name?' and then he saw the bodies lying there and wept.

Finally his tears subsided, 'I warned him not to return yet, there is a traitor nearby, we followed as fast as we could, but it seems we arrived too late. Did you not get the warning?'

'It was lost to us, yet I think it would not have done any good,' Daisy said with no trace of accent in her words.

'You are a wise woman?'

'I have been called many things Sir, but never that before.'

'But you see the future?'

'Aye, sir, most times, but there is little I can do to prevent events unfolding.'

'Then you know we must be away with all the speed we can make?'

'Lord Rothford?'

'I fear so'.

The packing was done with as much haste as possible. Jessie cried, James was less reluctant, wiping his father's great sword free of their enemy's blood, he was keen to press on.

Finally all was prepared and the horses saddled. Lord Stafford would take the girls to his home while James would stay nearby.

'Mother, you are not coming with us?' Stafford asked of the loyal maid.

'My place is here,' Daisy replied, 'the dead will have a good Christian burial.'

'Now James,' she bent her head for one last kiss, 'you must be strong, for you must go to the Astley's as your father wanted.'

'I cannot leave my sister,' he replied, though his eyes spoke of revenge, not just suffering.

'Yet it will be the first place that Rothford will look, and you must stay there, for one day soon there will be another king and Halleswell Hall will be returned to you.'

'You know this?'

'It is true,' she replied simply.

'We must leave now,' Lord Stafford knew that time was short.

Outside a wagon was ready and Stafford placed the luggage inside. Then he beckoned the two girls to join him.

'I don't see any cause to leave,' Sarah said, but Daisy whispered in her ear and the girl's face went white with shock. James kissed both girls, but his eyes lingered long on Sarah's fair face.

Daisy came out of the house and passed a bundle of books into James's arms.

'Read these, they are your father's and his father's. They will explain a lot to you. Now go and God be with you.' The wagon made good speed, but not enough to hide the servants slain in the gatehouse. It was the final straw in a long and heartbreaking day. Both the girls clung together, their eyes filled with tears for the innocents slaughtered in cold blood that day.

The villagers came, as Daisy knew they would, to see the Master and Mistress to their final resting place. Charles and Margaret would lie in the earth together, not branded, as Lord Rothford would have doomed them to be. She watched the cart as it vanished into the distance, too afraid to go with them lest her role would come to naught. She would keep up the pretence of a lived in house for a few days, long enough to let the children get away. The visions were coming faster now and every day she saw a new wonder. Halleswell Hall would go through many a difficult time, but one day there would be new blood here and a promise for the future, a good future after centuries of unease.

Now she felt her ancestors calling out to her to come home. She would take one last walk in Brannon's Wood before taking the poison that would seal her lips for all time. Nobody would know where Jessica had gone, or the child that would eventually change the course of the family's history.

Her footsteps took her straight to the clearing where the well was already becoming overgrown. Its time in the world would come again, but for now it would hide itself away from the wickedness of the world. The late evening light warmed the old stones and she sank back, grateful for the warmth.

The light came slowly, seeping through the undergrowth and spilling from her fingers.

'Are you ready now sister?' the voice asked.

'More than ready brother, it's been a long journey and now it's time to rest.'

'Hold your hand out, that's it, welcome home sister.'

Revenge and the Depth of Hope

'God's Teeth,' James swore for the third time that day, 'why would the girl not leave him alone?' For two years he had lived quietly with the Astley's, plotting his revenge on Rothford, but always keeping the memory of his sister and cousin in his mind. Now it seemed that he must put up with the devotion of a girl barely out of the schoolroom. Fiona was a pretty lass but now he was a grown man with a man's appetites and feelings. He could no more love her than Rosy, the maid at the coaching inn who gave him such good sport on a dull night.

Guiltily he thought of the Astley's who had taken him in and showed him such kindness, but he could not be expected to marry their only daughter. Despite his reduced circumstances, he was still a Lord, and hadn't old Daisy said that the king would return one day?

No, it was wrong to lead the girl to think of him in a romantic way. Even had he been a mere peasant, his heart belonged to another, so many miles away.

'I brought you some wine Sir James, mama thought it would chase the gloom away.'

'Thank you kindly child, but I am merely studying, not brooding.'

Meekly she cast her eyes down, 'my apologies, Sir, I had not meant to disturb you.'

Damn, now he felt even worse! The least he could do was to be civil to the girl, so accepting a glass of wine he thought of an excuse to escape.

'My pardon, dear child, I had not thought the hour so late, please convey my good wishes to your dear mother, but I will be dining out tonight.' He had to escape this prison, if only for a brief night. He blessed his father once again for leaving sufficient funds to last him for at least the next ten years. Gleefully he thought of Rothford, looking for gold and jewels and finding nought. Charles had taken the precaution of hiding his wealth where none but his own family could find it. Still he angered at the thought of Rothford's factor running his family home and estate. He rode to the village now and again, but the plight of his people tore at his heart.

Where once the villagers were allowed to take a plump bird or a rabbit to feed their family, from Brannon's Wood, now there was a gamekeeper who laid the evil mantraps for the desperate or unwary person.

His father would have turned in his grave at the sight of skinny children and empty grates in the winters chill. Forbidden the bounty of the trees, many had come close to death from the bitter winter that hung over the land. He gave what he could, but Rothford's spies were everywhere and a golden coin could hang a man merely for having kept it back from the extortionate taxes laid on them. It was easier and kinder to pay for goods at the local market and trust the food he sent through his friends would reach the empty bellies of those in need.

Thrusting the thoughts away he turned from his father's diaries and went to dress for the cold night's ride. At least he had been allowed to keep his own horse. James thought that maybe Rothford was relying on him to ride the stallion away to visit his sister; little did he know the plans already in motion. Draining the last of the good wine he went to his chambers in preparation for his night's outing.

Rosy laid back against the pillows with a satisfied smile on her face, James' head laid on her ample bosom and he was snoring gently.

'You have the best of both worlds,' she thought to herself. First the money from James, then the larger bribe paid for by Rothford. She regretted spying on James, he was a gentle man and clean, not like her usual clients, but money could not be sneered at. A pity then that she had little to report back. James paid in coppers with never a sign of silver or gold. Rothford was always angry lately, he accused her of holding secrets back from him and once he had blackened her eye after he went through her money chest.

31

'Where have you hidden it, dirty whore?' he said, his face purple with anger.

'I ain't hidden nuffing, I said as how he ain't got much money.'

'Then what is wine doing here?' he answered, 'most men drink ale or cheap brandy?'

He tipped his head back and drunk straight from the bottle, spluttering in disgust as the cheap wine went down his throat.

'You have changed this; no man would drink these slops.'

'James is barely a man,' she said, 'he would not know the difference; he drinks enough of the foul stuff.'

'I bet you charge him heavily for it as well,' was his only retort.

'I get's it where I can, I's a working girl as you well know, Lord Rothford.' She spat at his feet.

He had ridden off in temper but suddenly the money did not seem so important.

Now she thought it time to rouse her young lover from his sleep, 'James, 'she called to him, ''tis time for you to go.'

Just for a moment she saw the anguish flare in his eyes and then he cloaked them with his usual warm smile.

'Ah, dear Rosy, how well I sleep in your bed. One day, maybe when my estates are returned to me, then I can pay you what your charms are worth.'

'An pigs may fly, now get you back afore you scandalise the Astley's,' she giggled at the thought.

Jessica stood by the graveside, her son held tightly in her arms. She could not believe that her dear husband Charles was lying in the cheap coffin. Sarah held her by the arm and for a moment their fingers intertwined. The church was full, despite the threat from the roundheads. Charles had been a good man and people thronged to see him laid to rest. Now they were vanishing in the sudden mists that spring up so quickly by the marshes.

Sullenly his brother Robert stood by, watching as she cast the first earth into the yawning grave followed by a single red rose to denote her love.

For a moment she swayed with fatigue, but Sarah kept a firm grasp on her arm.

'It is time to go dear sister,' so they had called each other since leaving Halleswell Hall behind.

'You comfort me sister mine, but why is life so unfair? First I lose my parents, then leaving James behind and now…..' she faltered for a moment. 'I loved him, Sarah, even though he was old enough to be my own father; he was such a good man, so loving and caring. What will we do without him now?'

Sarah could not answer; the future was as bleak as her own heart. In one day she had found and lost her other family. There had not even been time to say goodbye to her parents before Sir Charles led them away. She had left reluctantly, knowing that by staying she might put her family in danger, but still she wept for her parents and her young siblings.

Instinctively she knew that she was the only Meverall child in her household, she had seen the dawning recognition in James' eyes and the look of love that had passed so briefly between them. On the long ride from Devon to Suffolk she had learnt much, how her grandfather, Thomas loved her grandmother, but could never marry her because of his position in society. How he took a bride and after fathering Charles, the heir, his rightful wife had gone to her grave. 'Poor Thomas' she thought, 'having to put aside his true love for the sake of both their reputations'. Jessica knew little of this; it had been Daisy that had told her of the family secret, never to be revealed, less Jessie learnt that her grandfather had never loved her own grandmother.

Now they were at the mercy of Robert, Charles' brother and heir who was already an embittered man. On the long journey to this place they had been chased by the enemy and Charles had suffered a leg wound. On arrival he found that his lands had been taken in the name of parliament and all they had left was a small farm. Jessie tended Charles while Sarah worked on the farm. It mattered little to her, for she had been working since she could walk. She had not been surprised when Jessie married Charles, she knew no men of her own age. Walter had been born some ten months later, but the wound in Charles' leg had never properly healed and now Jessie was a widow with a six-month old son.

The funeral supper was as dark as the day. Few people could afford to stay, less they too were marked as Royalists. Robert was soon drunk and Jessie was left alone with Sarah. Long into the night they talked about the future. If Jessie stayed then soon Robert would make a move towards her, but they were both penniless and where would they go? Back to Devon and into the power of Rothford's clutches? Even Robert was a more appealing choice. The plan was made that night, it required cunning and nerves of steel, but Sarah knew it was their only choice.

James was seething, this time Rothford had gone too far. A village lad had been caught poaching a rabbit and the sentence called for was death by hanging. Another year had gone by, a year in which James had practised secretly with sword and dagger. He had to challenge Rothford or die in the attempt. Dressed in his much patched clothes he rode Fleetfoot to the very gates of Winterbourne House, the ancestral home of the late Meverall's. Hammering on the door he waited for a reply, it wasn't long in coming.

Rothford's man, Heath, stood before him, 'Tradesman's entrance is around the back', he proclaimed haughtily.

'Tell your Master that if he has an ounce of courage in his heart then it would be wise to treat me with more deference,' he said, his heart hammering in his chest. 'I bear the true name of Meverall, which is more than he could ever aspire to, being just a man who bought his title.'

Heath yawned; this youth was nothing to him, but he took the message to his master, thinking there would be fine sport today.

James waited patiently; Rothford would keep him waiting to test his nerve.

'James, my lad, to what do I owe the honour of your visit?' he sneered.

The fist came sharp and fast, hitting the jaw straight on.

'I call you a coward and ask for satisfaction on the field of honour.'

'You dare to challenge me, boy; I could have you clapped in irons for such a threat?'

Simon, the Magister, stood forward from behind James, 'A dual is still perfectly legal in this land, I suggest you either respond or be branded as a coward.'

'When?' was the only reply.

'Dawn tomorrow, but if you prefer to settle it right now then so much the sooner you will be in your grave,' James answered.

Rothford could hardly back down now, but still he dissembled.

'I gather you are already prepared?' he asked, thinking to shake the boy into precipitate action.

'I have only my father's sword and my dagger; I expect that you wish to choose the weapons yourself. However, I have no funds for pistols since I lost my land to you, Master Rothford.' Nothing could have incensed Rothford more than that slur on his name.

'We shall meet now then, sword and dagger is acceptable, though I fear yours might be rusty from disuse?'

James held his fear in check; 'the rust stains from traitors' blood has long been washed away. The blade is keen as am I.' He answered quietly.

The dual was held on the village green, Rothford confident that he would get rid of this upstart sooner than planned. 'Maybe he could even wrest the whereabouts of his sister from him before he drowned in his own blood,' he thought with satisfaction.

Both men stripped to the waist and a gasp of surprise went up from the crowd. Rothford had the advantage in height and the way he held himself showed that he had fought before. Beside him, James looked exactly what he was, a young gentleman that had never fought a real battle before and had never lifted a blade in real swordplay. Yet he had worked, both in the fields and with a tutor more deadly than even his father had been.

His muscles rippled in the sunlight, the tanned body taut with tension as he sized up his opponent. Rothford may have the longer reach, but James was young and fast on his feet. In that moment, before they clashed blades, he remembered the advice of both his father and the veteran soldier who had arrived a year ago.

'Swordplay is like a dance,' he heard the words inside his head. 'Courtiers play at it, but when it is for real it is a dance of death. Keep your anger in check; make the sword an extension of your arm. As the making of a sword is tempered first by fire and then plunged into water, so you must cool your fire until the moment is right to strike.'

Warily they circled each other, Rothford looking for the quick and easy strike. His sword arced in the air, but James had sprung aside and now took up the offensive.

The first cut took Rothford by surprise; the younger man had slipped through the gap, striking at his sword arm.

Now the older man's experience came into play as he parried each stroke with an effortless ease born of long practise.

James fell back, his shoulder slippery with his own blood. Briefly he felt a fission of fear but then he recalled the words of the man who taught his own father the art of swordsmanship.

'Concentrate son,' he heard the words and entered the trance that comes from deep inside the soul of a true warrior.

The sun rose higher in the sky as the fighters parried blade with blade. Blood run freely from the many cuts inflicted on each man and still they played the deadly dance of death.

By now the spectators were hanging out of windows, sitting outside the tavern and keeping a close circle around the two men. Long minutes passed by and still the swords clashed together, steel ringing on steel as the two men sought for that opening to end the fight. James was tiring as he strove to lift the great blade above his head in an attempt to cleave his opponent in two. Rothford managed to dodge the two-handed swoop of the blade and again took up the offensive. James knew he could no longer carry on such an exhausting pace. Calling up his last vestiges of energy he slipped once again into that dreamlike state.

His feet blurred with the speed of a dancer as slowly he pushed his opponent backwards. Rothford had not expected this, the boy should be dead by now, how had he learnt to fight like this? The worm of fear crept inside his stomach but he was no weakling and started to gain ground. Confidence made him careless, as he lunged forwards his feet slipped in the muddy ground, tripping him up and landing him on his back.

Instantly the blade was poised at his throat, 'Yield now and I will spare your life,' James could not kill even a man like Rothford in cold blood.

'And what are your conditions if I do so yield?' the older man was trying to buy himself some time.

'That you leave my land and swear never to set foot here again.'

The crowd booed, they were out for blood and Rothford was not a popular man.

'I accept your conditions; now help me to rise with some dignity left.'

James was still an innocent in many ways. Lowering his sword he held out his hand and in that moment Rothford swung his sword catching James a glancing cut across his cheek.

The reaction was swift. James spun in a tight forward roll and his blade sank into Rothford's chest.

The crowd went wild with the scent of the kill. Sickened to his soul James called out for a priest to attend the dying man.

'I want no popery,' Rothford said with his dying breath.

James turned away in disgust. His head still ringing from the fight and with bloodied limbs he picked up his discarded shirt and stumbled to the tavern where he sank his body into the horse trough before calling for brandy and ale.

Early morning sunshine seeped through the thin curtains and James winced at the light and the pain in his head. He lay sprawled across his bed at the Astley's, fully clothed and stinking of the coppery smell of dried blood and cheap brandy. Somebody had pulled his boots off and a bucket was placed by the bed, obviously in case he had vomited in the night. He imagined that Francis Astley had helped with the only manservant, Sam, to get him to bed.

He groaned as he lifted his head from the pillows, 'how could he have allowed himself to get into this state?' Then the memory of the dual came back to him and heaving he emptied the contents of his stomach into the bucket. It was one thing to think about killing a man, but the reality of killing his first man did not sit easily on his shoulders.

There was a light tap at the door and gratefully he answered it to Sam. He could not face the family at this moment.

'I bring you water to drink, sor, an a drop o' brandy to take the shakes away. Jenny be drawing an heating water for a bath sor, an Master Francis says as how those there clothes of yorn should be burnt.'

37

'Thank you Sam, but I fear I will never drink a drop again.' James could barely lift the water to his lips his hands shook so.

'Drink the brandy sor, 'tis the only remedy for now.'

It tasted foul but it seemed to do the trick.

'Tell me, Sam, what did I do last night?'

'Nothing bad, sor, every man would have done the same, 'tis never easy to kill a man an stay sober. It were the villagers as got you drunk, not a drop o' the grog were paid fer, you mun be their hero.'

'Who was it that brought me home?'

'The master thought 'twere wise, after the cheering comes the tears an he would not see you blub like a babe in public.'

Once more James felt the guilt in his soul. These were good people and all he had done was to bring shame on their house.

How could he have acted differently though, when his life had been at stake? The Welshman, Ivor had taught him well. He had learnt little of the man's past except that he had once fought by his late father's side. Now he was gone, leaving James alone with the aftermath of his first kill. It was one thing to think of killing an enemy but another to actually do the deed.

He needed the brandy later on when the sawbones came to stitch up his wounds. Most were shallow, but one on his chest had nearly pierced the lung and the scar on his cheek would be a lifelong reminder of his first fight.

Fleetfoot cantered along the country lanes; it was now a good three weeks since James had ridden away with tearful goodbyes to the Astley's. The fatal dual was still legal and many had come forth as witness to Rothford's last treachery, still he had thought it wise to get away for a long while. The journey had seemed endless, but soon he would be on Stafford's land and reunited with Jessie and Sarah. Whistling cheerfully he could just imagine the look on Jessie and Sarah's face when he told of the revenge taken on Rothford. The hard ride had taken some of the guilt away and now he was clothed as a man of his status should be. His father's sword hung at his side and his saddlebags were filled with as much of the gold as he could carry.

Taking the turning towards Stafford's great mansion house, he felt a moment of unease. Here was the great oak-lined entrance, but there was no gatekeeper to bid him 'good day'. In fact the whole place had an air of neglect around it, but that could be an attempt to appease Cromwell's men, who were still roaming the land to bring down the last of the Royalists. Step by step he held his horse on a tight rein, something was definitely amiss and as he came into sight of the beautiful old house he realised what was missing. There were few labourers on the land and now he could see places where fire had scarred both the house and land. Before he went any further he felt it wise to retrace his steps and enquire of the farm he had passed by briefly on route to here.

The farm was adjacent to the Stafford lands, maybe a few acres; it too showed signs of neglect. Weeds choked the entrance and the farm gate was swinging on its hinges. However, two women were rounding up the herd of cows for the evening milking. Both wore bonnets to ward off the heat of the late August afternoon and one carried a young child strapped peasant-style to her back. James smiled at this homely scene until he drew near to where the women were leading the cows to the milking sheds. Cheerfully calling a 'hello' in their direction, both turned their faces to his and in that moment James' heart plummeted. Twin pairs of hazel eyes locked to his as he recognised the faces of his own sister and his beloved Sarah.

Jessie flung herself into his arms, the child held safely in the enclosing arms of brother and sister.

'James, my God, you are alive,' she cried, hugging him close to her. Sarah hung back, but he could feel her gaze on his and knew that she, too, was glad to see him alive and well.

'Let me look at you, God's teeth James, you look so grown up. But what has brought you here and dressed in such finery? Do you not fear the wrath of Cromwell's men to dress so?'

This was not the time or place to reveal his revenge or the safe passage he had sought through bribery. Many of the rival army had been drafted in by threats and were still loyal to the cause. Others were more than willing to take his gold. What concerned him was his sister and his beloved Sarah working as peasants in the fields.

'Sister what are you doing labouring as a peasant and Sarah too? Where Is Lord Stafford? I had thought to find you both living in comfort and safety; instead I see no signs of father's friend and the home of the Stafford family in the hands of rogues?' The man came around from the back of the barn, his lips wet from imbibing the rough cider.

'My brother is dead,' he said, 'killed by placing too much trust in the king's army. Now you see the ruin of our family. This,' he exclaimed 'is what he has brought us to, a measly farm and a few acres. Though I fear it's not to your liking I have done my duty by housing and feeding your kin though I know you not my fine gentleman?'

Jessie made the introductions. 'Robert this is my brother James, the last of the Meverall line and by our father's passing he is now Sir James Meverall as knighted by the king himself.'

'James, this is Sir Robert Stafford, brother to my late husband and also the last of the family line save for my son, Walter.'

Sarah took this chance to diffuse what was becoming a difficult situation; she knew well how belligerent Robert could become. 'Pray take James inside for some refreshment, 'tis a warm day and the dust of the road lie heavily on him. I will see to the milking and join you later.'

It was to be an evening of revelation to him. Here was Jessie, widowed and with a child to care for. There were no maids to wait on them, Sarah took that duty to herself and his heart bled to see her serve the plain fare and then seat herself to the meagre remains of their meal. Robert had started on the cider as soon as the meal was eaten and now was tossing back the brandy as if 'twere water. James learnt more than he wished to know that night. Not only had Cromwell confiscated the Stafford house, but also Robert barely held tenancy of Home Farm. Robert was now ingratiating himself to James, no doubt seeing the fine clothes he had bought for this visit and thinking that money would soon be forthcoming.

James knew that money would change hands, if only to free his women from this vile man, but worse was to come. In his cups, Robert let slip that he sought either Jessie or Sarah for his wife, not mattering which of the women he took to his bed.

When the household were all abed, James knocked quietly on Sarah's door. She answered the door still fully dressed. 'Come and walk with me awhile, dear heart,' James begged.

'Gladly I will,' she replied tiptoeing past Robert's bedchamber, though they could hear him snoring in a drunken stupor.

The night was still warm and he led her into a copse of trees. All his resolve was shattered in that moment; drawing her into his arms he kissed her passionately.

'Sarah, my love, how I have longed for this moment, you know I have loved you from the time I first eyes on you?'

'And I too, dear James, but there are things I must tell you now, before we go too far,' the pain in her voice was almost too much for him to bear.

'I know about your grandfather, it is in Thomas' diaries as shown to me by my mother. How he loved not my true grandmother and how his mistress bore a son, your own father. What does that matter to us, we may share the same blood, but many families have mingled like blood in the past and came to no harm?' His voice was full of longing.

Once again he bent to kiss her and his hands strayed to her breasts. Bending to kiss the arc of her throat, she suddenly pushed him away.

'Beloved, I have dreamt of this moment, but it cannot be;' now the tears were flowing freely down her face.

Lifting her shawl she held it tight against her, as if to ward away the passion they both shared.

'Thomas died young, he never knew....' For a moment she could not go on, but James had to know the truth.

'My mother was in service to Henry, she was an innocent when he took her in the stables and him so old.'

'But..?'

'Shush dearest, this you have to know, when she became heavy with child she was put from the house, alone and helpless she turned to the one man that truly loved her, Thomas' bastard son, my father John. Do not you now see, he raised me as his own, so I am doubly a Meverall, James, I am your sister in blood though not in name?'

Nothing could have prepared James for this revelation; he doubled up in pain as if struck down by the same blow he had once felt at Ned's funeral.

'A curse lies on my family,' he cried out, 'before me I see the only woman I can ever love and she is close blood kin.' Slowly he got to his feet and moved towards Sarah.

'I care not; I love you and always will.'

Sarah wished he had not returned to her, no more could she push him away, but she could never wed with him, not when their children could be cursed by the inbred blood. 'Sarah, come to me now, I care not for tomorrow, tonight I must lay with you or die.'

Sinking down in the grass they allowed themselves to express their love for the one and only time left to them.

James arose with a heavy heart. Today he had to face the future and provide for both Sarah and Jessica. First though, he had to get rid of Robert for the day. Over a late breakfast he put his proposal to Robert, though he hated parting with any money to this oaf. Between mouthfuls of bacon he outlined his plan. The timing had to be just right and luckily he had seen a handbill pronouncing today's hiring fair. Clapping Robert on the back with a false humour he said, 'Well brother, I have noticed you run a tight ship here. But there is no bull here except you?'

Robert nodded, well pleased with the reference to his manhood.

Drawing forth his money-belt James allowed a glimpse of gold coin.

'I believe there is a hiring fair today?'

Robert grunted his assent.

'Then what say you that we go and look for a fine bull to serve your cows?'

'Not in those fine clothes, you would be stripped of your money and left for dead. Nay, brother, stay here with your sisters whilst I can bid for lesser money.'

James knew the way the man's mind worked. He would spend the coin on a bull and then squander the rest on ale and loose women. He had to make sure that his plan would work though, so adopting a mulish tone he pretended to be offended.

'So you would leave me with the women while you fill your belly in the inns?'

'Not I?' Robert put on his sober face, 'I will be there and back within the day,' he winked at James, thinking him naïve.

'The cellar is stocked with some of my late brother's finest wines, get the women working and slake your thirst there. Maybe even walk to the village, I can recommend a good woman there to wake your manhood.'

James had to bite his tongue at the brutality of the man. He would not allow Jessica or Sarah to spend one more night in this hovel with Robert's greedy eyes upon them. If he could have chanced the scandal he would have run the man through for the insult to those he loved.

Once Robert was safely out of the way with two gold sovereigns to speed him along, James confided his plans to the women. 'We need just a short time away and I have the name of a good family that will shelter us until it is safe to return home. Cromwell's army need food and shelter, it 'twill not be long before we can return in safety. With Rothford dead the factor can not hope to run two large estates. The tenant farmers will work more gladly under my rule. As my sisters you will be under my protection, though we may have to play the puritan for a while.'

Jessie was troubled, 'if we did go back then what could stop another Rothford coming to claim both the lands and our bodies? I will not be sold to the highest bidder and my child slaughtered as the son of a Royalist. Think on it brother, would we have more freedom than we have here, I think not?'

In vain he protested, not wanting to be parted ever again from the two women. Had he fought Rothford to the death only for it to be an empty gesture?

'I long to go home, but what is there for us now? The memories of our parents bodies lying in their blood? And what of Sarah? Have you thought it through? We know she is our kin, but the villagers would only see her as another bastard Meverall, could you dare to fight them all brother?'

Numbly he had to admit the truth of Jessie's words, Sarah would be scorned forever. He had one last argument, 'Rothford's wife Helen has gone back to her mother's kin. The house now stands empty but for the servants and the overworked factor. We would hold the house against the King's return.'

Sarah's voice cut into the debate between brother and sister. 'I am sorry James but my mind is made up. Jessie and I have planned for such a day as this. We will take the ship to France where our welcome is assured in the court of Charles's wife. Maybe one day we will return if Charles regains his late father's throne.'

'We need to be away with all speed if we are to escape this nightmare,' Jessie was looking at her son as she said the words which would set them free.

There was nought else he could do. To allow his loved ones a chance of freedom and an easier life he would face the jaws of hell itself.

The evening sun cast its rays upon the ripples of the tide as James reined in his horse. The hired gig had placed the women in time to catch the ship to France. This parting was bitter as the two women he loved more than life itself were waiting to board for their new life, far from England's shores. With that flash of insight he knew he would never see them again in this life. Jessie stood apart, they had said their farewells earlier and he had given her sufficient money to set her up independently if she so wished. Now the moment he had dreaded had come, holding Sarah in his arms for the last time, he whispered once again his love for her and slipping off the great ring of the Meverall's, he placed it on her thickest finger. Both women had wept but that relief of feeling was not granted to him. From this day on, his heart would be of stone. The young boy had become a man, firstly when he had fought the dual and now, when his future loomed ahead of him, so bleak and empty.

He watched in silence as the ship drew away, the figures of the women receding in the distance.

'God be with you,' he uttered, mounting Fleetfoot and rode away without turning back.

Charles the Second was asked to take the throne back in 1660. England's civil war left a wake of tragedy with many of the Royalists unable to recover their lands. Halleswell Hall was indeed returned to James, as Daisy had once foretold, though a mystery surrounded the quick return of all he had lost. James married and bore two children, one a girl and the second his heir, a lusty boy he named William.

To the villagers he showed a kinder heart than to his own family.

A stern man, he commanded respect where it was due, and if sometimes he appeared to be lost in thought it was put down to the loss of his parents and his sister. Brannon's Wood was once again re-opened to the farmers and villagers alike. He died when William was just entering his manhood. Some said he died of a wasting disease, though others spoke of a broken heart.

The Reluctant Marriage

'Boom!' The cannon fired another round into the Spanish ship. It was a vision straight from Hell, with the guns pounding from both sides and visibility severely impaired from the smoke of battle. From his place on the bridge with the other officers, Henry tried to peer through the smoke at the ghostly silhouettes of men tamping powder into the heavy cannon.

Now he could just make out the Spanish ship, its sails in tatters and fires breaking out where the cannon balls from the English ship had left their mark. The Spanish captain was obviously trying to run, but it was too late and bowing to the inevitable he raised the white flag of surrender.

As the victory cheer sounded all over the British frigate, Henry felt proud that he was a part of this, his very first battle. He had but recently been given his commission and such a resounding victory lifted his spirits. Looking across at the other officers, he saw a gloating look on the Captain's face as he gave the order to board the beaten ship. Something about that cruel smile made his blood creep and a feeling of dread came over him. Still, he had his own job to do and shouting to the men he watched as the planks were laid and sailors crowded the Spanish ship. Henry watched as the Spanish captain handed his sword over in the ritual gesture of surrender. The remains of the crew stood behind him, many bloodied by battle. Henry found it difficult to keep upright as he slipped on piles of corpses; the deck was awash with the blood of the dying and maimed sailors. No amount of experience could have warned him what was to come next. Smiling evilly the captain turned to his first officer and said,' now shoot them all, Mr Frost.' Henry was horrified, 'But Sir you can't they are unarmed, they surrendered.' The words were out before he realised he had uttered them. It was too late to take them back now. The captain's eye was on him and it held as much benevolence as he had shown the Spanish sailors.

'You have something to say Lieutenant?'

It was too late to go back now and Henry was no coward, He straightened his shoulders and said, 'You can't do that Sir they surrendered.'

'And just who are you to question my decision. Number one arrest Lieutenant Meverall for insubordination.'

Henry tried to close his ears to the sound of gunfire that filled them as he was led away back to his ship, but it was no good the screams of dying men penetrated all his defences.

Henry's mind was brought back into the present as a large wave tilted his small fishing boat. Looking up he realised the waves had pushed him around the point while he had been daydreaming about the past.

Grabbing the tiller he tried to turn the boat back out towards the open sea, away from the cliffs now looming over him. The tide had his boat trapped now and with the headland cutting off the wind to his small sail there was nothing he could do to keep his boat from the rocks. Fear began to seep into him. Looking both up and down the coast, he could see nothing but the foaming of spray against the cruel rocky shores. Something caught his eye. There was a break in the white scarf that the cliffs wore, just behind a jagged outcrop of rock the waves seemed to continue to run rather than smash themselves into the coast.

A fleeting hope crossed his mind, was there a cove or bay hidden beyond that rock? Under his expert hands he guided the small craft nearer to the spot he had glimpsed. Slowly the bow turned in that direction and he hoped that his instinct was right. There was nothing to lose anyway, if his fate was to die right now, he would face it head on.

The left side of the boat scraped along the jagged rock and then the bow was pulled sharply left by an even stronger current. It was mere seconds before Henry's craft was shooting through a short tunnel underneath the towering cliffs. In those brief seconds his mind conjured up pictures of death and destruction. It was pitch black and he imagined an underground river where the turbulent waters would crush him to his death. It didn't happen, the bow came round and he found himself spinning slowly as the surf spent the last of its strength washing up on a tiny underground beach.

He was surprised to be alive, let alone to be in such a vast cavern. Sunlight was leaking in from some source, as his eyes were now adjusting to the thin light. Motes of sunlight glittered off the wet rocks and looking upwards he tried to gauge how large this cavern actually was, but it was still too dark. Turning the tiller he headed toward the soft beach and jumped out of the boat when it touched land.

He looked around, the cavern must be immense. He could not see the top or the far walls as darkness hid them from him.

It didn't take long for the question to come to his mind. 'What was he going to do now, how was he going to get out?' he had no immediate answer; his nautical mind said he should wait for the tide to turn and maybe he would be able to ride the outgoing tide. In the meantime the light had to be getting in somewhere so he might as well use the time while he waited for the tide to explore. Maybe there was a way out on the landward side.

It took him some time to find it, but eventually he found an exit. It was a small hole, and he was thankful for his lean frame as he squeezed himself out onto the wet grass at the back of the point.

His eyes took a few moments to adjust to the blazing sunlight. A sigh of relief escaped his lips as he wondered what he should do next. There was nothing for it but to walk back to Halleswell. His little boat would be safe until he either left it, or dared the opening once again.

It was only a couple of months after his adventure that a chance meeting occurred that would change his life for ever.

He had been out riding one day in early autumn and had decided to ride for the point. He had been there several times recently, but never had he seen a soul there before. He pulled his horse up sharply when he saw the shape of another horse standing on the headland. There was no rider in sight and he wondered if someone had come to grief. Riding closer he saw a man stand up from where he had been lying on the cliff edge. Henry pulled up but it was too late now to make out he hadn't seen the man and so he carried on his approach.

The man at the cliff edge seemed unconcerned to be found there.

'Good day to you Sir.' He said as Henry drew closer, 'a fine morning for a ride.'

Henry paused before replying, 'indeed it is, although it is not often I meet other company here?'

The young man looked sheepish, as if he didn't particularly want to tell Henry what he was doing there.

Henry looked closer at the man, 'Don't I know you Sir?'

'Yes Sir, five years ago Sir, I was a midshipman on the *Goshawk*, I was there the day you stood up to Captain Wallis, Sir and mighty proud I was too, even if it did no good.'

'Thank you, er, sorry your name escapes me.'

'Grimwood Sir, ex-midshipman Grimwood.'

'Ex?'

'Yes Sir I left the navy just after you was booted out for what you done Sir.'

'Oh, and so what brings you out here today?'

Grimwood looked taken aback by the sudden question and he didn't answer until prompted again.

'Well Sir I was looking for a cave that is rumoured to be at the foot of these ere cliffs.'

'Really and why would you want to know about the cave?'

'Ah, I am afraid that's something that I shouldn't divulge Sir, it would get me in a whole heap of trouble.'

'And what makes you think you are not already in a whole heap of trouble, acting suspiciously on private land. I think maybe I have a right to know what you are up to don't I?'

Grimwood was caught he didn't know what to say. At last though, he decided that he would probably be in less trouble not having done anything yet so he told Henry why he was interested in the cave.

'To hide a boat Sir, well a ship really.'

Henry was suddenly interested. 'Indeed, and why would you want to hide a ship, smuggling I presume?'

Grimwood didn't answer but Henry took the look on his face to be one of guilt.

'Come with me Mr Grimwood, I think we have a lot to discuss.' Chatting about old times, they made their way to the local tavern.

Henry loved the sea and wasn't happy unless he was aboard a ship with waves flowing under his feet. There was another reason as well. His family were bent on marrying him off to the highest bidder in the marriage mart. Henry didn't want to get married, so his jaunts on the sea kept him out of the persuasion brought to bear by his parents.

Together with Grimwood, Henry had quite a profitable enterprise in a surprisingly short space of time.

They had started off with buying a ship. That had not been easy. Their requirements were pretty exacting and there was not a great supply of ships for sale. Their ship would have to be fast, have a decent amount of cargo room, and be small enough and have a shallow enough draft to fit in the cave at Harland point.

In the end they found a man who was willing to sell them his brigantine with no questions asked. The *London Town* was a sleek craft, twin masts and able to carry a large amount of sail that gave her the necessary turn of speed. Henry renamed her *Ghost*. Modifications were made to make her as fast as possible and test runs saw her flying across the waves.

Both Henry and Grimwood had contacts with seafaring men who would not be adverse to a little illegal activity, and they soon had a full crew that they struck a part share deal with. A man will always put more effort in if he has a stake in the operation.

The first attempt at getting *Ghost* into the cave had been a hairy moment. The currents were almost impossible to read. Henry had to use all his nautical know-how and rely on a lot of luck to get the ship safely into the cavern. They had managed it with only a small scrape down one side and once they had her in they had been able to make modifications to her in secret.

Clients were not in short supply and it didn't take long for them to have more than enough cargo to make several runs a month. They started with short runs across the Channel to France but it had not been long before much more lucrative trips into the Mediterranean were the norm.

As much as Henry's seafaring life was going smoothly his home life was a stormy sea. His family knew nothing of his new business activities. As far as they were concerned he was still a rising officer in His Majesties Navy. Henry had thought it better to keep up the pretence for several reasons; firstly he had not wanted the inevitable ranting about bringing the family name into disrepute that he would have been bound to get from his father. Second it gave him the perfect excuse for being away for extended periods of time, which in turn kept him away from the question of marriage.

When he was at home his parents entertained quite lavishly. He could not object to this as apart from being the done thing, he could not afford the risk of being seen as a recluse. Gossip would spread and before long questions would arise about his naval career. It was easy for him to avoid the city of Bath, for his mother had just engaged a new architect to update parts of the Hall and money was needed for the renovations.

Still, he disliked the parade of spoilt, pampered young women that were flaunted in his presence.

He would be polite, of course, and occasionally he would steal a kiss from one of the willing women, but that was normally as far as he would go. There were plenty of village maids willing to share his bed, especially as his aloofness to the daughters of the gentry seemed to excite the peasant women. In the back of his mind there was a vague memory of a few drunken nights when his behaviour might have been...well, misconstrued, but he soon pushed that away.

Things came to a head one day in the middle of a hot summer. His father called him into his study. The look on his face didn't bode well and Henry was nervous by the time his father told him to sit.

'What were you thinking boy, do you know what you have done?'

Henry didn't, but he knew he was about to find out so he kept silent and waited.

'Catherine D'vere, does that name ring any bells?'

'No Sir should it?' asked Henry. He had a vague memory of a girl by that name having been at the house on his last visit, but he didn't want to admit it.

'Well lad, Catherine D'vere is to be your wife and be your wife soon.'

Henry was taken aback. 'I don't think so father, I hardly remember the girl, let alone want to marry her.'

'You have no choice you fool; it seems you were a little more than friendly with her on her visit and that friendliness has left her with child.'

Henry's jaw dropped, this was something he had not thought of. He could think of no way out of it either. His father would not let the family name be disgraced and he shuddered to think what the D'vere's would do to him if he didn't do the honourable thing.

Henry was caught and he knew it. He would have time to think on it, he had a voyage arranged and he hoped that he could put off his prospective bride until his return, but his father wouldn't allow him to set sail until the hasty marriage was arranged.

Catherine looked nervously around the great hall as her father; Sir John D'Vere took her arm in his. Today she was to become the bride of Sir Henry Meverall, a man that she only knew from a brief encounter that she now knew had been planned from the start by her own father and Sir William Meverall. The facts that a child was know growing inside her body did not bode well for the future. She had been trapped as surely as a rabbit in a snare and but for her religion would have thrown herself from the turrets of Granby Castle, their ancestral home.

She remembered that fateful night clearly, the grand banquet that had been put on by the Meverall's in supposed honour for her father, a true descendant from a Royalist family who had lost much in the civil war and was now near penniless. Halleswell Hall had glittered like a jewel in the Royal crown. The grand hall and stairs gleamed brightly in the myriad candlelight. At the time it had seemed like a dream come true, her debut into society at the age of just sixteen. Sir William epitomised all she thought sacred, his black hair lightly flecked by white and his stance and speech that of a true gentleman. The wine had flowed in fountains and her feet had ached from so much dancing. Yet she was happy for her parents who had spent lavishly on her ball gown. They had hoped for an alliance with her and the heir, Henry, although he was many years her senior.

Dutifully she had danced with him, knowing that her family could be saved from poverty by such a match. He was goodly of face and form,

his hair dark like his father's and the hazel eyes had twinkled merrily as
he swept her up in his strong arms with every lively dance.

The wine had gone to her head and when Henry had suggested a
breath of fresh air she had thought him chivalrous. There in the gardens
he had kissed her face and throat, his hands straying towards her breasts
with the low cleavage of her dress. What happened next had taken her by
surprise. The fumbling of his hands as he sought her maidenhead, the
fingers probing and prying until she beat on him with her tiny fists
clenched in anger. He had taken her like a mere peasant girl, sprawled
out on the grass and casually had cast her aside after it was over. She
had wept but her tears had only angered him. Her ball gown stained and
her virtue assailed she had crept inside where the lady Mary had
attended to her.

She should have been happy on this, her wedding day, but she
remembered how he had cast her aside that night. Now the hall
stretched before her, every surface decked out with early spring
flowers. Her mother had put the finishing touching to her dress,
while the French maid had dressed her hair in loops of gold. Her
dress was full, the petticoats making it hard to walk, but she
knew her dress was the best money could buy and if Henry
turned away from her then it would be from shame.

The music played as she walked sedately on her father's arm
along the vast expanse of the hall. Family and friends cast rose
petals before her feet but her eyes were on the man who waited
impatiently for his bride to join him. He looked distinguished in
his Navy uniform, yet whispers had reached her ears of his
disgrace and she wondered what would become of her in the
years to come.

The bedroom had been bedecked with flowers and her maid had
removed the lavish dress, leaving her in a silken robe which
caressed the rounded curves of her body. Catherine had put aside
her doubts and was awaiting the arrival of her new husband.
Surely he could not turn her away on this, their wedding night?
She paced the room with its huge canopied bed and paused to sip
from the chilled champagne, the bubbles tickling her nose and
making her laugh. He strode into the room, the uniform of his
rank in the Navy askew, his breath reeking of brandy. With delib-

erate motions he started to undress, the clothes cast on the floor as if he was deliberately discarding them for good. She took up another wine goblet and filled both to the brim with the sparkling wine,

'Come my husband; let us drink together for now we are one in the sight of God and the Holy Church.'

He took the goblet from her and drained it one gulp. 'So my bride wishes fair words and a civilised toast to our union? You can drink your wine and go to the devil for all I care. You trapped me into this sham of a marriage and if the brat survives he or she can also go to the devil for all I care.'

Filling the goblet once again he raised it to her lips, 'drink deep my wife, for when the tide turns then I go from you and may you have joy in this house for it's but a prison to me.'

Catherine's anger bubbled over. 'I beg to differ sir, 'twass you that stole my maidenhood and spoilt me for a better man than you. Now get out of my sight and take your drunken ramblings to a peasant maid, for I will not sleep with you tonight or any other night.'

'Is that so?' he grabbed at her and tore her gown from top to bottom. Once more he forced himself on her and when it was over he pulled away from her.

Catherine was beyond tears. She arose with dignity and walked across to the writing bureau where she picked up a silver letter-opener. Her robe hanging in tatters around her she advanced on Henry and held the tiny knife to his throat.

'I will never let you touch me again as long as we both live. This marriage is not to my liking and I say that the child I bear will not belong to you either. Now leave this room or I swear I will kill you.' In that moment she looked magnificent as a goddess with retribution in her hands.

Henry was appalled with the way he had treated her, his natural instincts were that she had trapped him into marriage and now he felt shamed. His own lusts were to blame, but even as he acknowledged this his thoughts turned to his ship and the feel of the wind in his hair, the roll of the ship as it breasted the turbulent waves. He could not find it in his heart to apologise but turned away and slept that night in the stables.

Catherine watched her husband as he walked out of the door and her young heart broke in two. Now she belonged to this strange family and in due course she would bear an heir to the Meveralls. She had no doubts that it would be a son, but for now she was just a young girl, robbed of her family and cast adrift in a loveless life. Throwing herself down on the bed she resolved that she would never give her heart to any man again. Her quiet sobs lasted all of the night, though she had had no idea what would come from her life with the Meverall family.

Having gathered his crew Henry wasted no time in setting sail. They had gone no more than five miles however before they found themselves confronted by two Navy ships and looking to the stern a third was blocking off their retreat. Henry thought about running and turned *Ghost* out to sea. That route was blocked too and with cannon on three sides Henry knew there was no escape. The trap had been well laid.

The Navy ships closed and one came along side *Ghost*. Armed marines boarded and it was not long before the entire crew were under arrest.

An officer approached Henry; there was the hint of a smile on his lips as he spoke.

'It seems that your activities in the smuggling business have come to an abrupt end Mr Meverall.'

Henry looked up at the use of his name. It confirmed his suspicion that they had been betrayed, he was known as Meverall only to the crew of *Ghost*, everyone else he had dealings with knew him as Samuel Cabot.

'Yes we know who you are Sir and what you have been up to for the last several years, I think you are in a fair amount of trouble are you not?'

Henry didn't answer; his mind was full of questions. How was he going to get out of this, who had betrayed him? He had no answers right then.

It appeared that the officer was of the same view and was not long in letting Henry know what was to be his fate.

'I have a proposition for you Mr Meverall. I have been autho-rised to offer you a choice. A man of your superior navigation skills could be of use to His Majesty. Of course it could not be done through regular channels as the King requires a service that can not be condoned or seen as anything to do with him or the British Navy. Your choice is to do this task or face the gallows.'

'Do I get to know the nature of this task before deciding?'

'Of course, but I think that is better discussed in private.'

Henry nodded and started to walk away from the gathering of his men and the marines. He noticed that several muskets followed his progress. His cabin was cramped but it was adequate for the purpose.

'There is a certain Spanish ship that his Majesty would like hunted down. It can't be seen to be any official action on our behalf, and of course the perpetrators of the act of sinking this ship would be condemned for their actions by his Majesty. 'So the officer gave the ultimatum.

'So my choice is the noose or a life on the run, neither choice sounds very attractive to me.'

'I am sure it doesn't, but the king is prepared to go some way to sweeten the deal. There is a plantation on a Caribbean island that he has promised to be handed over to you once the task has been completed. It will be in your name and be your property along with a statement of pardon. The only stipulation is that you do not ever return to this country.'

'My crew?' Henry enquired.

'Will be free to return or stay with you as they see fit and if they choose to return they will be issued pardons with the stipulation that they will be hanged should they be caught at smuggling again. Of course your ship will be forfeit at the conclusion of the deal.'

Henry was thinking fast, if this deal could be trusted it would get him away from the D'vere girl, he still didn't think of her as his wife, and he could live in the sun on a tropical island. This could work out in his favour.

'So it was no coincidence that led you to find us today then?'

'No we did receive certain information and it might flatter your ego that we have been chasing you for some time.'

Henry passed his eyes over his crew as if trying to see which of them had taken the tainted silver. It also crossed his mind to wonder if they knew about the cave.

'It seems there is no choice for me, is there, I don't fancy having my neck stretched just yet.'

'I thought you might come to that decision.' He pulled a packet from under his tunic and handed it to Henry. 'This contains your instructions and description of the target. It also details the rules of the deal we have almost struck ensuring fair play on both yours and His Majesty's behalf. That piece of information must not be imparted to anyone else other wise the deal is off. Do you understand Sir?'

'Yes I understand' said Henry taking the packet.

'Then let us shake hands on the deal as gentlemen should,' Henry was aware of the irony in the other man's tone. 'Good, then you will wish to be on your way, you have a long way to go. Good day to you Sir and good luck.'

And with that the marines left *Ghost* and returned to their own ship.

There was silence aboard *Ghost* as all the crew watched the Navy ships turn and make sail.

'Right lads, we have been given a reprieve but we are going to have to make a long trip. Mr Grimwood, set us a course for the Caribbean.' Without another word Henry turned and headed for his cabin. He needed to think, get this all straight in his head.

He sat for some time looking at the packet in front of him and he still hadn't opened it when there was a knock at his door.

'Come.' He said absently.

It was Grimwood. 'I have set us a course Sir but some of the lads want to know what is going on.'

Henry rubbed at his temples; he had a headache coming on. 'It's simple really, my friend. I was offered a choice; either enlist us all as privateers or face the noose. I didn't think many of you would want to hang so I took the job.'

Grimwood nodded, 'I had a feeling it was something like that, might I know what our task is Sir?'

'Simple, we have to go to the Caribbean, find and sink a certain ship.'

'I see, did they say why? I mean could it be a treasure ship. There could be a tidy profit in this don't you think?'

Henry smiled. 'I think you could be right Mr Grimwood. The Navy never said we couldn't loot the ship before we scuttled her.'

Grimwood turned to leave.

'One more thing Mr Grimwood, one of the lads must have turned us in. I think we might need to find out who the traitor in our midst is, so keep your ears open.'

'Yes Sir, I did wonder how they managed to find and trap us so easily. Might you have a word with the lads too Sir, let them know what's happening?'

They had been sailing for two days and were now well out into the Atlantic. They had a shadow; one of the Navy ships was following them at a discreet distance, obviously making sure they didn't renege on the deal. Henry wondered if they would be followed right across the ocean but by the next morning their shadow was gone. They were making headway and if the weather was kind they would make good time.

Henry sat in his cabin that evening, the packet still unopened in front of him. He didn't know why he was loath to open it, but he had a feeling he wasn't going to like the contents. Finally he broke the seal and pulled out the bundle of papers. It took him some time to go through them and when he finished he sat back with a sigh. He had been right. The Navy officer had neglected to mention a few things, like the fact that the ship they were hunting was in fact a Spanish Galleon. They were going to be massively out gunned and unless they could come up with a miraculous plan, there was little chance of them being able to sink it. So the navy had sent them on a suicide mission. They must have thought they had some chance of success though. They obviously wanted this ship dealt with and wanted it badly. There was no mention of the ships cargo or why they wanted it stopped, apart from the fact that it was a Spanish ship. Henry started reading between the lines. There was something about that ship that they didn't want it to reach its destination, for the plan of attack suggested a lonely location. The more he thought about it the more intrigued he became. All sorts of things were going through his mind and the more he thought the more excited he got. There must be something valuable on it, and he made up his mind that he was going to find out what it was and make it his.

A week later one of Henry's problems came to an abrupt conclusion. Grimwood had a quiet word in his ear and with a nod Henry followed him below decks.

'I think I have found our traitor Sir. I don't have any concrete proof but Cooper has been acting oddly since we had our run in with the Navy. He jumps as soon as anyone goes near him and he has a look of fear in his eyes whenever he is spoken too. Not much to go on but it might be worth a chat to him; see if a bit of persuasion will make him admit it.'

'Thanks Tom, send him to my cabin will you. I think a little chat might be in order.'

It was not long before Cooper was ushered into his quarters. The man was clearly ill at ease, but many of his crew would have reacted in a similar way. In all fairness Henry knew he should give the man the benefit of a doubt.

'Ah Mr Cooper, kind of you to come, can I offer you a drink?'

Cooper looked terrified. 'No Sir, thanks all the same.'

'Right, you don't mind if I do, do you?'

Cooper didn't answer; he was too busy chewing on his bottom lip.

Henry sat behind his desk with his legs outstretched across the corner. He didn't say anything but just looked at Cooper, a sardonic smile lighting up his handsome features.

It was not long before he got the result he was waiting for. The man was clearly guilty and suffering the pangs of his conscience. 'You know don't you Sir?'

'Know Cooper? What is it that you think I know?' He wasn't going to make this easy.

Cooper didn't answer, he looked at the floor and the look on his face said that he would rather be facing a dragon than his captain right now.

'If you mean do I know that someone took tainted silver and condemned his shipmates to death, then yes I do. If you mean do I know that you are the traitor, then I think your demeanour since you entered the room pretty much speaks of your guilt doesn't it?'

Cooper continued to examine the floor of Henry's cabin. Eventually he looked up. 'What are you going to do to me Sir?'

'We are privateers now Cooper, that makes us one step away from being pirates and you know what pirates do to traitors don't you, yes Mr Cooper you will feel the lick of the cat.'

'No Sir, please, I don't want to die please I beg of you.' The man buckled at the knees and shivered in fright. The Cat had been known to kill men, or even worse, to let them live on in agony.

'You should have thought of that before you took the silver shouldn't you. Now outside!'

The men were gathered on the deck, all aware that something was going to happen. As Henry spoke the words that branded Cooper as a traitor angry murmurs were already spreading through the sailors. It was one thing to cheek the captain, but to put all their lives at risk was an entirely different matter.

'Grimwood, lash Cooper to the mast,' Henry ordered.

Grimwood complied although it was no easy task with Cooper near faint from fear.

Henry wasn't looking forward to the passing out of the sentence either, but he had to control his crew, many hardened men with little left to lose except their lives.

Henry took his place and addressed the assembled men. 'Cooper here has already pleaded guilty to taking silver from the navy officers to turn us in,' his voice rang out clear in the noontide air.

'Now I must pass sentence on him, but first I will know what my crew think.' With that the angry men started to roar out, twenty lashes O' the Cat, no fifty, said another. The bosun spoke with scorn, 'I took me a hundred lashings an' still here to tell the tale.'

Henry finally agreed on fifty lashes, yet he had little stomach for the proceedings. Grimwood ripped the shirt from Cooper's back and gave the Cat an experimental crack in the air. The crew quietened down at once, a few had been licked by the Cat before and knew what was coming. The first stroke seemed almost a caress. So lightly did it fall, yet Cooper howled in pain as an angry red welt bruised his back. By the end of ten lashes he was beginning to whimper as the blood started to flow. After twenty lashes he was crying like a baby and Henry was finding it hard to keep looking at the man.

On thirty lashes Cooper briefly lost consciousness only to scream at the next ten strokes. By now his back was starting to resemble a piece of bloody meat and Grimwood gave Henry a questioning look.

He could have stopped it at that point, but the men were aroused by the sight of the blood and were chanting 'Death to the traitor.'

'What could he do?' he thought. 'Any sign of weakness and his crew would never respect him again.' Then he had an idea. Calling to Grimwood he shouted, 'Tom you need to rest your arm, and I have a thirst. Let us have a tot of rum.' Opening a barrel the crew were soon tossing back the rum and Henry was able to get Cooper cut down. He was still breathing but he was gasping like a beached fish.

'Haul up a bucket O' seawater,' Tom said, 'twill aid the healing and might yet save 'un.'

Cooper hovered between life and death for the next three days. The crew were satisfied with his punishment and each took turns in applying both salt water and then the salve to his back.

Yet he died on the night of the third day and the crew accepted that it was God's will. Not so Henry, he had never yet condemned a man to death and the feeling was enough to make him vomit. He was there the next day though, when the shrouded body was cast over the side of the ship to feed the fishes. Henry's education in the school of life was now complete.

It was a long and sometimes hard journey. The weather had for the most part been kind to them but storms had often lashed their craft with terrifying displays of nature's ire when thunder rolled, lightening scorched the sky and huge waves had pummelled them for days on end. It was early one sunny morning that the call they had all been waiting for came at last. 'Land ho,' rang down from the crows nest. Immediately the crew dropped what they were doing and stared ahead to catch the first glimpse of land that they had seen for weeks. A resounding cheer went up as the misty blue of a possible island appeared over the horizon. Over the next few hours the land came in sight. Through the telescope the largest land mass, a towering mountain came into full view. Henry had his sharpest crew member look out for signs of life on the rapidly nearing island, for island it soon proved to be.

They hove too just off the island and boats were sent ashore with most of the crew aboard. For many this had been the longest voyage they had made and it felt good to have the feeling of dry land under their feet once again, even though it might be just a short reprieve. They stayed on the island long enough to restore their stocks of food and water before setting out again. Henry was eager to get going again, but he saw the necessity of fresh food to lift the men's spirits. The island was quite large and populated by a good amount of fresh game in the form of wild boar, plump birds and an inland lagoon where the fish seemed to leap straight into their nets. He would have liked to explore further but it was time to go in search of their quarry. Looking over his charts Henry had the course the galleon was headed on and the rough date when it should be in the area, but it wasn't going to be easy, that he knew. Still, he had time on his side and a crew that were eager to see action after such a long time of doing naught but waiting on his instructions. Ensconced in his private cabin with Grimwood he poured over the charts and tried to plot a course that would take them as near to the Spanish galleon as possible.

They had only been sailing a few days when it seemed that luck was on their side. They had rounded the tip of Bermuda and were heading out to sea when a shout caused Henry to reach quickly for his telescope. There was a sail on the horizon. It was in the right area at the right time and it was not long before Henry decided the distant ship must be the one they were looking for. He could not believe they had found it so easily but he was thankful all the same.

Now came the difficult part however. How were they going to capture and sink the massive galleon? Henry called Grimwood and together they started to hatch a plan, it was desperate but both men thought it had at least a small chance of working.

'But Sir, I can see so many holes in this plan, if it works I can certainly see them surrendering, but all the timing and the luck would have to be on our side. We have the speed but we are relying on them not understanding what we are doing and changing course to broadside us.'

'I know Tom, I have seen it done once, many years ago and the Spanish captain turned and ran, if this one does the same then it will work, if not then I think we are in trouble. We are not on a Navy frigate now.'

'Sir, forgive me if I overstep the mark but what is the point of this, I mean why is it something the Navy couldn't handle, they have been sinking Spanish ships for years, what's so special about this one that they won't take responsibility?'

'I'm not really sure, from the little they have told me in my instructions, it is a delicate matter that would possibly cause all out war between England and Spain should responsibility for sinking that ship be laid at English feet, but if they happened to get waylaid by pirates, meaning us, then there would be no English involvement and they would get what they want.'

'So we are pawns then, used just to keep the King's hands clean?'

'That about sums it up, plus it is all that is keeping us from the hangman. I don't think failure is an option. If we don't succeed I think we are going to be listed as pirates with a price on all our heads. I don't know about you but the idea of that does not appeal to me.' Henry laughed ruefully, at least he retained his sense of humour!

'Sir, me and some of the lads have been thinking, if as how they want this ship sunk so much we reckon there is something valuable on it, there almost has to be doesn't there?'

'Not necessarily, Tom. Think about it. The navy would be risking at least one of her ships to take down that galleon and have to pay for the privilege. Getting us to do it gets the job done risk free. It costs them nothing and has the added bonus of being able to say that it was nothing to do with them.'

'But what if there is, we wanted to suggest capturing her rather than just sinking her, what do you think, could we give it a go?'

Henry smiled; he couldn't fault Tom's heart, or the rest of his crew's for that matter. 'I don't think so Tom, we would be outnumbered three to one and they are bound to have well trained marines on board. I think it would be suicide. We have a small enough chance as it is.'

A knock on the cabin door interrupted the debate.

'Come,' said Henry, annoyance flashing across his face.

Grimes poked his head around the door. 'Sir I think you had

better come an 'ave a look at this.'

Henry was on his feet immediately and heading out of the door as he answered. 'What have we got Grimes, they haven't seen us have they?'

'No Sir, we are keeping our sails below the horizon, but if you look past her that is what you need to see.'

Henry took the offered glass and raising it to his eye saw what Grimes meant. A grey line was appearing on the horizon, widening by the second.

'Fog!' Something clicked into place in Henry's mind. He had his plan. 'Tom you might get your go at taking her after all!' Much heartened by this change in fortune he called out,

'Pile on sail Grimes I want every knot of speed we can get now.' Now came the opportunity that he needed. It was to be a race then. If the galleon reached the fog bank they would lose it for sure

'Aye aye Sir,' said Grimes, before bellowing at the crew to add more sail.

Ghost was soon flying through the water, cutting through the waves and leaving a foaming white trail behind them. They had their chance, Henry knew the wind would be much lessened near the fog bank, slowing the galleon and giving him the chance to cut the gap between them fast. They would be spotted of course but if they could get near enough fast enough….. Henry turned to Grimwood, 'Tom time for us to open the gun cabinets and make ready to board.'

Grimwood smiled and the glint in his eyes said he was looking forward to this.

Henry remained where he was, the telescope switching from the ship ahead to the fog bank, it was going to be close and of course it was a gamble. If the galleon's captain chose to turn and fight instead of running for the fog then they were in trouble. Abruptly he laughed, 'we are damned if we do and damned if we don't,' he thought.

One advantage *Ghost* had over the Spanish ship was in its speed, being the lighter ship of the two. Faster the sails filled and the sleek craft started to gain on the galleon. Henry watched as the sails on the galleon went slack as the wind died before the grey curtain, looking lower he could see oars appear, they were making a run for it then.

'Give me every ounce of speed *Ghost* has,' shouted Henry, not taking his eyes off his quarry. It was going to be close, they were catching up fast now but Henry knew they would lose the wind in the same way as the galleon had before too long.

'Make ready oars but keep them shipped till I give the order,' he called to his first mate as he joined him on the fore deck. They might have need of those oars before long, but Henry had a loyal crew, not like the Spanish who often used slaves on the oars.

They were close enough now for Henry not to need the telescope, he could see the galleon's crew rushing around the deck trying to get more speed out of their ship.

Again Henry wondered why they hadn't turned to fight; they must have known they had their pursuers outgunned. Maybe they did have something valuable on board, something that they couldn't afford to risk in a gun battle, maybe that would work in his favour.

The galleon reached the fog bank. The grey curtain swallowed the ship up slowly as though enveloping it in a blanket.

At that moment *Ghost* lost the wind as they approached the fog.

'Cast oars,' yelled Henry. He knew that with the last of their speed they needed that extra impetus. *Ghost* glided into the fog as the rowers made rapid headway towards the point where the galleon had gone into the fog-bank. 'Ship oars.' The command was soft but relayed to the rowers.

There was silence on *Ghost*; all ears were straining to hear any sound from the Spanish vessel. Henry expected it to be still a little way ahead of them. Their surge of speed had certainly closed the gap but had the galleon altered course as soon as it entered the fog? *Ghost* would still be moving faster than the bigger, heavier galleon. Could they have missed her?

'You hear anything Tom?' asked Henry his own ears straining for any sound. There was none apart from the waves slapping the sides of the ship. The fog deadened sound, and Henry knew that they would be very close when and if they heard any noise from the galleon.

'No Sir, not a thing,' answered Tom.

And so it went on, the cat and mouse chase conducted virtually by sound alone.

Time went on and Henry began to have doubts, what if she had changed course in the fog? What if they had used the fog to turn the tables and start hunting them? What if... Enough of the 'what ifs, they had to be close; this was their best chance to capture her with minimum chance of loss of life. He had to be right, just had to. We should have caught them by now, how wide was the fog bank? Henry shook his head, there were too many questions invading it, too many doubts.

The fog seemed endless, visibility was down to a few feet and the temperature had plummeted. It seemed the rest of the world had disappeared; all that remained was their little patch of gloom.

A sound cut through the fog, a clink of metal on wood, it was close, very close.

The dark outline of their quarry was suddenly right there in front of them.

'Hard a port,' hissed Henry.

Ghost swung round and the grey shape of the galleon slowly appeared ahead of them. Once again the oars cut into the sea on Henry's command. 'Starboard now,' he whispered and *Ghost* swung round next to the galleon.

Musket fire flew at them from the deck of the galleon whilst cannon fire attempted to rip into the heart of the smaller vessel. *Ghost's* crew returned fire, their own cannon balls smashing through the Spanish hull. Gun smoke added to the fog making visibility virtually zero

The two ships ground together and immediately Henry led his crew over the hastily laid planks, swarming onto the galleon under cover of the dense smoke and fog. Brandishing cutlasses and muskets they looked like pirates and that was the cry of alarm that went up from the Spanish ship.

The battle that followed was short but bloody, with the better-trained Spanish officers trying to hold back Henry's men who seemed to be everywhere at once. Bullets flew through the air. Men screamed in agony as both bullets and swords found their mark. The outcome should have been to the advantage of the Spanish crew, yet it was Henry's scorched and bloody crew that won the day. Some of Henry's men hurried below to take the gun crews, others lined up the surviving Spanish soldiers on deck surrounded at gun point while others took control of the cabins.

Henry had escaped with a singed ear and a slight skin wound that nevertheless was bleeding quite profusely. Impatient with Tom worrying around him, he ripped the shirt from one of the Spaniard's back and bound it tightly around the wound. Inwardly he was delighted by how the battle had gone and not a little contemptuous at the lack of backbone shown by his foe. It was not long before the entire company of the stricken galleon were sitting on the deck casting angry, and not a few frightened glances at the armed men standing over them.

'Captain, come and look at this,' shouted, Smith. It took a moment for Henry to find the location of the voice in the dense fog, but a glimmer of light caught his eye. Smith had lit a brand and by the light of it he looked down into the hold, reeling back with the shock and stench of what he now witnessed there. He was shocked by what he saw. As a torch was held over the opening he could see a little movement which told him there was something alive down there. Taking Smith's torch he thrust it through the opening. Eyes were reflected in the light, dull eyes of hopeless souls. So this was a slave ship. Henry was sickened, he of course knew that such a trade went on and had to admit that he had never thought much about the fate of the poor souls sold like cattle and treated worse. But now with the stench rising from the hold he felt an overwhelming sympathy for them.

'Get a ladder down there and get those people out,' said Henry. The anger in his voice added bite to his orders.

Another commotion made him look up away from the slaves. More of his crew were marching three women toward him. The women didn't seem too pleased at being forced, especially the one in front. Her haughty expression was built from anger more than anything. She marched right up to Henry and demanded an explanation.

'What is the meaning of this; you have no right to board a ship going about its legal business,' said the woman in a strong Spanish accent.

Henry had to smile; she was showing more backbone than

the crew of her ship had. He was struck by her beauty too. Even in her towering fury her brown eyes melted his heart.

His staring seemed to catch her off guard and for a moment she flushed and looked away, it was only momentary however and her words when she turned back to him were full of venom, reinforced by more fury at her reaction of the moment before.

'I demand you leave this ship immediately and let us continue our journey.'

'I don't think so my lady.' Henry gave her his best smile.

'Are you mocking me Sir?' her flung back hand came round as she tried to smash Henry around the face. Henry saw it coming and stopped the blow easily.

'No your ladyship I am not mocking you in the slightest. I am overwhelmed by your beauty and you certainly have the heart of a lion, which is more than can be said of your crew I fear.'

'Pah, cowards the lot of them, they should have fought to the death, not given up like slaves.'

'Glad you mentioned them, your ladyship,' said Henry with a meaningful look at the weak and gaunt slaves that were being helped from the hold.

'What of them?' answered the Lady apparently unconcerned at the wretched state of the slaves.

'I see you are unconcerned at the treatment those PEOPLE have received at the hands of the masters of this ship.'

The lady didn't answer but the look on her face told Henry all he needed to know. Disdain and irrelevance were written all over it.

'What is your name milady?'

'You may call me Donna Isabella, I think that is all you need to know about me for the present.'

'Well Donna Isabella, it is my pleasure to make your acquaintance,' said Henry with a bow

Donna Isabella didn't think their meeting was much of a pleasure and she didn't hold back in telling Henry either.

There was silence for a time as the last of the slaves were carried out of the hold; these last few were obviously dead. The sailors laid them out along one side of the ship and for the first time emotion crept across Isabella's face, something close to horror and sudden realisation.

'Some of those people actually died down there?'

'Oh so there is some emotion in the ice maiden,' said Henry although he wished he hadn't almost immediately.

Isabella's expression returned to stiffened immediately.

'And what is to become of us Captain, are we to be your hostages? I am sure you would get a fair ransom for our safe return.'

'I am sure I would your ladyship but I am not a kidnapper and the less I have to do with authority, both your countries and mine the better I like it. And why would you be worth such a ransom, are you of some import in your country? I would guess that you are as you speak very good English, you must have had a good tutor.'

One of the other ladies stepped forward, perhaps made bold by her lady's bravery or maybe in frustration at the way Henry was speaking to her.

'Do you know who my Lady Donna Isabella is Captain?' She didn't give Henry a chance to reply but continued.' My lady is the half sister to Louis François, Duc d'Anjou; you should have more respect when you are in the presence of royalty.'

'Well Your Majesty, I do humbly beg your forgiveness,' said Henry with a courtly bow. 'We are in the presence of royalty lads,' shouted Henry. This was met by a loud cheer from *Ghost's* crew and not a few of them offered Isabella a bow.

Marie was on the verge of another outburst to berate Henry once again but Isabella interrupted, 'Enough Marie, be quiet.' Isabella was fuming and Marie with one glance at the look of towering fury on her face retreated with muttered apologies.

Turning back to Henry she looked at him. 'Well?'

'Well what, Your Majesty?'

'Well what are you going to do now, are you going to let us on our way now that you know who I am or do you intend to hold us hostage for a ransom?'

'I am afraid I can't let you go and as I said before I am no kidnapper, so that does leave us in a quandary does it not?'

Isabella looked slightly worried at that, not knowing what to read into Henry's words.

'What is the purpose for your presence on this ship anyway?' Asked Henry quickly, he had been hoping to catch her off guard and it seemed it had worked because she answered without thinking.

'I am to be married; I am on the way to meet my prospective husband.'

'Another arranged marriage,' said Henry bitterly.

Isabella was surprised by his reaction but she added, 'I am to be married to Alfonse Carreño who is Governor of Puerto De Plata.'

Although Henry kept up his show of cocky bravado inside he was starting to wonder what he had got himself into. This was more serious than he had been led to believe. Whatever he did now he was going to end up a hunted man, either by the Spanish or the British or more than likely both..

'Enough of this, very enlightening as it is we can not stay here forever discussing it. Mr. Grimes, take all the officers and put them adrift in a boat and give the rest of the crew the option of joining us or joining their officers, the slaves we will free. I am not sure how we are going to manage that so just keep an eye on them for now.'

'Mr. Grimwood, take mastership of this vessel and follow *Ghost*, keep some of its crew and a few of our lads to help you. I will take the rest of the new recruits over to *Ghost* and lead the way. The ladies will come over to *Ghost* with me, if they would be so kind,' said Henry with a bow in the direction of Isabella.

'What about these?' said Grimwood with a look at the slaves.

Henry thought for a moment, 'any of you speak English?' He asked the group in general. One man slowly raised his arm as though admitting to speaking the language would earn him a beating.

'Good' said Henry, 'that will make this easier, can you tell your friends that you are all free.'

The man looked stunned as if he couldn't believe what he was hearing. He turned to the other slaves and spoke; they all had a similar reaction to the first, disbelief and a fear that this was some trick.

Henry could see that they didn't know what to do. 'This is no joke or trick, you are all free men. If you wish you can stay to work with me or I will set you ashore when it becomes convenient.'

70

'I thank you Sir,' said the first man who had spoken, 'we are most grateful but where would we go if you set us free, we would be hunted as escaped slaves.'

'Then stay and work for me, I will see you fed and watered and you will be free to come and go as you please. All I would ask is for your loyalty the same as I ask of anyone who works for me. You should know that there is some danger in being associated with me and my crew as I think that we are not going to be popular with either English or Spanish but rest assured that you will come to no harm by my hand or those of my men and you shall take orders as a free man not as a slave. How do you say?'

There was a moment's pause before a resounding answer of 'aye' came from all the gathered voices.

The spokesman had further to say, 'master, we are not sailors and would work on the land, will this be possible?'

Henry had no answer at that moment. 'I don't know yet, we will see, I have to think a few things through. Rest assured I will not abandon any of you though.'

With that Henry turned once more to Isabella, 'Ladies if you would like to accompany me to my ship I would be most grateful.'

Isabella and the others followed him; there was nothing else they could do.

When they arrived at Henry's cabin Isabella looked round, she was horrified. 'You expect us to stay in this?' she exclaimed, waving a hand to indicate the none too clean, very cluttered room. 'There is only one bed, this is outrageous, why could we not stay in our staterooms on our ship, at least they were clean and airy.'

'And the ship is full of sailors who have been at sea for weeks without the scent of a woman, it is for your safety that I brought you here where I can keep an eye on you and make sure my crew don't get too interested.'

Both Isabella's maids pulled their shawls closer around them and even Isabella blushed slightly, her reply was none too coy though. 'Thank you for your concern Captain but I am sure your men could be expected to contain their urges as well as you can.'

Henry laughed, 'you know little of men then milady and even less of seafaring gents if that is what you think.'

'Now if you will excuse me I have some things to do. Oh and please do not leave this cabin without my permission; I would not want you to come to any harm whilst you are my guests.'

'Your prisoners by any other name,' said Isabella under her breath, she didn't think Henry had heard her.

After he had left the ladies he made his way to the ships wheel and issued orders to get them underway. Soon planks and ropes were hauled in and sails were raised and as they took the wind both ships started forward. To where though? Henry realized that he had no idea where to go or what to do next. He was in real trouble. He hit the wheel with his fist. Suddenly he wished he had done as instructed by the Navy, sink the galleon and take the reward. He couldn't do that now, the King's scheme had obviously involved the princess being dead and she was very much alive, a passing thought, maybe he could still come out on top if he killed her and scuttled the ship. He shook his head; he couldn't do that, suddenly what happened to Isabella mattered to him. He realized he liked the woman, they had only just met and her tongue had been vicious toward him but maybe that was what attracted him to her. She was a feisty one that was for sure, he almost pitied the man whom she was to have married, but there was something else, not pity but jealousy. Stop it, he thought she obviously hates me so no point in having thoughts in that direction. He had more important things to worry about than that woman anyway.

He couldn't go to the plantation he had been promised, the navy would know exactly where he was, he couldn't go home, he would be killed on sight. He had no money to speak of, most of his wealth was buried in the cave under Harland point. There must be money on the Spanish ship, Isabella must have had a fair dowry, his men had not found it but there must be a safe hiding place on there somewhere.

Henry made up his mind, their next move would be to go to some deserted island and ransack the galleon for every penny they could find, and then he would take them to a French or Portuguese run island. He quite fancied the idea of running a plantation, he had all the manpower he needed to run it in the freed slaves, they would work the land for him and willingly should he ask it of them. He now had two ships at his disposal as well, chances to make some profit there as well, either legit or illegal, it didn't matter too much out here.

Handing the wheel over to Grimes and ordering him to keep a straight course he made his way below to find his maps. They were somewhat incomplete but showed the majority of the known islands and crucially which country ran them. He dared not land on any British or Spanish owned island.

For now though one of the smaller uninhabited islands would serve him very well.

Two days of hard sailing had brought them to a small island. They had anchored both ships off the reef and had gone ashore in the longboats. Henry had gone to the Spanish galleon and together with Grimwood had started searching for the secret hiding place that must hide the valuables belonging to Isabella. He had brought the ladies with him so they could change their clothes and freshen up as they had put it. Isabella appeared at the door, watching Henry as he tapped the walls in various places. Henry was taken aback when he looked at her. She was dressed now in britches and a white cotton shirt, although it was the sort of thing a man might wear, no man would look that good in it.

'If you are looking for something Captain you could have just asked you know.' Isabella sounded amused and there was a slight grin creasing her face. Henry had to admit that the smile she wore suited her and made her more beautiful than ever.

Henry found that he was embarrassed and he laughed nervously. What was the matter with him? He was normally so assured and confident with women but suddenly he was unsure of himself in her presence and that annoyed him.

His annoyance made his answer harsher than he intended but the words had left his lips before he had a chance to think and he regretted them immediately 'I would not have thought Your Majesty would have been too keen on helping me rob her.'

'You would have been right then wouldn't you, but then after all a prisoner has no rights and I would not have been surprised if whereabouts of my wealth would have been beaten out of me by a pirate such as yourself.'

The good humour of her entrance was gone, the haughty princess was back and Henry mentally kicked himself, he had missed an opening, probably the only one he would get but his pride wouldn't let him back down now, an easy apology might have brought her round but he wouldn't do that. 'I could have it beaten out of you, or maybe beaten out of your maids, maybe that would have more effect as I think you might even enjoy a beating.'

'You dare to threaten me, well you will get no help from me, find it yourself if you can,' and with that she turned on her heel and left.

'Damn' said Henry as his pounded his fist into the wooden paneled wall, something else he immediately regretted.

Isabella was furious, damn the man, she wondered for a moment why she cared. She was even more surprised to find that she was crying, she didn't know if it was from fury or upset but she decided it must be the former.

When she entered the cabin she shared with her maids of course they immediately wanted to know what the pirate had done to her.

Strangely she found herself defending him. 'He has done nothing but knock back my attempt to improve our position.'

Marie and Louisa fussed over her and sympathized which ended up in them crying at their fate. Isabella needed some air; she needed to think things through. She was confused and although she hated to admit it there was a tiny part of her mind that was scared of what the future was going to hold for her. Leaving her maids she went up on deck and headed for the bow where she could be alone and think things through.

She had dressed as she had to visit him in an attempt to prove to him that she was not just a useless woman, thinking maybe that she could persuade him to deliver her to Puerto De Plata, wrong ploy, he hadn't even noticed her change of attire. Grrr, that man was enough to infuriate a saint.

As she thought about it she realized that she didn't want to do her duty, to go to Puerto De Plata and she certainly didn't want to marry the man she had been given to. This was her chance to escape her fate, to get out of marrying an older man she had never met and doubted that she would ever like let alone love. Did she really want to live a life of a dutiful Governors wife, endless parties and entertaining dignitaries? Sitting bored at home whilst her husband did his governing duties? The more she thought about it the more she realized she wanted more from life, but what, the concubine to a pirate? She started, where had that thought come from?

She was not sure she liked the direction her thoughts were taking her, yes he was handsome and well built, and didn't he know it too. He was also uncouth and she was sure there was a cruel streak in him a mile wide, but still even though she didn't want to admit it she was attracted to the man.

So what was she going to do next? Her strong adaptable woman ploy had failed miserably so there was only one thing left for her to do. She decided to do what she did best, dress in her finest, dazzle and intimidate the man into doing what she wanted.

What was it about the woman? She was haughty and certainly looked down her nose at him, not at all like the simpering women he was used to, those girls who were so easy to manipulate, young ladies that fell at his feet. No this one was different, he knew she wouldn't simper for anyone, maybe that was what he liked about her, the fact that she had the character to stand up to him. The more he thought about her, the more he thought of her as a challenge that he had to best. He would have her in his bed, of that he was sure. It would be fun to have a challenge to get her there rather than just having to smile and utter a few sweet words to have them eager to do his bidding. He thought how different Isabella was from Catherine. When he occasionally thought of her there was nothing, but Isabella, she certainly sparked his interest.

The next few days saw Henry busy organizing the re-supply of the ships. The galleon had been much better supplied than *Ghost* so some of the rations were moved over to her and both ships were topped up with what could be gleaned from the island.

Henry decided to invite Isabella to dine with him. He sent one of the sailors to cordially invite her to dine with him. She sent back a polite acceptance and Henry set about organizing the evening. He wanted to impress her so put all his efforts into ensuring that they would have the best food that they had available to them.

Isabella had been surprised to receive such an invitation to join the English Captain, Henry at dinner in his private quarters. Despite her pride she was intrigued to know how the English dined, besides she was bored with being cramped up with her maids alone in the tiny cabin they shared. To share a room with a mere maid was an insult that she could no longer tolerate, so she accepted the invitation. Tonight she would dazzle them with her best gown and then see how Henry would come crawling on his hands and knees to worship at her feet!

A tiny worm of doubt tried to enter her thoughts, Henry was a man used to being treated as royalty by his crew. He was also very handsome with his dark hair and flashing black eyes. Compared to the old man she was destined to marry, Henry cut a dashing figure with his white shirt open to the waist, the dark chest hair proclaiming his manliness.

'No! She would not think this way! It was insult to her proud family name!'

As he inspected the food before it was cooked Henry had to admit that the crew had done well in collecting together reasonable fayre. It would have to be something special for Isabella to be impressed. He shaved and put on clean clothes and even had a dip in the sea to get his body clean in readiness for the evening.

The evening arrived and Henry stood in the cabin, bathed in candlelight as he awaited Isabella's arrival. She was late.

For once she had an honour guard to the Captain's quarters. Yet it was spoilt by Grimes who insisted on wrapping a large cloak about her. 'Heavens Missy, sure you could not go out dressed like that?'

'And why not, English peeg? My gown, it is beautiful, n'est-ce pas?' These fools could not speak Spanish, though a few spoke French quite well.

'Yes, well I have to speak as I find, it is your bosom Madam, sorry, I meant Donna Isabella.'

'You do not find my "bosom" to your liking?'

'I like it too much and so will the rest of the crew. They ain't seen a woman in months, one look at those Bristol's an' they would revolt.'

'Pah! You speek like a fool.'

Isabella arrived with imperial grace; she floated into the room, her embroidered gown swishing across the planks of the cabin floor. She looked stunning, her long black hair was immaculate and intricately woven with strings of pearls and her gown, revealed when she removed, with some disdain the cloak that Grimes had insisted on, hugged her in all the right places and flowed to the floor in a cascade of grandeur. She approached Henry and held out her hand for him to kiss; she was in her element here. She knew how to be regal; she had done it all her life.

Henry kissed the proffered fingers with a bow and led her to her seat at the table; he was going to show her he knew how to behave too.

Once they were seated they waited for Grimwood to bring in the soup. When it was put in front of her, Isabella sat and looked at it and then poked at it with her spoon, she took a couple of sips before putting it down.

'The soup is not to your liking?' asked Henry as he ate his with gusto.

'I have had enough thank you,'

Henry finished his and Grimwood came in with the main course. Isabella was not impressed with this either and her regal manners slipped.

'How could she eat this pigswill? The beef was tough, the vegetables mushy and the wine very inferior to what she was used to.'

Grimwood was refilling Isabella's wine glass when he caught his foot in her gown and spilt wine down her precious dress.

'Bastido! Son of a dog! How dare you, my gown, it is ruined. Captain, flog this man, I demand it.'

Henry had enough of the bitch's sharp tongue. It was time to teach her a lesson.

'It was an accident Milady, I am sure Mr Grimwood is very sorry.'

Grimwood was trying to dab at the spilt wine whilst trying to avoid touching Isabella's displayed cleavage.

'consiga de mí, cómo el atrevimiento usted me toca.' Isabella was so furious that she lapsed into her mother tongue.

Henry tried to calm her for a moment but finally he lost his temper, 'Grimwood. Out! And you Milady, I think it is time you were taught a lesson.'

Isabella uttered a gasp of shock as Henry grabbed her arm and dragged her to the couch where he put her over his knee and proceeded to spank her. Isabella was screaming incoherent obscenities at him, kicking and punching any part of him she could reach.

Eventually Henry stopped and he sat Isabella upright on his lap. Her reaction was not what he had expected. Instead of jumping up and continuing to rant and rave she looked into his eyes and dropped her lips to touch his. Henry was not about to let her have the initiative, and so wrapping his arms around her returned her kiss with all the passion he could muster.

Isabella pulled back, her breasts were heaving in her tight bodice, a fact that didn't escape Henry's notice. Isabella saw where his eyes were glued and slapped him around the face. That slap held no malice however and Isabella was not really displeased to have her body examined.

She made no complaint as Henry started to work on the many buttons and hooks that held her dress. In the end he was not going fast enough for her liking and started to undo the fastenings herself. She had to stand to let the gown fall to the ground and she stood in front of him in her undergarments, her chest was heaving again, this time out of anticipation. Henry wasted no time in removing the rest of her clothes and she returned the favour by ripping his shirt from his back and they both worked on his britches. Once all their clothes were mingled on the cabin floor Henry picked Isabella up and carried her to his bunk. He gently laid her down and joining her gently kissed her before doing it again with rising passion. His hands wandered across her body, fingers caressing nipples that rose to meet his touch. Soft groans of pleasure escaped Isabella's lips as she enjoyed his touch. His fingers slowly worked their way down the length of her body, caressing her thighs before finally finding her most secret of places. Isabella was not going to let him take control of the situation and her hands roved over his well muscled frame and closed around his rising member.

Henry adjusted his position so as to enable him to enter her and for a moment they looked into each others eyes before his lips joined with hers and their bodies completed their union.

Sated they lay together, Henry's finger lightly brushing away loose strands of Isabella's hair from her face.

They slept until the first rays of the new day's sun crept across the room waking Isabella. She carefully escaped from Henry's arm that still embraced her and finding her clothes she left the cabin and hurried back to her own. Once there she made sure her maids were still asleep and proceeded to dress once more in her shirt and britches and then headed for the deck. She had to think about what had happened last night, she felt such a mix of emotion, anger at herself for letting it happen, embarrassment for enjoying it but most of all she was surprised to find that her overwhelming emotion was happiness.

Henry sat on the porch and looked out at the setting sun as it slowly sank into the darkening ocean. It was hard to believe they had been here for nearly two years now. In some ways Henry's life had undergone some profound changes in that time. He would never have believed he would have enjoyed running a sugar plantation. It had been a natural progression from when they had decided to stay on the island. He had a ready made workforce and natural resources in abundance. Their island was a paradise and was thriving. Of course his crew had not been happy with the lack of female company and had set out rectify that situation. They had soon found willing partners in the pirate ports and not a few from ships that called at the island that now had a small port. So now there was quite a community on the island.

The galleon, that Henry had renamed *Donna Isabella* was used to transport the cane they sold and to import goods that the community needed.

Ghost however was hidden away. Henry was not satisfied with just the plantation and his love for the sea was sated by frequent trips in *Ghost* to hold up Spanish shipping.

The plantation had become almost a front for Henry's more secretive business and it had all fitted together very well indeed.

His relationship with Isabella was something that both intoxicated and infuriated him. To say their relationship was fiery would be a gross understatement. Henry had made the mistake of trying to bend Isabella into a more malleable person. He had learned the hard way that Isabella was going to be subservient to no man. With a wry smile his fingers found the scar on his arm where she had cut him during one of their fiercer discussions. He would have it no other way really, it was the fire that burned inside Isabella that had attracted Henry to her in the first place. Without it he doubted whether their relationship would survive or indeed would ever have started.

There was just one thing that was playing on his mind, it nagged at him and he wondered at it. He had a child in England he knew, a child that he had never seen or had news of. As time went on more and more he thought he wanted to see his child. It was irrational as there was no room in his life at the moment of offspring but he just had to see it, to acknowledge his or her existence.

He came to a decision that night as he watched the sun set. He would make the trip to England and see his son. There was just one obstacle in his way, Isabella; he didn't think she would be too keen to let him out of her sight for several months. Trust was one thing that she was short of in his case, he couldn't blame her really at the start of their relationship he had not exactly been faithful to her. When he looked back now he had been foolish in the extreme to think he could get away with kissing other wenches. And now he would not want any other women. Isabella made sure of that both with words from her tongue and the way she used her body to keep him faithful.

Isabella was an intuitive woman and she knew there was something troubling Henry. When she found out what it was she surprised him by not only agreeing to him going but saying that he should go because if he didn't he would be wondering for the rest of his days.

Decision made Henry didn't take long to get all in readiness for departure. He had decided to go in *Ghost* as she was faster than *Donna Isabella* even though there was more of a risk of being hunted by the Navy in his own ship. It was a risk he was prepared to take to get him back to where he now called home as quickly as possible, plus at least if he had *Ghost* under his feet he would have a chance of running from any navy vessels if they encountered any.

THE WINDS OF CHANGE

Catherine drew her cloak tightly around her as she slipped out of the servant's door. Her restless night's sleep made her long for a breath of fresh air but it was so hard getting away from the women of the house who thought that women in her late stages of pregnancy should lie abed all day. It had been quite easy to get away with half the kitchen staff still abed and the scullery maids struggling to light fires on this blustery January day. She trod carefully, the light at this hour of morning just beginning to streak the sky with a hint of dawn. A gust of fierce wind threatened to blow her off her feet and she very nearly turned back, but that would be giving in and one thing that Catherine did not lack was courage.

Brannon's Wood was taking a battering; the ancient trees whipped up by the wind sent smaller branches tumbling through the air, whilst the thunderous roar of the storm drowned out all other sound.

She would head towards the lake through the ornamental gardens whose hedges gave a little shelter from the storm. Gasping with the effort of staying upright she paused for a moment and surveyed the scene before her. Swathes of grass rippled down towards the choppy waters of the lake. In the half light of morn grass and waves blended into one, a grey-green sea of movement capped by white edged spume. The sight made her momentarily dizzy and she laid one protective arm around her mounded belly. She had not wanted this child, but since it had first kicked inside her she had grown to love it. The child would be hers alone, she had not seen or heard from her husband since their wedding night.

Another gust blew her hood from her face, tendrils of blonde hair escaped from their snood and danced in the breeze. Suddenly she felt a moment of freedom and laughed out loud for the thrill of being young and alive. She would survive this prison and make a life for herself and her child. After all, she was bearing the child of the heir to the Meverall fortunes.

It was then she heard the whimper under the noise of the wind. It sounded like an animal in distress and her warm heart was touched by the plea. Taking a few careful steps backwards she reached the line of the hedges and peered inside for the source of the sound.

He was half-hidden by the bush that had trapped him. Nicholas, Henry's brother, was trying hard not to cry as the brambles caught at his clothes.

'What are you doing here?' she asked and then realised the question was a moot point; he was scared to death by the trickle of blood running into his eyes where a bramble had grazed his cheek and temple.

'I am sorry Kate; I didn't mean no harm, only I thought you should not be alone out here with the storm getting worse.' He was trying to be brave and Catherine knew she should not treat him harshly. It was difficult to keep that resolve though as Nicholas followed her everywhere like an overgrown puppy.

'Take my hand Nick and let's get you out of there quickly. If I try to untangle all the knots we will be here all day,' she tried to sound decisive knowing he could easily panic.

'But I can't see, Kate, have I lost my eye, it hurts so much?'

Gently she wiped the blood away with the sleeve of her dress, 'there now, it's only a small cut 'twass the wind in your eyes and a bit of blood.'

Still she was starting to worry. The wind was freezing her hands and a low misty drizzle of rain was making visibility poor. Gripping his hands tightly she pulled him towards her and at that very moment she felt a warm rush of something between her legs. Had she wet herself, or mayhap it was blood? The fear blanched her face and set her shivering. She had no mother to tell her the rites of birth and she had feared to show her ignorance to the women of the house.

Nicholas was busy picking the burrs from his coat and failed to see his beloved Kate collapse on the ground. When he did look up his heart froze in his breast.

'Kate, oh Kate, what have I done, please get up,' his eyes were filled with tears mingled with his blood. She was lying on the ground, her breathing ragged and her eyes closed. Frantically he looked around but the mists and rain that fell so suddenly in this part of the country had descended on them both. They were hopelessly lost and he feared to leave her. 'Help! Please God help!' he cried as the wind tossed his words away. Now he wished he was a grown man, not a thin boy of scarce thirteen years. All he could was to strip off his coat and place it under her head while he chaffed her icy hands. Should he risk trying to get back to the house or to stay and hope that search parties would be sent out as soon they were both missed? Looking at the pallor of Kate's face decided him. He could not leave her here alone and so cold. With one last cry of 'Help', he laid his own body around hers and prayed they would soon be found.

He must have dozed for a moment for he felt a wet tongue lick his face. The dog was preceded by its owner, 'By all the Holy Saints, what has happened here?' he heard a woman's voice with that soft accent that spoke of a local woman.

'Please help us,' he uttered, his voice breaking.

The woman bent forwards and gently nudged him out of the way. As she examined Kate he noticed that even in this cold weather she wore only a shawl around her thin blouse and full skirt. Her boots were sturdy though and she held herself square against the rising wind. Kate's eyes flickered open with no surprise at seeing a stranger. 'Can you sit up Milady?' Kate nodded yes and Nicholas rushed to help her up. Calmly the woman looked at him and spoke, 'Meg is my name lad and birthing is one of my trades. The lady is going to have her baby this day and needs help.' She looked at him as if assessing his strength. 'You'll do fine my boy, now this is what I need you to do.' Unwinding the length of rope that held the dog she handed it to him. 'Fix this tight around your waist. I will hold one end while you follow the hedges back to the gardens. From there you should be able to find the house clearly. You do not need the rope, but I will come and help you if you become afraid. Can you do this task?'

Nicholas nodded, the steady eyes had reassured him and he felt he could do anything. But one question tugged at his mind,

'Why can't you go Meg, for I am sure you would find the house more quickly than I?'

'What do you think the fine ladies would do if such as I knocked on their door?' she smiled gently, 'they would take me for a Tinker and send me packing. They would also want to know what I am doing on their land, do you understand that lad?'

'You will take good care of her?'

'As if she were my own sister,' was the reply and with that he was content.

Thomas Edwin Meverall was born in the early hours of January 29th 1728 after a long and difficult labour. But for the insistence of Nicholas and Catherine herself both mother and babe would have died, but as Meg was widely considered to be a skillful midwife and had kept Catherine alive when Nicholas went for help, the women of the house tolerated her. Despite his wounds and a chill that only warmed brandy could ease, he had paced up and down the hallways as if he were the father of the babe. Nothing would induce him to go to his bed until both mother and babe were pronounced out of danger, and then he slept for twenty four hours not even breaking his fast.

Thomas was small as he had been born before his proper time, but he was pink and healthy and took to the breast straight away. Henry's mother, Louise had tried to procure a wet-nurse for the baby and was near scandalised when Catherine insisted on feeding Thomas herself.

'Tis but a fancy Milady,' Meg had intervened, 'the poor mite came near to death's door so 'tis natural that she clings to the child. She had a queer turn and 'twas lucky that Master Nicholas saw me walking in the woods and called for help.' So it was that Meg's presence was explained, and lucky she had been that the doctor agreed that Catherine should be indulged in all things with her so weak still.

If anyone had queried the doctor they would have found that he often called on Meg for help with the birthing. She was clean, skilled and had a special touch with frightened women, but it was a closely guarded secret.

Sir William was overjoyed with the birth of an heir and sent several messages to the Navy to tell his son of the birth. It appeared that Henry was on a special mission and could not yet be contacted and with that he had to be content. Catherine blossomed as the weather became milder and little Thomas finally managed to put on weight. Both Louise and Mary, Henry's sister doted on the child so that Catherine began to feel as if her role as mother was being usurped. Her one delight was in Nicholas, who had seemed to have grown up overnight since that fateful day when she had nearly lost her life and that of the babe. Sitting in the nursery with the pale light of March awakening the frozen earth she crooned to Thomas as he slept in his cradle. Nicholas would find her there, his arms full of early spring flowers. Brannon's Wood gave up its bounty with a display that surpassed the ornate garden flowers. Early primroses gave way to wood anemones, stately irises mingled with the pink of cyclamen and March brought its treasures of daffodils, crocus of every colour, the sweet perfume delighting her heart. Nicholas would sit at her feet as she carefully stitched tiny garments for Thomas to wear. He would make her laugh with tales of the villagers and the mysterious tinkers that told fortunes for rich, pampered ladies.

Her greatest pleasure though came from the way he sang to Thomas or coaxed a smile from the baby with his antics. Once when she weary from sitting up with Thomas who had developed a nasty cold, it was Nicholas who sponged the baby's hot brow and smoothed the golden hair with a tenderness that brought tears to her eyes.

Soon Thomas would have to be christened, but Henry had sent no message and she dreaded the day when he came to see his son, for then she would have to play the dutiful wife or carry out the threat she had made on their wedding night.

However, a year passed by with no news from Henry and when a second year brought no news it was feared by Sir William that something had happened to his oldest son and heir. Catherine was glad of the reprieve though she knew that in Henry's absence the friendship between her and Nicholas was becoming more than that of brother and sister. Though separated by nearly five years in age, Nicholas was fast becoming a man and though she tried hard she was finding it difficult to think of him as a love struck young boy any more.

Nicholas and Catherine were enjoying a walk around the gardens on a late April day when their attention was caught by the sound of horse's hooves galloping past at a dangerous pace. Catherine's hand flew to her mouth to stifle the sudden scream of fear, for she thought she recognised the arrogant man under the filthy clothes he wore. Dismounting he called 'hey boy' to one of the stable lads and without a backward glance ran lightly up the stairs and into the house. 'It's Henry,' Nicholas said flatly, 'and in a great haste by the look of it. Oh Kate, what if he has come home to stay? I could not bear that.'

'Yet he is my husband by law and the father of dear Tom, though I see no resemblance in his sweet face. Come, dear Nick, and get this torture over with.'

Both hastened to the nursery and Catherine cradled Tom in her arms. Anxiously she awaited the sound of footsteps on the stairs outside the nursery, but they were long in coming. Instead she could hear raised voices and the sudden slamming of a door.

Sir William was furious and did not care who heard his foul language. He paced the floor of his study, unconsciously flicking his riding crop. This was not the way he envisioned the return of his son and heir. The man who had strode into his private sanctum and demanded ale and brandy was a filthy lout, not the gentleman he should be. To make matters worse he had neglected the care of a good horse, leaving the stable boy frightened and unsure what to do next. 'Damn it all,' he thought, 'even a peasant would have more care for an ass, let alone a fine horse.'

Henry, for it was indeed his errant son, was sprawled in HIS armchair with his dirty boots resting on the edge of a low table. Glass in hand he was gulping back the brandy he helped himself to and was laughing at his father. 'Crack!' William swung the whip at his son's boots.

'You Sir, WILL behave with some manners in my home, now get your dirty feet down before I whip you in earnest.'

'I thought that removing boots was the job of your servants, father? As to taking that silly riding whip to me, maybe you should know that I have wielded a far more dangerous thing than that little toy?' he sneered at his father.

'Damn you to hell, I will not be spoken to so in my home. By Gad Sir, you are a bounder and if I see right you are a disgrace not only to the family name but to the Navy.' William was now struggling to regain his composure, not wanting to discard his heir and the boy he once loved so well.

'Come father, do you not see that I have ridden long and hard this day. If my manners are so rough and ready to you, think not what it has been like these many years, far from any proper civilisation?' Now Henry was acting the penitent and expecting his father to bow to his every wish. William was not to be taken in so easily though. Instead he looked at the long tangled hair, the matted beard dripping with the dregs of the drink and wondered if there was anything left of his son inside this boor.

'Well, father, I take it you do not approve of my appearance? Oh yes, I know that look of old. I suffered it enough as a child but now I am my own man,' here he stood up and a look of venom crossed the handsome face. Laughing again at his father's anger he coolly poured himself another large brandy. 'I see the smugglers keep you well supplied with France's finest drink.' William began to swear again and the whip hovered dangerously near to Henry's face. 'Deny it all you may, but I found the secret cellar long ago. Who knows, that very fine brandy could have come from my very own ship?'

If William had been hot with anger before, now he turned icy cold and Henry took a step back.

'His Majesty's Navy are above petty smuggling. You are a liar and a scoundrel. I should whip you within an inch of your life if you have brought scandal on the family name.'

'Come now father, let us not argue, for the prodigal son returns to see what manner of son my wife has born me.' William liked this tone of voice even less, but the man had a point. Like it or not he was Thomas' father and entitled to see the child.

'Of course you may see him, but first you wash or you enter the nursery over my dead body.'

'That could be arranged,' Henry muttered, but he could do with a hot bath and a plump maid to scrub his back. Besides, he still wished to see his mother, the only person here that would be glad to see him.

Washed, fed and considerably drunk Henry finally climbed the stairs to the nursery as the sun was going down in a red ball of flame. The child was asleep in his crib and Catherine stood by, her face a mask of hatred. Nicholas had been made to join his father in the study, although it went hard with him to leave Catherine on her own.

Boldly Henry crossed the room and made as if to scoop the child up in his roughened hands.

'Pray do not wake him, sir, for he has only just gone to sleep,' Catherine tried to keep her voice even though she was shaking inside. He ignored her completely and picked the sleeping child up so quickly that Thomas began to bawl with the rough treatment. For an instance Catherine thought she saw a flicker of something akin to tenderness but then it was gone and the usual sneer was back on Henry's face.

'Whose is this puling weakling, for he is no child of mine?'

'How dare you say that you...you bastard?' she screamed at her tormentor.

'For certain it is the child who is the bastard and I say again this is no child of mine.' With that he went to drop the baby back in the crib but Catherine grabbed Thomas away from him and placed the baby gently back in his crib.

'I am ashamed to say he is your child, though God help me, I wish 'twere not so.'

'You jest Madam. Look at his tiny body and his pale hair. The Meverall family have dark or chestnut hair and are strong and sound of limb. I repudiate him as I do you.' This was serious. If Henry failed to claim the child as his she could be put out with the child to return to her father, who would die of the shame.

'My hair is the same colour and anyway, a child's colouring changes when he grows. Neither is he a weakling, he was born a full three weeks before his time. He is barely past two years old so you cannot judge his colouring yet.'

Suddenly Henry looked bored, in truth he had been momentarily surprised by the thought of his child and the feel of the boy in his arms. That was one weakness he could not afford to give into if he valued his life style and Isabella would not welcome a child of his. Still, he was angered by his thoughts and up to some malice before he left.

Pulling Catherine to his body he grabbed her by her hair and forced his lips to hers. Filled with hatred she could not stop herself and hit him across the face with all the force she could muster. He looked momentarily foolish and then that same arrogance was back again.

'What a boring little milksop you are Catherine. I like my women with meat on their bones and a fire in bed. You would chill the blood in the veins. Mayhap a spanking would put some life in you,' and with that he went to put her across his knee.

At that moment Nicholas came hurtling into the room and threw himself at his brother. Things may well have gone ill if Sir William had not been right behind him. Swishing the riding crop he brought it down on Henry's arm which had gone around his brother's neck.

'Get out of my house right now,' he yelled his face suffused with blood. 'I have no son save for young Nicholas here. He is twice the man you will ever be.' Henry may still have done an injury, but he could not afford to be detained here right now. 'Ah, I see it now, two milksops together mooning over each other. But remember Catherine is still my wife, so the boy shall bear my name and you can want each other all you like.' Seeing Nicholas' face he knew his barb had struck home.

'As for you, father,' he spat the word out,' look after the child well for I fear you will have no more grandchildren.'

Taking the stairs in great bounds he stopped only to pick up his old clothes, for he still needed his disguise. His horse had been groomed well but he had need of both speed and a cloak of darkness. Glancing quickly around, he espied his father's great black stallion. Let them have the Arab horse, the black would suit his need. Laughing like a demon from hell he bound away and vowed never to come to Halleswell Hall again.

The door to the cottage swung upon and the cloaked figure was ushered quickly inside. Though the room was small it was clean and smelt sweetly, not like some of the hovels in the village. Firelight lit the corners where the sparse furniture was revealed, a pallet strewn with clean straw, a wooden rocking chair and by the fire a handsome straight-backed chair. 'Sit you down there,' Meg motioned to Catherine who welcomed the warmth from the fire for it was a bleak December evening and she had walked far by secret ways.

'Mistress Kate, you took a great risk coming here tonight, why did you not send the stable lad to me with a message, for he's kin and would keep quiet on pain of death?'

'Hush, Meg, do not worry, for none would recognise me even without the cloak.' Letting the garment fall she was revealed dressed as a young lad might if he were a-courting a maid.

Meg had to laugh, for Kate (as she was now called by all except visitors) looked the part with her skin still lightly tanned from the harvesting and her golden hair tucked back under a dark wig. 'Shall I fetch you some elderberry wine, it's been a fine year for the making?'

'Please Meg, I should like that.'

Catherine had never been inside the cottage before now though she had often met the wise woman in the woods or about the kitchens of the Hall. Though she kept to the servants' quarters, it was no secret that the other women of the house would chance to appear when she visited. Meg's skill with herbs was matched by her skills with powders and potions to make the skin appear pale and unblemished. Her elderberry wine was much sort after for it's delicate taste and heavenly aroma. Many a local gentlemen swore that her poultices were far superior in the treatment of gout than the good doctor, though none would mention it in society.

Kate eased the boots from her feet, glad of the respite from the stuffing of straw that made Nick's boots fit her tiny feet. Now Meg placed a small tray between them as she pulled up the rocking chair to the fire. There were two earthenware mugs set by the bottle and a plate of flat cakes still warm from the oven. Privately she thought the cakes good enough to grace the table of a Lord, but to say that would only embarrass her friend and her errand here tonight was too important to be denied.

Meg kept her silence, knowing that Kate would need time to broach the question on her mind. While they sipped the wine and nibbled at the cakes she had time to think over the past few years and the changes that had taken place up at the Hall.

She knew of Henry's disgrace, of course, village gossip had kept it alive for many months. What was more surprising was the way in which Nick had taken to following the factor around the estate and even helping out with the harvest. When the rents were due he would sit in the factor's office and although he kept his silence the first year, by the second he was greeting the farmers by name and even asking about their families. By the third harvest following Thomas' birth, Kate had asked if she could help in the main fields belonging to Halleswell Hall. It was no small measure of the respect the women had for the Mistress of the house that allowed her to do light duties in the fields. Some women gossiped it was to be near Nick, for the growing love between them could not be missed. However, the men folk soon stopped that, for there was never more than the familiarity of brother and sister between them. In public they displayed great restraint, though few of the landed gentry now called at Halleswell Hall with no young girls to court. Sir William and his wife were growing older and the elder sister Mary had never shown any inclination towards marriage. So all things told, it was generally a happy household only marred by the dishonour of Henry.

'Meg, I asked you a question, have your thoughts strayed back to your native land?' It was well known that Meg had family in Wales and some thought mayhap in Scotland as well.

'My pardon Mistress, my thoughts were rather nearer to home, but come now, this is no mere social visit, though glad I am to see you.'

Catherine shifted uneasily in the chair, 'can you divine the future?' she asked.

'By all the Saints Mistress Kate, what do you think me to be? Such arts are the works of the devil and his misguided followers. Even the tinkers pretend no such thing, for they have their own code of honour. Some have the sight but that is a gift from God and never to be used lightly.'

Catherine hastened to calm her friend's fears down. 'I did think you may have the sight, but please believe me I meant no harm or idle question. The thing I have to ask you is of great importance to me and to one I love. Before I asked you that I needed to know if there were any other hope, for now I have none.' Her eyes filled with unshed tears and her hands started to tremble. 'What I ask now goes against the Christian church but I see no other way.'

Poor Meg, she had expected the question. Indeed she had spent much time in prayer, for although her herb knowledge was great she was a true Christian and only worked for the good. Sighing deeply she made it easier on Kate. 'You want to ask if I have a herb or potion that will stop a man's seed growing in your womb. I have such a remedy but it carries a great risk if you wish to be with child at a later time. Normally I give it with reluctance and only to a woman who has already too many mouths to feed. No, do not interrupt,' for she had seen Kate about to speak, 'with knowledge comes power, but also a great responsibility. You wish to ask this of me for the love between you and your husband's brother. That love is beginning to tear you both apart. You see no moral answer for it is a sin to commit and yet I don't need the sight to know the burden of grief you both bear. Nicholas is still very young and may yet marry, though if the fire consumes him then he may commit an even greater sin, that of lust and not love. I am right in this, you have spoken to him?'

'Spoken? Yes Meg, we have done naught else. Once, maybe...a moment in the fields, the sun hot and both of us drunk with the day's delight. A kiss that sent my heart souring, my legs weak and a feeling in my body such as I have felt before. Oh Meg, he cried as he pushed me away, swearing eternal love and that he would never put me in that position again. Since that day we have tried to stay apart but daily he must visit Thomas who he counts as his own son.

'Father knows, of that I am sure. But what can he do when he needs an heir to run the estates until Thomas comes of age? Nick loves the land and he loves the people.' Now she started to cry in earnest, 'he will make a good Master and so I must bear this burden or leave, yet that would break Father's heart and Nick's as well.'

Gently Meg embraced the distraught Kate; for she had suffered greatly over the past five years since Henry had rode away. She remembered the feelings of youth and the desire to lay with a man she loved. Yet her own calling had lead her to many places over the years, the skill of healing was upon her now and always, still she thought of the man she had left behind. Kate had first thought of Nicholas as but a boy, it was only since the last two years she had seen him as a man. Their love had blossomed, and yet their conduct was without any blemish. Wiping Kate's tears away she knew that she would help the lovers.

'Take heart, Mistress Kate, for I will give you the herbs you require, but use them sparingly for only God can say what the future might bring?'

Nicholas buried his face in Kate's abundant hair, his heart still hammering from their recent bout of love-making. 'I love you more than life itself,' he murmured for the umpteenth time. She drew his beloved face to hers and gently traced the firm lines of his face, the strong chin, the long lashes that framed his expressive eyes, and the full bottom lip that told of his sensuality. Never had she expected such delight in the act of love, for Nick was both gentle at times and passionate at others. The chamber was lit by a few candles that cast a benign light on their entwined bodies. Stretching out one arm, she found the goblet of wine, and taking a mouthful of the sweet wine she laid her mouth on his and deliberately allowed a small amount to trickle from her mouth to his.

'Oh my darling Kate, do not tempt me so, for soon I must get back to my chambers before dawn lights the sky.' The only answer was a light giggle as she sought his manhood once again, her greedy fingers coaxing it back to life.

'Just once more, my love, I beg of you, for soon our visitors will arrive and you will not be able to come to me for nigh on a week.'

'Wanton hussy,' he laughed back, but his body betrayed him once again as the wine continued to pass from mouth to mouth. He groaned with the rising of his manhood to her touch, but this time he held back, slowly teasing her as the tip of his penis rubbed against her most sensitive spot. Her breath was starting to come fast, but now he pulled away from her. They would have no more time together for a while, as his father was once again holding a ball to bring eligible women to parade before him, in hopes of a marriage that would bring more children to the Hall.

He wanted nothing of these women, for who could capture his heart and soul as his darling Kate had done for as long as he could remember?

Rising above her, he displayed his taut, tanned body to her gaze, knowing that she loved to look on him before the act of love. Now he took her dainty foot in his hands and starting to suck the big toe he caressed her feet. The sheets still slippery from their previous love-making, he lay prone as his tongue started to move slowly from her feet to the calves, stopping once to lick the sweat from behind her knees. Kate groaned but still he would make her wait, for he knew her appetites as well as his own. Gripping one leg in his strong arms he used his tongue to trace the inside of her thighs, slowly working upwards as she started to pant with desire. Lightly touching her bud with the tip of his tongue he felt his own desire as a force so strong it could hardly be contained. Yet still he sought to stay in control as his tongue explored her belly button before moving upwards to gently flick her taut nipples.

'Oh God, Nick, I need you now inside me,' she implored him as the juices began to flow from her secret place. Raising himself above her he looked into her blue eyes blazing with passion and all control was gone. Once, twice, he entered her before she curled her legs around his body and drew him deeper inside her, the hot stream spurting as her body convulsed under his. They lay quiet and spent, their fingers intertwined as their hearts beat in time together.

'Kate, oh Kate, my darling woman, how can I stand another night without you?' his voice broke with emotion, yet he knew it was but a dream, for how could they ever marry and beget the children he wanted so much, when she was still married to his hateful brother? For nigh on two years they had been lovers and every night he wished that they were free to marry. Instead they had to creep around, hoping that they would not be seen.

This time the ball was postponed as rumours of the dreaded disease, Smallpox, had reached the ears of the noblemen. From the gentry right down to the peasants fear was in the air and trade had almost ceased. In the grand houses the lords and ladies hid behind perfumed handkerchiefs, whilst the servants hung pomanders around the rooms to ward off the evil fumes of the disease. For the peasants there was no such protection as they struggled without trade to feed their families.

In vain Nicholas and Kate urged them to keep working on the land, for lack of food would surely make them more vulnerable to the disease. For themselves they did not fear, but Halleswell was in grave danger with Sir William and his wife so old. Kate worried for Thomas, for if he died she would lose her only child. If anything happened to him or Nick then her life would be over, but still life had to go on and the villagers were ill-prepared for such an emergency. August was nearly upon them and though the weather continued hot, if the harvest was not brought in then famine would kill those spared by the disease. Kate had some knowledge of the Smallpox and knew that few would survive. Those that did would be horribly scarred for the rest of their lives, if hunger did not kill them sooner.

At such times people turned to God and each day the churches were filling up with people begging for their lives and that of their children.

Kate knew that cramped places bred the disease more quickly, but how could she convince the villagers of that?

The family Physician was of no help either. He recommended that the house should be kept apart from the world whilst praying for deliverance, for with the smallpox no family was safe. So far they had been lucky, for the house and the surrounding villages were isolated. Many misguided people had converged on places such as the town of Bath, where the waters were said to have curative properties, but each day brought news of new places where the deaths from the disease were wiping out half of the population. Kate's family had originated in the North of the country, so she knew that cramped quarters only spread any disease more widely. While the family were safely behind closed doors they would stand some chance of surviving, but at what cost?

Daily she would travel around with Nick, trying to persuade the farmers and the villagers to keep working on the land and to avoid places like the churches. A few hardy souls agreed to help with the harvest and those families had food to eat. But in the poorer parts of the village children sat listlessly around, there empty bellies protruding through the thin flesh. Fishing boats lay idle in the harbours and vegetable plots were raided daily by the thieves and the idle. Nick had set up a special force of brave men to keep strangers away, but it was a short term measure and both knew it.

It was then that Kate decided to consult Meg, who had stayed away for a long time now. This time she wore no disguise for desperate times called for a brave stance. The cottage was close to Brannon's Wood and for a moment her spirit dropped as she could see no wisps of smoke from the chimney. Meg was working in her herbaria and did not answer for a while. When she did it was with a pleasant demeanour and Kate realised that she should have visited long before now. She had not seen Meg since collecting the herbs that kept her from getting with child. That had been six months ago 'Meg, my dearest friend, how I have missed you,' she cried, hugging the older woman close to her.

'Mistress Kate, well this is a nice surprise and you look so bonny, I hope that life is good with you and your family?'

Kate scrutinised her friend. She looked much older and more careworn since last she had seen her, and yet there was still the twinkle of mirth in her eyes. She decided that pleasantries should be set aside for now and addressing Meg she came straight to the point.

'I, well we... need your help dear friend, for surely you have heard of the disease that threatens the lives of all?'

'I am aware, in fact I have recently returned from a visit to a countrywoman of mine who knows somewhat of this plague they call the Smallpox. I have learnt enough to think that I may be able to hold it at bay, but I am afraid that the early signs of fever are already beginning to show in the village. It is a very bad thing, Kate, the fever lasts a few days and then the body erupts with sores. There is no cure and many die in agony. The few who survive will bear the scars for the rest of their lives. I am afraid this is not what you wish to hear?'

'Oh Meg, surely there is something you can do with your herbs and potions? I ask of this not just for my family, but for those who cannot help themselves. There is already hunger in the village and many will die. Please tell me that you can help us?'

There was a strained silence for a while and then the wise woman spoke, 'You ask a lot of me mistress, but I have heard how both you and Master Nick have tried so hard to help the poor. It goes in your favour that you have not asked of me for help for your own, but for all who may surely die. Yet if I agree to help there may be many who would put the name of witch on me and that could also be said of you. If I take this risk then you take the same on your shoulders, are you willing to take that chance?'

'Gladly I will and this I promise you now. If any speaks one word against you then I shall stand up and say that 'twass I that made you do this. Is that sufficient for you, dear Meg, for my heart and mind are set on this course of action?'

The women embraced before they retired to the back of the cottage where Meg kept her herbs and simples. What Meg was preparing to do was something that Kate needed to know about for it was something that had never been fully tried before.

They took for the first trial a young boy who was displaying the first symptoms of fever which Meg knew was the first stage in the disease. As an orphan there was no one person who would enquire about his health, although he was a sturdy lad and well used to hard work. Meg explained what she was doing as Kate was stood by.

'My kin have noticed over the years that dairy maids rarely develop the Pox, though they were not sure why this happened. We asked the tinkers to report back to us on any other cases where people who worked with cows had not caught the disease. Tinkers travel far and wide, so soon we were able to notice a pattern beginning to emerge. All over the country there are isolated communities where cattle are the mainstay of the community and the people there rarely catch the disease. Some may show mild symptoms but make a full recovery. One of my kin in Scotland found that some cattle have a mild illness that is called Cowpox. By the means of taking a small amount of the pustules and then scraping this onto the skin of people the Pox is either not caught at all or they only display mild symptoms. This, Kate, is what I hope I may try here. It will require courage and faith and many would not accept the treatment. For these I will try such herbs as will give a promise of some recovery, though 'tis in the hands of God himself. This is the battle we face and it will not be easy, but we are fortunate that cattle breed well here so we may hope that deaths will be averted as much as we can tell. That is the situation Kate, if you wish to back out now I will not blame you.'

It was a long speech and much for Kate to take in, but in her mind she could see Thomas writhing in agony and her mind was made up. She would work with Meg and pray at the same time. She would not lose Nick or any of the family if it was in her power to save them.

So she watched as Meg made a small cut in the boy's hand and applied a paste she had made up earlier. The boy would stay with Meg and in doing so would be well fed, for Kate would supply food from the Hall as both she and Nick had been doing for the poor of the village since this crisis had started.

'When will you know if the treatment has been successful?' Kate enquired.

'When two days have gone by and the lad does not show any signs of the sores. Yet even this could be the lad's strength and he may well have recovered of his own accord. In this case it may take many trials and still I might fail. We will have to wait and pray that the disease does not spread, for then I would not be able to treat so many. Indeed, I may contract the disease myself, for my first trial was on myself alone and that was just three days ago.'

Kate looked at her with new respect, for what courage must she have to expose herself to such a degree? With scarce a moment she spoke what was in her heart, 'then take me for your next trial, for I am healthy and would wish to share this burden.'

Meg looked horrified, 'you know not what you ask of me, for if you die then that would be a disaster beyond belief. Your family need you, the villagers need you as well, for who would care for them as you do? Pray, do not ask this of me.'

Had she known how magnificent she looked in that moment, the Lady of the great house facing the wise woman?

'For nigh on two years now I have taken your herbs that I may be as a wife to Nicholas. I have not grown heavy with child and so, my dear friend, I place my trust in you that I may also be spared by God to help in this endeavour.' Drawing up her sleeve she exposed her arm and the blue vein that stood out in the crook of her arm. 'Make the cut here where it will not show. Please Meg, do it now before my courage fails me.'

There was no gainsaying her. Meg made the cut and watched as the blood began to spurt. Hastily she applied the salve and then pressed the wound to stop the bleeding.

'Go home now and rest. Do nothing that may reopen the wound. You may feel a little feverish for a few days, do not worry as this also happened to me. If you are free from the sores in three days time then return and may God in his infinite mercy watch over you.'

Nick laid his hand on her brow and was alarmed to find it hot. His darling Kate had refused all food that day and now he started to worry, for a few isolated cases of the fever had been found in the village. 'You should not be here,' she said, 'send Mary to me lest our secret be revealed, for your countenance is dark with worry.' Her smile was tremulous but something in her eyes must have reassured him for his face softened. 'For now I will be guided by you, though if the fever worsens then an army of all the demons from hell would not keep me away,' bending his head to kiss her she pushed him lightly away, 'Nay, my love, I would not have you exposed to this illness. Happen it may be a passing thing but 'tis my wish that you stay away for two more days.' Anticipating another argument from him she added, 'One thing that I wish you to do is to take Thomas out in the fresh air, for if not he will weaken in this stifling atmosphere.' It was certainly true. On Mary's orders all the windows had been closed and the heat was stifling in the August sunshine. Not a breath of wind stirred the air and she feared for her son. She could not yet confide in Nick about Meg's experiment for his anger may lead to exposing their clandestine love.

'That I can do and gladly, for Thomas is restless. We shall take a short ride in the woods before I leave again to oversee the harvesting'

Two days later Kate managed to take some broth. The fever had reached a pitch the night before and now her brow felt cool to the touch. Rising slowly from the bed she beheld her whole body in the mirror, there were no sores and although she still felt a little weak she knew that her gamble had paid off, she would not get the Pox. It was another day before Mary pronounced her fit enough to take some air. Her immediate reaction was to ride to Meg's cottage, yet prudence won over her heart's desire. Mary looked tired so she could not add to her burden, for now both Sir

William and his wife Louise were showing signs of the fever. From her bedroom window she could hear the sounds of Nick and Thomas at play in the gardens. She would surprise them by joining them in their games.

Slowly she dressed, knowing that to call the maid would spoil the surprise. Though her limbs felt weak she could not wait to leave her hot and stuffy room, besides, she missed her lover and her son.

It was Thomas that saw her first as she walked hesitantly towards them. With a cry of joy he abandoned the game and ran to her side, his golden hair gleaming in the sunlight.

'Mama, you are well again,' his joy sending tears to his eyes. 'We have been so afraid for you, haven't we, Uncle Nick?' he turned as Nick came bounding up to their side. There, in the gardens backing onto the trees of Brannon's Wood the three made one as they closed arms around Kate. Nick's voice was throaty with relief and desire 'God be praised, you are well again my dear.' Kate laughed, her joy was complete. 'Yes, my dears, I am well again by God's good grace (and the skills of Meg, she thought to herself). Ruffling her son's unruly hair she thought he had never looked as healthy as he did today. The sun had touched him with a light tan of gold, his blue eyes reflected her own and yet...she caught her breath, he had the strong Meverall chin, the long eyelashes of Nick. But for the colour of his hair he could pass as Nick's own son. Hugging him tight she took a light tone, 'I have interrupted your game, so what do you think, should we have a picnic here on the grass?'

'Oh yes, mama, that would be such a fine treat. Uncle says that you are too thin, shall I go and ask cook for some food?'

'That would be wonderful, my son, for I am so tired of broth. Let's see, I think I would like some chicken or maybe Quail if cook has it, also pastries, both savoury and sweet. Some boiled eggs, hunks of fresh bread, butter and honey, ripe peaches and a few bottles of wine. Do you think you can remember all that?' She smiled at him lovingly.

'Of course Mama, I have a memory like an elephant, so uncle says, though I have never seen such a beast.'

'Then fly away little bird and bring me back such dainties to put roses back in my cheeks.'

'You are sure you are well?' Nick asked, 'I could not stand that worry again.' How he longed to take her in his arms but though few were about they could not take that chance. Instead he held her hands in his, knowing that she had sent Thomas on an errand that would allow them to talk for a while. Briefly Kate told her story, putting a finger to his lips when he sought to interrupt her. 'I have to ask you if you will visit Meg and see how both she and the boy fares, for I came through the fire and I am restored to you in health, though my spirit is troubled. I cannot ride for at least a day or more and would have tidings. This could be the cure we have prayed for, as I took the chance and am fine.'

'My God Kate, did you not think what it would do to me if I lost you? Why put yourself at risk?'

'Do not look at me that way,' she replied as she saw his face darken. Sometimes she could see the look of Henry in his face, when he was worried or angry, but he was still her own sweet love. 'I did it for the love of you and Thomas. Oh Nick, can you not see what this could mean? We could save our family and many of the village folk if this works?'

'Promise me that you will let Meg treat both you and Thomas, 'she implored him, 'promise it on your love for me and I will know it is then true.'

'I swear that I will do this for you on my love and my life.'

'Then I am content with that, my love, for I could not live without you both.'

He let out a long sigh of relief, for had she not come through the ordeal unscathed? How could he then tell her that many would not accept this cure, if it proved to be real? The poorer folk would accept it without question, for what did they have to lose, but to persuade his family would be another matter entirely. Still, he could not dampen her spirits for he would take the chance and so would Thomas if there was the slightest chance of survival.

'I will ride there tonight, beloved, but allow us this one day of happiness with our son by our side.'

The picnic was a grand affair with cook finding any delicacies she could, for Catherine was much loved by the servants. She ate well and teased Nick by popping dainty morsels in his mouth. Replete, they lay side by side as Thomas played in the gardens and ventured near the woods. On the morrow she would keep him by her side, for Nick had promised to bring news of Meg and the boy she had treated. It was to be the last idyllic day for some time to come.

August had come and gone, with the best part of the harvest safely gathered in. Nick had used every able-bodied man and woman and sometimes the children as well. The boy that Meg had treated was fully recovered and now working in the fields as part of the Meverall staff. When she could get away Kate worked with Meg, trying to persuade people to accept the treatment that both had wisely spoken of as merely herbs from Brannon's Wood. Such was the power of belief in that Holy place that many of the stronger people recovered well. The death toll had still been high, with the aged and the youngest too weak to fight the disease. Compared to other places they had come through with a much lower mortality rate than surrounding areas. The biggest problem had arisen when other folks had tried to enter the village. Though Nick's men had held many off, there were some that got by and were beaten to death by the scared people. Now the grain was stored there was no respite as the late vegetable plots had to be dug by hand. Soon the apples would be picked, some set by against winter and some left to produce the local cider. Though Nick had tried to say that fruit was needed for the bare winter months, still the men would make their brew, using the very foods that should be set aside against a long hard winter.

Thomas had survived and now led the children in the picking of blackberries to make jam and other fruit to bottle. Kate loved to see him with the village children, as an only child he had often been lonely at the Hall. Both her mother-in-law and Mary had been near scandalised by the boy running wild, but Sir William approved, saying that a good master should know his own people. Therefore it had come as a bitter blow when both William and his wife developed late fever. Nick and Kate discussed the options with Meg. Should they try the vaccine and be held to account if the old folks survived? Mary would never accept such a cure as she believed that only God could have saved the people. Sadly Meg told them that their parents would probably die anyway, few of the older folk had survived and those that did still bore the hideous scarring of the Pox.

For a week Kate took turns with Mary so that the nursing was constant. On the third day Louise broke out with the sores, and though the herbs eased her suffering she died in agony two days later. Now Kate took turns with Nick, for Mary was worn out with the endless cold baths and the effort to wet the swollen lips of her patients. Many of the servants now ran away in fear, for all knew of Kate's friendship with Meg. Bitterly Kate thought of all they had saved and how short their memories could be.

On the Sabbath day she sat with Sir William and confessed what she allowed Meg to do and how she had helped. 'Dear father, will you allow me to treat you as I have treated so many? It may yet save you,' bursting into tears she held his frail body close to hers.

'My dear child, do you not think I know of all that goes on with my estate? I have great respect for the wise woman, but it is my time to die.' Gently he patted her hand. 'I am old Kate; I have lived my allotted span of life and do not wish to linger on as an old man in his dotage. You have blessed this house with your presence, I am only sorry that you had to marry the wrong man.' She let out a gasp of surprise, for she had thought their secret safe.

William smiled, 'Do not blame yourself my dear, for I knew long ago that my son, Henry was never the man to settle down. Still, I would have seen his face before I go to my maker. Louise never gave up on him, to the end she thought he would come home.' A sudden coughing fit kept him breathless for a while. 'Now I know the joy you have brought to this house and to my younger son. Nay, do not deny it, for I saw the love grow between you both and it is fitting in my sight. I wish you to know that I have changed my will in favour of Nicholas, so that if Henry dies you will be free to marry. I have left some small sum to Henry, for he is still my son, though I doubt he will ever return. Nicholas knows of this and has agreed that he will forfeit any right to the estate when Thomas reaches his majority. Do not look so sad, daughter, for so I protect you all. Now could you indulge an old man, as I wish for a pipe and some rich wine?'

Kate hastened to do his bidding, only stopping to call Nick to her side. Between them they lifted the old man into a sitting position. Nick lit the pipe and Kate poured the wine. William smiled and asked to see Thomas alone for a moment. So it was that Thomas looked on his grandfather for the last time and saw him at peace with his favourite things about him.

Sir William was buried alongside of his wife with his old body free from sores. In the end he had just slipped away quietly, the doctor said his heart had just given out. He lay with his venerable ancestors in the Meverall family plot, with his remaining family about him and a parade of people from far and wide weeping openly at his funeral.

Nick openly put his arm around Kate as she wept for the man she had so briefly called father.

Thomas stood solemnly throughout the service and when it was over he turned to his mother and the man he now openly called father. 'Let us go home now,' he said.

Henry was desperate to get back to his island home, desperate to see Isabella again.

He was glad he had gone to England however. It had got things out of his system and made him certain that his new life in the Caribbean was the life he wanted. There had only ever been the tiniest sliver of doubt in his mind, but now that he had been and seen how things would have been for him in Halleswell hall he was certain that his life with Isabella would be as different for him as heaven and hell.

Nothing much had changed on the island since he had left. Isabella had been very pleased to see him and she had expressed those feelings as only she could. Henry had been exhausted after Isabella had finally finished greeting him. She did rather spoil it by interrogating him about other women he had met in England. For once Henry had been able to be completely honest in his denial of any wrongdoing.

The plantation was doing a fine trade, Isabella had shown herself to be a fine business woman and they were making a goodly profit from their crops of sugar cane.

The plantation was only part of their enterprise however and the illegal side was much more profitable, if much more dangerous. Rich Spanish galleons were easy pickings for the crew of *Ghost*. And as the years went on they became infamous for their skill at taking Spanish vessels. This of course led to the reward for their capture getting ever higher.

Isabella wasn't content just to stay at the plantation, although she did enjoy the cut and thrust of the business world when it came to the sugar selling, she did find the day to day running of it a bit boring. She had come to love the sea, almost as much as Henry and the adventure of fighting the sailors on the galleons they attacked was something she found that exited her about her new life. Henry hadn't been happy when she had first told him she would be sailing with him; neither had the crew for that matter, superstition about it being bad luck to have a woman aboard was part of it. Isabella's temper was something else that put them off. It didn't take long for them to get used to her presence however and they soon realized that she was an asset to some of their dealings, being able to speak Spanish she was able to put the Spanish sailors in the picture very plainly what would happen to them if they didn't cooperate. It didn't seem to matter to her that the ships they attacked were her ex-countrymen although it was something that Henry had thought about, but he came to the conclusion that if she was not worried then why should he be.

Isabella always dressed in cotton shirt and britches when she was on board ship and Henry thought the look definitely suited her, many of the crew did as well and many times an enquiring look from Isabella sent them scurrying off after being caught staring. Isabella thought it was funny and not a little flattering to have so many men wanting to watch her every move but she couldn't let them see that she was enjoying herself.

Three years their reign of terror lasted, sending many a Spanish galleon to the bottom of the sea. They had some narrow escapes in that time. Both the British and the Spanish Navies were after them and but for the speed of *Ghost* and Henry's guile they could have been caught several times.

Eventually however all good things come to an end as they must, they could feel the net closing in, the time had come for *Ghost* to be hidden away and mothballed. Henry and Isabella had more money than they could ever spend in their lifetime and the crew were now well off as well. Some of them had families and children as well and so after discussion between all of them it was decided that they should hang up their pirate boots before they ended up at the end of a noose.

It was not long however before Henry's sea legs started to itch, there was something else as well. News from England was not good. Smallpox was stalking the land like a grim reaper collecting souls. Many had died and those that survived were horribly scarred.

Henry began to worry about his family again, something he hadn't done for years. He wondered if they were alright indeed whether they were still alive.

He eventually discussed this with Isabella, he expected a big argument from her telling him that he was not going but this time she surprised him by agreeing that he should go without making a fight of it at all, of course she had an ulterior motive, she wanted to feel the sea beneath her feet again as much as Henry did. Henry did halfheartedly try to persuade her to stay at the plantation but in truth he didn't put any conviction into his argument. He knew anyway that when Isabella made a decision, there was no power on this earth that would make her change her mind, and woe betide any who were foolish enough to try. He wanted her by his side as much as she wanted to be there, and so it was that this time when *Ghost* sailed the Atlantic Isabella was part of the crew. He had wrung one concession out of her, she had promised to stay on *Ghost* when Henry made the trip to Halleswell, he couldn't risk her contracting the disease of course but that was and sounded like an excuse. The real reason being that he didn't want Isabella coming face to face with his wife, that would not be a pleasant meeting, and in Henry's view one to be avoided at all cost because Catherine was liable to end up dead. That wasn't something even Henry wanted on his conscience. Even though he had decided to go back he needed news before he could do it.

So every now and again Henry risked calling into a friendly port to gather the news from England. Part of this was because he wanted to know if he was still being hunted down, but another part of him (one he would never admit to), was for news of his family. His bloody father could go to hell for all that he cared, but he missed his mother who had been the only person that really understood his changeable moods. When they put into St Kitts the governor, not knowing of Henry's disgrace, had wined and dined him in a splendid fashion.

The old uniform had been kept clean, guaranteeing him such welcome when needed. It had been seven years since he had walked away from the family home, though he knew he would always get a welcome at Harland Point.

The news from England was not good. An outbreak of the Smallpox was devastating whole towns and villages. For once he thought of his mother. She would be in her late sixties by now and very vulnerable to any disease. He would have to risk the journey even if was only to say 'goodbye' to her.

He took just half the normal crew, leaving the rest on the Island they had found. He needed a fast trip and fair winds. Arriving at Harland Point he had hired a fleet horse and dressing as a gentleman he thought to throw off the pursuit. He laughed at the 'wanted' posters; they showed a much younger, bearded Henry. Now his hair had lightened with the sun and glowed with reddish tints.

His arrival had been too late; his parents had been buried just a few days before.

A Different Shore

A few days after the funeral Thomas was laying wild flowers from Brannon's Wood on his grandparent's graves. He missed them so much and although the late roses from the formal gardens made a grand display, still he favoured the sweet honeysuckle, the bright-eyed daises and the water lilies. So deep in thought he started when a sudden noise came from behind him. He had never seen such a man before now. He was tall and his features were browned by the sun. Thomas took in the fine lawn shirt, open at the neck to show the same deep colour. Yet his britches were well made and the leather boots shone in the sunlight. The long dark hair was burnished with a touch of reddish highlights, tied back with a black bow such as his father now wore in mourning. Now he remembered his manners, 'Good morrow sir, have you come to pay your respects?' for why else would a stranger be near the family plot? The man looked at him with a keen eye and Thomas shivered for a moment under that steady gaze. Then the man's face broke out in a smile and he relaxed.

'Good morrow to you young man, my pardons for intruding on your grief, but I see that you have been recently bereaved?'

'My grandparents passed away within a week of each other, but surely you know this and have arrived too late for the funeral mass?'

'Aye lad, far too late I fear. I am a distant cousin and knew your grandparents well. My duties as a Naval Officer have taken me too many distant shores. I heard of the Pox and came as soon as I could, but pray tell me, how do your parents fare?'

'They are well sir, both were ill for a while but by God's great mercy most of our household have survived.' He was loath to tell this stranger that the man he called Father, was not in truth his real father. Yet he was a Naval man and might have news of his real father. He should be cautious and invite this man to meet his parents, for surely they would know him if they were kin? Sketching a hasty bow he introduced himself, 'My name is Thomas, Sir, I fear my manners are lax, for you should be welcomed to the house. Now I extend a welcome to you, though I know not your name?'

Henry looked at his son and replied, 'say only that I am cousin to your father. My name is one that I will greet them with, but for now I would pay my respects as you so rightly guessed.'

Thomas hastened away, leaving Henry to say goodbye to his parents. Kneeling, he touched the grave of his mother; she had always loved him so why did the sight of his father's grave touch his heart? He had travelled fast once the news came of the Pox in England, dodging the navy patrols as only he and his crew could do. Should he go to the Hall and risk being reported to the patrols? The sight of his son had thrown him off balance, for the lad was sturdy and had shown great courage in facing him. He was certainly a Meverall, of that he had no doubt and yet he would never acknowledge his son for he had Mistresses enough with Isabella and the sea. Making up his mind he untied his horse and rode slowly towards the Hall.

'Calm down son, I need the story from the start,' Kate tried to sooth the excited boy, for who else could the stranger be than Henry, after all these years? She had sent a lad to fetch Nick from the fields and prayed he would get here on time, for what would Henry want but to claim his right as Master of the estate? Once again Thomas told of the strange meeting and was to repeat it once Nick arrived.

'Tom, I would have private word with this stranger, for he may not be what he seems. Ask Nell to bring food and ale to my study, then you might like to see the new pups that Lady has born,' Nick needed some time to think and all boys loved to see new pups.

'Thank you Papa, but may I see the stranger again if he is kin?' His parents agreed and Tom went off on his important errand, for now he would wait and see.

Henry had changed a lot, although his arrogance was still there. He was ushered into the study by Nell, who removed his boots with a sly glance. Both Nick and Kate welcomed their guest although both stood up, Kate leaning against the chair. Henry took the mug of ale and irritated by his poor welcome he bade them both to be seated, 'For the love of God, cannot you unbend a little? Come, brother, join me in a mug of ale, and Catherine, stop fidgeting and take a glass of wine. You look on me as if I am a monster, yet here I am, being civil as I can.'

Nick relaxed a little and decided to take the ale, though he drank but little and that only after hard work or at the dining table. He poured Kate a glass of wine, noticing how her hands were shaking. There was nothing to do but to come straight to the point.

'I cannot say I am pleased to see you brother, I am not a hypocrite. But for the sake of our parents I welcome you as much as I can.'

'Good, we understand each other well, though I wish the welcome to be warmer. Come, kiss your husband Catherine.' Dutifully Kate moved forwards and laid a light kiss on his cheek.

Nick's hands clenched but then Henry started to laugh. 'Oh this is such sport, but you need not fear me, I came home to see my mother, not to force myself on you both.' His face changed, the haughtiness was there but overlaid by a real grief, 'Tell me, brother, did they suffer much?'

'No, both passed away peacefully, mother spoke your name at the end. Father had a change of heart as well, though I think the terms of his will might not please you,' Nick had no heart to speak of their mother's agony.

'You swear this is true, Catherine?' Henry asked her.

Yes, 'tis true, why should I lie?'

'Would you bring me brandy Catherine, for I have a great thirst and much sorrow to bear?'

She gave him a fierce glance but judged rightly that he was shaken by his mother's death.

The air was still and for a moment an uneasy silence fell amongst them.

Nick broke the silence. 'I have here father's will if you should like to read it?'

Henry laughed, 'Why bother, he disinherited me long ago? Besides, do you see me as a farmer? It might suit you, brother, but the sea is my life and I have no wish to leave it.'

'Yet it is my duty and I have to say that father left Halleswell Hall to me, though kept in trust until Thomas comes of age. He also left you a large sum of money and mother's wish that you should take any of her jewels as you should want.'

Henry looked uncomfortable but then his natural exuberance came to the fore, 'By God, I never thought the old man had it in him. He repents on his death bed and offers up the estate to my son? Well that's a pretty picture for sure. Shall I stay and claim my wife? Let my brother run the estate for me and reap the benefits when Thomas comes of age?'

Catherine's face darkened and Nick looked as if the devil himself had taken over his wits.

'What a jest,' Henry smiled with the thought. 'Nay, do not look so glum, I have money aplenty and,' here he looked at Kate, 'you may have more meat on your bones, but I would free us both from this loveless marriage if I could. I would like something to remember my mother by, though.'

While Kate instructed cook in the meal for that night Nick stayed with Henry as he looked through his mother's possessions. It was a strange feeling for both and Nick felt more at ease with Henry since he had been a small child who worshipped his older brother. Now he could not tell from one moment to the next what the expressions that passed across his brother's face would be. 'Here's a pretty thing,' Henry said, picking up a dainty gold cross with a single ruby set in the middle. 'I do not remember mother ever wearing this?'

'Mother was a secret Catholic; she had this as a young woman when Catholics were persecuted. It's Welsh gold and very valuable, but there are other gems more precious and costly. Father told me that she kept this next to her skin for many years until the Protestants took the throne. Then the family joined the high church and mother hid this away. It was in her hands the day she died. I sent for a priest to absolve her of her sins, for so she believed.'

'This I will take, in remembrance of our mother, if you do not object?'

'I have all I need right here, but won't you take more?'

'No, brother, I have no need of wealth; I ask only that I may take the portrait of mother, the miniature of her with father?' Nick found the miniature and placed it in Henry's hands.

Now they were free of the past, Nick could feel some of the love they once shared.

'You have brought my son up well,' Henry said, 'he's a fine lad and a credit to you both.' Looking on his brother's face Henry read the troubled look, 'Do not worry, I will not take him from you, but speak no more of me, for already the lad sees much that should be hidden.' In a rare moment Henry decided to tell the truth, 'I am a privateer and now a pirate. Do not look so shocked, I think that father always knew. I would rather that he called you father and not suffer the disgrace if I am caught. I would hang for sure and what would that do to the child?'

Nick was speechless, grasping Henry by the arms they embraced for the last time.

Dinner was a happy affair and made more joyful when Kate took the wedding ring that had belonged to Louise and gave it back to Henry. 'I have a feeling that another woman will wear this with more grace than I,' she replied simply when Henry started to protest. That night Henry rode away with haste for his ship would sail with the dawn. He knew not that he was followed that night by more than the King's men.

The letter arrived a week later addressed to Lady Henry Meverall. The message was brief. Henry had died in combat and His Majesties Navy offered their condolences to the widow. She wept a little for the father of her son, but Nicholas kept the secret to his grave, for his most trusted men had been there when the soldiers fired at Henry and saw the living body carried away.

Henry rode away from Halleswell Hall at midnight, hoping that the soldiers would be in their cups by now. The hairs on the back of his neck prickled, he was sure he was being followed.

'Damn,' he thought, 'there was a buxom lass in the Smuggler's Arms and he had been looking forward to some real English ale. 'They caught him up at the crossroads where the turning led to Harland Point. He only hoped that his crew were still sober enough to make their escape. He ducked and dived as the bullets pinged around him. Riding almost prone he noticed that not all the bullets were aimed at him. Casting a quick glance behind him he thought he recognised one of Nick's men. Distracted for a moment he felt the bullet bite into his leg. There was only one thing he could do, galloping on for a few hundred yards he passed into a wood and rolled off the horses back. The King's men ran on, but one man stopped and Henry held his breath.

'Sir, 'tis I, Matt from the smithy, Master Nick said to get you away to safety. Hurry now, afore the soldiers see they'm chasing a riderless horse.'

So it was that Henry returned to *Ghost*. The ship was far out to sea before the soldiers realised they had no body to take back. But fearing their Captain all swore that he had fell mortally wounded into the sea. So the legends say and who would question the King's men?

Henry was in pain, his leg burned and he was having a hard time trying to stem the flow of blood. By the time he reached *Ghost* he was wavering on the edge of consciousness. Isabella was the first to see him coming and she rushed down the gangplank to catch him as he finally collapsed when he was safe inside the cavern under Harland point. More crew members rushed out to help and soon Henry was lying in the bed in the cabin.

Isabella found herself the one that the rest looked to for instructions now that Henry was out of action.

She had to weigh up several things. Was Henry being chased, was he followed, were they safe here? She didn't know but thought there was a good chance that he had been followed and their best chance was to run for it. Once they had clear sea under their keel she knew they would be able to outrun any pursuit. She was worried about Henry though, she didn't know if the rolling ship would make his injury any worse, she decided that it had to be worth the risk, they couldn't stay here, if they were found they would be caught like rats in a trap. Her mind made up she issued the order to set sail and they cautiously emerged from the cavern half expecting to see Navy ships waiting for them, the sea was empty however and they had the luck of the tide running the right way which aided their attempt to get to the open sea.

Isabella stayed on deck long enough to see them on the way

before telling Grimwood to keep a good eye out for navy ships and to set a course for home. Once they were underway and the wind had filled their sails Isabella rushed back to Henry's side. He was moaning softly to himself wavering on the edge of consciousness. Isabella looked at his hand, thinking to hold it in hers but he was gripping something in his hand that he wouldn't let go of. She wondered what it was that he held on to so tightly but his health was her main priority now and so she checked the bandages she had applied to his leg and then sat down to wait for him to awake.

As darkness fell Isabella fell asleep and didn't awake until she felt a hand stroking her hair. Looking up she saw Henry was awake. His face was creased with pain but he managed a smile when he saw her look up at him.

'How do you feel my love' asked Isabella, it sounded an inane thing to say but she could think of nothing else, such was her relief at him awakening.

Henry had no energy for speech but did manage to grip her hand tighter in response.

It was a long journey, especially for Henry. The pain of his wound was made worse by the movement of the ship, it made every day a waking nightmare for him but he made himself face it for Isabella's sake as much as his own.

On the third day Henry revealed what he had been holding in his hand. It was the cross he had brought from Halleswell Hall. He held out the cross he had held in his hands for the last days.

'This is my gift to you Isabella, it is a piece of England made in Wales, a reminder of my home that I would give to you as a token of my love and as a symbol for the rest of our lives.'

Isabella had tears in her eyes as she reached out her fingers to touch the gold cross. 'No my love you keep it until we get home, it has been a good luck charm that has kept you alive for this long, maybe it will sustain you until we get home and you have regained your strength.'

Sight of their island home was a very welcome sight for all the crew and the welcome they received when they docked was enough for all of them to feel that the trip had been worthwhile for that alone.

Henry was pleased that their lookout system must be working for all of the islands inhabitants to have got warning of their arrival and had time to make their way to the dock. Wives and children cheered enthusiastically eager to greet fathers and husbands.

Henry stayed at the helm and watched the joyful reunions that were happening all along the quay. It brought a warm feeling to his heart to see it, something that he wondered at, he must be getting soft in his old age.

Isabella came to his side. 'Are you ready to go home Captain?'

Henry smiled, it was good to hear the word and now for the first time it actually meant something to him.

He still had a very noticeable limp but he managed to get to shore under his own steam. Isabella hovered by his arm ready to catch him if he stumbled. She had mellowed too thought Henry with a grin although he was sure it was only temporary and it wouldn't be long before she returned to her fiery self.

That night they had a celebration party. It was a magical night; lanterns lit the gardens in front of the white plantation house, bathing it in an orange glow. Palm trees added the paradise feel of the night and music mixed with the tropical food and large amounts of rum made it a night that none of them would ever forget.

They danced the night away, Henry took a turn on the dance floor but his wound limited him to one short dance but he was happy enough to sit and watch as Isabella whirled around, laughing and having the time of her life as she danced with partner after partner coming back to sit on Henry's knee when she finally had to give in to exhaustion. Henry kissed her and looked at the golden cross that glittered in the glow of the lamp light, he smiled, his thoughts back in England as he thought of his son, he was growing up to be a fine lad, would he ever see him again? He asked himself, probably not was the answer but he knew he was well looked after by Nick and Kate and he was happy enough with that.

Finally it was time for the party to finish, none said as much but it was just that time when everyone mutually decided that it was time for bed. Although a good number of the adults would not be sleeping for some time yet.

Weeks and months passed in peace on the island. *Ghost* had been hidden away and for some time the shipping in the area had been safe from being attacked by pirates.

Henry was content to stay on the plantation, riding and walking with Isabella through the fields of cane or along the side of streams running down the side of the mountain that dominated the island at its northern end. His leg became stronger as time passed and eventually he had only a slight limp to say that he had ever been shot.

Henry and Isabella were soon accepted into Caribbean society and often received invitations to society balls on various islands. Henry found it amusing that they were treated as equals, indeed they both had backgrounds that made them members of that society but little did they know they had former pirates in their midst.

This life might have gone on indefinitely, but Mother Nature intruded upon their tropical paradise.

The day started as any other, bright sunlight reflected off the blue ocean that gently wove its way through the coral reefs that protected most of the island's shoreline. A light sea breeze made the palm trees sway with a soft rustling as their leaves caressed one another before it moved on to the cane fields to make them bow before it.

The plantation awoke slowly. Henry stood on the porch of his home and greeted the morning with a stretch. It had become a ritual that he did every morning and it took him a moment to notice that something was different. He couldn't grasp what it was for some time but it suddenly struck him. There was no bird song, always the sound of the many birds that inhabited the island greeted the morning along with Henry, but not today. Henry wondered at it. He looked around but could see nothing amiss and with a shrug he went back indoors and forgot about the birds as soon as he saw Isabella coming down the stairs. He felt that familiar pulling inside him as he fell in love with her all over again as he did every morning.

After a leisurely breakfast Henry had his horse brought to the house for his morning ride around the plantation. As he left the house he glanced at the sky, there was a darkening on the horizon, looks like the rainy season was going to start early this year.

As morning drifted into afternoon Henry began to keep track of the growing dark smudge, it was beginning to look like they were going to have a storm.

It had started as a strong gale, they had been through worse and so no one on the island was unduly worried. It was not long however before they realised that the wind was not going to stop increasing. This was going to grow into a full blown hurricane. Palm trees were uprooted and the cane fields flattened by the torrential rain and howling wind. Everyone was now taking shelter in Henry and Isabella's house; the less robust dwellings had been demolished one by one as the storm grew in intensity.

It was dark; no lantern could withstand the wind. Fear crept into every heart as the weather systematically destroyed all they had spent so long in building.

A window blew in sending slivers of glass flying across the room like a host of tiny daggers, screaming cut through the sudden darkness as lanterns were extinguished by the unrelenting wind. It had found a way into the house now, had a foothold from which it grew, more windows smashed and then the door blew in. It was the beginning of the end. Their home was being destroyed piece by piece. Screams of pain came from every-where as flying glass and furniture flew across rooms, destroying anything or anyone that had the misfortune to be in the way.

It all stopped, suddenly there was silence. A silence made all the more pronounced for the terrible noise it replaced. Those people who were able sat where they had been hiding and stared around at the devastation around them. Not a few bodies lay unmoving, dark pools of blood marring the tiled floor grew around them from where flying glass or debris had ended their lives.

The survivors slowly roused themselves, Henry took charge.

'Come on, everybody, we need to move, we are in the eye of the storm. We have a little respite to get into the wine cellar. Grab what food and water you can and then get down below ground.'

It wasn't long before they were huddled in the cellar, ears straining for the sounds of the returning storm. Henry looked around, there were so many faces missing. As best as he could judge half of their number hadn't come down to the cellar. This was a disaster for all of them both a personal tragedy and for their future.

Many faces he saw had cuts and bruises, raising his hand to his own he could feel the slick wetness of blood. Moans from the injured were the only sound as they waited. The wind hit so suddenly that many of them jumped as the roar crashed in on their senses. Sounds from above of their previous lives being destroyed went on and on as if the wind never wanted to release them. All night they sat there, some slept, most didn't.

It went on for so long that when it stopped it took them a little while to realise that silence had returned and it was even longer before they dared to come out of the cellar. When they did finally emerge it was to a scene of total devastation. Everything was gone and with it their hopes and dreams of a life on this island.

That one day had undone all they had worked for since their arrival, it was uninhabitable now. Shock was the expression that marred every face as they realised they had nothing left, people wandered here and there looking for any of their possessions that had survived. There was very little to be found.

The victims of the storm, and there were many, were buried together in a makeshift graveyard near the site of the ruined plantation house. Henry felt that was the end of their island adventure and after talking it through with Isabella called everyone together a couple of days later.

'Our lives here are over, there is no point in me speaking of false hopes, we have less now than when we arrived. We have to accept that we are going to have to leave, to start new lives somewhere else. I have made up my mind what I will do and it is for each of you to make a choice. *Donna Isabella* is due back in two days, pray god that she was spared in the storm. I am taking *Ghost* and any that wish to accompany me. The rest can take *Donna Isabella* and go where they wish.'

There were mumblings of discussion in the small crowd of listeners. They all realised they could no longer stay here and they knew that wherever they went they were going to struggle to build new lives. Both choices Henry had offered were taken up and so it was that as soon as *Donna Isabella* returned both her and *Ghost* made ready to leave the island for the last time. All had a heavy heart to be going, many had left loved ones buried in the new graveyard, yet it was still a fond farewell to the paradise they had all called home.

Henry had one more surprise for the people that chose to leave on the *Donna Isabella*. To each he gave a pouch of gold, something to start a new life with wherever they chose to go.

To the new crew of *Ghost* he gave the same. They were set on a different path, a path of piracy, discovery and adventure.

As they set sail Henry stood with his arm around Isabella at the wheel, they looked back at their island for the last time.

'Where will we go my love?' asked Isabella as she looked up at him.

'Who knows, we have the whole world, we can go where we please, anywhere would be paradise with you by my side,' said Henry with a fond glance down at Isabella, 'we are free to do as we will and go wherever the wind takes us. I have always fancied the Orient, maybe our new life will be there.'

Isabella answered by squeezing his arm and moving her body closer into him

'Time and the wind will tell us,' he said more to himself than to Isabella.

A New Horizon

As Henry started in his new life, little did he know that on the other side of the ocean his son was marking out his own path.

The hot summer sun beat down on Thomas's body as he urged the men on. After two years of hot summers and little rain the crops were once again beginning to wilt in the heat bringing the real possibility of starvation to the estate and the villagers. In the year of 1757 many parts of the county suffered the same fate and imported grain was bleeding the coffers dry. The lake had almost dried up, leaving the swans stranded and the fish flapping on the shore. It had taken much persuasion on his part to get the men hauling water from the well in the woods, for it was regarded as a holy place by many. The barrels that once were full of ale were now used to water the fields that Thomas judged to be the best for the holding of water.

A few had spoken against his choice, arguing that the fields near to the marshes would better serve their needs, but a conversation with an aged Meg decided him against that course.

'Heat combines with the marsh water to breed disease,' she had told him, and remembering the years of the Pox he agreed with her. Those that disagreed were soon swayed as the grain from those fields rotted and died.

The estate fields were too large to water, so Thomas had persuaded the farmer who had fields near to the woods to allow them to grow the grain for the whole area. Now as they hauled up the cool water he hoped that the large payment from his parents would keep Master Godwin in a good humour.

'Let us take a break now, 'he said as the women from the village brought the savoury pies and jugs of the local cider. For himself he only allowed water to pass his lips, for though the cider was refreshing it only made the thirst worse later. He had broken his fast on plain bread with honey and now, as he bit into the pastry his mouth watered with the taste. Thomas had partaken of many fine foods, some the village folk would never taste, but the pastry with its meat and potato filling balanced with the apple filling to make a meal fit for a king. Now they would take a nap before drawing water for the evening watering.

There would be no such rest for him as he mounted his horse and rode on to check the other crops. Although it was early in the month, already children were digging up the potatoes before they became infected from the blight. Thomas had worked out a rotation of crops so that some would be gathered early and others left to grow larger in the ground.

Fresh greens would be the problem and to this end his parents had rode to the town of Bath, where jewellery could be sold to buy such foods as would not grow. Later this year he would set sail to the land of the Welsh, where the late snow would melt off the mountains to water the fields below. There he would trade for the greens they needed.

The sun was setting as he finally made his way home. Hot, tired and thirsty he stripped off down to his underwear and using an old horse trough he immersed his body in the cold water. His parent's chaise was back in the stables so he wrung the water from his hair and entered the house through the kitchen quarters. 'Nell, bring me a clean shirt, 'he asked as she ran up to him with her usual jaunty look.

'You mun look respectable, for the guests,' she said, 'shall I lay out your best clothes?' He felt a moment of annoyance, for why should there be guests when he was exhausted already? Still, he had never known his parents to do anything without justification He went to his room and dressed as well as he could under the present circumstances.

He was to thank Nell later on; for all that she was a hussy the girl had spoken true. He entered the smaller dining room that seated a smaller number than the grand room in the hall. Candles blazed from the great chandelier sending a soft glow over the dark table with its pristine white clothe. The table had been set for five. His mother came forth to hug him and his father clapped him on the shoulder. But he only had eyes for the two guests that hovered uncertainly in the background. They were without a doubt brother and sister, for their features were almost identical.

Soft brown hair framed the girl's heart-shaped face and her deep green eyes peeked out demurely from under her long lashes. Her brother had the same colouring, although his features were manlier.

His father bade them step forward and introduced them to him as David and Elizabeth Stafford. Elizabeth smiled prettily and a dimple appeared on each cheek. David went to make a courtly bow but Nick stopped him with his words. 'No Stafford should bow to us however they are lowered by chance alone. Thomas, meet your distant cousins for so their family was once held in high esteem.'

Over dinner Thomas leant much more. The Stafford family had been loyal supporters of King Charles and had lost both land and title when the civil war had stripped them of that right. Now they were descendants of a family line that once was allied to the Meverall family. They had met with his parents at the assembly room in Bath, where both sought to interest the richer families to buy what jewels and plate as they could sell. Kate had raised enough to buy in more grain if the harvest failed, whilst David Stafford had sold the last of the family jewels, save for the family ring and the silver locket that Elizabeth wore around her neck.

'I had to invite them here,' Kate exclaimed. 'Imagine such a timely meeting, though both were ready to go back to their farm. I said that surely the labourers could manage without them for a while though Master David thought they would slacken off without his hand to guide them.' So the conversation went with Thomas admiring the determination of David as they both talked about land and crops, though it was so hard for him to keep his eyes off the lovely Elizabeth.

Their courtship was a short affair. From the moment that Thomas had set eyes on her he knew that Beth would be his bride. That she shared his love was a miracle to him, who had never fallen for any other lass. His liking for David was another factor, though he had to leave to supervise his own small land. Beth stayed on and as the July rains finally fell they laughed and sported like children. Thomas's gamble had paid off. Not only was the harvest a great success, but Beth consented to become his bride at the harvest festival. Nicholas and Kate were overjoyed. No children had been born of their marriage, so the prospect of grandchildren had eased their hearts. Thomas and Beth were married in a simple ceremony in the month of October. Though she had a name that would have graced royalty, still she preferred a country wedding which suited Thomas well as his love was for the land and not great titles. David stood as a father to Beth, since their own father had died young. The celebrations went on all day, with the bride and groom presiding over first a family meal and later in the evening joined the villagers as they feasted on roast deer and a suckling pig. Kate and Nick started the dancing as the fiddlers played a merry tune.

'Are you happy, my love?' Thomas asked of Beth, for he would have given her the moon and stars if she had asked it of him.

'Dear Tom, I could not have wished for a better day. I only wish that we could live as simple folk, for the running of such a large house weighs heavily on my shoulders.'

'Have no fear, my love, for my parents are still young. They can be Lord and Lady while we live in the great house and leave such entertaining to them.'

'For certain they both look young for their age and yet they must be older than they look to have a son of your age?'

'We Meverall's age well, dearest, I shall live to be a hundred,' he joked as he swung her up in his arms for another spirited dance. One day soon he would have to divulge his secret though it would hurt him deeply, for hadn't his father Nicholas been more of a father than that shady character he met briefly beside his grandparent's graves?

He was to remember that conversation in years to come. The estate prospered with David, now very much a gentleman farmer, travelling abroad to learn of such methods as drainage to put the more barren land to use. Fields that were once dry benefited from the new system and the marsh lands were now put to use with drainage channels carrying the excess water away. Nick and Kate continued to entertain the other gentry while Tom and Beth worked together on the land. Their firstborn child was a solemn child that they called Grace. Their next child was a boy that they named James in honour of their ancestors. In the year of 1762 Kate developed a harsh cough and as the year turned she died of the consumption. David put in a rare appearance at the funeral as by now he had married a girl from Holland and had sold the farm to live with his wife in their own homestead. Nicholas lost heart after Kate died and Thomas was obliged to work less on the land and more on estate business.

With King George ascending to the throne in 1761 a time of peace and prosperity lulled England into a sense of stability, so that many estates became more prosperous. Beth gave birth to two more stillborn children and Thomas took joy in his only living children. His sister Mary had gone into a convent shortly after his grandparents died and little Grace showed signs of leaning towards a similar life. In complete contrast James showed an interest in soldiers from a very early age, leading both Thomas and Beth to wonder if any of their children would ever show any interest in the house and the estates.

Beth accepted the inevitable truth that there would be no more children, so it came as a surprise to her when she fell pregnant in 1778, after all she was coming up to her fortieth birthday. Thomas was delighted and even Nicholas seemed to rouse a little from his customary gloom. The boy was born in early 1779 and was given the name of George. Nicholas lived long enough to see the boy christened before passing quietly away in his sleep. He left the family journals to Thomas who pondered on them for a long time. He had always known that Nicholas was not his real father, but more surprising was the fact that Nicholas had played a part in ensuring his real father, Henry, had probably escaped the very night when he had first met him. Of course he would not be alive now even if he had survived the wound that had disabled him that night. Still, he wondered about his father and what kind of life he had lived as a pirate. The journals were then locked away to pass on to his eldest son when the time came. How was he to know that James would join the army and set sail to fight against the Americans in the civil war, after all he had not even had his sixteenth birthday when he ran away to join up?

So he lavished his love on young George in the hope that at least one of his children would take to the land in the footsteps of him and Beth. George grew into a sturdy lad who seemed to enjoy the pursuits of a gentleman. He kept a fine seat on a horse, mingled readily with both the gentry and with the factor, yet

Thomas sensed restlessness in the boy. It came to a head when the lad had just passed his fifth birthday. He had gone with a local lad to see the Naval ships come into the port. One of the junior officers had taken a liking to the boy, taking him aboard. That night his childish chatter had been of the great ships and the thrill of actually being on the sea. Once he had been put to bed then Thomas had taken Beth aside, showing her the journals and telling of his own birth.

'Oh Tom, why didn't you tell me all this before now, I would have known better.'

'Maybe he inherited it from my father, maybe it was just meant to be. I can't answer that, I only know that my heart has always belonged to the land and that the first time I went sailing I was seasick within minutes. I am sorry my darling, but I think this may be your burden. I would wish it different. I am getting old Beth; time is not on my side. Let the boy go his own way in life for he will never be happy again if he is forced to become what he can never be.'

Beth looked at her husband. She had not seen it before now, the touches of white in his hair, the crinkling around his eyes.

'Come to bed beloved and let me show you that you're not old.'

That night he made love to his wife for one last time. It was the gentle love-making born out of familiarity combined with a love so pure and abiding that they lay together long afterwards, there hearts beating in perfect unison. Tom could not sleep. Instead he watched his wife's face peaceful in sleep. After all these years together he still marvelled at her beauty that welled up from a pure and loving heart. Now he understood why his parents had defied the conventions of the times and how his true father Nicholas had given up everything for her sake. 'I love and adore you Beth,' he whispered as he arose and dressed in his riding clothes. Mayhap he could find some comfort in riding out in the early dawn.

They found his body lying near the hill that faced towards the moors. The horse had apparently balked at a ditch and thrown him, instantly breaking his neck. Yet his face was in repose and showed no signs of trauma. He was buried alongside of the two people who had taught him the meaning of love, Nicholas and Catherine Meverall.

WAVE DANCING

Elizabeth looked across the great hall from her seat by the fire. Her aging eyes were not surprised to see George standing lost in thought at the base of the stairs. He would often be found there, deep in a world of his own, gently stroking the face of Eve that had been so loving carved there centuries before.

She studied her son, tall and slender but with a wiry strength evident in the way his shoulders moved. His long dark hair tied at the nape of his neck added to his lithe stature.

A mother's concern was evident in her eyes as for the hundredth time she wondered what George was thinking. She had asked him several times but had always received evasive answers.

There was much about George that she did not understand, he had been born to her late in life, the second son she had given her beloved Thomas and in many ways he was an odd boy. She had to smile in spite of herself, she still thought of him as her little boy but a boy he was no longer, twenty now and every movement showed her he was a man. The smile was brief as her thoughts returned to what he was doing. He disappeared for days at a time. He told no one he was going and told no one where he had been when he returned. His wordless communication with the carving would become more frequent when he was about to disappear, that his mother realised, was why she dreaded seeing him standing there now.

Turning, George saw his mother's gaze and a smile creased his handsome features as he crossed the room to her. Kneeling in front of her he caught her wrinkled hands between his and brought her fingers to his lips.

Neither said a word and George rose and left the room. If he had looked back he would have seen a tear escape his mother's eye.

He hadn't looked back, and now he had much more pressing matters on his mind. He stood at the wheel of his ship as it passed silently out of its hiding place under Harland Point. Even though he had done this so many times it didn't get any easier. It took his full concentration to guide the craft through the rocks and high swell of the waves that buffeted them and tried to stop them leaving.

It was a smallish ship, two masts provided the means to set sail footage to make the ship fast and light, too light sometimes in the storms that could and did occur in the English Channel.

The ship had a small crew, all local lads from the village and even a couple of workers from his home at Halleswell Hall. He trusted them all with his life and they the same with him. They had been together for a long time now, they had all known each other from a young age and a common bond of a love of the sea had first brought them together and had started on the road they now followed.

Smuggling, while illegal, was not investigated too closely and had provided a good living for all involved. Now though, things were slightly different. The trouble in France had provided them with new opportunities to make a profit transporting British nobility out of France to the safety of English shores.

Such was the purpose of this trip. It had not started well, the sea was high and the strong wind was in the wrong direction, making them have to fight to gain any forward motion. They were headed into a storm, dark clouds hung heavy on the approaching horizon and rain fell in a curtain, the light failing even though it was two hours before dusk.

Looking up into the sky George could see the black clouds roil and merge. The storm was going to be a bad one, of that there was no doubt. Fleeting thoughts of returning to shore crossed his mind. His ship was not built to withstand heavy seas. His honour would not let him give up, there were people waiting for him on the French coast, people that were relying on him to take them to safety, he would not, could not let them down.

The sea continued to rise, waves crashed over the bow as it rose and then fell down the next trough. They made little headway against the wind and the rain which now fell in a dark curtain. Things were getting serious, even battened down as they were, water was finding its way into the hull faster than the pumps could pump it out.

The wind suddenly changed direction, there was no warning but suddenly they were running before the wind instead of fighting against it.

The rain tore at George's face, blinding him as he fought to keep control of his craft. There was a crack followed by a ripping noise that was louder even than the howling rain.

Peering upward George could just make out the tattered remnants of the mainsail flapping wildly in the howling wind, ripped down the middle, the sail was useless and in fact it was worse. The remains blew about so erratically that steering was made almost impossible and the whole ship began to lurch dangerously from side to side seeming to be in imminent danger of capsizing.

Sailors struggled to climb the rigging up the mainmast cutting the ropes that held the ruined sail. Once released it took off, the wind carrying it away from the foundering ship. They were in trouble now, without the sail forward motion was at the mercy of the cold grey waves. Sinking was now a real possibility. All George could do was hold the ship with its bow into the storm and hope they could ride it out. It would be dark soon making it impossible to judge the swell. There was a real danger that they would be overwhelmed.

'Get that sail raised,' He yelled as loudly as he could over the howling gale.

Shouts rang out from different parts of the ship, all but lost in the noise of the storm. Sailors began the treacherous task of setting another sail. At any moment they could be lost overboard, all were aware that should they go over there was no hope of rescue. Even though most were attached by safety lines, they were still in peril of their lives.

Thunder crashed, lightening illuminated the ship for long seconds, leaving an afterglow that blinded as the light faded once more.

At last the new sail was set and it boomed out with terrific force as the wind caught it.

George had to alter course slightly to catch the wind properly in the sail. He prayed silently that this one would be strong enough to see them through.

The ship gained speed and was soon flying before the wind. Now they were going too fast, where as they had been riding the swell now their speed had them outrunning the icy dark water beneath them. The top of swells saw the bow leave the water to come crashing down on the back slope of the next trough. The little ship was not going to take much of this sort of battering. The sail was going to have to be furled once more. A task that was going to be nigh on impossible with the power of the wind forcing the sail taut as it was.

Wiping the rain from his eyes George peered into the darkening gloom, straining to see anything that would tell him that the far shore and safety was getting closer. He could see virtually nothing; even the prow was lost in the downpour.

A shout from the bow was the first warning he had; instinctively he hauled round on the wheel, forcing the ship to turn sharply. Wood and sailcloth complained loudly at this treatment and the ship was turned almost onto its side as a wave hit them broadside.

Looking to his left George could just about make out dark cliffs rising high above. But for that warning yell and his quick reactions a few more seconds would have seen then smashing straight into the gigantic rock wall.

There was no time for relief; they were still in desperate trouble. The force of wind and wave was intent on pushing them into the cliffs. It was all George could do to keep the rudder over enough to stop them being dragged into the crashing foam of the waves as they smashed into the cliffs.

Nature took mercy on them after half an hour of desperate struggle. As they approached a headland that stuck out into the sea like a huge finger, the wind moved round a few points and pushed them slightly out to sea once more and the waves were now racing down the coast instead of smashing into it.

Rounding the headland George steered into the leeward side where the wind was cut off behind them by the towering cliffs. It was but a brief respite as George knew that once the waves pushed them from shelter then the wind would catch them once more. That few seconds was enough, the sailors scrambled up the rigging and got the sail furled.

Looking desperately to the shore George searched for a hint of somewhere he could beach his craft. There was no hope of reaching a harbour, that much he knew. He had no idea where they had made landfall but just getting solid ground beneath his crew's feet was his priority now.

He felt more than saw the coastline soften and he took a gamble, steering left he guided the ship towards the coast once more, praying that his instincts were right. Staring through the rain he half expected to see the cliffs looming over them again at any second but they didn't appear and with a final push the sea threw them up on a sloping beach of shingle. The hull scraped and screeched over the stones before coming finally, thankfully to a halt.

George didn't move, relief held him rooted to the spot. He still clung to the wheel that he had fought with for the last desperate hours. The wind still blew and the rain was falling hard as ever, but George experienced a moment's peace before shaking himself and galvanising his crew into action. Grabbing kit and equipment they were soon all climbing over the side of the ship and dropping down onto French soil.

The rain seemed lighter now they were on dry land but the wind was as strong as ever. All the crew were exhausted and in need of shelter and warmth but they didn't dare venture far in the pitch darkness, France was not a safe place to be now, especially for people in their line of work.

They trudged up the beach and found trees lining the top of the beach. The trees cut out some of the wind and most of them just threw themselves to the ground, leaning against sturdy trunks. George thought they could risk a small fire and issued orders to find any dry wood they could.

Soon they were all huddled round a small blaze, its warmth leeching out some of the cold from exhausted limbs. They were too tired even to mount a watch and sleep finally overtook them and none knew more till morning.

The morning brought a dramatic change in the weather. The

storm was gone as though it had never been. The early morning sun worked its way through the leaves dappling the ground beneath with bright rays, ever changing, as the breeze moved the branches above.

George awoke with a start and immediately berated himself for not setting a watch; there was no excuse for such laxity even after the experiences of the previous night.

Looking about him, he wondered where they were, nothing looked at all familiar. Maybe he would see more if he got out of the trees and with that thought made his way between the tall trunks until he came to the far side of the thicket. He shaded his eyes against the sun and looked out into the expanse of country-side. Gentle green hills marched their way inland as far as the eye could see. Moor land that looked peaceful in the morning light. There were no landmarks that he could see although there was a rough track going along the coast not too far in front of him. It didn't look a well travelled route, weeds were poking their way out of the packed earth in many places and there were only old looking wheel ruts marking the tracks surface.

As he was just about to go back into the trees a movement caught his eye. Turning toward it he saw a man on a horse riding hard down the track towards him. Ducking back into the trees he watched the rider approach. As he grew closer George could see that the horse was lathered up and had obviously been ridden hard. The riders black cloak was flying behind him allowing George to see that the man was armed with a sword and he had no doubt pistols as well. George's hand went automatically to his own blade before he recognised the man and running from his hiding place he hailed the stranger.

'Louis, Louis, up here.' He shouted, waving his arms over his head.

The rider glanced up to where the shout had come from and hauled on the reins to bring his labouring mount to a halt. Turning he rode to the bottom of the slope and dismounted with a flourish and walked toward George.

'George Fletcher, my friend I had almost given you up, I was beginning to think maybe the storm had beaten you.' He spoke good English but with a heavy French accent, his smile was universal though and conveyed pleasure and relief at their meeting.

George had to smile at the use of the name he used in France, such a common name to hide his identity. Louis embraced George and then his face suddenly became serious and businesslike.

'Things are getting dangerous here my friend, we had best get under cover. I can not be seen meeting you here or anywhere else for that matter.'

George was not surprised at this statement although he was slightly worried by the fact that Louis was. He had never bothered about the danger before; in fact it had seemed to be the danger and adventure that drove Louis in this venture. Not much older than George himself he cut a flamboyant figure in his black clothes and wide feathered hat. He knew it too and many a time his handsome face and image had helped him find his way into a maid's boudoir.

While he had been thinking Louis had retrieved his horse and was leading it up the slope and then into the trees. Looking round he checked to see that George was following and then continued 'It is good that you didn't make it to the normal place, it is being watched now and is unsafe for any English craft.'

George grunted, deep in thought he wondered at the change in Louis, something must have happened. He showed little of his usual joviality and that troubled George.

'Where is the *Wave Dancer* moored George?' asked Louis over his shoulder.'

George tried to lighten the mood. 'Moored, that's a laugh, she is beached just through the trees. Hopefully the crew are checking her over although they were all still asleep when I came through the woods.'

Louis didn't seem to see anything funny, he just continued. 'Then we must get you floated as soon as possible, I will send some people to help you get back into the water.'

George stopped, he had to know. 'Louis what has happened I know something has?'

Louis stopped but he did not speak for a moment. Eventually he turned and George was disturbed to notice a tear slowly working its way down his cheek.

'It is my father; George. Soldiers came upon him alone on the road a few days ago and tried to arrest him. Of course he put up a fight but it was to no avail, there were too many of them and a sword thrust from behind ended his life, the cowardly bastards, they couldn't take him in a fair fight.' There was pride in his voice as well as the pain and a note of defiance that was evident above all.

George was stunned. James De Castellan had been a great man, English originally George thought although it had never been confirmed to him. That was what had driven him to helping English nobles escape the guillotine. Between them, and with George's help, many people had been saved from a gruesome death. The profit to be made was beside the point in all their eyes, just recompense for the risks they ran.

James had been the brains behind their operations. It was he who had first approached George a couple of years ago and broached the subject with him. George of course had leapt at the opportunity for many reasons, not least the uncanny resemblance that the De Castellan family bore to his own. The first time George had met Louis he had been stunned, it was almost like looking in a mirror, they even wore their dark hair the same.

'I don't know what to say Louis, I am so sorry. I know we all knew there was risk in this venture. But I would never have dreamed of it coming to this.'

Louis shrugged, 'mercie boucoup mon amie.' He said, almost embarrassed as he lapsed into his native tongue.

They came out of the trees to find, as George had expected the sailors were working on the *Wave Dancer*. He couldn't help a proud smile creasing his face. He had a very good crew that would do almost anything for their captain.

Louis didn't seem to notice, he was still subdued. 'I will send some trusted people to help you get off the beach this afternoon. Then if you will accompany me back to my house I will introduce you to your passengers. I think you had best wait till dark to set sail. There are many ships being searched at the moment, some even confiscated or sunk if they are found to be wrongdoing.' He remounted his horse as he was speaking and started off without another word.

George was deeply disturbed. James' death had come as a shock to him and he found that he felt the loss deeply, but Louis' reaction had told him that it had affected him badly and George wondered if he could still rely on him. What they were doing was very dangerous, although they had always made light of that. Now though George was thinking that maybe Louis was going to try something reckless and noble to avenge his father.

There were things to do and getting them organised took George's mind off James and Louis for a while. It seemed the *Wave Dancer* was still whole and there was surprisingly little peripheral damage.

The main problem facing them was that the ship was deeply embedded in the shale of the beach and it was going to take a huge effort to get her back into the water.

The crew had done all they could and had even started to dig the ship out when help arrived. Men came down to the beach either singly or in small groups. Louis arrived with one small group and told George that they had to go in small groups to avoid raising suspicions. All the men were carrying ropes and tools that would help in the struggle to get the ship afloat once more. There was laughter and joking in the air as they arrived and they started work as soon as they reached the ship. They had obviously done this before as they knew exactly what they were doing.

Louis stood and watched for a while. His demeanour was still grave but there was the odd hint of his good humour as he watched his men as they struggled to get the ship into the sea. He even made the odd comment when something went wrong or if one of the men slipped or fell.

At last the ship was once more where she belonged, gently rocking as the surf rolled under her. She was moored a little off shore now and the crew were using a rowing boat to go to and fro as they made preparations for their departure.

Louis' men left as soon as the ship was back in the water, but Louis himself stayed on long enough to ask George to accompany him to his home.

George knew that he would be meeting the people who were to be his passengers but there was something else, something that had been bothering Louis.

They walked up the beach with Louis leading his horse.

'I have something to ask of you my friend. It is something my father bade me ask should any harm befall him. It is a risky undertaking and I know not how you will proceed with the second part.'

George was silent; inwardly he was wondering what might be so important to Louis to make him nervous of asking a favour of a friend who owed him many a life debt. Neither said a word as they reached a barn where a horse was tethered, awaiting George. Mounting they raced off in silence, Louis leading the way to his country estate.

Passing through a low arch they entered the De Castellan estate. A wide avenue of trees bordered the road that cut through the parkland in a direct line to the house. House, castle would be more like it. In fact it was called Le Chateau De Castellan. Many turrets stood atop the white stone walls that reflected in the large lake that fronted the castle, making the castle look even larger than it was.

George had often wondered why the revolution had not forced the De Castellan family to abandon their home as so many others had, but Louis had shown him the small army he had to call upon, and the castle itself would take an army to uproot its residents. George frowned. It was obvious to him that that was why James had been waylaid on the road. He considered imparting that knowledge to Louis but then thought that he must have realised that himself, not that it stopped him travelling on his own or lightly guarded.

A groom was waiting for them when they dismounted and he took their horses.

Louis showed George in and he followed through a stone floored hallway. The walls were lined with portraits that seemed to inspect the visitor. George wasn't sure if he had their approval, such were the stern expressions.

The hallway opened out into a large hall, again lined with pictures and heavy drapes. Furniture was sparse, a huge dark wood dining table surrounded by dark, high backed chairs took up the centre of the room and a few smaller pieces of furniture stood along walls, looking almost as though they were trying to hide so as not to detract from the impact the dining suite made.

Louis bade George to take a seat at the table and then ordered wine from a servant who was awaiting them. As they sat and drank, Louis much more than George, a small knot of people entered the room and approached the seated pair. Louis stood to greet his guests. They were well dressed and were of obvious high standing. Three men and four women crossed the room.

'Ladies and Gentlemen, please take a seat and join us in a glass of wine,' said Louis.

The new arrivals did as they were asked and a servant poured them all a drink.

'Some introductions, Captain George Fletcher, these fine Ladies and Gentlemen will be your passengers for your return journey. Lord and Lady De Lacy, Lord and Lady Cambridge and Sir and Lady Astley and their daughter Rebecca.'

They all acknowledged their introduction with varying degrees of enthusiasm although all of them seemed to think their station held them far above a mere ships captain.

George recognised the names and had a vague memory of meeting Lord De Lacy many years ago but George only had eyes for one face, that of Rebecca. His heart had missed a beat the first moment he had seen her. He knew that face, had been in love with it since he was a young child. Rebecca's face was that of Eve from the carving at his home. The likeness was uncanny. The same eyes and high cheek bones, even Rebecca's mouth had the same turn up at the corners, giving the impression that she always had the hint of a secret smile just waiting to be released.

With a start George found he was staring, Rebecca seemed amused. The hint of a smile widened slightly and her eyebrows rose as if to enquire why he was staring at her.

George hurriedly averted his gaze and he could feel the colour rising in his cheeks as he fought to control his emotions. With a start he discovered that Lord Astley was addressing him.

'Sorry.' Said George, 'you were saying.'

'I was asking what facilities you had on your ship and if we would be getting separate cabins, if you can take your eyes off my daughter for two seconds.' Lord Astley was not amused at his staring.

'Sorry Sir, no Sir you will all be in my cabin for the journey. *Wave Dancer* is not a large craft and is built for cargo more than passengers.'

Lord Astley's humour was not improved by this statement

but he chose not to pursue the subject.

'Captain, how long will our journey take? My wife is not the best sailor,' said Lord De Lacy. He was the eldest of the group and had a frail look about him. George wondered if he was more worried about himself but he answered 'We will be in England by midday tomorrow, my Lord.'

Lord De Lacy grunted, he didn't seem impressed with that at all. Louis stepped in as he saw George was about to add something. 'My Lords and Ladies The Captain would like to sail as soon as the sun sets, so if you would ready yourselves for the journey I will have my carriage made ready.'

They all rose together and started to leave the room. Rebecca was the last to leave and George's eyes followed the sway of her hips as she followed her parents. He wondered if she always walked like that or whether it was for his benefit.

Louis grinned. 'An attractive young lady is she not.'

'Indeed she is,' answered George dragging his eyes away from the doorway.

Louis was still grinning when George turned to him but that faded as soon as he saw he had George's attention.

'George, I have something to ask of you as a friend. It will add somewhat to the danger of your journey but it is something that my father wanted and I would be in your debt should you carry out this task for me.'

'I am in your debt many times over my friend. Ask and I will do your favour if it is in my power.'

Louis rose and crossed the room to a cabinet. Drawing a key from his pocket he unlocked it and drew out a large casket which he brought back to the table and placed in front of George.

'This was my fathers. It was his wish that if ever anything happened to him he wanted this casket taken to England and returned to its original owners. He never said how he came by it. I would guess that he either bought it or it was from a customer and for some reason it never got sent back to England.'

He ran his fingers over the ornate carving on the lid, lovingly almost as if touching it brought him closer to his father.

'My father said something odd as well. He said that you were to deliver it and that you would recognise the contents and know where to take it.'

George said nothing; he was puzzled.

Louis passed the casket to George who pulled it in front of him. He sat looking at it for a moment before flipping the catch and lifting the lid. Inside was a king's ransom. Jewellery of all sorts lay in the velvet lined interior. Necklaces and rings, bracelets and even a tiara revealed themselves between George's exploring fingers. One piece caught George's eye, a signet ring with an inlaid crest. He recognised that crest immediately as it was his own families coat of arms.

Staring at it he said quietly. 'Yes I do recognise the contents and I do know where to deliver them.'

Louis was watching George, his face was unreadable.

George looked at Louis and said. 'I think it is time for me to tell you a few things.' He still held the ring in his hand and he passed it to Louis saying, 'This ring bears the coat of arms of my family, the Meverall's. I know you know me by the name of Fletcher but my real name is George Meverall from Halleswell Hall in Devon. I have had my reasons for keeping my identity a secret, maybe I should have trusted you with it, but it is a well known name in society and for the operations we have been carrying out I thought it better to keep who I am a secret.'

Louis did not seem surprised at this information, merely nodding. He still held the signet ring in his hand, looking at the crest embossed in the gold.

It was some time before Louis spoke. 'I knew Fletcher was not your real name and I understood your reason for the charade so I did not pursue it, although I must admit to being intrigued. What you have just told me makes many things clear. My father knew or at least guessed your identity I think, or why else would he entrust this casket to you and you alone. That was a secret he took with him to the grave. Now it is my turn to surprise you my friend.'

George looked at his friend, wondering what he was about to say.

'We are related, distantly but my family comes from Meverall stock as well.' He smiled. Another small masquerade, made necessary by circumstance. I...'

He was interrupted by the door banging open and an armed

man rushing across the room. Both seated men turned to see what was happening.

'Monsieur là sont des soldats approchant le château, un grand nombre qui nous dépassent en nombre dix à un. Ils ont également l'équipement de siège. Ils doivent vouloir dire pour prendre le château.'[1]

'What?' Said Louis, jumping out of his chair he crossed the room to look out of the window. There was indeed a large body of soldiers approaching the castle.

Louis was calm and business like once more when he turned from the window. 'Looks like we are in for a fight my friend, I think it is time for you to move out before we are surrounded.' He did not sound unduly worried by the forces outside.

'Marcel, a placé les défenses et envoie quelqu'un pour chercher des invités de capitaine Fletchers. Ils partiront maintenant'.[2] He said to the man who was awaiting instructions.

Immediately he left to do his masters bidding.

Louis turned to George, 'Your guests will be ready in a moment.' There was a smile on his face that spoke of his amusement at the discomfiture of the nobles that would be most put out with being told to get a move on. Marcel was not the most tactful of men and he would get them moving one way or another.

'There is a passage that will lead you out of the castle. I do wonder if it is a coincidence that has brought these forces upon us today. Could it be something to do with your mission?'

George had been thinking the same thing. He had dallied longer than he should. He should have picked up his passengers and left, but he hadn't so there was nothing to do but make the most of the situation as it stood and get his guests to safety. He just hoped his ship had remained undiscovered, although his crew knew how to look after themselves and would do their all to protect the ship even if that meant taking it out to sea. That could be a problem if he arrived at the beach only to find the ship was gone. He berated himself silently for coming here, Louis was speaking to him once more. 'I can not spare any men to accompany you but you should be safe in the tunnel, just be careful when you get to the other end and keep your wits about you my friend.'

Marcel entered once more, leading a disgruntled set of nobles.

'What is the meaning of this? Your man virtually pushed us out of our room?'

'We are about to be attacked My Lord and it is time for you to be gone.'

Lord De Lacy's demeanour changed immediately. It was almost possible to see the colour drain from his face. 'Of course we should leave, what are we waiting for?'

It didn't take them long to make their way down the long tunnel and soon they were waiting by the entrance, hidden behind a large bush while George scouted the area, not least to find out where they had come out and what direction they would have to follow to find the ship.

All was clear and they were soon hurrying through the parkland at the rear of the castle. George had a good idea of where they were and led the way in a circular route. They were soon at the boundary of the Chateau lands and hurrying toward the coast.

The soldiers had scouts out to stop any such escape and a group of three riders came upon on as they crossed an open stretch of grassland. They didn't hesitate but charged with swords drawn. Their intent was obvious and so George drew his weapons and waited. There was nowhere to go; running would only offer their backs to the oncoming horses. The soldiers obviously thought they were coming in for an easy kill and showed no reserve as they charged.

The first shot from George's pistol took the lead rider full in the face, throwing his lifeless body from his saddle. The other two came on, George parried a wild swing from the next rider's blade. There was nothing he could do to stop the third. His swing almost removed Lord Astley's head as it connected with his neck. He was dead before he hit the ground. Screams of the ladies mixed with the thunder of hooves.

The riders had split up, making it impossible for George to stop both of them. Their next charge would result in another death. That was a certainty.

The rider to his right never started his charge however. A shot rang out from a thicket and the man fell lifeless to the springy turf. Suddenly there were men charging from the thicket toward the terrified group of nobles. The last rider lost his nerve and bolted. He didn't get far, a shot took him between his shoulder blades and he gracefully slid from his saddle.

'Good timing gentlemen,' said George with a grin as members of his crew approached. His grin faded as he turned to see Lady Astley cradling the lifeless body of her husband. Rebecca was there too, a look of shock on her face as though she couldn't believe what had just happened. George hurried toward them. He was gentle but firm as he said. 'Come we must be away from here. My men will look to Lord Astley's body. We must get to the ship, and fast.'

An hour later, they had made the *Wave Dancer* and were at sea, the coast of France receding into the late afternoon sunset.

The nobles sat in George's cabin, silent except for Lady Astley's weeping. George entered when he had ensured the safety of his ship. The nobles looked up as one. George saw that the haughtiness had been wiped from all their faces. A mixture of terror and relief showed on all their features. The only face that remained resolute was that of Rebecca, and George found he could not read her expression at all. Their eyes met and something passed between them that neither understood.

Sometime later George was standing at the prow of his ship. He had a lot on his mind. So much had happened in the last few hours, the adventures he had enjoyed for the last few months had turned sour. He had to admit that the danger and adventure were why he had made so many trips to France, but the seriousness of what he had been doing had been brought home to him with a big bump.

He realised that one way or another it was over now, it would never be the same after today that much was certain. If Louis survived then he would have to leave the castle eventually. The revolutionaries wouldn't stop now, even if this first assault did not work. Where would Louis would go? He didn't know. If he came to England they maybe they could meet up once more, if he ran elsewhere then maybe they would never meet again. George hit the rail with his fist. He had so many unanswered questions that he knew Louis had the answers to. What was their blood relationship? Where had James got hold of the lost Meverall treasure? He looked at the Meverall crest that adorned his hand. It looked right there somehow. Questions filled his mind, so many questions that he didn't know if he would ever find answers for.

His thoughts drifted to Rebecca. He had found the woman he had been in love with for so long. The statue of Eve had been his love for as long as he could remember. He had always known somehow that that face was the face of the love of his life. Little had he known the manner of their meeting. Now was not the time to pursue his suit though. It would be improper to make advances with the death of her father so raw.

There was a movement behind him. He turned and saw Rebecca, wrapped in a long cloak, for the sea breeze was cool as dusk faded into night. She walked straight up to him her eyes locked on his and eased herself under his arm. There was no mistaking that she had already made up her mind.

WAVE DANCING – PART TWO

George stood and stared out of the window of the great room of Halleswell Hall. He didn't really see the sun rising slowly out of the dawn mist. The mist had settled over the parkland in front of him during the long hours of darkness as if covering Halleswell Hall in a natural shroud. Hours of thoughts and memories tumbling over one another passed unnoticed by George as he had stared into the darkness, waiting for the dawn. Hours of tears and smiles had passed as he had remembered. There were no tears now, he had shed them throughout the night, maybe that had been the point of his vigil, remember and mourn so as to be strong in the morning.

He had dressed in his finest yesterday, not really knowing why. He just knew that he had to stand vigil for the night and greet the dawn of the day when he would bury his beloved Rebecca.

The house was silent, none stirred in the household yet, or if they did they were silent, respecting their masters mourning. His children still slept, he knew for they had been late to bed last night, unable to sleep with the knowledge that this would be the day they said goodbye to their mother for ever, old enough to understand, his three girls had cried themselves eventually into a restless slumber while his baby son knew nothing of the tragedy at his birth nor how it had brought despair to his kin.

His mind was elsewhere, in another time. A happier time, in fact the happiest time he had known in his life. A happiness that should have been his for many a year but that life had been wrenched from him by cruel circumstance.

He lifted a glass of brandy from the windowsill and raised his glass to the dawn. 'Rebecca, love of my life.' He said to the dawn but the dawn didn't answer.

The mist slipped away as George's thoughts melted back to the sun warmed deck of the *Wave Dancer* eight years ago as he guided his ship into the hidden sanctuary below Harland Point.

George was flanked by a beautiful woman, a woman who's slightly smiling mouth and sparkling eyes had captured his heart as soon as he had seen her.

The crew bustled about the ship, making ready to moor. Apart from Rebecca, the rest of the nobles George had rescued from France stayed below in his cabin. Lord Astley's body lay in the hold with his wife, who had refused to leave his side. Thinking of Lord Astley, George glanced at Rebecca, she showed no outward sign of how the death of her father had affected her but George knew she was hurting inside. The fact that she had remained on deck with him for the duration of the voyage had as much to do with not wanting to face the fact that her father was dead as wanting to be in George's company.

It had been a relieved but saddened party that had arrived at the doors of Halleswell Hall to be greeted by George's mother. How she had known they were coming she had never let on, but somehow all was ready to receive the body of Lord Astley to be laid out in the parlour and readied to be laid to rest. The rest of the group had stayed at Halleswell Hall until arrangements were finalised for Lord Astley's funeral.

Although it had been a subdued atmosphere, George and Rebecca spent the days of her stay together, just sitting and talking or walking in the grounds of the Hall. George had never been happier and Rebecca was in good spirits most of the time, although thoughts of her father coloured her mood without warning every now and then as realisation that her father was dead hit her again and again. There were tears, but George was always on hand to offer his embrace when the tears took hold of her.

It had been late on the first evening following their arrival when Rebecca had seen the carving of Eve.

Candlelight flickered across the features of the carving which were so obviously those of Rebecca. She had been stunned as she looked, almost as if in a mirror, at the beautiful carved face that looked unseeing back at her. George had watched her, gauging her reaction. She had touched the carving with something approaching awe.

George smiled and said softly. 'I have been in love with you for as long as I can remember, even though I had not met you. You have been my talisman all my life and now you have been made flesh my life is complete.'

Rebecca had answered by reaching for his face and gently brushing her lips across his.

Carriages had arrived and the noble guests had departed. Rebecca had gone along with her mother as they accompanied Lord Astley's body back to their family home. George had promised to follow in a couple of days for the funeral. Rebecca had looked back at a waving George with a look of longing in her eyes. George had known that they would not be parted long but that didn't stop him feeling a lump rise in his throat as the carriage sped away from him.

The mist was there once more, brighter now as the sun became stronger and the mist started to lose its battle for existence. George had a smile on his lips, remembering that time made him feel lucky to have had his dreams become reality but at the same time the hurt cut deeper, wounds that would never be healed in this world.

Of course that first few days had been wonderful but their wedding day, now that had been something special. The mists receded into sunlight once more as he thought of that sunny July day when all had seemed right with the world and he had felt he was the happiest man alive. A secret smile passed his lips as his thoughts slid back a little to the night before the wedding.

The evening sun was slowly disappearing over the horizon, taking the light with it but it was still warm as George and Rebecca strolled through the parklands of Halleswell Hall. The lights of the hall twinkled in the growing dusk. Decorated in readiness for tomorrow, the Hall for once looked a splendid and warming sight. Some of the brooding menace that normally flowed from the hall was lightened, almost as if the house itself welcomed the forthcoming happy occasion.

The young lovers moved slowly, skirting the edge of Brannon's Wood. They talked of the wedding tomorrow and also of what their mothers would say if they knew they were out here in each others company, when they should be separate in their own rooms contemplating the enormity of tomorrow's ceremony.

Both had laughed at their superstitious mothers, about them telling them it was bad luck to see the bride the night before the wedding. A fox barking deep in the wood startled them. Rebecca gasped and then laughed at her fear as she leaned into her husband-to-be. George had pulled her even closer, raising her chin he kissed her gently and then more passionately as she had returned that first kiss.

The breeze in the leaves of nearby Brannon's Wood had a slightly erotic feel to it making the moment perfect for the young lovers.

Slowly they had sunk to the grass. Rebecca's arms folding around George's neck as he sank to lie beside her. Laying back they both looked up at the sky, now dark but suffused with the lights of a million stars. The silence was complete as they lay there, happy in each others company.

George broke the silence. His voice was suddenly nervous as he said 'I don't think I can wait till tomorrow, my love.'

'Me neither,' said Rebecca. George could not see the way she had chewed her lip after she had uttered those words. George was not the only nervous one.

Fumbling nervous fingers battled with buttons and clasps as they undressed each other. Naked they stopped, unsure as to what to do next. Rebecca took George's hand and placed it on her breast. Slowly and gently he caressed her, nerves and a rising passion making his hand shake slightly as he stoked her soft flesh. Time stood still as they explored each others bodies. A soft moan of pleasure escaped Rebecca's lips as George touched her most secret of places. Slowly their movements grew in intensity. Instinct and passion took over, banishing their nerves as they made their love known.

George smiled again as he glanced toward the ceiling. That had been the night that Sarah had been conceived, his beautiful eldest daughter who had such a look of her mother about her.

They had fallen asleep in each others arms, waking only when the first light of dawn had touched their naked bodies. Sitting, they had looked into each others eyes and laughed. They had dressed and ran hand in hand back to Halleswell Hall. Thinking to sneak back to their rooms. But an amused voice had startled them as they stole through the great hall toward the staircase.

'I wondered where you two were,' said a familiar voice from his seat by the fire. Louis De Castellan had an amused smile on his handsome face that only widened at the guilty looks that George and Rebecca exchanged. Realising that Louis knew exactly where they had been sent a mortified Rebecca scurrying up the stairs. Louis' laugh followed her only to be lost when she closed the door to her room.

'How long have you been here Louis?' asked George as he took the seat opposite his friend.

George's thoughts turned to Louis De Castellan. They had shared many an adventure over the years. They had got in a few scrapes too, mainly due to Louis' tendency to court danger. The two of them had been a team, brothers although their blood relationship was somewhat more distant.

The journey that had brought Rebecca to Halleswell Hall had been the last time he had seen Louis for some months. At first George had thought that Louis would be in his element fighting off the soldiers that were assaulting his chateau. Time had passed however and George had begun to wonder and worry more and more when they had no news of him. Rebecca had been the one who eventually sent him to France to find his cousin. She had got so fed up with George's increasing moods that she even went so far as to pack a bag for him when he protested that he was needed at home.

George had to smile, Rebecca had a very forceful character when she put her mind to it, but truth be told he had not needed much persuading; he was desperate to find Louis. For their friendship, but also for unasked questions that he had been desperate to learn the answers to. Louis was the one who had held the key to unlock the things he had to know.

It had been the first time *Wave Dancer* had been to sea since that last fateful rescue mission. George felt free and at ease as soon as he had guided his ship away from the coast. He had loved his time in the company of Rebecca but part of his soul lived riding on the ocean. It had been a smooth trip and it was not too long till the French coast came into view.

George hadn't known where to start but the chateau had been the last place he had seen Louis so that was the logical place to begin.

Arriving at the chateau had been a sobering experience. Although it looked the same as it had the last time George had seen it, apart from a few battle scars. George knew it was abandoned. It had that feeling about it. The feeling a place has when it is empty, an atmosphere that is recognisable as soon as it is felt.

Shocked and worried for Louis' life, George was not to be put off and he was soon making enquiries of local people. Some he vaguely recognised, but none knew him and he didn't find anyone that could or was willing to tell him what had happened to Louis. Either it was loyalty to their Lord or they really didn't know what had happened to him. George had a strong suspicion that the former was the truth.

He had spent the night in the chateau; although it had been locked up George had easily found the escape tunnel entrance and gained entry that way. He had hoped he may find some clue inside as to what had happened after he had made good his escape on his last visit. There was nothing, a covering of dust on the floor told him that no one had been in here for months. He did take heart from the fact that the doors had been secured. Someone had enough time to lock the place when they had left, and the very fact that it had not been ransacked spoke of a victory in the fight he had escaped.

His memory of that day was of being afraid, slightly panicked and at a total loss as to how to proceed but salvation had arrived in the morning. A young boy was in the grounds when George left the chateau. The boy had spotted him and had cautiously approached and proceeded to tell him what had happened that day months ago.

The soldiers had brought up cannon and had been intent on destroying the castle. What they had not expected was for the people of the locale to take up the cause of their lord with a ferocity and guile that would have been a joy to the eye of any military commander. An attack from the rear and both flanks had destroyed the soldiers, even though they were far better armed, surprise had been their downfall. They had not expected any attack from outside the castle and were found wholly unprepared.

In the aftermath, Louis had made the decision to take flight, not for his own safety but to stop any reprisals his enemies might take out on the local population.

George had discovered that Louis had taken refuge at the home of one of his father's friends, a man that was slightly known to George, so he had no qualms about heading off straight away expecting that he would find welcome in the home of distant relatives.

He had found Louis and found that the experiences of the last months had much changed his friend. He had still been jovial enough and delighted to see George, but there was something about his demeanour that George found slightly worrying. There was something about the way Louis looked at him, a slightly haunted look. George put it down to the still raw emotions of the death of his father and the loss of his home. Later he had found out that that was not the whole reason for the change in Louis.

They had many chances to talk while George stayed. He got answers to questions that had been playing on his mind for months. The jewellery that Louis had given him to take home was one of them. How had James come to own them, if ownership was the right word for stolen goods? Louis could not be exact as to where his father had acquired them, but seemed pretty certain that they had come over from England some years previously and had been bought by an aristocrat on a whim as a gift for his mistress. It seemed however, that the mistress had recognised the Meverall crest and by coincidence also knew of James' heredity and so had passed the casket on to him. George didn't ask in what context James knew the lady in question well enough to confide secrets like his real identity to. Louis didn't say and George had not wanted to cast aspersions on his father's honour.

The kinship between himself and Louis was something else

that George had needed settled. He knew Louis' grandfather had disappeared from the Meverall house many years ago, shortly after the theft of the jewellery and the associated disasters that had befallen the family. George still couldn't believe there had been a whole other branch of the family that he had known absolutely nothing about.

Louis had been able to fill in some of the gaps. His grandfather had arrived in France after short stints in the army in The Americas and a trip to Russia. Louis had not known many details of his Grandfather's life but it seemed that he had been an adventuresome character. Eventually he had met and married Marie De Castellan and had inherited the chateau which had passed down the line to Louis.

If times had been different when the two men had met then things might have been different, but at the time the English aristocracy was not popular with the French people and so secrets had been kept that in another time might have been more open.

George wondered if that would have changed what had happened, probably not, but then matters of the heart were a law unto themselves.

The trip to find Louis ended with George asking Louis to stand with him at his wedding to Rebecca. That question had startled Louis and at first he had refused, claiming prior engagement and other reasons why he would not attend. George had been surprised to say the least. He wondered at his friend's reluctance but the real reason did not even enter his head.

Eventually Louis was persuaded but he had still not been happy about it. He did promise to be there the day before the wedding though and that was enough for George.

Their wedding day had been spectacular. Halleswell Hall was decorated and had never looked so inviting as it had that day. Flowers adorned every available surface, bows and ribbons intermingled with the garlands, even the maids had flowers in their hair. It had been Rebecca's wish for the blooms, a request that George's mother had been only too happy to accommodate.

His mother had been shocked when she first met Rebecca. The likeness to the statue of Eve had been uncanny and not a little disconcerting. It hadn't taken her long to start treating her like her own daughter however. Rebecca had that effect on people. A smile from her was enough to endear her to anyone.

Carriages had started arriving quite early in the morning as guests arrived for the celebrations, friends and family from all over the country and together with friends and family of Lord and Lady Astley; it had been quite a gathering.

Once the ceremony had started in the family chapel all those faces had blurred. George only had eyes for one face, the radiant face of Rebecca that had a glow about it as she walked slowly down the aisle toward him. The sun shone through the window and followed her progress giving her a halo of soft yellow light. She had never looked so beautiful.

A glance at Louis beside him had shown a look of awe on his face but there was also that haunted expression there again. George wondered at it briefly again but it was forgotten when his eyes turned once more to the stunning sight of his bride.

The rest of the day had passed in a blur that all weddings seem to for the bride and groom.

A secret smile crossed George's face as he remembered their wedding night. That was not a blur and something he remembered fondly.

The sun had burnt off most of the mist now and the household was stirring, making ready for the day's ceremony. None disturbed George though.

It had been the prescribed time after the wedding that George had been blessed with his eldest daughter, a beautiful baby that George had lost his heart to as soon as she was born. Halleswell Hall was a happy place for a time as if it too welcomed the new arrival. The Hall was full of relatives close and distant who came to view the new arrival. Rebecca hardly saw her husband as his time was taken entertaining various dignitaries and looking to do business deals while their wives doted on the new arrival. Rebecca found herself at a loose end, she loved showing off her daughter but found that with all the female attention she had time on her hands away from her child. Time that was filled in a way that maybe she regretted.

The smile faded from his face as more memories flooded his

mind. These were not so happy.

After the wedding George had persuaded Louis to stay at Halleswell Hall. Louis had shown the same reluctance as before but had eventually agreed. Life had been fine for a while; they had hunted together and made trips to Bath and even went to London together. But there was something growing between them as time went on. George noticed but knew not the reason. It was as if Louis was putting up a wall between them and George could not knock it down.

Matters had come to a head one afternoon that autumn. Louis had entered the hall with that haunted look that normally was only hinted at on his face in full view. He said not a word to George but had gone straight to his room and packed his bags. He had been up there for some time and when he finally came back down he said nothing to anyone. He had cast a guilty look at George but just headed out of the door. George hailed him but was ignored. He had rushed to the door to follow him but a sight met his eyes that almost stopped his heart. Rebecca was walking slowly around the lake. It was obvious she was weeping and was hugging her arms around her in a way that scared George. He glanced at the retreating back of Louis and then at his weeping wife. Torn for an instant, he knew not which of the people who meant most to him he should look to. Rebecca of course had been the one he had rushed to. At first she had not wanted his arms around her, but eventually she leaned into his embrace and her weeping was renewed.

Neither had said a word as they had stood there by the lake. George looked up at the sound of hooves on the gravel and had seen Louis riding hard away from the house and out of their lives.

George's mind was in turmoil. He hadn't known what had happened and it had been some time before Rebecca had composed herself enough to talk to him. Even then she had been vague and evasive. George had not dared to question her more closely even though horrible thoughts were running through his mind. Thoughts spun that he was desperate to have answered but at the same time was dreading hearing.

Later that night a maid had found George sitting alone in the great hall. She had silently handed him a letter before rushing from the room, almost as if she was afraid to be in her master's presence.

George had recognised Louis's handwriting immediately but it had been some time before he could bring himself to break the seal on the letter.

George my friend.

By now you will know that something has happened, something that should not have happened. I feel I have betrayed you my friend and hope that you can forgive me although I doubt that you will find it in your heart to do so.

I have been in love with Rebecca for a long time now. That is why I was reluctant to come with you in the first place and reluctant to stay with you in your home. I knew it was a hopeless love and a love that would not, could not be returned and it was like a knife entering my heart every time I looked at Rebecca.

Over the past days I have spent more and more time in her company until today, when my feelings got the better of me and I told Rebecca how I felt. I was surprised to see hesitancy in her denial of returning those feelings. I took advantage and kissed her. She returned that kiss but finally pulled away denying to herself that she had just done that act of betrayal to you. Suddenly she was weeping and ashamed. I tried to comfort her but I fear that may have been the wrong thing to do and she mistook my offer of comfort for something else. She ran from me in fear and I abandoned her. I cursed myself for being a fool and a coward but knew not what to do.

I am sorry for my actions today, more than you can know but I know there is no future for me here and I must leave whilst I still have some honour intact.

Please convey my regrets and apologies to Rebecca although I fear that neither of you will forgive my actions this day.

Louis.

George had sat staring unseeing at the letter for some time. His emotions were all over the place, he felt betrayed by the people he loved most in the world. He also felt love for both of them that neither had let things proceed, but the betrayal was the stronger emotion and that was something that would taint the rest of his marriage. Rebecca had come to him in the night. She just lay with him unspeaking and George had known not what to say to her.

That day had not been mentioned by either of them as time had passed, almost as if speaking about it would tear them apart. George could not help being distant from his wife as weeks dragged into months and years. It became almost ingrained in him and became a habit that he could not break out of, Rebecca accepted this almost as a penance. She had acquiesced to her duties as a wife but the joy was gone from their love-making and slowly over the years it seemed as though producing an heir was the only reason they shared a bed.

George stared at the sun on the morning of his wife's funeral. Tears were once more running freely down his tired face. His night of remembrance had brought things into focus for him. Too late now he realised that he had let one event colour the short time he had with his love. The betrayal would be there for ever but where was the forgiveness and the understanding? He had loved Rebecca with all his heart but that love had become tainted in his eyes. Now looking back, he saw that had he but shown compassion and understanding and possibly his own fault in the whole affair then how much happier their lives would have been. Too late now and that was something he was going to have to live with for a very long time

A polite cough behind him made him turn, 'It is time my Lord'.

George grunted, not trusting himself to make a longer reply and headed for the stairs to collect his children. When he reached the stairs his hand rested on the face of Eve. It felt different and he paused to look. The face of Eve was cracked from her eye to her chin almost like a tear furrowing down her cheek.

George was taken aback. It hadn't been like that before, he was sure of it.

A Victorian Christmas

The carriage slowed and came to a halt as it approached the front of Halleswell Hall. The black horses drawing it snorted, their breath steaming in the frigid winter air.

The door opened and a distinguished gentleman stepped slowly onto the gravel. Dressed in black boots and a long black travelling cloak he cut a dashing figure. Closer inspection told of an older man, careworn and tired after his journey but there was a twinkle in his eyes that belied his age and spoke of a quick wit and humour. His face wore a pensive expression, nervous, almost as if a part of him wished he was not here.

He stood beside the carriage and looked around; his eyes drinking in the house, the lake and the parkland that frost had turned white and sparkling in the morning sun.

Memories awoke behind that gaze and the pensive expression turned to one of sadness and regret. Shaking his head as though to dislodge the memories he turned to the door and swinging his cloak aside raised his gloved hand. He hesitated only slightly before tugging hard on the cold metal bell pull.

There was a barking of dogs inside in answer to the bell followed by admonitions to be quiet before the door opened and a brief discussion led to the man being invited inside.

'Sir, there is a man outside who begs a word with you. He would not give his name but said that he hoped that you would give him a few moments of your time. He is an elderly gentleman so I have asked him to wait in the parlour while I spoke to you Sir. I hope I did right?'

'Yes, yes that's fine,' said George looking up from his morning paper.

'I will come to the parlour to greet our guest.'

Entering the parlour George stopped dead in his tracks. He recognised the man in front of him even though he had his back turned to him. It had been fifty years since they had seen each other last.

Louis de Castellan turned and looked at George. 'George my old friend, I knew not what welcome I would find at your door but I had to see you. We are getting no younger and I didn't know how much longer I would be able to make the trip over the Channel.'

George didn't know what to say to Louis, their parting had not been a happy one and he had thought he would never see the man before him again. Now that he did he felt his heart soften. Louis was an old man, the same age as himself. Perhaps he wore his age better, perhaps the pain and bitter life George had led had made him age more than he should have done, who knows but suddenly the two old men were in each others arms. Tears fell from both men's eyes.

Finally they split apart and stood looking at each other. Both men seemed at a loss for something to say. George turned and reached for a brandy bottle, inviting Louis to join him in a warming drink. The invitation cut the tension and handing Louis a glass he gestured to him to take a seat. Both men sat, each nursed their drink, thinking about the same thing but neither knowing how to speak their thoughts aloud.

'It has been a long time Louis; the years have treated you well.'

'Thank you, life has been kind to me for the most part since we last met.'

Silence again, the subject touched on but still the way forward blocked by fear of saying the wrong thing. With a deep breath George played the opening gambit. 'You know Rebecca died giving birth to my son I presume?'

Done, the walls were breached; there was no going back now.

Louis looked at his glass and swirled his brandy around. 'Yes I did hear George, and I was in more than half a mind to come here then, but fear of how I would be received held me back.'

'Perhaps that was for the best, I was not the easiest person to be around at that time. What happened that day Louis, Rebecca never would say exactly and I have wondered for many a year?'

Louis paused for a moment before answering. 'I left you a letter; I had hoped that you would have taken that for an account of what had happened and why I left as I did.'

George rose from his seat, crossed the room to a cupboard and removed a silver casket. Inside laid a very old sheet of paper. 'This letter?' said George as he lifted it from the box. 'Yes I read it, read it a thousand times over, wondering how I could be so blind. How could I not have seen anything between the two of you.'

'I have regretted that day from then to now, George and I will for the rest of my days. When news arrived of what happened to Rebecca, I was on a horse and on my way here before I came to my senses and realised that I would find scant welcome at that time. After that I just put it off and off until my courage failed me entirely and I thought I would never come back. A few nights ago however, I suddenly felt I had to come, there was nothing of the old fear and I knew that I had to get here before Christmas day. I know not what made me so sure but here I am and glad am I that I followed my feelings this time.'

There was silence again as both men sank back into their memories.

'I think I forgave any part you may have had in those times long ago Louis. Maybe it was for the best, what might have happened if things had gone further should you have stayed. I don't know, you did the honourable thing and although my marriage to Rebecca was never the same, I believe that the fault lay with me and me alone for the way I treated her. I would not let it go and let it cast its shadow over our lives together. That I have regretted more than anything. Had I known that we would have such a short time together I wonder if I would have handled it differently.'

'Thank you George, you do not know how much I have longed to hear those words. Many times I have thought what might have been had I but managed to keep my feelings under control, but history is set and there is nothing that can be done to alter what has gone in the past.'

'True enough and now that we have been reunited I would have us end our days in friendship, let us lay events from the past where they belong. Now tell me what have you been up to for the last fifty years?'

December came in, cold but bright. Louis De Castellan was still George's guest and showed no sign of wanting to go home.

After their first awkward meeting relations had improved between them. The day after Louis' arrival they had made an emotional trip to Rebecca's grave. Long they had stood silent, each deep in their own thoughts that they did not care to share with each other. The fact that they stood there side by side was enough to make their reconciliation complete.

December progressed and so did the two old men's relationship, as days slipped into weeks they became at ease with one another and had told each other tales of things that had happened to them in the fifty years they had spent apart. Some of it George had never told another soul.

George had told Louis of a problem that had been eating away at him for longer than he cared to remember. His son James. 'I did not deal with Rebecca's death well, in fact I went to pieces and subconsciously perhaps blamed her death on James, unfair I know but for a long time I wasn't thinking rationally.'

Mental pictures flooded into George's mind as he spoke, fleeting glimpses of shouting and beatings. Looking back it was hard to believe what he had done and how long it had lasted. It had become a habit that neither he nor his son had seemed to be willing or able to break.

'Finally I came to my senses, too late I thought, too much had happened between us. It was about five years ago. I was writing my memoirs and as I wrote realisation of what I had done hit me. I had destroyed my relationship with my only son in the same way I had my marriage. I had been a fool and at that moment I had wondered if I could save my relationship with James. I was getting no younger and suddenly I feared dying with my son hating me.'

George gazed at the mahogany panelled wall of the study as his mind went back to the day he had first tried to make peace with his son. He had sat in his favourite armchair, the two dogs curled around his feet. James stood awkwardly. It was rare now that his father invited him into his study. Memories of standing here in his childhood threatened to swamp him.... So many occasions when he was beaten for minor misdeeds came back to haunt him.

His father seemed to guess what he was thinking as he invited his son to take a seat. Where do I start to explain? he thought fondling Bonny's ears? 'So much time had gone by and James deserved an explanation for his cruelty and neglect. Would his son understand and maybe grow closer to him?

Slowly…haltering over the painful past he started to speak of Rebecca and the grief that had torn his heart into two. It was a long story though James never interrupted once. Occasionally his eyes would betray the deep hurt inside though he barely moved an inch from where he sat in silent judgement.

'I was wrong son; I see it now,' his breath trapped in his throat as he waited for some sign of forgiveness or the beginnings of understanding.

James rose slowly to his feet. Crossing the room to the sideboard he poured two glasses of wine. It was something he had never done before but the last hour had opened up a gap in the relationship between them both.

'You ask forgiveness, father, yet how can I forget so many aching years when I strove hard to please you?'

Wearily George took the offered glass. James was now striding back and forth, trying to take it all in. Would he ever get another chance? Suddenly that seemed more important than anything to him.

'I am sorry, father, but I must think on this. You denied me not only your love but the memories of a mother I never knew. I was just a child; I had a nanny but no parents. Nothing I did ever pleased you, that is the cross we both must bear,' saying that he turned to the door.

George suddenly realised Louis was talking to him. 'Sorry Louis, what did you say?'

'So how did it work out with James? Did you manage to work it out?'

'Eventually, it took about two years for us to start feeling really comfortable in each others company. It was never going to happen overnight, there was too much history to be made up for but I am glad I have finally sorted myself out. I have caused so much pain and unnecessary heartache to those that I should have loved and cherished the most. I do so regret that now I have wasted half a life with self pity and selfish disregard for what others have gone through.'

Louis paused for a sip of brandy before answering, 'but you have come to terms with it George and you have made your peace with all of us. It is all history and can't be undone but you have the future. Enjoy it to the full my friend and I think others will enjoy it with you.'

A couple of days later George and Louis were sitting by a roaring blaze in the large great hall fireplace, shadows danced on the walls as the flames played and cavorted their way up the chimney. Both men were at ease after a filling supper and were now settled to a brandy and a chance to talk.

'You know what you said the other day about me enjoying what remains of my life, well I have been thinking on that and I am thinking of inviting the whole family over for Christmas. It has been too long since Halleswell was full of happy children. You will still be here for Christmas of course won't you?'

Louis nodded, 'that's a good idea George I think that would be a fine day.'

Theo woke early. The house was quiet; indeed there was not a sound to be heard. Unusual for a house the size of Halleswell Hall but this was Christmas and things were always different at Christmas.

Theo climbed from his bed and padded down the great staircase. The staircase looked enormous to a little five year old boy. Today the stairs were dressed in garlands of green and white. Theo let his hands trail through the decorations as he hurried down the stairs, running his hand over the cracked face of Eve as he reached the bottom.

Reaching the great hall at the bottom he stopped. His mouth opened as he drew a deep breath of amazement. He had never seen such beauty before. A Christmas tree stood on a large table in the corner of the room, decorated with an amazing assortment of sparkling shiny baubles and beads. The sunlight from the window made rainbows where it stuck silver and gold.

Theo could not take his eyes off it.

A door must have opened somewhere; a slight breeze moved the rainbows, making them dance and sway, evocative and trans-fixing. Theo stood unblinking, not even hearing the footsteps that came up behind him. He jumped as a voice behind him said, 'Merry Christmas Theo. Do you like the tree?'

Theo turned and smiled up at his Grandfather, 'it is beautiful Grandfather, more beautiful than anything I have ever seen.'

George smiled, little Theo was growing up fast, he was already a tall lad, not exactly skinny, but did look like a good meal would do him a bit of good.

'Where are the rest Theo? I thought all you youngsters would have been down here, seeing what gifts Christmas has brought to you?'

Theo lowered his eyes; he had been so transfixed by the tree that he had not even seen the pile of gifts on the linen clothed table beside the tree. He made no move toward them however, preferring to admire them from where he stood.

His grandfather stood there with him, his wrinkled hand resting lightly on his Grandson's shoulder. Both of them looked up as a wish of 'Merry Christmas' rang down the stairs.

James and Elizabeth stood arm in arm at the top of the stairs. Theo broke from his grandfather's arm and rushed up to them.

'Mama, Papa come and see the beautiful tree, it is truly wonderful.'

James smiled at his son, 'of course Theo, we are coming now and we too want to see it.'

Reaching the bottom of the stairs, James greeted his father; it was a warm greeting, one that James had yearned for since he was a child and was now happy to receive.

Elizabeth's greeting for George was even more enthusiastic. She embraced him and planted a kiss on his cheek. If George found this show of affection from his daughter-in-law embarrassing he didn't show it, in fact he welcomed it. His life had been too short on affection, maybe partly his fault but not wholly.

Other members of the family made their way into the great hall over the next hour, George's younger daughters Grace and Jemima came down together, followed by their children. They showed the same awe as Theo had done at the sight of the glorious tree.

Not long after Sarah arrived in a carriage with her husband and two children. They were warmly welcomed by her sisters and all the children.

George waited in the hall for the new arrivals, the morning air was brisk and his lungs could not take it.

Sarah came straight over to where her father sat in his chair by the fire.

'Father,' she said, as she threw her arms about his neck. George returned the embrace; it had been some time since he had seen his eldest daughter. He had missed her cheery presence in the hall. They parted and George looked into her eyes, as usual when he saw Sarah he felt a pang of pain, as it was like looking into the face of his Rebecca, so similar were they.

It had been nearly fifty years since Rebecca had been so cruelly taken from him. Not a day went past without him thinking about her, and seeing his daughter made those memories so much clearer, maybe that was why Sarah didn't come to visit that often. She knew the pain her visage caused her father and had wept over it many times over the years. Her mother's death had blighted more than one life. It was not only her face that mirrored Rebecca, her son, Richard had come to her late in life and perhaps the life she led was the one that Rebecca and her father should have enjoyed. Maybe that was just an over active imagination and was not something that anyone had ever wondered out loud. The whole family had been affected deeply and all of George's daughters missed her terribly, even after all these years. George had done his best, but he was so wracked with grief and pain that much of their upbringing had fallen to the maids of the house. The girls did not blame their father for it now, although they might have done in the past.

The family was all gathered now; happy laughter rang out in the great hall as a mass of children waited impatiently for the present giving to begin.

George watched from his chair. Christmas always raised a smile on his face and this year was extra special, having the whole family together for the first time in many years. There was nothing like the look of joy on a child's face.

Theo loved his new wooden ship that his Grandfather had hand carved for him. It was beautifully detailed and he had even painted on the name at the front. It was *Wave Dancer* of course.

George told him that the real ship would be his one day and he hoped he would treat her with the same love that he had. Maybe the words did not mean that much to a five year old boy but they were something he would remember later in life.

Toys were soon spread all over the floor as children played with their new gifts. Adults too were busy thanking each other for presents that they gave to each other on this most special of days.

Soon it was time for the whole family to make the short journey to the chapel for the Christmas morning service. Great coats covered the black morning suits of the men and top hats were donned along with gloves to complete the men's ensembles. The women were soon wrapped in fur muffs and fur hats covering the wide assortment of crinolines, and hooped skirts were held up above the grass that had been moistened by the rain during the night.

A carriage had been brought to the door for George and Louis. George was not up to the walk. Although he protested that he was, his daughters would have none of it and he soon realised that they would be fussing over him all day, so he had better get used to it and give in gracefully. In truth he didn't put up much of a fight, he was starting to feel tired and the day had hardly begun.

Whilst the family was at church the servants of the house worked rapidly to make the hall ready for the sumptuous feast that the family would enjoy on their return. The massive table was set with the best silver cutlery and bone china, today was one of the few times in recent years that the family finery had been brought out. In fact it had not been used for so long that the staff had struggled to find some of it, hidden away in cupboards as it was. Delicious smells came wafting up from the kitchen adding to the party atmosphere that would greet the family on their return.

All was ready when a crowd of laughing revellers removed their overcoats and furs and handed them to servants who waited to receive them. There were gasps at the table that now groaned under the weight of tureens filled with steaming vegetables and gravy boats steaming and adding to the tantalising aroma. Decorated with holly and the best silver candlesticks it was an impressive sight indeed, light flickered off the polished crystal wine glasses and decanters, that wine filled, prismed light in all directions.

As was customary the family seated themselves with George at the head of the table with his daughters around him. The chair at the other end of the table was left empty and when all were seated George stood and made a toast.

'To you all, may you have many a happy Christmas and especially you little ones. And to you Rebecca we all miss you always.' And with that he raised his glass and saluted the empty chair. Everyone followed suit and there was a moments silence before the happy chatter once more filled the room with sound.

Soup tureens were taken around the table and for a time the only sounds were that of silver on china as the family enjoyed the appetizer for the many courses to come.

As soon as the soup course was finished staff bustled around the room removing the empty bowls. George rang a small bell. This was the moment for the staff to bring out the meat, a large goose was the main attraction but there was also pheasant and even a brace of quail, a special treat for Sarah, who adored them.

Soon the sound of cutlery on china mingled with the chatter as the meal begun in earnest. All had plenty to eat and then some, whilst leaving room for the sweet course that all were looking forward to. Mrs Cooper was renowned for her skill with pastry and she did not disappoint on this occasion. Steaming puddings were brought to the table to ooh's and ahh's from the awaiting revellers. Cheese and fruit followed by coffee and all washed down with wine and port.

Eventually the men withdrew to the parlour for a brandy and a cigar, leaving the women to chatter amongst themselves and to watch the children as they were freed at last to once more enjoy their presents.

In the parlour George sat himself by the fire and closed his eyes. He loved Christmas, and this one was more special than most, but at the same time it always brought back memories of broken dreams.

He opened his eyes to see James looking at him, a worried expression creasing his face. He came over when he saw George had caught him staring and pulling a chair to the fire, he joined his father.

Neither spoke for some time but eventually James said, 'are you alright father? You look tired out.'

'I'm fine,' said George, 'just a little weary, its funny how tiring Christmas is isn't it. I feel like I have done a hard day in the fields.'

Eventually George rose. 'Come with me James there is something I would show you.'

Glancing across the room he called to Louis. 'Come with us Louis if you would.'

James got up and followed his father to his study. George went to a locked cupboard and opening it, removed a casket and brought it to the desk where James and Louis waited. George said nothing for a moment but opened the casket and turned it toward James.

'Do you know what these are James?' He said as James dropped his eyes to the contents of the carved box.

James shook his head, his eyes remaining on the rich jewellery that lay before him. It was a king's ransom, all antique and of beautiful quality. He didn't touch the contents of the box but he looked up and asked his father a question.

'Why are you showing me this now father?'

'Because soon you will be master of this house and you need to know that your financial future is secure. This jewellery is part of that security. It is worth a great deal and holds a good piece of our family history with them also. Louis is here to act as witness to my wishes. Also I think this is a good time for me to give you this Louis,' said George pulling his Meverall signet ring from his finger.

'No Louis, no protests, I have made up my mind. I would have my ring as a link between our families that shall last as long as our families do. James I ask you to be witness to this, and to hold that should ever a De Castellan ask for aid then our family shall give it freely and willingly.'

Neither said a word for a long moment, George's mind had drifted back to the time he had first laid eyes on the fortune that now lay before James, a time in another country, in another life. It had been in the castle of the De Castellan family, a branch of their own that he had first seen them; in the company of Louis who he had found out at that time was actually his cousin.

James looked again at his father's aged features. Pain and grief had etched themselves on that face and age had made their effect even more marked. James didn't know what to say, his father had never talked to him about inheriting anything let alone Halleswell Hall.

Louis was humbled by George's speech; to him it was a final act of forgiveness.

'Thank you George, that means more to me than you know. I am humbled by your generosity.'

'And I will keep my side of that bargain, father and will do my best to be a good master to Halleswell Hall, when the time comes.'

'That is settled then, now let us rejoin the festivities, they will be wondering where we have got too. You coming Louis?'

'In a minute George,' said Louis, his mind still in France.

The pair of them re-entered the great hall to see a happy Christmas scene. Louis stayed in the study, his fingers running along the carved casket, his mind had gone back to a time when his own father had shown it to him, in France so many years ago.

It was dark now and the candles had been lit, their soft light casting shadows around the room. Grace was seated at the piano and both Sarah and Elizabeth were singing Christmas carols. All the children were sitting listening and occasionally joining in with snatches of the songs that they knew. The adults stood around them, some with drinks in their hands and some with children on laps.

George took his seat by the fire and James came to stand by him.

Elizabeth left Sarah to finish alone and came over to her husband, collecting a tired looking Theo on the way. She smiled as she deposited Theo into his Grandfather's lap. Theo was asleep in seconds. George said nothing but the smile on his face spoke volumes. He ran his hand through his grandson's blonde hair as he slept on his lap.

The singing continued and when they ran out of carols Grace changed the tempo to more soothing tunes.

Louis came back a while later and was immediately surrounded by children, all clamouring for a story. Louis smiled at them holding up his hands in mock protest. He loved telling the tales as much as the children enjoyed listening to them. The noise had awakened Theo and he quickly summed up the situation. Jumping from his grandfather's lap he hurried over to Louis. 'Tell us a tale of *Wave Dancer*, Uncle Louis. Have you seen the model grandfather gave me? Wait I will go and get it.' He said all this without pausing for breath and was off up the stairs to fetch it before he had even finished the sentence.

On the way down his hand brushed the face of Eve, had he but had time for close inspection he would have seen that the face of Eve was smooth once more and there was the hint of a smile on the beautiful carving's lips.

George smiled and settled himself once more into his chair. His eyes passed over the room, taking in the faces of all that were dear to him. Theo smiled when George's gaze fell on him.

Sarah had come over and was sat at her father's feet, resting her hand on his knee. George glanced away from Theo and his eyes met those that his daughter shared with his beloved Rebecca. George realised he was happier now than he had been for as long as he could remember. He had all his family around him after a happy Christmas day. He felt a peace in his heart that had long been missing.

He closed his eyes and his thoughts wandered back to *Wave Dancer*. Rebecca stood by him at the helm of the ship and she asked him a question. 'Are you ready my love?'

'Yes my love I am ready, all is settled now and I yearn to be with you once more.'

George Meverall passed from this life on that Christmas evening 1853. He was buried in a grave with his beloved Rebecca and the headstone read simply, 'reunited for eternity.'

THE COMET PARTY

Vicky perched on the end of her bed, her soiled muslin dress leaving patches of grass and earth on the pristine white sheets. For a brief moment she was tempted to lie down and add her muddy boots to the carnage, but common sense finally prevailed. Sinking her head into her hands, the reddish-brown hair tumbled unbound around her shoulders. Screwing up her face into a hideous gesture wasn't going to work right now; the tears fell from her startling blue eyes and ran through her fingers adding streaks of mud to her lovely face.

'I want my Ayah,' she screamed into the empty room, but only echoes bounced back at her. Baba Mama was left behind in India along with the only real family Vicky had ever known. Her father was still an alien figure to her, as were her brothers, Rupert and Tim. Sent back to an English boarding school at eight years old, both were strangers, even though Rupert was five years older than her at eighteen and Tim just turned fifteen. Her mother was a mere memory now of a pale faced lady dressed in white and gold. Vicky remembered colours; India was a land of great contrasts with colour overwhelming the sounds and scents of the beloved country she had been forced to leave behind.

Slowly her sobs started to fade as she remembered Kiku, the houseboy who had helped her to learn some of the local languages. Guiltily, she thought of the time when she made him climb a tree to fetch just one ripe coconut when there were plenty already in the kitchen. Then there was Suki, the maid who crawled into her bed and held her whilst the fierce tropical storms raged all around her frightened senses.

These were part of her rich heritage, the silent maids and the cheeky houseboys. Her Ayah's adoration and that of her sisters who praised her looks and her quick grasp of the native language. Dressed in the finest of silks, she would parade before

169

her father and mother for a goodnight kiss, before shedding her finery as a snake sloughs off its skin and running through the darkness to her Ayah's village. Draped quickly in a sari, she would skip and dance in her bare feet until she was too tired to carry on. Soft arms would then hold her and place her back in her bed. No words would be spoken. Who had need of words then?

Once again she was in disgrace for roaming through the woods with her friend Jenny from the village. She hated this cold and ugly place, although it did look quite striking when the sun finally appeared. With her quick wit she soon had some of the family secrets and the old legends planted firmly in her mind. She had persuaded a very reluctant Jenny to help her look for the fabled holy well in Brannon's Wood. Putting on airs and graces came naturally to Vicky, had not she seen this game played out so many times before?

'My father now owns all this land' she had said with conviction, neglecting to say that it had yet to be handed over by her repulsive uncle, Theo. So why should she be blamed when both had tumbled down a bank and landed near the river? Sent to bed without any supper was no hardship for her, but poor Jenny would be beaten for the state of her clothes. Resolving to take some of her spare clothes to Jenny's mother, she started to pull off her heavy boots.

That was when she heard the whispers on the nursery landing. It would not be the maid Florence, who often sneaked some food to her; Uncle Theo had been remarkably knowledgeable about his household and had forbidden any of the staff to go near her that night. So who would be skulking around here at this hour when supper was near to be announced?

One voice was definitely her brother Rupert, but the other was muffled as if he or she was wrapped against the April chill.

'Father isn't fit to be the heir,' she heard Rupert say.

'Would you then have another?' The voice was low and almost hissing.

'I need proof, damn you,' Rupert spoke again.

'I know where the journals are kept.' This time the voice was really threatening.

'You would take it for yourself then, you rogue?'

'Careful, my friend, I merely warn you that there are others with just claims.'

'I knew it, damn you; you would lull me with false promises while you stake your claim!'

'Be careful what you say, our family is an old one with long memories, it would not be wise to cross us.'

Vicky cowered at the threat in the voice, only once before had she heard such venom and that from a powerful medicine man, she hoped Rupert would not do anything silly.

'There is the ritual?' Now the voice was wheedling, and Vicky felt, more than heard a rustling as of dried leaves in an autumn wind.

'Damn you to hell, I promised that it would be so,' Rupert answered.

'Hush, I feel a presence nearby.'

'Creaky boards and hungry mice,' the other voice was mocking.

Vicky realised that despite the balmy April weather she was shivering. That voice, the menace, it was like stepping into a tiger's den. She had seen much that the English would never understand (not counting herself as English right now); she sensed violence in the air, but who would listen to her? Now she hardly dared to breathe as the memories washed back over her.

She was in a jungle clearing, pressed close against the ground in case the Tiger man heard her. Much of the speech had been too much to understand, but some second sight told her that the incantation was meant to bring Tiger's spirit here. Holding tight to Kiku's hand she felt herself say, 'he knows we are here.'

'The tiger spirit burns bright in you tonight; otherwise you would be dead by now.' She heard the words as in a dream.

'No,' I will not be part of this,' she started to rise from the ground, and in that moment all the breath left her body.

He was beautiful, this Tiger spirit, his fur gleamed red and gold in the firelight, his eyes shone with a radiant light as they looked deeply into hers and then passed back to the eyes of the Shaman.

His hands moved with speed and the image of a corrupt English official vibrated in the air.

'Shanu Akra Imbas' he said and the tiger roared just once before vanishing completely.

'Come child,' he spoke in perfect English.

Vicky rose shakily to her feet.

'Let me see your hand, Tiger daughter.'

Vicky held her hand out.

'Ah, Tiger daughter, yours will not be an easy path, but you will triumph over many enemies, this I see when the dragon takes to the sky.'

Was it a dream? The mangled body of the official was discovered the next day. Among his papers were found damning evidence of fraud and illegal smuggling of slaves.

Now Vicky shivered again, the house was filling up with guests from far and wide, all to see the fabled Comet that spoke to her of destruction and despair.

Was this the time to fulfil the prophecy made so long ago? She only knew that forces for evil were gathering, and if the answer lay in her Uncle's old journals, then she had to find them before anyone else. But what could she do, one young female child that was hardly ever noticed? Maybe that would be her advantage?

Hastily undressing, she slipped between the muddy sheets and dreamt all night of dragons in the sky and pain such as she had never felt before.

Slipping silently through the door, the cloaked figure hastily dropped it to the floor revealing a deep green satin gown that showed to perfection her trim figure and deep auburn hair. Casting her old slippers off, she donned a pair of matching silk dancing shoes and patting her hair into place she slowly descended the stairs for supper. How quaint these old traditions were, she thought, when most people regarded the late evening meal as dinner. Indeed they had dined earlier at six of the clock, but now it was nine pm and she found that her appetite was indeed coming back. Clutching her shawl about her shoulders she felt a twinge of unease. Had she been seen leaving her room? Placed as she was in the older wing, she doubted that very much.

Inwardly Charlotte suppressed a shudder of revulsion mixed with anger, how dare they treat her as an old family retainer when she was carrying enough jewellery to buy this house many times over? Deliberately she had left her emeralds in her safety box, maybe Theo was too old and jaded to recognise real wealth, but she wasn't here to display that, her purpose was her own and not to be compromised by vulgar displays of her position in society. Perhaps Theo had some inkling of her worth, but she had been invited on what seemed a mere whim. Maybe she should trust that inner voice which spoke of dreadful deeds and hard times to come?

'Charlotte, my dear, please come and sit by me, I feel faint for the lack of female company.'

Must I put up with Lady Astley's twittering? She thought, but knowing the importance of the next few days she was inclined to be lenient tonight. If only the meal would not drag on then she could see it through without the longing to stifle the pompous bitch.

'You are related to the Meverall's of course?' The old biddy was waiting for gossip.

'Merely a distant cousin, but glad of the invitation,' she replied in a steady voice.

'It must get very lonely in the wilds of Scotland?' Her neighbour inquired. 'Could not your dear husband accompany you on this long journey? Of course we didn't have far to travel, being close cousins as you may know?'

'I am a widow,' she replied, 'but this is not an occasion to ask questions,' that put the old bitch in her place.

Theo was drunk, not mildly tipsy but roaring drunk. Supper was supposed to be a light affair, a mere top up of food to placate his guests who would never understand his longing to get away from company as quick as he dared. Dinner had always been served at six pm, his excuse that he had to be up early to settle affairs of his estate. Instead he retired to his study as soon as decorum allowed and then would partake of both brandy and the opium that Richard had brought to him.

Ah Richard, he thought now, 'so aware of a grown man's needs.' He was almost certain now that he would be leaving Halleswell Hall to Richard, but the party was also to make sure he was about to make the right choice. If he had known that stupid, blundering Rupert was aware of the secret journals, then he may never have allowed them to return. The darkest secrets of all the Meverall family since the Hall had been built were written in those journals. It was the family's own unwritten code of honour that all remaining Meverall's should know of their existence, but they had passed in an unbroken line throughout the centuries to all the eldest Meverall sons.

Maybe a pillow secret had been shared with man and wife, or knowing the Meverall history, through man and mistress? He thought and a dry chuckle escaped his fleshy mouth.

Drawing deeply through the pipe, he felt that calm sensation wash over him once again and reclining on his bed he drifted into a semi-sleep, where wanton women displayed their bodies to him and the entire damn Meverall's had gone to their own fiery doom.

The tapping on the door brought him back from his pleasant dreams and without considering his guests he barked out 'Go to hell, you bastard!'

Richard entered, completely in command of the situation though his eyes betrayed the glassy look of one who had smoked the pipe himself.

'My pardon, Uncle, but I thought you might need some more... err... refreshment before the night was through.'

'God damn you Richard, but I suppose you may be right,' he agreed.

'Then allow me to top up your pipe and your brandy glass for just a moment of speech with you', and without waiting for a reply he carried out these duties with scarce a tremble of his hands.

'You want something!' Theo yelled.

'Hush, Uncle, this is a private matter and not all here are friends.'

'You know something?' Theo said.

'Merely a rumour, Uncle, but it is wise to be careful.'

'Who, damn you, tell me right now?' Theo spluttered.

'Calm yourself, a man such as you should already be aware that not is all that it seems,' Richard replied with the air of the diplomat he once had been.

Theo wasn't that stupid though; even drunk he kept some of his wits about him. 'You speak of the unrest in the village?'

'Partly so, uncle, your position on this is not a strong one. Brannon's Wood was left by the first Meverall, Thomas, to be untouched for all time and open to the villagers except for the usual hunt when the villagers were warned.' Anticipating the next remark he hurried on, 'but times were hard then and in the years to follow. Now the estate is more prosperous I think a rent rise would be in order?'

'Very clever Richard, you would give with one hand and take away with another?'

Richard looked down at his white hands which had never known a real day's toil, 'it is business, plain and simple. I could have the documents ready for you in two days time.'

Theo laughed, this was a man after his own heart, but cleverly Richard had sidestepped one important remark, 'then who is against us?' he demanded to know.

Crossing to the door, Richard checked that nobody was in earshot.

'It is like this,' he said.

The dawn was still a half hour away when Tim went quietly through the kitchen, helping himself to new baked bread and honey. After only a few days, Flo knew every need of the guests at Halleswell Hall. Munching on the bread he took a slow walk down to the lake. Setting up his easel and sorting out his paints took little time; Tim was used to being hurried from one place to another. With luck he could capture that elusive moment when the sky lightened and the first rays of dawn swept over the land, dappling the lake with a myriad of colours. Drinking from his flask of small beer, his breath caught in his throat as he saw the majestic white swan glide into view. Now if he could only lure her here for a few minutes more then the pink light of dawn would create a background fit for this lovely creature.

Taking up pencil and paper, he quickly sketched her outline in as she dipped her proud beak to take a little of the bread. In one of those rare moments of magic she stayed where she was, as the sun rose over the brow of the hills and tinged her feathers with pink and gold. Further out a fish jumped as if to greet the new day, sending ripples through the still waters. Brush in hand; Tim tried to get as much in as possible. Later on he would have to work by memory, but with his background, memory came easily to him. It was the presence of the two Labradors that first told him somebody was nearby.

Please God, he thought, don't let it be Tristan with his golden hair and manly physique. It was getting harder each day for Tim to hide the attraction he felt towards him. Yet Tim was not ready to cross that line between loving men instead of women. Many times he had prayed to God to ease his burden, but God never replied.

'Sorry to disturb you, Tim, my dear, but I was walking the dogs and couldn't help seeing that glorious spectacle, may I see your drawing?' Alex asked. Tom merely nodded, grateful it was this harmless man.

'You have a rare talent there, my son, have you ever considered the Royal Art School?'

'Father would never allow it,' Tim replied, 'it's not considered a manly pursuit by him.'

'Ah, I understand,' Alex said, 'let me tell you of a friend of mine.'

Tim nodded again; he was a polite young man with an eager curiosity.

'It was when I was quite young you understand, maybe sixteen or so. Anyway, father had been posted to Russia and I spent most of my childhood there.' He paused as if lost in memories of long ago. 'I had this friend, Sergei; he was about your age or maybe a year younger. He was in the "corps de ballet", you understand? '

'Yes, I do, I have a fondness for the ballet myself,' Tim replied.

'It is considered a great honour in Russia to dance, but his father was a military man and wanted to take his son out of the school. In despair he turned to me as a friend and a comfort. We were young and indiscreet. Sergei was disgraced, of course.'

'What happened to him?' Tim asked, caught up in the story.

'His father disowned him, but he went on to become a great artiste, of course. I saw him dance one time before the Tsar himself. We were never the same again, he had the ballet and I was destined to become married and father Zara in due course.'

Tim hung on his every word, 'you must have missed him very much,' he said.

Sadly Alex hung his head, 'I made an awful scene, demanded he declare fidelity to me, but like the swan you have just drawn, you cannot capture a free spirit.'

'But', Tim started to say, and then fell silent. He could not bear to see the pain on Alex's face.

'Be yourself, Tim, give love where it is due, but never try to hold onto a dream. God has given you a great gift, use it wisely and never ask of yourself that which can never be changed.'

Tears pricked Tim's eyes as he saw this stately man pull his past around him as a cloak against a storm. Changing his mood, Alex said, 'race you to breakfast?'

Tim laughed with delight, but deep inside he kept Alex's words in his heart and vowed the swan painting would belong to Alex one day.

Breakfast was a dismal affair. Theo stayed in his room and Richard seemed to be slightly the worst for wear. Rupert and Tristan lounged back in their chairs, expecting to be waited upon. Alex was quite jovial, but beautiful, petulant Zara was in a foul mood. Charlotte was in command and dutifully helped to dish the food out. Vicky went to help her, lifting the cover off various dishes and exclaiming with delight when her favourite little rice cakes came warm from the oven.

'What on earth are these?' Remarked Tristan, helping himself to eggs and bacon.

'Little rice cakes seasoned with spices and honey,' Vicky ventured, 'it used to be our breakfast treat, but no doubt you have forgotten them?' She looked at Rupert whilst saying this.

'They smell lovely,' remarked Charlotte, 'can you spare me a few?'

'You can have mine,' said Tim, his appetite suddenly gone by the touch of Tristan's hand on his thigh, 'I seem to have lost my appetite.'

'I too', said Zara. 'Where is the caviar on toast?'

Mildly Alex admonished his spoilt daughter, 'this is English fare my dear, caviar is a luxury few people can afford here.'

'How absolutely tedious,' Tristan replied, his hand attempting to creep up Zara's gown.

'Would you care to accompany me on a drive this afternoon; I hear that many delicacies can be found nearer to the harbour and such a pretty lady should be indulged on such a day as this?'

Zara coloured slightly, 'I have no female escort,' she replied prettily, looking around the room for aid.

'My pardon, mademoiselle, but I am to help provide towards this evening's feast,' Charlotte inwardly shuddered at her close escape.

Florence chose that moment to arrive with hot buttered toast and fresh coffee.

'Do not look at me,' she stated boldly, 'the Master has stirred up a hornet's nest in the village with his plans for hunting and shooting. I must work all day with hired help for this here party.' She added.

'Damn cheek,' replied Zara under her breath, but it would not do to upset the servants at a time like this.

'We will take Tim and Vicky then,' she said.

'My apologies dear cousin,' Vicky thought up her excuse on the spur of the moment, 'we have to gather early strawberries and such fruit as can be found at this season. We are not a rich household, as you may have guessed by now.'

Zara fumed inwardly, her father must then accompany them.

The breakfast over all went their separate ways.

Nathan was up early as always. Going from stall to stall, he patted the horses' heads and wondered what would become of them in the years to come. Hero danced away from him, but it was merely a playful mood, not the alarm he caused when anyone except his mistress tried to get on his back. Checking the others was second nature to him, brought up as he had been in the saddle by the age of five. Wind-dancer was unusually lively this morning; whilst Theo's large stallion, Blackfoot, was as staid and steady as ever.

The mares, Starlight and Moonbeam were eager for their breakfast and caused him no problems. Settling down with his pipe and tobacco he watched the family as they ventured out for the day.

For four long years he had played the part of the spy in an enemy encampment, never knowing when Theo would strike out at the family he had come to think of as his own. He knew of their backgrounds, of course, that was something he had been carefully schooled in. But he was bored with the whole charade and wondered whether he had been placed here on a fool's errand

How he longed for his own home and the luxuries he missed so much. A stable hand was treated as a slave in this house and if not for the oath he had sworn on his father's deathbed he would be away back home. He also did it for the love of the lady and for fear of her impending doom. It was like a chessboard, he thought, all the players in their correct places and one hand lightly resting on the board.

From this vantage point he could see how the day's play turned out, but later on he would need to sleep to be ready for come what may.

'Morning Nat, I've brought you a fine breakfast,' said Flo, 'seems us country fare is not for the likes of them. Reckon you could put away some bacon, eggs an maybe a kipper or two?'

Nathan laughed; there was some compensation for being a groom after all.

'Must you get back now dear lady, I could do with a drop of the gossip?'

'Aye and the small-beer too no doubt?' She laughed back.

'We'll share it,' he replied.

'What, you lazy bugger, don't I have a feast to plan for tonight, what with all these proud ladies and gents and half the blooming countryside to boot?'

'You will love every minute of it, a chance to show off your cooking which,' here he paused for a moment to savour his feast, 'is the best in the whole of Devon. Now sit you down for a moment, for I need answers to my questions.'

'Nat, you will get us all in a trouble with these questions of yourn. Why not let things be?' Florence was getting upset.

'How many years have you been here Flo?' Nathan asked.

'You know right well,' she replied, 'since I were a kitchen maid.'

'There, we have it, you know more of this family than I do.'

'Be that as may, master Nathan, but I reckon as how you could tell a tale or two if you could?'

'Peace dear lady, we are on the right side.' Nathan said.

'I'll take a jug of ale then, reckon as how this could take an hour or two' she replied.

'Did not I promise you a centrepiece of iced swan?' Nathan smiled.

'An pigs may fly!' She answered boldly.

'Have I ever broken a promise to you?' He sounded hurt.

'No, and you ain't going to start now.'

Heads bent together they talked whilst watching the activities from the house starting out.

The car sped down the country lanes taking little notice of passing horses and tractors. Tristan was in his element here, courting danger was as much of an arousal as getting a woman (or a man) in his bed. Zara was screeching with delight as she held her scarf around her hair. Alex sat in the rear seat, cramped, uncomfortable and near to throwing up his breakfast.

'Can't you slow down Tristan?' He asked, 'automobiles are still quite rare in this part of the county, we could easily cause an accident.'

'Papa, don't be such an old fuddy-duddy,' Zara replied, 'this is so much fun.'

'Like bayonets and guns?' Alex said, reminding her of the country they had left behind.

For a brief moment a shadow crossed her pretty face, but she soon came back with a retort, 'mere peasants, father, did not the Queen herself tell us so?'

Alex could not answer. He had seen the unrest in the people, the conditions they lived in where a loaf of bread could hold back one more day of starvation. If the people had to chop up furniture to keep them warm, then where was the point of building an ice palace to stun the nobles? He had seen enough of poverty and human misery to last him all his life. Still, he felt for the family he had just left behind. If there had been anyone available to take Zara out of Russia he would gladly have stayed behind. His daughter meant the world to him, but she had been brought up to luxury and this strange invitation from Theo seemed like a godsend at that time. Theo had called on every Meverall, whether they bore the name or not. Although the family name was Stewart, everyone knew that he was descended many generations back from an affair with a Meverall and Charles the Second. A name change didn't hide that line of descendants. All he wanted was to see his lovely, but pampered daughter settled into marriage, far away from the Russian court and its intrigues.

His own father had been an ambassador from the young Queen Victoria, and on his father's deathbed he had taken up the role, eventually becoming an advisor to Nicholas the Second. He had married a young Russian girl, but while he was on a visit back to London, she had vanished, leaving him with a daughter to bring up on his own.

For four years now they had served Nicholas well, Zara had been a good friend to the older girls, Olga and Tatiana in particular. It was Alexis that his heart went out to, maybe if Alexis had not been born with Haemophilia then Nicholas would have had the support of his wife, Alexandria.

His thoughts were rudely interrupted by Tristan yelling 'we're here!' Gingerly he stepped out of the car and surveyed the scene before him. Barnstable was the sort of village he approved of. The market streets were bustling with busy shoppers and near at hand were fishermen who were now displaying their morning's catch. Instinctively he knew that no caviar would be found here, these were honest but ordinary fishermen. Tristan seemed to have come to the same conclusion, as he was busy shouting at the crowd.

'Up the coast,' one said, 'yer need the big harbour.'

Alex spoke awhile to a few old salts then turning to Tristan he said, 'there's a larger fishing port just up the coast at Ilfracombe, you might find caviar there, but none here can guarantee it.'

Tristan looked petulant, 'I need some food and a drink,' he said.

Zara looked furious, but a few words from her father soon turned her mood around.

'The locals recommend a dish called lobster; it's said to be twice as expensive as caviar but much more filling and suitable for the King's table.'

'Then buy some and allow us to have a light lunch,' Tristan said.

'My dear young man, I'm afraid I thought this was your treat, I have maybe enough for a pint of ale on me.'

Tristan glowered, but he wasn't about to lose face in front of this man, throwing a few guineas to Alex he said, 'then buy sufficient for myself and your daughter,' and with that he walked into the nearest alehouse.

Zara stuck her pretty little nose in the air and held up her lacy, scented handkerchief, 'This..this peasant hole stinks of fish, I demand to be taken back to more civilised places, even that miserable heap of bricks called Halleswell Hall is better than this ....,' here she swore in Russian, words Alex had never heard from her before now.

'Then I fear you must either wait on Tristan or join with me in an excellent Inn recommended to me by the carter who will later take us back on a slightly less dangerous route', Alex spoke mildly, but he was fed up with the whole day and even more fed up of the company of his spoilt daughter.

He watched with some relief as Zara entered the same Inn as Tristan, although he loved his daughter he was looking forward to some time away from her excessive demands. Eagerly he followed the smells of good honest cooked fish and a pint of the local brew. Zara could take care of herself, he longed for a good gossip with the locals, a pint of ale and some down-to-earth company.

The Comet Party – Part Two

Pushing themselves through the undergrowth was not an easy task. Tim pulled briars from his hair and flung himself down on the ground. Vicky merely laughed.

'Come on lazy-bones it's only a few more paces.'

'You said that twenty minutes ago,' he grumbled.

'Please Tim, this is ever so important,' she replied.

A few more minutes saw them in a small clearing where dog roses vied with the heavy undergrowth to keep them out.

'Why does it have to be exactly here?' Tim said, 'I see no difference from the rest of the wood.'

'It's a holy place, 'she replied simply.

'Well, I see nothing holy, but you brought me here for a purpose,' he said, knowing that his little sister never did anything lightly. If there were a purpose behind this visit then she would reveal it in her own time.

Briefly she told him about the conversation she had overheard and her own need to find the journals that seemed so threatening. Tim was lost for words. Vicky could be impossible at times, but she had never lied to him.

'What hare-brained scheme have you come up with now?' He asked.

'The comet party is tonight, Theo will be wining and dining his new friends hoping to make a good impression so he can get people up here for hunting. Dinner will be about seven pm so the guests can look at the sky about nine or ten o'clock. We can slip away easily and raid Theo's study. Whatever is going on is to do with the journals. We have to see them.'

Tim thought a while, 'don't you know that will be ideal time for Rupert and his accomplice?'

'No silly, they must be on show for most of the time, father is quite insistent on it, he wants to have the Hall for himself.'

'Well, that's natural, there isn't any competition.' He said smugly.

'Lady Charlotte has a claim, and so does Alex.'

'How do you know that?' Tim felt quite cross with his sister, he had no idea of this.

'Forget their names, Tim, both Charlotte and Alex have an equal claim, can't you see the family resemblance?' Vicky said.

Yes, blinded by his infatuation with Tristan, Tim had not really taken much notice of the people who were kin to him. Alex had the dark hair and the regal bearing of a true Meverall; also he was well thought of by the monarchy as well as fast becoming his own friend and Uncle. As an heir he could bring prosperity to the Hall and he had a very attractive daughter. Charlotte may seem plainer in contrast, but she could have easily been Vicky's mother with that rare combination of the Meverall red hair.

'So how do you propose to break into his study?' He asked.

'With this,' she said, showing him a key.

'How the hell did you get hold of that?'

'From Flo, she has duplicate keys for all the rooms in the house,' She said calmly.

Casting aside all thoughts of how she had got it, Tim remarked, 'so how does Rupert get in?

'He'll pick father's pocket of course.'

Tim was completely dumfounded, how Vicky ever got to know this he couldn't say. But he had one last argument that even Vicky couldn't have thought of, 'how do we get Tristan out of the way, he seems to be everywhere?'

'Flirt with him, of course, that will get Zara's back up and between you both you will keep him busy.'

Poor Tim was almost speechless, but Vicky put him at ease. 'Dear Tim, it's so obvious to me that you prefer men to girls, did you think I would love you the less for it? But, please, just flirt, Tristan is dangerous in his own way and I would not see you hurt.' Kissing him lightly on the check, she said, 'and now we must go back.'

Full darkness had descended as the first carriages started to arrive at Halleswell Hall that April night. Closer to the house lanterns hung in the trees lending extra light to the glittering display that the Hall had donned for that night alone. Lights shone from every room and the new chandelier made every part of the great hall glitter with jewel-bright lights. Guests had flocked from miles around to witness this new prosperity of the ancient line of Meverall's. Rumours had spread of the great wealth brought back from India and the almost kingly status of the Russian ambassador. Every wealthy family had sent at least one, if not two guests and some had arrived *en fammilie* to enjoy the feasting and dancing. Few were that concerned with Halley's Comet, for most it was just an excuse for a party and to see if Theodore had really opened up Brannon's Wood for hunting. Women with single daughters sought an opportunity to display their daughter's charms to possible suitors whilst many a penniless lord thought to make a wealthy match.

Theo struck an imposing figure with his dark evening suit and courtly manners, most borrowed from a bewildered Alex. Richard shone in his full ambassador's suit and medals, whilst Alex himself had played down his role, only adding the badge that Nicholas had bestowed on him, not realising that the older families knew of that importance. The younger males were suitably clad in sober black, although both Rupert and Tristan wore their Oxford ties. Tim surveyed the scene with mixed feelings. On one hand he had seen many more glamourous occasions than this, in waiting on his father, back in India. But the English nobility certainly knew how to dress and behave. Oddly, then, he had a vision of peacocks displaying their tails and nearly laughed out loud. How he would love to paint this scene and capture every nuance of behaviour, but his promise to Vicky was not to be broken.

Zara descended the great stairs, pausing by the carving of Eve to show off her beauty. Tim was unmoved by this ice queen displaying her figure in a tight white sequinned dress, but he felt the eyes of every man in the room turn on her. Rupert and Tristan seemed mesmerised by her. She certainly knew how to dress to advantage with her dark hair falling in ringlets around her face, whilst a silver tiara nestled in her hair. How was he supposed to divert Tristan when Zara made such an impact?

Once more the crowd gaped as they heard the introduction of the Duchess of Dunloman. Looking up in surprise he saw

Charlotte regally descending the stairs in a way that Zara could never have achieved. Her ivory gown was covered in an over mantle of reddish gold that captured the tones of her hair, but it was her bearing that shone over everyone there.

Last, but by no means least, he heard the heralds announce the Right Honourable Lady Victoria and knew then that tonight would change all their fortunes for good or ill.

Charlotte had come unannounced earlier to Vicky's room, where a state of near chaos had descended. Poor Vicky was in turmoil as she looked through her wardrobe of children's clothes and knew that her father had made no provision for her tonight. On one hand the childish clothes would make her look less than her age, but the few limp evening gowns would only hamper her movements later. Also she felt a moment's envy for the beautiful Zara, with her fine dresses and glittering jewellery.

The discreet knock, she took as one of the maids, but opening the door she was confronted by Charlotte looking every inch a Queen.

'Well, young lady, are you going to stand there gaping, or do I have to wait outside?'

Vicky had no idea if she could trust this distant relative of hers, but calling on her inner sight, she believed there was more to her than met the eye.

'You can call me cousin, but I think aunt might be more appropriate,' she said, looking steadily into Vicky's eyes.

'H...How did you know what I was thinking then?' Vicky was flustered.

'Why do you walk around that place in the hall?'

'All that blood, all that sorrow,' Vicky replied, and then, without thinking she blurted out, 'you see it too?' Her eyes like saucers.

'Of course I do, I am at least half a Meverall' she replied.

'But what's that got to do with anything?'

'No time now my dear; we have to get you spruced up.' And with that she started going through Vicky's clothes. Armfuls of muslin and petticoats were flung everywhere, whilst Charlotte looked for a suitable garment. Reaching into the depths of the wardrobe she suddenly cried out with delight, 'just the thing, I couldn't have done better myself.'

Vicky looked at the high-collared silk coat, with its rich emerald and gold colouring and the Tiger design so skillfully embroidered on the back. There were loose silk pantaloons in white to go with the outfit, but it was a court officials dress, not a ball gown.

Again Charlotte seemed to read her mind. As she fussed around she casually declared. 'You will be the belle of the ball and afterwards it will be handy to move around quickly, I take it you still want to go through with this silly adventure of yours?'

'It's not silly, it could be a matter of life or death,' she said, glaring at Charlotte, 'and if you know so much about me, you will know I never give up!'

'Peace child, believe it or not I am on your side in this, but I cannot see the outcome of tonight's work, it's a blur to me and I like it not.' With that swift manner of hers she suddenly asked, 'have you got the Tiger's claws, for I am certain they will used tonight?'

Vicky never hesitated this time, 'I have both sets, blessed by the shaman and given to me for times of trouble. Both will fit easily into the pockets of the jacket, it was made for such a purpose.'

Charlotte looked deep into Vicky's eyes as if assessing her very soul. She felt her fate tied up with this child, who could have been her own daughter. Acting on instinct she hugged the girl close to her.

'Promise me Vicky, that whatever happens tonight, you can trust Nathan in the stables, I cannot answer questions now, but Nathan has some of the answers.'

So it was that Charlotte, Duchess and friend to princes was followed down the grand staircase by Lady Victoria, a stunning beauty in her emerald coat with the Meverall family hair tumbling abound around her shoulders in cascades of rich Auburn red.

Theo blanched when Charlotte's full title was given out; he knew she was a lady of some renown, but a Duchess? Why had not his spies told him of this, it could change all his plans for the future? Vicky also gave him pause to shudder briefly, in her the blood of the Meverall's ran pure and true, also her strange attire was somehow both regal and frightening at the same time. Glancing at Richard he saw the same shock mirrored in his face.

'What a strange way your daughter dresses tonight,' he asked, 'I don't like it at all Richard, make her change it at once.'

Richard's face was ashen in the glow of the new chandelier, but still he kept his wits, 'it's too late Uncle, people have already seen, we would both looks fools if we made her change now, also it seems that she keeps rich company we cannot afford to anger.'

Theo saw the sense in this, 'then let us retire for some fortification.'

Zara was fuming with anger at this slip of a girl; she vowed silent revenge before the night was through. Both Tristan and many of the eligible males were watching Vicky with eyes lit with that fire that should belong only to her. Indecision haunted Rupert's eyes and she wondered if tonight would bring disaster on them all.

Only Tim seemed at ease with this vision of beauty, but then he knew his sister's gift for drama. 'Well done sis,' he said, 'you look like a queen, but that coat, isn't that carrying things a bit far? Father and Uncle Theo looked like they were about to die from an apoplexy at the sight of you?'

'It was Aunt Charlotte's idea,' she replied, 'but I think it was a good one.'

'Since when did she become Aunt, I thought we were to trust no one?'

'We have to trust someone, Tim, and she is family after all. You must not forget our purpose tonight. Anyway, I can see you are becoming firm friends with Alex.'

Heads together, they discussed the night's plans until the great gong was sounded for dinner.

Half of the great hall had been partitioned off, but now the drapes had been pulled aside to reveal a feast, and what a splendid feast it was. People spoke later of the great banquet, as much as the strange affairs that followed.

Course after course was served, with lobster bedded on a colourful salad as the start to the meal. All eyes were drawn to the centrepiece though and not a few of the guests hastened through the meal to sample the great white swan, made of ice and spun sugar. Women twittered and the men wondered if Theo indeed had hidden riches to hire a master chef to produce such a masterpiece. Nathan smiled inwardly as he served the chilled wine, only hesitating when he topped up the glasses of Charlotte, Tim and Victoria. With the other guests the wine flowed freely so by the end of the meal more than a few were already well into their cups.

Once he bent and whispered something into Charlotte's ear, but she merely nodded in reply. 'He tells me how my horse is faring,' she said to a suspicious Tim. 'Perhaps after he's finished serving you might like to see the horses, I hear you are a good judge of horseflesh?'

'I am bound to another service tonight, my lady, maybe tomorrow I will have more time?'

Charlotte inclined her head, 'such delays sometimes can prove beneficial,' she said mildly.

Once dinner was over guests started to move out onto the terrace. Others climbed the nearest hilltop hoping to get a better view of the night's proceedings. Tim was in this latter party with a few of the other guests, but more importantly, Rupert, Tristan and Zara. Each had a bottle of champagne and glasses whilst Tim had only his blanket, his sketch board and pencils. Tristan sidled up to him in a manner that was very suggestive. Seating himself on Tim's blanket he offered him champagne from his own glass. 'Come now, my dear fellow, you have hardly touched a drop all night, surely you want to mark this occasion with a drop of the best bubbly?'

Tim's hands were sweating, he had to keep alert, but Vicky had said to keep them occupied, so with a slight shrug he drained the glass in one go.

'Bravo, little brother we will make an imbiber of you yet,' laughed Rupert.

Zara knelt beside him on the rug and suggested an act that had Tim blushing, but then a hush fell over the crowd.

It appeared first as a mere lightening of the night sky, but then slowly the head of the comet came into view, flashing across the night sky and blanking out some of the stars. How long it hung there until its tail became slightly visible, Tim would never remember. For that moment he felt something bigger than him and his petty desires. He longed, yearned, to capture that moment forever on canvas, but knew he could never do justice to this, one of the sky's children. Open mouthed he gaped and felt the rich taste of brandy on his tongue as Tristan leant forward and gave him a drunken kiss.

Heady with the sight of the comet and Tristan's body close to his, Tim returned the kiss passionately and if not for the other people nearby, Tim may have capitulated completely; even now he felt his legs weaken as his erection pushed against his trousers.

'Frightened, Tim?' Tristan leered at him and in that moment Tim felt a great shame wash over him. He had been skillfully played and now he could no longer see either Rupert or Zara.

'Go to the Devil,' he yelled back as he remembered his promise to Vicky.

Vicky had been sat by her new found Aunt when the comet appeared, awed by its magnificence but knowing what she must now do. Just as she went to turn away she felt that usual dizziness that preceded what she now knew was the sight. Nothing had prepared her for such horror though and she felt her knees tremble and the tears springing to her eyes.

'I know what you saw, child, I am afraid that nothing can stop it coming true.'

'Oh Aunt, all the death, the carnage, the mud, the blood, the sky weeping for the fallen. Why did I have to see this?'

'It's our curse, yours and mine, but don't you have something you must do urgently now?'

For a moment Vicky felt the old suspicions come back, but her purpose was now set. Without a word she slipped quietly away from the revellers.

Getting into Theo's study was easy with the master key in her hands. Cupping the candle gently she laid it on the desk and surveyed the room. Alarm bells were ringing inside her head, the study was far too neat, in fact she could hardly feel any remnants of humanity in the room. Her senses were still on heightened alert after what she just witnessed, but she still looked around the room for anything that might look like the old ledgers. Fear and curiosity overcame her instincts as she took down from one shelf a journal marked simply, 'Brannon's Wood'. Now her uncle's plans were laid bare before her as she read through some of the pages. In growing horror she saw the extent of his plans, not just now, but for years to come.

In hindsight she remembered Jenny saying something about the felling of trees on the outskirts of Brannon's Wood, but wood was often cut down for many purposes. Now she thought about those trees and how many years they had once stood there. Possibly for at least ten centuries, she thought now.

Vicky may not have been born or brought up in England, but she felt the scars as if the ancient trees were wounds in her side. Her ancestors had lived for centuries on this land. Where an occasional oak tree had been taken for shipbuilding at times of war; always her ancestors had planted young saplings. She had felt too the ancient power in the woods, the power of Saint Brannon, but also a darker power, born from myth and legend. Here were Theo's plans for a new road to cut through the forest, gaining him rich revenue. But the road would also cut through the village and many people would lose their homes. Here was her father's writing, deeds ready to sign to rob the villagers of their lands. All that was missing were the original deeds of the inheritance of both Brannon's Wood and much of the village with the farmlands around.

Theo would use her father and then hold out on the money and the inheritance due to him. Vicky knew her fathers weakness for the opium and that he was weaning Theo onto the poppy. Between them there would be left nothing, something her brother Rupert had no doubt discovered. All they needed were the documents, she thought and who better to find them than her! She gasped as the candle spluttered out and strong hands took hold of her on both sides. Rupert said 'just in time dear sister,' in that mocking tone of his, and as the gag was forced roughly in her mouth she sent out a mind message, loud enough to be heard by anyone with the sight and hearing.

Tim heard the message as he groped his way through the unlit study. He knew of Vicky's powers but never before had he become the recipient of them. Blindly he followed down the stairs where a servant's passage led to the garden and onwards across the lawn to the edges of Brannon's Wood. So intent was he that when the cloaked figure touched his arm, all the breath left his body, he was caught and now there was no one left to help Vicky.

'Do stop struggling Tim, I am no enemy, I am here to help you.'

The cloak parted and revealed a woman dressed in men's clothing, it was Charlotte, and looking as if she had a fierce headache.

'Yes, I heard it too, nearly split my skull,' she said, 'now speed is of the essence if we are to save your sisters life. Take this,' she handed him a storm lantern, 'wait here for Nathan, he'll be along soon.'

Still Tim could not trust her; this house had been his undoing from the very start. 'I'm sorry,' he said grabbing hold of the lantern, 'I must go to my sister's aid,' and saying this he ran blindly towards the woods.

'Damn it all.' Charlotte swore, all the powers were bent on the destruction of Vicky and her two brothers. Only she could give any aid and now here she was, blind with only her inner sight to guide her. She would have to wait herself for Nathan and that would take up valuable time. 'Hold on Vicky,' she sent the thought loud and clear, knowing the folly of letting herself be known, but anxious to offer comfort to her niece. All her choices had gone astray this night, she should have spoken to Vicky before now and also to Tim, made herself known and damn the consequences of her actions.

Nathan wasn't far away, stopping only to pull on stronger breeches and arming himself with pistol and knife he sped across the lawn, unerringly reaching the spot where Charlotte was waiting for him. No words were needed; Nathan had felt the blast throughout his head.

'Thank God you are here,' said Charlotte, 'you feel the gathering forces?'

'The balance is close,' he replied,' but are we up to it?'

'I don't know,' she answered truthfully, 'if Vicky only keeps her powers in check and use them only for the good, then we may have a chance, but I fear that the tiger spirit may be unleashed in anger and then God help us all.'

Nathan had no need to be told further, taking Charlotte's arm they picked their way cautiously through the woods.

Vicky choked on the gag, the scent of opium almost overpowering her, but that calm voice spoke in her head, *you will triumph over many enemies, the voice of the shaman came to her. Remember though, that Tiger spirit can only be used in defence, let it turn to vengeance just once and it will consume you.*

She was lying on her back in a clearing not far from the Holy well. Rupert was arguing with some hooded strangers and it seemed as if he was not winning the argument. She tried hard to see with her inner vision, but the opium had blocked that route to her. Drifting through strange visions she seemed to hear a voice calling out to her, 'stay calm, stay focussed, the effects will wear off very quickly if you don't fight it.'

The visions came fast with an unusual clarity. She saw a woman much like her, her hair streaming behind her as she rode a lathered horse. Then she was in an unfamiliar house with a woman crying over a bairn. A voice came strong and clear, 'Sarah, you must leave him behind, these people are good, but childless, they will give the boy a chance for the future, whilst we ride into danger and maybe death.'

The vision left her for a while and then she saw another baby, this one loved and cherished by no less than a king and his consort.

Mists gathered and time stood still as she saw an unfamiliar shore and a boat, which had ridden on the wings of a storm. More pictures flashed through her head and suddenly she was back in her own body.

'Vicky, have they hurt you?' She saw Tim bound with ropes nearby her and knew that both of them had been lured into this trap. Now she saw her captors clearly, two women of an interminable age and a man wrapped in a cloak of power so strong it made her feel nauseous.

Tim made as if to speak again, but a booted foot caught him in his chest and he doubled up in agony.

'There was no need for that,' she heard herself say. 'I am the one you want.'

Rough hands unbound her feet but left her hands bound together. 'You will lead us to the Holy well,' one woman spoke.

'What makes you think I know the way there?' She said defiantly.

'Vicky, just tell them what they need to know,' Rupert said uneasily.

'Show them yourself traitor, 'she spat in his face.

'I don't know the way, but please co-operate Vicky, I never meant it to come to this.'

The man held up a knife that glittered in the fading light from the passage of the comet.

'Show us the way or watch me carve both your brothers up into tiny pieces,' the voice spoke with power and authority.

Vicky laughed, a strange sound in that gloomy place, 'so they played you false as well Rupert, what was to be your reward, the ownership of Halleswell Hall?'

Before he had time to answer one of the women kicked out at her feet, Vicky fell to the ground. 'Get up bitch, we want what is ours.'

'The Holy Well, is that what you want? But you dare not step inside,' Vicky said, rising unsteadily to her feet.

'Oh, but you can and you will,' said the younger of the two. 'Many years we waited for this day, through birth after birth we have always come back with the memories of our kin behind us. We were here before Brannon came to this place and ousted us from our lands and kin. Now the Meverall's fight amongst themselves, our power has waxed,' holding her arms up high she reached towards the sky.

'Get up girl, your power is nothing here.' Slowly Vicky was dragged towards the clearing.

'They said a ritual,' Rupert almost screamed at her, 'I thought a mere blood letting in exchange for knowledge of the journals, please believe me sister, I had no idea.'

Vicky said nothing; she walked towards the clearing where the Holy Well lay hidden from all except for those with the power for good. Three powers were warring here tonight, that of the ancient folk, the Druids who had been slaughtered almost completely by the Romans. Then there was her own power, that of the shaman and the tiger cult. Brannon was here too, with his staunch Christianity and power to heal. In unleashing Tiger spirit she would shatter the presence of Brannon, but rather let him be shattered than bound to the evil forces.

'I am ready,' she said, and a great sigh ran through the clearing, 'what would you have me do?'

'First climb into the well and bring up all you find there.' The man spoke.

'No, I refuse,' she said though her legs trembled.

'Then bring her here,' one of the women spoke up, 'her life is now forfeit and with the sacrifice the well will be open to us all.'

Rough hands forced her down and her coat was opened for all to see. The knife hung poised above her heart and in one last gesture of defiance she turned to her brothers and bade them farewell. Slowly the knife descended until it pricked her skin and a trickle of blood ran down her breasts. At the last moment she found the strength to don her tiger claws and to dig them deep into the hand that held the knife.

Vicky was never sure what happened next, there was a scream and suddenly the clearing was filled with the sounds of blades clashing. Two slim men were fighting with the women and as the man brought his blade down one more time he was knocked off his feet by a power so vast it darkened the stars themselves, she had unwittingly called up Tiger spirit and now he had to feed. Vast claws tore at the throat but the man was determined to finish her off and the knife came down once more. The scream ripped through her soul as she felt the knife enter Charlotte's body and tear slightly at her own skin. At the last moment her aunt had hurled her body on top of Vicky's, a soft groan escaping her lips as the knife robbed her lungs of breath and stopped her heart with its cold touch. With a strength born of desperation she managed to shove Charlotte's lifeless body off her and she stood slowly and looked around.

Distantly she heard the voices of her brothers as Nathan set them free, the screams of the women echoed in her mind but all she could feel was a vast emptiness and anger so great she could not contain it. In that space of time she was no longer an innocent young girl, but an avenging spirit born of wrath and bitter grief. For so many years she had been alone, the memory of her mother long gone. In her newly found Aunt, she had discovered a kindred spirit and one who both shared and understood the sight. The fake steel tiger claws dripped blood from her fingers as the wrath built inside her mind. Shadows turned her slight frame into a powerful figure and from her mouth there issued words not of her making.

'I call upon the spirits to witness this death of an innocent woman, brought about by greed and avarice. I curse the Meverall's from this day forth, all will die, their house will fall into ruin and weeds will grow on the graves of the innocents.' The voice that issued from Vicky's mouth was not her own, struggling with grief and possession she saw the figure of Brannon standing a little way apart and in one great effort she managed to soften the curse,

'Until the day that one true hearted Meverall descendant finds peace in Halleswell Hall and the well once again belongs to the people.' Her body slumped over Charlotte's and laid still.

The ground started to rumble and stones to fall. Hastily Tim and Rupert dragged Vicky away from the edge of the well whilst Nathan tried to drag Charlotte's body away. It was too late. The avalanche took both friend and foes deep inside the well as the stones sealed the gap where once the holy well had stood. Nathan looked on in horror and despair as Charlotte's body passed from sight. Bending over Vicky's body he felt the slight breath on his hand. 'Help me get her to the stables,' he commanded the shocked brothers.

'But she needs a doctor,' Tim whimpered.

Nathan just glowered at the brothers, 'you would see her in prison for witchcraft?' He said to Tim, noticing that Rupert was beginning to recover from the shock.

'He!' pointing to Rupert, 'will not let this pass by, he's in it too deep and there are still women of the ancient kin hereabouts. They may yet come for her, even though their foul purpose has been swept aside. Tonight I have lost my mother. I will not allow Vicky to share the same fate!'

Tim started to protest but then felt Alex's arms restraining him, 'you should have confided in me,' he said, 'but Nathan is right, this scandal will not die down for many years and Vicky needs to be safe.'

Kissing his sister's pale face Tim watched as she went out of his life forever.

So it was that Nathan, last Duke of Dunloman, left his mother's body under tonnes of rock and riding Hero with tears running down his face took Victoria to a place of safety. There she leant about Sarah and the legacy she had left behind. The boy named Duncan, offspring of half-brother and sister was no monster, but a bright and comely boy who would go on to found the dynasty of Nathan's kin. In time she came to know the history of the Meverall line unknown to all but a few and to mourn the loss of her aunt. From Nathan she learnt the story of Sarah who had once returned to Halleswell to leave a letter for James in the secret recess in the well, telling him of the perfect child she had born.

Of the Meverall's and Vicky and Nathan, this story does not tell, but Charlotte could not rest easy, not with her bones lying in unhallowed ground.

Long after the scandal died down, still voices could be heard in the Hall and the villagers shunned Brannon's Wood in fear of the great cat that was said to roam there.

Memoirs of the Damned

Alex sat in his chair next to the fire. The firelight cast deep shadows on the walls of the parlour. There was no other light in the room. He spent most of his time there now. Halleswell Hall had become an unhappy, silent place in the last few years. So much death and disaster had befallen the Meverall's. It was hard to believe that so much heartache could visit upon one family in so short a time.

The clock in the main hall struck midnight. Alex waited; moments after the echoes of the clocks chimes died away the unearthly scream added its counterpoint to the end of another day. Alex felt no fear at that scream; he had grown used to it and almost looked forward to it to mark the passing of another day.

On a table by his high backed leather armchair sat a parcel, wrapped in brown paper and tied with a piece of string. Alex looked at it for a moment but instead of picking it up he stood and headed toward the stairs. There was something he had to do before he could bring himself to open that parcel.

He made his way to a locked door in the farthest reaches of the house and pulled a key from his pocket. With a sigh he unlocked the door and entered. Although it was a sight he had seen many times before it was still a blow to his heart. His daughter Zara sat at the dressing table brushing her hair, not an uncommon sight, but the constant combing had pulled out most of the strands, leaving sparse clumps of hair that only added to her nightmarish appearance. The mirror reflected back to him the blank look on his daughter's once pretty face. It was a look he had never got used to and he quickly tried to avert his gaze. She did not see him from her sunken eyes, didn't even register that there was anyone there at all. Zara was painfully thin; she had barely eaten for weeks, not since a letter had arrived telling of the heroic death of her husband Rupert.

Zara had not cared for her husband when he had been alive. The marriage had not turned out the way she thought it would. She had seen it as a means of escape from here. Back to the high life she had enjoyed in Russia. Her husband had other ideas however, he would not leave his home, even though things had gone so badly wrong for the family, he would not desert them.

The call to war had been the final blow to Zara. Her tenuous grasp on sanity had slipped and she had taken to spending long periods in her room. None knew what she did in there. She had screamed and thrown anything that came to hand at anyone who dared disturb her. Eventually Alex had been the only one who dared to visit her and so he was the only one who had seen her descent into madness.

It would not be long now, thought Alex. His daughter's torment was nearly at an end. Silent tears ran down his face, sinking into the tired lines of his prematurely aged face. He shook his head to clear it, knowing that he would be the only one to shed a tear for his daughter's passing.

Without a word he gently closed and locked the door. He had one more thing to do before he retired to his chair to pass the long unsleeping night hours.

Flo was readying tomorrow's breakfast as Alex walked slowly into the kitchen. She looked up as he entered and noting the tired look on his face said. 'You have been to visit HER then. Is there any change?'

Alex took that to mean was she was still alive, and he answered with a sigh. 'No change Flo, none at all.'

Flo thought he sounded exhausted but knew he wouldn't retire for many hours yet. She had given up trying to get him to keep regular hours and to get much needed sleep. Thoughts of leaving had crossed her mind many times, but she couldn't abandon Alex. He knew nothing of her feelings, never would, but they held her here stronger than any shackles.

She was scared, so many things had happened in this house and who knew what else lay in store for anyone who dared to live here? It had all started with the comet and the death of the Lady Charlotte. Vicky had laid a horrible curse on the family that night and that curse had not lost its strength over the years, in fact there was not a Meverall that hadn't been touched by that curse and even the Lady Charlotte had not escaped. Her spirit was trapped here, the ultimate reminder of the woes of the Meverall's. It was her spirit that kept visitors away, even the villagers were afraid to set foot on Meverall lands and none would enter Brannon's Wood now, not even to collect the fire wood that had been their right for centuries.

Flo's thoughts wandered to all the unfortunates, to Theo whose addiction to opium had led to an overdose and a premature death and to Richard, accused of administering the fatal dose of opiates; he had died in shame in Highgate prison in filth and squalor. Alex had not escaped the curse either, it was his curse to watch all those he had once loved die one by one and finally leave him alone.

Even Vicky herself had not escaped the curse although none knew her fate, or that of Nathan who had disappeared with her.

Flo had made Alex his cocoa, and with a word of thanks Alex made his way back to his seat by the fire. Settling himself into his chair he picked up the package wrapped in brown paper that had been left on his table. He sighed, he knew what that package contained and he stared at it for ages before finally bringing himself to untie the string that sealed the parcel. Inside was a pile of clothes with a sketch pad and a book resting on top of them. An official form and a letter completed the inventory. Alex glanced at the form and then picked up the letter. He saw that it was addressed to him. After a moment he slit open the envelope and took out a single sheet of paper.

Dear Uncle Alex,

Thanks for your last letter; it came at the right time, as I have been feeling pretty miserable for the last few weeks. A few of the lads in our company bought it, sorry, I can't give names, but you will know what I mean when I say it wasn't a pretty sight. Please keep telling me about the woods in summer and the swans on the lake, does "she" still come back, you know my favourite swan? As long as there is a little patch of home to hold onto, I can keep going.

Yesterday we passed through the village that was once M, I can imagine how pretty it once was and I only hope we can both come here in more peaceful times to see the beauty of the countryside. The men made a billet in an abandoned house. They managed to find an old gramophone and a record that they keep playing over and over; I guess we all have different ways of getting through this war. Last night, just as dusk was falling, I saw a lone bird in flight, somehow that made me feel as if there is still a world where life goes on.

Despite the nightly shelling we are all in good spirits & I can still hold my pencil steady enough to keep up my drawings. I write in my journal every night, so that if I don't make it through then you will have something to remember me by. I hope the censor lets this through; after all, you are my next of kin now, unless you have heard anything from V.

Goodnight, God Bless, Tim

The letter was undated and Alex wondered when Tim had written it. Refolding it carefully, he placed it on the arm of his chair and turned his eyes to the dog eared book that lay on top of the pile in front of him. The title, written on the cover in Tim's flowing script read.

The journals and experiences of Timothy Cavendish-Meverall.

Picking a page at random Alex began to read.

March 14th 1916 was the title at the top of the page. It was slightly obscured by muddy fingerprints and there were brown smudges that looked like blood had been smeared along the top of the page.

I have just arrived at the front for the first time with the French army, my other assignments have kept me out of the firing line but losses of other front line observers have led to me being ordered forward.

I have never seen anything like this Uncle, I am fairly sure that unless you have seen it with your own eyes you would not believe such a sight is possible on this Earth.

Imagine for a moment that you are staring up at the moon on a clear night when her landmarks stand for all to see. Imagine that desolate landscape on earth and that does not come close to the horror that France has become. Imagine that landscape as mud, as blood and water and the rotting remains of French youth. That would bring you closer to what I can see before me.

But there is a strange kind of beauty underlying the horror.

When the guns start they bathe everything with an orange glow. Although we know that death will follow when the guns stop and the whistle blows there is not a man that isn't transfixed by the sights and sounds that invade every sense.

Thousands of shells are flying over our heads, slamming into the enemy positions; hopefully they will soften them up enough to make our advance safer.

There goes the whistle, time to do our duty.

March 15th

Here we are back where we started uncle. Last nights efforts were totally wasted and only about half the men who advanced have returned. Uncle it is terrible. Terrifying is too small a word to describe it. I don't think I will ever forget last night; it is going to haunt my dreams and follow my waking thought.

I would use words like futile and stupid but they are frowned upon and called defeatist by the officers and the high command.

I have seen both sides of this conflict now uncle. It is no wonder the regular soldier feels aggrieved; we are doing the dying whilst the officers are drinking their wine in safety miles from here.

It is impossible to describe the filth we are living in, the mud means our feet are continuously soaked and the cold means they are numb too. The food is more suited to the rats we share these holes with than for humans. How we are expected to fight in these conditions is beyond me.

I suppose the only thing to even the balance is that the Germans facing us must be in as bad a state as us, or at least we can hope.

The sun is shining this morning, the only sound I can hear is the screams and the shouts for help that come from no mans land. There is no hope for those poor souls. Their shouts will only bring the Germans to them to put them out of their misery. They are out of range of our rifles and the Germans know it. They will mop up those unfortunates throughout the morning.

April 22nd 1916

It doesn't seem like there is a war on today. Our unit has been given a few days leave. Most of the lads hopped on the train and headed for Paris but I decided to take a leisurely break in the countryside. We only have three days and I didn't see much point in spending most of it on a train. So here I am, sitting in a field on a hillside looking out over a rolling landscape with fields of green and gold shimmering in the sunlight. Beside me is a friend I have made. He is a handsome young lad from my unit. He hasn't told me his age but he doesn't look to be much over eighteen. He comes from Somerset so not too far from home. He is a nice young man, scared of being here like so many of us, but there is a determination too to do his best for King and country. He has a keen eye for painting and we have spent a blissful afternoon sketching the French countryside. The hills here are not too different from home and it doesn't take too much imagination to think we are on the hill overlooking Halleswell Hall.

I hope I will be able to see that sight for real soon but I think we are going to be here a while yet. I have been missing home lately, it seems a long time since I have been there and the homesickness seems to be getting worse as time goes by.

May 11th

The endless drilling and inspections are becoming a drag now. The lads are eager for action just to break the monotony and free us from the eagle eye of the sergeant major. A real tyrant he is, none of us would be unhappy to see the back of him. Some of the lads have even sworn that next time we go to attack the German trenches the sergeant major won't be coming back with us. I don't think I could go that far but I can see the lads' point of view.

I'm not so keen to see action again. I am one of the few here who has seen the horror of a battle and although I have tried to warn some of the men what it will be like I don't think they believe me. They still think that it will be a glorious charge ending in them being given medals and honour. I am afraid those lads are in for a shock when it finally comes to battle.

The weather is awful and drilling in the pouring rain is miserable, half of us have had one illness or another. Character building they call it, I call it torture.

It is funny, social rank seems to mean nothing here. I was speaking to a lad from our village the other day. Tom the son of old Brian from Long End farm, you remember him don't you uncle? I think you caught him trapping rabbits in Brannon's Wood once, gave him a right hiding as I remember it. Anyway we had a long chat and talked as equal men, no social class comes between regular soldiers here, and we all have enough to moan about with the officers so we tend to stick together. Would I have spoken to him the same had we been at home? I would like to think so but somehow I doubt it.

June 20th 1916

Today has been a good day; no attacks have been ordered or come from the enemy. There is an air of expectancy in the air. Something is expected to happen soon, we hear that the French are still having an awful time at Verdun and we do wonder what is going to happen here, but for now it is a peaceful enough place to be.

The sun has been shining and a lot of the lads have been playing football behind the trenches. I have spent the day drawing, it made a nice change to be able to draw the men playing and laughing rather than dying under the guns and in the wire. The mud does not make a very good pitch but they do not seem to mind. Everyone is filthy anyway so sliding about in the mud doesn't matter much.

We got post today too, always a great moral booster to get news from home. It is a great boost to me to hear what is happening to the folk of Halleswell Hall. It gives me a sense of purpose, gives me a reason to be here and makes some sense of what we are fighting for. Thank you for sending the paper too Uncle, it was great to see my picture adorning the front page even if the subject matter was not what I would have liked it to be.

It is a bit frustrating to be told what to draw and photograph, those pictures do not tell the real story of what it is like here but then I guess the people at home would not really want to know, or at least the government would not want them to know. I have a large pile of sketches and photographs that do tell the real story, I wonder if they will ever be seen by the public, I somehow doubt it but they will act as reminders to me if nothing else.

July 1st 1916

Something is brewing Uncle; the tension in the air is unbearable. Everyone is quiet and withdrawn into their own thoughts. Mortality and fear are high on the list of things on our minds, along with thoughts of home and whether we will live through today to see it again.

The smiling faces of just a few days ago are gone now. The reality of war is about to hit home to the young men here, some are little more than boys. Along with the fear the lads are eager to see action. My viewpoint is somewhat different. I have seen the horror of Verdun and have some inkling of what lies in wait for us. I have to say I am terrified, Uncle, so much death and agony is about to be unleashed and the poor lads that are going over the top don't know what is about to hit them. The tone seems to be "let's get at them," how long is that going to last after the dying starts I wonder.

It has started Uncle. The first shells passed over our heads a few minutes ago. Since then the barrage has been relentless, deafening as thousands of artillery pieces send their shells to rain death on the Germans. The whole battlefield is bathed in an orange glow as shells explode one after another in an endless stream.

If it wasn't so terrifying it would be beautiful. I don't think anyone has ever seen such a sight and I hope that no one will again, although I fear this will not be a one off.

It won't be long now Uncle, the guns have stopped. There is the first whistle. The men are stood ready. I look into faces. Fear is etched there but also an eagerness to get on with what they are about to do. Some of it is the fear, just wanting it to be over but excitement is on many a young face. That scares me more than anything, that a young man can be so eager to go to his death, but I suppose youth has its own thoughts of invulnerability and thoughts like "it won't happen to me." I fear a large proportion of those lads will find out very soon that it can happen to them.

July 2nd

I made it back, unlike thousands of the other poor chaps. Looking around now faces only hold horror at what happened last night.

They were waiting for us Uncle, the artillery barrage that we had hoped would have softened up the Germans seems to have had little effect and their machine guns just mowed down our lads like a field of wheat, hundreds died before we even knew we were in range and thousands more lost their lives as we were driven on.

Finally we broke and ran for cover. Getting back, too many of the faces that I had looked into when we left were missing. It is hard to take, when you read about losses in war they are just faceless numbers, but being here and knowing the faces that will never see home again is something else. Some of those lads I had been laughing and joking with only a short time ago and now they are gone. Mothers will sit at home not knowing what has become of their sons and won't do for some time. So many have died and it is only the first day. How much death is yet to come, I shudder to think

July 16th 1916.

Today was the not first time that a gun was pushed into my unwilling hands by a Corporal, but I swear it will be my last. In vain I argued 'I can do this no more.' But the words fell on deaf ears and I was threatened with being shot as a coward. General Haig seems to think that this will be the final push, but already over fifty thousand English soldiers have been killed in a single day. I can't stand it any more, the constant shelling, the men that go 'over the top' and wander aimlessly in "No Man's Land" as the Germans' pick them off one by one. Oh uncle this is hell on earth and I long to be out of it for good. Death would be kinder than watching and waiting for a bullet to end my life.

If this ever falls into anyone's hands I could be shot as a coward, but rather a quick clean death than those I have been forced to witness. Oh God, I can't face another day like this. Dawn was streaking the sky as the order came, 'Up and over and give then a pasting.' But you can't fire at what you can't see. The German troops are in deep bunkers, our men can't reach them and it's like watching ducks at a fairground, just aim and watch them fall.

I was in the last push when the retreat sounded and I fell into the trenches, ankle-deep in mud and blood, with the rats ready to chew at anything that appeared not to move. We bludgeon them to death with our rifle butts; there is scant ammunition to waste on them. I tried to stop my ears to ignore the sounds of the dying, left alone in pain and fear, even the medical orderlies have to stand back and cry because we cannot spare another man.

I was supposed to be drawing a picture of our valiant men going fully armed and anxious to engage the enemy, but then I heard Walter cry out in agony and my heart lurched in my chest. Uncle, he was just a boy of 16, and he's hanging on barbed wire with half his intestines falling out. He's crying for his mother and I want to end his misery but it's another round of ammunition wasted as far as the army feels. I can't stand it, I want to scream and never stop screaming.

I couldn't stand it anymore. He's been hanging there crying for most of the day. Another push was ordered late afternoon and this time I was one of the first over. I could not get him off the fence, just cradled his head in my arms as he cried bitter tears. The rest is all a blur. I remember asking him where he came from, somewhere in Essex I think. He talked of bringing in the harvest and how he would now miss it. 'There's always next harvest' I said, but his poor body was nearly gone by then. 'Tell Eleanor I'm coming home soon,' he said, his breath almost failing. 'I'll tell her,' I said as I drew my knife across his throat.

Can't stop shaking, I'm trying to light a fag and burning my fingers.......

Alex could see big splodges of tears on this page, running his fingers over the tear stains he realised his own face was stained with the same show of emotion. Fearing what he would read next he turned the page.

August? 1916.
Cannot remember what day it is. Our troops are going back to N, for a brief rest. Just trudging, boots worn out and blisters on our feet... doesn't matter, it's a respite from the pounding of the guns, but I think I will hear them forever.

Uncle have you ever heard a horse scream? They say I was hallucinating but he did scream, I swear it. He was lying on his side in the mud with one eye rolling white from fear. Half his side was shot away. There is no God. He would not allow a creature to suffer so. I took out my pistol, but hands now shaking all the time. Evans, yes it was Evans. Has a farm back home. Tenor in the choir, he says to me, "Sir, we can't leave him, not in the road like that." I nod, he steadies my arm and the shot rings out. At the last moment I thought it was Hero. Same coat, same spirit.

"Stupid bugger," someone says, I try to say about Hero but only Evans listens.

Tried to draw him, "no they say," and it's crumpled up in a ball like life here, it means nothing.

Tired now, Evans sings a song in Welsh. He says it's a lullaby but it sounds sad and......

14th September 1916

Something has happened Uncle, I don't know how and I don't know what will be the outcome of it, but I fear the worst. I have been arrested and thrown in military prison. I am terrified of being here and what it means for me. I fear that I shall face a court-martial for a moment's madness. You have probably heard of my dishonour Uncle, and I would not blame you if you wished to disown me for the disgrace I have brought to you and the Meverall name.

If you have not heard, and to leave my side of the story I will tell what happens here, for I fear any court-Marshall will seek to gloss over the facts and pronounce me guilty for the good of the army.

We had just got back from another fruitless charge and after throwing myself back into the relative safety of our trench, I found myself sharing the trench with the same lad I had met so briefly before. He was in a terrible state, shaking and crying and unable to move an inch for fear of being shot at. I am sure I am not allowed to mention his name, but what could I do when he was sitting in the filth and muck of the trench and did not seem likely to move. I helped him to his feet and he threw his arms around me and was suddenly sobbing into my shoulder. I knew not what to do so I just held him, he seemed to gain some comfort from my embrace. Long we stood so until eventually he seemed to have regained some composure and he straightened up. A look passed between us and then it happened. I cannot remember who kissed who but suddenly we were locked in a passionate embrace.

Of course we were discovered immediately and both of us were dragged off.

That is all there was too it Uncle. I don't know how it happened and do not know why, maybe relief at surviving the enemy guns once more, maybe just a lax of control. I don't know and don't think I ever will.

I will not lie to you Uncle, I am terrified at the thought of what will happen to me and to that young private.

I can write no more this night, I am tired, so tired.

It is over, the farce that I knew it would be. They were going to find me guilty before I even entered the courtroom. There is no justice or compassion here, Uncle; everything is for the greater good of His Majesty's army.

Does that sound bitter? I suppose it does and I have to admit that bitterness and anger are taking up a large portion of my soul now. Both are emotions that I am not used to having to bear but I find myself unable to hold the feelings back now. I have been condemned to death for showing compassion to another human being. How can that be justice? How can another man be so callous and disregarding of a fellow soldier's life? These are questions to which I have no answer.

I had better tell you what happened at the trial because it concerns the family and that is something that you may never be able to accept.

I was led into the courtroom in irons like I was a dangerous criminal and forced to stand before a desk, behind which sat four officers. Three I didn't recognise but the fourth was someone you know Uncle. It was Nathan; a member of my own family was sitting there waiting to condemn me to death.

Poor Nathan, I have never seen the colour literally drain from a man's face, as his did when he saw me. The look of horror on his face was enough to tell me what the outcome of the trial was going to be.

It didn't take long, the charge was read out and each one of the officers said their piece, condemning what I had done as a crime against God and His Majesty. Nathan was in tears as he said his piece. Something that earned him disapproving looks from his fellows. They asked me if I had anything to say in my defence to which I replied that I had done what I had out of compassion for a fellow soldier, but they thought that such a thing had no place in the army.

Judgement was pronounced; each stated their verdict, Nathan in a croaked whisper as he uttered the word 'guilty'. I don't blame him, he had no choice, he was in an impossible situation and I'm sure it is something that is going to haunt him for ever and for that I am saddened.

I hope that one day he will read this journal and take my words as absolving him of guilt at his decision, and giving him my forgiveness.

17th September 1916

Today is the day Uncle, the day I leave this cruel life. Army justice is swift, it is only three days since my trial and with no appeal my fate is due to be carried out in a few moments.

I didn't sleep last night, but neither did I dwell on thoughts of what will happen to me this morning. I did spare a prayer for the young private who will share my fate, but my thoughts mostly dwelt in the past, thoughts of home, of England and the family.

Do you remember the swan Uncle? She featured strongly in my thoughts last night, wondering what had happened to her, if she was still alive and well and if she was what she was doing. As I dozed I felt her presence, maybe my imagination, but to feel her near gave me comfort through the long hours of darkness.

They have let me write a letter to you Uncle and you will have read that before this comes into your possession but I will state here that I hope you can forgive the disgrace I have brought to the family name, and hope that you will not look unkindly on my memory.

I leave this life now with my only legacy my words here and the pictures in my sketchbook.

Farewell Uncle.

Alex closed the book with a sigh and wiped tears from his face. He had never received that letter, maybe the army had stopped it, maybe it was lost somewhere but at least he knew now how Tim had perished. He could not find it in his heart to be angry with Tim over the reason for his death. For a while he too had felt that love that sprang from a youthful adoration of another young man. Tim's only failing had been his generous heart and the way he fought so long to conceal his true nature.

Putting aside the journal he opened the sketch book and gasped. The first picture in that book was a pure work of art, beautiful and wonderful even as it was terrible in the death it portrayed. Another followed and another as Alex flicked through the book. Each was a masterpiece in its own right and given the context of its subject was a fantastic commendation of Tim's talent.

This book of sketches would act as a true legacy which in future years would mark Tim as one of the finest war artists to work in the whole conflict.

For now though Alex was content to sit and remember Tim, the son he never had.

ARMISTICE DAY

London had gone crazy. Everywhere people were dancing, laughing, throwing their arms around complete strangers with no care for the brisk November day. Many were crying, tears of joy mingling with tears of sorrow for loved ones never to return, but only one person in this teeming mass of humanity appeared to be untouched by the day's events.

He stood alone for a moment, the weak autumn sun catching a glint of burnished gold in his dark auburn hair. In contrast to the revellers he pulled his greatcoat around him, not for the chill for he had felt much worse cold than today, but to hide the uniform he wore underneath. There had been no time or inclination to change into civilian clothes but he had at least removed the medals bestowed on him for nothing more than trying to get himself killed in the heat of battle. The irony was not lost on him, for despite his death wish he had come almost unscathed through battles so terrible that even now he shuddered to think of them.

Leaning heavily on his cane he felt almost proud of his wound, that jagged scar which ran from his hip to his right calf.

I deserved to die, he thought for the umpteenth time. Instead he had had been called a hero and promoted through the ranks to become a Major. Even the wound had not stopped him from charging the enemy lines although the bayonet had nearly severed the artery.

Somebody jostled him, the coat swung open and before he knew it a bottle of stout was pushed into his unwilling hand.

'You're a bloody hero mate,' the little wizened old man called out, attracting unwanted attention.

'Drink up man, there's lots more where that came from.'

Suddenly he became the centre of attraction as young women came to hug him and it appeared that all of London wanted to shake his hand. Pasting a sickly smile on his face he drunk the ale in one long draught, though all he wanted was to be left alone, it would be impolite to shove the crowd away. These people had suffered terrible losses, but here they were on Armistice Day, cheering at the end of four long years of pain, anguish and fear.

'Here mate, have another one,' this time it was a fellow soldier proudly displaying his private's uniform.

'Please accept my apologies, I have a train to catch,' this time the smile was more genuine.

'Got a girl back home?' The man didn't wait for an answer but called out to his mates.

'Get yer arse over ere Arry and you too yer bloody lazy lot. This ere man 'as to catch a train, going home to 'is sweetheart an' not a minute to waste.'

The crowd suddenly parted and Nathan was jostled along with remarkable speed to Paddington Station, the good-humoured soldiers plying him with drink all the way.

'Where's yer going to mate?' One asked and on being told that Exeter was the destination ripples of laughter ran through the friendly mob.

'Christ almighty you'll be lucky to get as far 'as half the way there, bleeding train drivers is 'aving a booze-up same as us.' Harry laughed.

Nathan hadn't thought of that. Of course people wanted to celebrate, but his time was limited and he felt a surge of dismay.

It must have shown on his face, for the man he gathered was called Eric screwed up his own face.

'I reckon the driver can make it 'alf drunk 'tis nothing to it' he beamed.

Striding along the platform he made his way to where a train was standing idle. Sure enough there was a man inside slumped across the driving seat and another man, obviously the stoker snoring away on the nearby bench, empty bottles of stout littered around their feet.

Eric paused for a moment, and with some hushed asides to his mates they gathered together and emptied the contents of the nearest water tank onto the sleeping men.

'Wassat? ' The driver came up spluttering, 'can't a man 'ave a bit of sleep here?'

At that moment he caught sight of Nathan, whose greatcoat

had parted briefly to show his uniform. Staggering to his feet he made a sloppy salute, 'sorry Sir, you caught us 'aving a bit of a kip.'

Nathan just smiled, 'forget the Sir bit, today we are all in the same boat and I'm sorry to have spoilt your celebrations, maybe I had better return tomorrow?'

'No fear Sir, we 'as done our jobs right through the war an we 'aren't going to let a man down now,' with this he prodded the stoker with the top of his boot.

'Look lively Jed, seems as how we have a bleeding hero here an we still have our jobs to do.'

Jed came slowly to his feet and took in the crowd that had now gathered. With a feigned nonchalance he took in the situation and before anyone could stop him he sunk his entire head into another of the precious water butts. The driver barked out an order,

'Eric, Harry, get us some of that piddling stuff that passes as coffee, we 'as a train to run.'

The next hour passed in a bewildering amount of motion as Jed and Sam, the driver, brewed the Camp coffee and slowly sobered up. Huddled around the glowing embers of a fire in the waiting room, as Nathan put his feet up onto the bench he briefly wondered how he was going to get from Exeter to Halleswell.

His right leg would not allow him to drive with any confidence, but he needed to see Alex as soon as possible. Resigned to a long wait he took out his flask of rum and passed it around to the other men.

Soon the waiting room filled up with other men and a smattering of women, all eager to join the sole train even if it meant it wasn't going in the precise direction they needed. No doubt they would use their wits to scrounge lifts in their general direction. Soldiers newly arrived passed around some of their precious rations, women dug deep for soggy sandwiches and one remarkable old lady seemed to have copious amounts of pickled eggs, no doubt filched from under the noses of unwary publicans.

This was a part of the spirit of wartime Britain Nathan had never seen before, and for a brief moment he felt some of his inner grief lifted.

Dusk was falling by the time the train was ready to leave.

Nathan managed to get a carriage to himself, and as the train chugged out of the station he allowed himself to drift into an uneasy sleep. His long legs started to unwind as he passed into a deeper sleep.

Hero was cantering away from Halleswell Hall with Vicky clinging to his back as if her very life depended on it, which of course was true. Earlier that day his mother had warned him to be prepared for a swift flight and now the saddlebags contained emergency rations along with important papers and his mother's fabled emeralds. The rest of the jewels had been left behind in their haste to escape, but he had sufficient money to last for a very long time. He was more concerned with Vicky's wound, which had been bleeding steadily for the last few hours and soon he would have to stop to rest and to rebind it. He wasn't too worried about pursuit at the moment; it would take some time to sort out the mess they had left behind.

Fortunately he had made plans for a rapid exit within his first few years at Halleswell Hall and soon they would arrive at a friendly house. He had not planned on being with Vicky though, but the tears for his mother would have to wait until a more appropriate time.

Turning from the main road he followed a cart track to the farmhouse that would be their shelter for the next few days. Willing hands were ready to catch Vicky as she fell from the saddle and he followed behind, exhaustion nearly overwhelming him.

He awoke to feeble sunlight filtering through the homely lace curtains of a large but prosperous farmstead. Stretching out his legs he felt a mass of bruises and fatigue in all his limbs, they would not be going anywhere else today. Fresh clothes had been laid out and he descended the stairs with some trepidation, would Vicky be all right?

Greeting his hosts with a quick 'Good Morning', he stepped outside to relieve his full bladder before entering the kitchen where a simple but filling breakfast had already been put on the table. Vicky was still asleep; her wound bound and pronounced by his hosts as merely a flesh wound. More worrying was her state of mind; she had been in a fever of anxiety for most of the night.

Later on he visited her with the good wife acting as a chaperone, not that they needed it, but country folk set great store by doing the correct thing.

Nathan stirred in his sleep, the flashes of memories now coming thick and fast. For a moment he opened his weary eyes, but on seeing nothing but darkness outside the window and the echoing promise of the driver to wake him at Exeter station, he soon drifted back to the memories of that mad dash to safety in 1910.

Parting with Hero had been a wrench that both felt keenly, but they were about to set sail for France the following day. This time their hosts were longstanding friends of both his parents and Hero would have a good home here in Kent. They had sailed on the next tide, the cliffs of Dover receding as both said their final farewells to England, leaning against the ships rails Vicky had looked up at him and in that brief meeting of gazes he knew his fate would be bound with hers forever.

As dreams go the next scene jumped to their arrival at the home of the Laurent family. Situated in the outskirts of Paris it was an ideal place for Vicky to grow up. Here she could study at a Catholic school and he would then be free to track down some other branches of the Meverall family.

Instead he had stayed for almost a year unwilling to part with Vicky, but finally his curiosity had gotten the better of him and he started on the long journey to the home of the de Castellans. Here he found many answers to his questions and marvelled at the way his mother had traced the roots of the family through many generations. He would bring Vicky here one day, he vowed, even if the old castle was suffering from the neglect of poor finances. They would ride together and exorcise the ghosts of the past. It was not to be though, the outbreak of the war had put paid to that with Nathan returning to England to fight for his country.

The sudden jolting of the train woke Nathan from his dreams. The train was slowing down and he guessed rightly that they were nearing Exeter. Wearily he said his goodbyes to the driver and tipped both him and the stoker heavily. What need did he have of money now when the whole of his world had gone crazy? Besides, he received a steady income from the Scotland estate and could, if he wanted to, have gone home to claim his rightful inheritance.

The night was well advanced and knowing he could go no further he took the advice of Jed and made for one of the smaller hotels that were then just beginning to open up again after the war.

The room was clean and although small it suited his purposes. He'd eaten a small meal put up by the landlady who was thrilled to have a British officer in her small establishment. Once more he had been subjected to the ubiquitous bottles of beer and even a small brandy, he would sleep well tonight he hoped.

Once again he was in that room with the stench of fear permeating every wall. This was one duty that he had never performed before and as he summed up the petty officials around him, he swore it would be his last. Why, why, why, his brain had screamed as they led the prisoner into the room. He had heard of the court marital, mostly lads of sixteen or seventeen, but many a seasoned soldier had snapped under the pressure of the endless pounding of the guns and seeing their comrades blown to bits in front of them. Christ Almighty, it was rest and hospital care these men and boys needed, not death by firing squad.

It was then that his worst nightmare happened to him. He lifted his head with loathing for the whole procedure and gazed into the eyes of Vicky's brother, Tim. He felt the shock as a ripple down his spine, chilling his blood and making his hands shake. He leant over to the nearest officer, just one rank above him and whispered that surely he should be spared this as the prisoner was kin to him. 'You'll do your duty Captain or suffer the same fate,' he was answered. Why didn't he get up then and walk out of the room? Was life so precious that he could partake in this bloody farce? His only justification was that maybe he could somehow swing the verdict by his own testimony.

Tim spoke well, although Nathan could see the telltale signs of severe shock in his every word and gesture. Passionately he spoke of this young officer's dedication to duty, his bravery in trying to rescue his comrades, the need to protect those young men, even though he was barely older than them.

One of the officers had the gall to yawn and Nathan nearly snapped at that point. Was it cowardice or knowing that somehow he had to spare Vicky this knowledge that finally made him utter those damming words, 'Guilty"?

He awoke with that word on his lips, guilty of sending his own cousin to the firing squad, guilty of his own cowardice, guilty of still being alive after he had done everything to get himself killed. Lying in bed looking at the ceiling he knew he had duties he could not put aside. Torn between visiting Alex first and going to Vicky, he chose the former, for he knew the old man would be in as much turmoil as he himself had been. Would Alex forgive him for his part in the proceedings or would he turn him away? At least he could tell the old man that Tim had not disgraced himself, but had done something he couldn't have easily done himself, he bore the end with dignity. Wearily he got to his feet, the right leg aching as usual. Quickly washing himself in the old sink he dressed and made his way downstairs, knowing that he would need to eat to keep his strength up even if it tasted like ashes in his mouth.

Breakfast was a pleasant surprise, two thin rashers of bacon, a fried egg and lashings of buttered toast. Despite himself he enjoyed it and wondered how his hosts had managed such a feast. Soon he would have to find some civilian clothes; he was tired of getting extra attention because of his rank. Little did he realise the lines of strain that made him look much older than his years, or the pity that welled up in the hearts of ordinary people when they saw him lean heavily on his cane. Thanking his hosts for such a delicious breakfast, he asked about transportation to Barnstaple, after that he could maybe get a lift from a farmer, or maybe even walk the ten miles to Halleswell Hall, it was the least he could do.

'You're in luck Major,' Mr Tanner replied, 'my nephew is going to Barnstaple this very day, fishing has been right good lately and we can make a fair profit from fresh fish. Not that it's easy for the boats to put out, but I reckon as how we could all do with something different to eat. He'll be starting off early, about ten o'clock, would that suit you?'

'My thanks Mr Tanner, that is good news for I have an elderly Uncle to visit and a tale that may not be to his liking, but such are fortunes of war that the young carry tales of much misery.'

His host looked at him with a keen eye but added no more. So it was that Nathan was perched on the back of a horse and cart an hour later. Chris was an amiable youth about seventeen years old but not very bright. That suited him fine as the silences were not uncomfortable and once again he could turn his thoughts inwards.

He remembered the day he had given Vicky the emerald necklace, it was on her 16th birthday and just before he had left for England. Some of the fire had gone out of her eyes but the emeralds had rekindled some of that spirit making him see her in a new light. Before, he had felt his fate tied with hers, but now she was showing signs of becoming a breathtaking beauty and in that moment he knew that he was in love with her and always would be. She had cried bitter tears on their parting, but he held back, thinking he was far too old for her. Now he wanted to go back to her and feel that life leap into his tired soul. He had only managed one brief leave when he was in France. The family had moved from their home in Paris to their summer home in Tuscany, there he had found her strangely subdued, and on their few evenings together he had learnt of her wish to nurse the sick and dying. He had accused her of trying to atone for the curse and they argued for the first time. Later on he had regretted that argument deeply, firstly when he had to tell her of the death of her father and later of her brother Rupert. The letter telling of Tim's death had never reached her, for by then she had taken that step and joined the growing ranks of nurses, lying about her age. As soon as he had seen Alex he was going back to France to find her and bring her home.

Chris broke into his thoughts, 'Mr Nathan, sor, we are almost there where does you want to be set down?'

'How about I help you load the catch first, then I'll see if I can find some farmer to take me nearer to the Hall?'

Chris beamed with delight, 'you is a fine gentleman sor, we'll load up and then we'll have us some ale and find you a farmer, I knows jus' the place to find 'un.'

Nathan actually enjoyed the physical labour, although it made his leg ache he had learnt to compensate by building up his arm muscles. Before long the catch was safely stowed away and packed in ice to keep it fresh. He had also haggled with the fisherman getting a better price than Chris, with his slower brain could ever have done.

Soon they were seated in the Anchor and downing a good quality ale. Nathan found a willing farmer to take him within a short walk to Halleswell Hall. Sometimes his uniform did have some advantages, but he vowed to buy some civvy clothes as soon as possible.

By the time he reached Halleswell Hall Nathan worried that it may be too late in the evening, but a few words from the taciturn farmer dispelled that notion. It appeared that the villagers were still very wary about the house, but could confirm that lights could be seen in the Hall as late as midnight. He was tired from his long walk but nothing could have stopped him now. Walking up to the main door he rapped heavily on the knocker and sat back on the porch to wait. By now the moon was high in the sky and casting long shadows across the lawn and the distant lake. Nathan shivered; he could feel the presence of something just beyond his reach and thought once more of his mother. The great door swung back with a lot of effort and he saw Flo, now older and looking frightened.

'Lord Almighty, it's master Nathan, come in quick.'

'Please forgive me Flo, I couldn't get here any sooner, but I'll make it up to you.'

Flo led him into the house, noticing the limp and the strain about his eyes. He would need some fortification before seeing Alex, so she took him into her kitchen where she poured him a large brandy.

'My thanks Flo, but I think I should see my uncle as soon as possible.'

'Mr Nathan, Alex is much changed and I think it wiser if I went ahead to announce your presence here. Could you wait a while longer, you see he doesn't sleep much these nights and I was about to take him his nightly cup of cocoa.'

Nathan glanced at the clock, it was nearly 11, and suddenly he thought how selfish he had been arriving so late.

Catching his eyes Flo knew what he was thinking, he had no knowledge of how things went at the Hall. Her old eyes softened instantly.

'Maybe you should wait until morning, but the master would welcome your company if you are not too tired?'

'I'll wait, I don't sleep easy myself.'

On entering the study Nathan was shocked by Alex's appearance, just eight years ago he was a fine figure of a man in the prime of his life. Now he looked a good twenty years older than his true age. Little did he know that Alex was appraising him in much the same way?

'Come in dear boy, sit down and make yourself comfortable,' Alex said.

Instead Nathan crossed the room and, bending awkwardly, he took Alex's cool hands in his own.

'Forgive the late hour uncle, but I swore an oath that I would come to see you as soon as possible. I understand if I am not welcome here but I had to come.' The tears were flowing unchecked down his face as he looked into those kindly old eyes.

'You are more than welcome, indeed I have longed for this day for nearly two years.'

'But...how can you even bear to look at me after what happened?' Nathan managed to say.

'I would welcome you for the love between our kin, but also I yearn for any solace you can bring me in the wake of Tim's death. He was like a son to me in the years before the war.'

Nathan looked stunned, but he could see the compassion in the old man's eyes and something gave way deep inside his soul.

'Tim was a good man, kind and gentle but fiercely protective of his men, some barely younger than he and some much older. He was scared, of course, we were all scared, but we couldn't show it. From his men I leant much. That he was always there when someone needed a kind word or some gentle encourage-ment. No man was untouched by his generous soul and many loved him as a brother, a friend, an oasis of calm in a world of uncertainty and bitter death. He had a best friend, a Welshman called Evans; they were together from the first day in France. Tim told him about his early years in India, of the holidays he spent from boarding school in England and how he loved the gentle rolling hills of Devon. Evans told him about his home in Wales, the soaring mountains that made him feel he was close to heaven, the terrible struggle of the miners to scrape a bare living from the deep coal-pits and how sometimes his family would go hungry when times were lean. Many times both would share the watch together and Evans would teach Tim the songs of his childhood, lullabies to sooth the spirit and songs to stir the blood. Tim sung in the language of the Ayahs, who looked after him as a child. Neither saw any class distinction; they were just two men making the best of a war that made no sense to them.' Tears rolled down Nathan's face as he remembered all the tributes he had listened to.

'This hurt you deeply,' Alex finally replied. 'Yet you barely knew Tim before the war?'

'I knew him well, uncle, my mother had a gift of the sight; I was not a young man that would settle easily into running a big estate. I loved horses and spent more time in the stables than with my tutors. I was just sixteen when mother sent me to Halleswell Hall. I was a stable hand, sent to watch over my kin because of a vision of doom that my mother saw. I was the lad that first put Tim on the back of a pony, the one that was there when Tim was scolded for wanting to paint and draw. He shared all of his hopes and dreams with me but I could never tell him of our kinship. I wish now that I had, I wish that I could have told him how proud I was of him and that his feelings were not unnatural, but those of a gentle soul.'

'I never guessed,' Alex murmured to himself, not until the night of the Comet party and by then it was all too late. Holding tight to Nathan's hand he lifted him to his feet, only a slight tremor betraying his agitation.

'Tonight I feel in need of something stronger than cocoa, could you ring for Flo and tell her that she should go to bed. There is something I need to show you and tonight I would ask you to join me in a glass or two of brandy, for I feel you and I may need it before the night is through.'

Bemused Nathan did as Alex had asked; although Flo was loath to leave her master.

'Do not overtire him,' she had said and he had assured her that his intentions were to put Alex's mind at peace.

Both learnt much that night, Nathan once again broke down as he read Tim's journals and Alex was both comforted and appalled at Nathan's account of the court martial.

Suddenly a scream rent the air and glancing towards the clock Alex saw that it was well past the time he normally visited Zara.

'Please forgive me Nathan but there is something I must do, perhaps we could talk again in the morning?'

Another scream made both of them jump.

'I know little of this matter, but I can tell a human scream when I hear it, let me help you Uncle,' Nathan replied in a cool, calm voice.

'Nobody can help us, I am sorry Nathan, this was something I failed to tell you but now I have to go to her.'

'I will come with you,' there was no denying that firm tone.

Briefly, Alex outlined Zara's descent into madness as they climbed the stairs.

Alex opened the door onto a scene that shook Nathan to the core of his being. The room was filthy, with food splattered against the walls and broken china everywhere, but he had eyes only for the frail figure that was about to launch into another hysterical scream. Alex went to take her into his arms as she cried out, 'Papa they have all gone away, long gone..' her voice trailed off until she caught sight of the man standing in the doorway.

'Get him out,' she screamed, 'go away, go away, make him go papa.'

Undaunted Nathan moved into the room, whereupon Zara hurled herself at him, scratching his face and beating at him with her puny fists. They stayed that way for nearly ten minutes, with Nathan making no move to protect himself from her fury, until at last she subsided sobbing into his arms.

Alex looked on with wonder as Nathan led her towards the bed and gently laid her down, still stroking the sparse hair and crooning to her in a gentle voice. For just a brief moment something like lucidity shone in her eyes and with just one word, 'horses', she sank into a deep sleep with her thumb in her mouth.

Pulling the blankets up to her chin, Alex crept quietly out of the room with Nathan following.

Back in the study Alex bathed Nathan's face where deep scratches had drawn blood.

After a very strong brandy Alex stopped shaking while he regarded Nathan with awe in his eyes.

'How did you do that?' He said, 'she hasn't let anyone near her in the last three years.'

The reply was slow in coming as Nathan wondered how he could tell this broken man what he should know about Zara's condition.

'I saw many such scenes while I was convalescing in the hospital. The doctor's called it "shell-shock" but the army failed to recognise it as a medical condition. The mind is a powerful thing but it can only take so much before the shutters come down and then retreat back into their childhood where all was safe and mama or papa could kiss it better. I suspect that Zara has a similar condition and I'm afraid the prognosis is not good.'

'The doctors said it was lunacy and that I should have her put away, but I couldn't do it to her. Some days she smiles at me and then my heart overflows with love for her. Only Flo can now bear to stay here and I'm afraid it won't be for long. What am I going to do then, it would kill me to have her locked up?'

There was another long pause as Nathan thought about his longing to find Vicky, but he could not turn his back on the man who had absolved him of so much guilt.

'I have some ideas uncle, but I suggest we both try to get some sleep and see what tomorrow may bring.'

'Of course, dear boy, you must be very weary. I have had a bed made up for you on the ground floor; I thought it would be easier for you than using the stairs.'

Crossing the room he kissed Nathan on the cheek, 'goodnight, God Bless,' he said echoing Tim's words.

Dawn crept through the curtains waking Nathan from his usual snatched sleep, but today he had a purpose and for once he hummed to himself whilst he was dressing. Though the urge to find Vicky was still paramount in his thoughts, he had a plan that might just make his uncle's life a little easier. Instinct and knowledge told him that it would only be a temporary solution. He had seen Zara's condition and knew that death could only be delayed, not averted. In some small way he felt that by helping his uncle he was also helping himself to come to terms with Tim's death.

Breakfast was a cheerful affair and he even managed to flirt a little with Flo, God knows she could do with a bit of banter in this gloomy house. Once more he would have to walk into the village but even if there had been one horse remaining he doubted his ability to ride one now.

Whilst Alex was trying to coax Zara to eat he managed to talk over his plans with Flo, who was frankly amazed at the proposals he had put forward, but if they worked it would make her life much easier.

'Not a word to Alex mind, I wouldn't want to raise his hopes,' he told her.

'I'll tell the master I'm spring-cleaning the room for you,' she laughed, and then in a more serious tone she enquired about the length of his stay.

'As long as it takes, but I pray that it won't be too long as I must find Vicky before she comes to serious harm.'

Alex was waiting for him as the little pony and trap pulled up outside the doors to the Hall. Nathan looked weary, but as he helped his passenger down he smiled at Alex.

'Uncle this is Betsy Miller, she's going to be helping you to look after Zara.'

Betsy dropped a neat curtsey, then stepped forward and shook Alex's hand.

'Mr Nathan said as how this was going to be a trial of sorts, my mother and me, we'm grateful for the chance, 'specially as she's in the family way again.'

Alex looked perplexed, but now was not the time for questions, taking her arm as if she was a grand lady he led her inside to the kitchen, thinking that Nathan had brought her mainly to help Flo. Certainly she appeared unafraid of the house and that boded well. Meanwhile Nathan was bringing in all sorts of strange packages and parcels. Flo appeared to know more than she was letting on. She greeted Betsy as an old friend and set about making tea and offering her delicious scones around.

Nathan eventually joined them and outlined his plans to a shocked Alex.

'Betsy comes from a large family and needs to work to help her family. She has ten siblings and one of them was unfortunate to be born without her full wits, if you understand what I mean?' The girl nodded as if to say go on, clearly there was no embarrassment about her young sister.

'She's been looking after Rose for nearly six years now, and she had a very special way with the child. Fortunately the girl is now of an age that all the family can pitch in and keep her safe. I've been privileged to meet her and she's a bonny lass. Betsy wants to earn some money as her father is often out of work, but more than that she feels sorry for the young mistress of Halleswell Hall.'

Alex looked alarmed; he had no idea that the villagers knew about Zara.

'Have no fear Uncle, there are few who know of the situation, but Betsy has a lively mind and she is not scared of the rumours, being a good Christian girl. What say you Uncle, shall we try a little experiment, Betsy is a willing girl and strong with it?'

A few minutes later Nathan stood with Alex and Betsy outside Zara's door, Alex looking as if the very devil was riding his back, Betsy clutching one of the parcels and Nathan hoping this would work. Evening was falling fast and Alex clutched the oil lamp tight to him as he slowly turned the key in the lock. Zara was sitting by her mirror running the brush through her hair. Hearing the door she turned slightly and opened her mouth ready to scream. But Betsy forestalled her by walking in boldly and without a pause took the brush from Zara's hands and started to brush the sparse hair herself, all the while crooning softly as if to a young child.

Now Nathan walked slowly forwards and unwrapped the parcel. He handed a beautiful china doll to Zara.

'Zara, this is for you, I think you lost her a long time ago but I found her and I want you to take good care of her, can you do that for me and for your papa?'

Cautiously she took the doll and cradled it to her.

'Livvy gave her to me but I lost her long, long ago.' Smiling at her father she spoke in a childish voice, 'thank you papa, I will hold her and cuddle her and never, ever lose her again.'

Now she turned her attention to Betsy and her lip started to pout as if a tantrum was about to erupt. The atmosphere in the room was charged with tension as she turned her face to the strange woman who was brushing her hair.

'Are you my new maid?' She spoke clearly, 'papa sent the other ones away and so shall I if you don't suit.'

'That is right and proper my lady, but I think you an me, we'm going to be friends, that's if you'll give me a chance,' Betsy said in a firm voice.

The light dimmed in Zara's eyes, the moment of clarity had gone although she still clutched the doll to her sagging breasts.

'I think that's enough progress for one day,' Nathan said, 'these things take time, although I think it went well.'

The following days were a hive of activity, as Nathan helped Betsy with her new charge to visit the nursery that had been turned into a playroom for a young girl. Flo had done wonders with it, and while Zara was out of her usual room both Nathan and Alex pitched in to clean the room and turn in into a haven of peace for a young child. Scrubbed clean and hung with bright curtains, it looked more inviting. Now the bed had a new mattress and a covering in pink together with pink flounces to match the curtains. The carpet was a lighter shade of pink and the dressing table held lots of curious little jars of creams, lotions and a new set of mother-of-pearl brushes. In one corner stood a newly carved and varnished rocking chair, and from somewhere Nathan had found a lovely lacquered music box that played a soothing tune. Poor Alex was totally bemused by all the preparations but the improvement in Zara's moods more than made up for it. Gently Nathan explained that there would still be mood swings and tantrums, also that Zara would never make a recovery, her poor mind and body were too sick for that to happen. At least she would be comfortable and maybe even happy in the time left to her. Betsy was wonderful with Zara, holding her tightly while the tantrums lasted and dressing her in pretty clothes so that Alex could see the last faint bloom of youth in his daughter's appearance.

Two weeks later Nathan announced his departure the following day. He had done what he could and now was aching to take up the next stage of his life. That night he spent with Alex in his study and both men were overcome with the sadness of parting.

'You will write to me?' Alex asked.

'Of course Uncle, you are more like my own family to me, I only wish I could stay here longer, but maybe soon I can persuade Vicky to come home to Halleswell Hall.'

'Then I have something to show you and I pray you won't take this amiss.'

Crossing to his writing bureau he brought out a thick bunch of papers and handed them to Nathan.

'This is my last will and testament; I leave Halleswell Hall to you knowing that you think of it as home. No, please don't refuse it; I see the pain in your eyes. I know that my time is limited as is my daughter's; I would lie at rest knowing that you will one day come home. My last years will be better for the things you have done for me, you brought some sanity back to me and for that I am forever in your debt. One thing only I ask, that if some day the world changes you will bring Tim home to lie next to me.'

'I will try uncle, I swear it on my life, but don't be too eager to embrace death, I would have you see my children, for it is my hope that I find Vicky and persuade her to marry me, I have loved her for so long.'

Both men embraced and another burden was finally lifted from Nathan's shoulders.

He stood on the quayside waiting to embark on what he hoped could be the next to last voyage of his life. Vicky had left six months ago for India and finding her may take him years, but he would find her and hope to bring her home. The sun was sinking into the sea as he moved a pace forwards; the tall man with auburn glints in his hair leant on his cane and never guessed for one moment what a striking picture he made.

COURAGE AND SACRIFICE

Vicky straightened up from the bedside, trying not to wince at the pain in her back. With her one free hand she made to wipe the sweat from her face when a brown arm appeared with a cool cloth to bathe her aching forehead.

'Thank you Amita, although you should really be resting,' she addressed the older woman that now stood quietly to one side.

'I rest when you do Vicky, will you come to eat soon?'

Despite her tiredness, Vicky could still summon up a smile for this wonderful woman who had cast aside all her upbringing to help her 'English miss.' Amita was a Hindu of a fairly high caste, but after losing most of her family to the pandemic she had followed Vicky around everywhere, even into the men's ward. Now Vicky looked back down at her patient, a young man of about her own age who was in the last stages of the deadly virus which had swept through India like a scythe through a field of wheat.

Already he was coughing up blood, his lungs drowning in it as he struggled to breathe. Vicky knew the next few hours would be crucial, his chances of surviving now completely gone. She hardly had the energy left for the overwhelming sorrow that always swept over her when yet another patient died. In the last four months death had become a constant companion, although it went against her nature to give up on even one person.

'There is nothing else to do Amita, but the least I can do is to sit by him until the end comes, I don't think it will be long now. Is there anyone here who can say a prayer over him, I can't even tell if he's a Hindu or a Muslim?'

'The holy men, pah! They have all run away. Only the English father with his beads and book is left. His prayers will reach the Gods, wherever they are.'

Vicky just nodded, here in this nightmarish place it did seem as if every God known to man had deserted them, but she was surprised to hear Amita say it. The older woman had always been a devout worshipper even as her husband and sons had been taken from her. She relied heavily on Amita to tell Hindu from Muslim, Buddhist from Christian. With all dignity taken from the victims, sometimes the presence of their holy men could ease their terrible passing from this hell on earth.

'Could you get one of the boys to find Father Francis, I think I saw Kumar around a while ago?'

'I go myself, my English it get better every day I think?'

'Its very good Amita, I am glad you are here with me. I only wish there were more like you to help us. We need more nurses and doctors, men to take the bodies away, women to help us cook and clean, but I think they are too afraid.'

'I go now, find the father. Maybe take a little while with all the prayers he make to your God.' With that she walked away, her sandals slipping slightly on the bloodstained floor.

She was so tired and much in need of a bath. Why did Amita never answer her question about more help? She had been in Bombay for four months now and except for a few older children the disease appeared to be hitting only the people from twenty to about forty, just the wrong age-group when they needed every able-bodied men and women to help out, not only in the hospitals but in the fields. Already food was rotting in the ground with so few of the people left to get the harvest in. Amita was a rare woman, an educated woman in her mid-fifties, but still she was a member of the ruling classes. If she could overcome her aversion to working along different religions and even talking to men, then there must be other older men and women somewhere who weren't at work in the fields?

Once more her mind went back over her arrival in India, first to see if she could find the medicine man to lift the curse she had unwittingly laid on her family, but as soon as she had seen the bodies already piling up in the streets she had reported to the nearest hospital. She had no fear for her own life ever since she had heard of the deaths that occurred in her family, but she would have spared Alex, Zara and Nathan if she could have.

Suddenly her patient started that racking cough which signalled that the end was near. Hastily she pulled up the plastic sheet, which was the only thing that protected her uniform from the terrible discharge of blood soon to come. Gently she took one of his blue hands in hers, despite the risk of infection; it was all she could do now that cyanosis had taken him over. Blood gushed from every part of his body; even his eyes were weeping bloody tears.

She heard the calm voice of Father Francis behind her, his litany of absolution for the soul that was about to depart. Blood splashed his robes as he knelt next to her and made the sign of the cross on the man's forehead. One last sigh and the soul left the body, a bloody husk, empty of life. She didn't even realise that she was crying again until she felt a tug at the hem of her dress.

It was little Kumar, a young boy of about seven or eight, who had lost every member of his family and now ran around the hospital taking errands and curling his body up on the mat at the foot of her bed to sleep.

'Come missy Vicky, doctor man says you need food and rest. Grandmother go to heat water for you.'

She smiled through her tears at the honouree "grandmother" bestowed on Amita by all the children. So many had arrived here alone in the world, while the few elderly people left were too busy trying to raise their own grandchildren and till the fields. Many had been taught a smattering of English already and the few that hadn't were soon picking the language up.

Thanking Father Francis she followed Kumar out of the ward.

Once she had thoroughly scrubbed herself clean she sat down in her tiny room to share the sparse meal with Amita. It was the usual fare, rice mixed with some unknown vegetables and a few things that could be some sort of beans. Bread was scarce, but there was the flat doughy stuff that filled her up, even though it wasn't very appetising. At least there was still plenty of the dark Indian tea she had come to enjoy without milk or sugar. Remembering to use her right hand, she scooped the food up with her fingers and some of the doughy bread. There was plenty of cutlery but it saved on the washing and sterilising process. Once the meal was finished she went behind the small screen that offered a modicum of privacy and changed into her cotton night-dress. Amita then took her leave, preferring to sleep in a small house nearby that hadn't yet been taken over for nursing the sick.

There was a light tap on the door and Kumar entered now clad in a clean dhoti and ready to say his prayers with her. Gladly would she have just fallen on the bed, but she kept the ritual up for the sake of the boy. The first time she had knelt at the side of the bed Kumar had started laughing. 'Why you greet the bed?' he had giggled as she put her hands together. That was her introduction to the Hindu greeting of namaste. Hands clasped in the same attitude of saying prayers, she soon learnt that this had great significance to the people, who would bow their head slightly with hands in the same position and say namaste (which was something like an honourable greeting with some religious meaning to it.)

Now Kumar joined her every night with his strange mixture of Hindu and English prayers. After that he would curl up on the mat at the end of her bed, much as a guard dog would do for its master.

Sleep came instantly after her twenty-hour shift, although her dreams were often troubled by memories of the past. In some she was fleeing with Nathan, in others she was in France receiving the letters that told of her family's deaths. Nathan had spared her the details of Tim's death, but she had known from the moment he was shot. The sight was still with her although it had become easier to live with over the years. Now she saw herself as she had left her comfortable home to take up nursing in 1916. How she had crept out of the window late at night and was accepted without much probing into her past. Nathan had been furious, but there was little he could by the time he had leave to visit her. Dear Nathan, how she missed him but somehow she could never use her sight to find him.

Now the dreams started to turn dark and frightening. She was in a field hospital barely a few miles away from the trenches. The pounding of the guns and the screams of the dying were doubly sinister with the lights in the tent often dimming or going out altogether only to be shocked back into focus by the blinding flashes of the mortar bombs.

None of her brief six months training, acting as a general intern could have prepared her for the sight and sounds of the real action, where surgeons struggled with only the barest of instruments and precious little medicines. She soon learnt how to hold a man down as a doctor had to amputate an arm or a leg, sighing with relief when the patient passed out with the pain of it. Sometimes there would be rum or whiskey instead of chloroform or a quick blow to the jaw administered only to save the man from pain. Hardening herself to carry out her work took time but without it she could never have carried on. Tired and sick to her soul, she often took over quickly as the surgeon passed on to his next patient, sewing up wounds and helping to cauterise stumps.

Then there was the mad scramble into the ambulances as the battle drew nearer, the curses of the doctors, as a man newly operated on would die of shock or the jolting of wagons over ruts.

Vicky turned uneasily in her sleep and then woke up instantly as an arm grabbed hers.

It was only Kumar awakening her to another long day and night of toil. Without thinking, she asked him what the time was in English and when he just looked at her she switched to a rough form of his own dialect.

'The sun is so high,' he replied making a gesture that told her it was about ten in the morning.

'Missy Vicky have good long sleep, doctor say so.'

He was right, she had slept for nearly nine hours her rumbling stomach told her so even if she hadn't judged the time for herself.

'Grandmother have food ready soon,' he said.

Groaning to herself she quickly washed in lukewarm water and put her cumbersome uniform on. If she had her own way she would have gladly have worn the baggy trousers of the Muslims, but then she would be bound to offend someone. The days were getting chilly anyway with the winter season in its second month.

Ah well, she thought to herself, better go and get some breakfast even though it would be the usual fare of rice and whatever else could be found.

However she was to be pleasantly surprised by the sight of two boiled eggs on a china plate and a few slices of very thin bread. Amita beamed at her from her place at the small table.

'My cousin Meera she arrived last night from the country. Much problems getting here but bring hens and trade with soldiers for bread. Also bring lazy old men who hide in house afraid of much sickness. I say old lazy men do not die, Miss Vicky say so.'

Vicky was so pleased she nearly hugged her friend before remembering to ask permission to do so.

'Much change with sickness Vicky, now you are little sister to me and can hug big sister.'

This was even better than the breakfast laid out waiting for her. Healthy men to help with the mounds of corpses, although she didn't think they would like it much. Even better was Amita's total acceptance of her, which was something to be able to take some comfort from.

'Now little sister eat good food and then we work.'

That was the old bossy Amita back but Vicky just smiled and set to with gusto.

Soon she found out that Amita's 'lazy old men' was completely false, more a term of affection than anything else. As the epidemic spread to every part of India she was doubly grateful for the help of any able-bodied person. Silently she wept as every day the streets of Bombay piled up high with more bodies, some dropping dead en route to the hospital. Still the starving people and the refugees flooded into the city, making the disease spread even more rapidly. The men would push carts laden with bodies to the vast funeral pyres as far from the city as possible, the smoke a constant reminder of the frailty of life.

In the hospital doctors and nurses died indiscriminately as the disease progressed, adding to Vicky's grief as one by one the other nurses that sailed with her were mown down.

Now her only joy was with the children, their solemn faces soon turning to smiles as they found jobs to do in and around the hospital, to take their minds off the carnage they saw every day. 'Once this is over I'm going to take them away somewhere,' she vowed to herself, 'somewhere where they could learn to be children again, not carriers of messages or extra hands to cook and clean.'

It was a beautiful warm sunny day in early March and outside the children were playing a form of football taught to them by a kindly British officer, but inside the hospital it was as gloomy as night. Patrick Mahoney laid in a tiny alcove off the main ward, his lifeblood draining away with each wracking cough he made. Vicky sat beside him, helping to lift him forward with each laboured breath. With the last of the morphine gone she had begged for a bottle of whiskey and surprisingly had got it. Not that it had made much difference to the young Irish doctor who had fought so valiantly for every one of his patients. Now it was his turn to die, a man barely into his thirties with a wife and three young children waiting back home for him. She wanted to scream at the injustice of it all, but she was too busy mopping in vain at the blood gushing from his drowning lungs.

Father Francis sat at the other side of the makeshift bed, a tall white-haired old man with more of an eye to the whiskey bottle than to the soul of his charge.

'Don' burn me,' were the last words he said before collapsing back onto the bed.

Hastily the Father made the last motions, but then he shocked her by his callowness.

'He'll have to go in with the others,' he said in a mild tone.

Vicky was suddenly furious, her hand shot out but Amita caught it in time before she hit the priest.

'He deserves a place to himself and I don't give a damn where you find it, but by God you will find it if you have to search all of Bombay to do so.' With that she burst into tears and hurried out of the room to fling herself on her bed.

Why, God, why? She whimpered to herself as the full truth hit her, now there would be only two British doctors left alive, and a handful of Indian doctors with accents so strong she could barely understand them. Rocking her body with pain and fear, she nearly hit out again as warm arms attempted to hold her close. If it was that damn catholic priest she would rip his heart out. Instead she heard a familiar voice speaking softly to her, 'Vicky, dearest, it's alright, and I'm here now.'

'Nathan?' and again. 'Nathan, am I dreaming?'

'If you are then so must I be,' he replied smoothing the hair away from her face and gently kissing her swollen eyelids. His grey eyes regarded her steadily, but she could see the lines of strain on his face and the agony in that look. Lifting her hand she touched his hair and then said something so stupid she could have kicked herself, 'but you've got grey hair, here and here,' frantically patting at his face.

'One for every day we have been apart,' he said, but now he was smiling.

'How, when, why?' and suddenly she was crying again, but tears of joy mixed with love and compassion for this dear man she had never thought to see again.

'Darling Vicky, do you think an ocean could have kept me away from you? It would take the entire world's oceans and then some more,' his voice was husky and so full of love it shocked her out of her tears.

'You called me a damned brat the last time I saw you in France,' she hiccuped.

'And so you are but you are still my damn brat, or so I hope,' he suddenly looked uncertain.

'Oh Nathan I do love you so, surely you know that by now?'

'So much that you first run away from home, and then send me half the way around the world to find you,' he replied and now tears filled his own eyes.

'Every moment of every day I woke and thought of you. Even in the heat of battle, when I thought I wanted to die your face would be in front of me begging me not to throw my life away.'

'Hush,' putting a finger to her lips, 'I have done many things I am not proud of, some that I am deeply ashamed of, but one thought, one feeling kept me alive through it all, that one day I would see you again and have a chance to explain before you sent me away.' Now he sounded deeply troubled.

Hesitantly he told her about Tim and the part he had played in that awful day. As she stayed quiet, her eyes looking into the distance as if to seek the truth of the matter, he went on to tell her about Alex and Tim's journals. Still she stayed silent and he wondered if he had lost her forever. If so he had lost his last reason to live.

She came out of the trance-like state slowly as if she was waking from a dream.

'I saw it happen,' she said, 'but there was something I could not see, something that took the fear from his eyes and…yes, now I know, it was forgiveness and a touch of regret for all the things he would never see again or go on to do. He would have been a fine artist, no; he is a fine artist for I see more clearly now the papers in a pair of worn hands. Alex has Tim's drawings, I am right, aren't I?'

'Yes, Alex has Tim's drawings and one day I am going to show them to the world, that's if you can bear to allow me near them,' with that he hung his head in shame.

So gently she lifted his head up and looked deep into his eyes. 'You were never to blame for any of it; it was I alone and that awful curse I put on all the Meverall's, never thinking it would apply to those of the blood, not just the name. That's why I came here, hoping to find someone to help me lift it. I stayed here when I saw the terrible suffering. I wanted to spare you and anyone who still lived, but now I know there is no stopping what I began that day.'

'Please Vicky don't talk like that. I admit there were times that I wondered if such a thing could be, but after living through the last four years of hell I think we make our own destiny. Could we have stopped this war merely by wishing? Can we stop what is happening now? If it's God's wish then there is nothing we could have done to avert it, though I'm more inclined to think of this as the work of evil men.'

'Nathan you have to leave right now,' she said springing to her feet. 'You may not believe in the curse but I do and now you are here where people are dying faster than the flies that feed on the corpses. Oh God, what have I done, I've brought you to your certain death?' Again she started crying but with an edge of hysteria to it.

Slowly he stood up and picked up the cane that had fallen from his hands.

'Look at me Vicky. After Tim died I became reckless, I had a death wish, I charged headfirst into every battle and came away with a mere scratch.'

Vicky appraised him with her nurse's glance,

'That's no scratch; I would hazard a guess at a bayonet wound?'

Angrily he pulled up his trouser leg and exposed the jagged scar. 'Yes it was a bayonet scar, and it came within an inch of an artery. I spent weeks in a filthy hospital tent while young men with lesser wounds than I died from gangrene. After that there was the channel crossing, with German Zeppelins bombing us night and day but I didn't die. I spent six months learning how to walk again, and every night I thought of you out there in the heat of battle and I cried like a bloody great baby. So I don't believe in your damn curse and I'm never going to let you out of my sight again.' With that he sank exhausted onto the bed.

'Do I get any say in this?' she asked smiling now.

'No, you don't,' he snapped, expecting to be rebuffed any minute.

'Then come here and have a hug before I tell you what you've let yourself in for,' and with that she threw her arms around him.

KARMA

Tea-black night embraced Vicky as she glided on silent feet towards the edges of the compound. An onlooker would be hard put to discern the quick glimpse of white against an ebony sky, pregnant with inscrutable meanings belonging only to the initiated. The moon lay on her back allowing only the light of the distant stars to intrude on a soul beset by troubles.

A faint breeze ruffled her hair and spoke briefly of the imminent monsoon months. Nostrils flared as the many perfumes vied with each other for ascendancy. Far away but unmistakable, the scent of sandalwood carried on the errant breeze, mingling with a hint of jasmine. Cinnamon and cardamom mixed with the delicate fragrance of saffron invoked memories of the previous evening's meal, whilst the pungent smell of ghee threatened to overcome each and every odour.

Occasionally a yip or a yowl disturbed the silence, whether of wild dog, or a lone wolf it was hard to tell. Vicky had already tuned out the sound of insects and now listened carefully for any sounds of danger, but she could not feel anything that would threaten her. A moth came within inches of her body but veered away towards the distant lights of the clinic, where Dr Nadeem was literally burning the midnight oil once again. Even the whir of mosquitoes seemed absent, another warning that the short dry spring was about to end.

Slipping through the only entrance, she allowed the feeling of stubby grass to soothe her tired feet, it had been a long and arduous day with only the promise of her nocturnal forays to look forward to. She knew that Nathan worried about these midnight walks but she needed them to sort out her feelings of something bearing down on her, an inescapable threat to overshadow the love between them.

A short walk led to one of her favourite places, an abandoned temple on a grassy hillock. From here she could look at the sky and ponder on the questions that had recently been troubling her every sleepless night. Spreading out her silk wrapper she lay down and scrutinised the heavens as if they might have some answers to her questions. Maintaining an even breathing she slipped into the light trance that always followed her mediation.

The world soul was Braham that encompassed the universe and was, to the Hindu religion, the ultimate expression of their religion. Braham was the world made flesh and every living being, human, plant, animal, landscape, in short everything that populated the world that could be seen. Of the unseen world that was the province of the enlightened and the triumph of good over evil. Of the gods there were none, just a huge collective consciousness that any soul could eventually aspire to. There were the 'avatars', gods that took on many aspects including that of humans, but they weren't actually worshipped, more used as a teaching aid. Vicky knew this was a very simplistic idea of a very complex faith but it appealed to her in a way that other religions did not.

Now, as she watched the stars in their eternal dance of the skies above she could sense a pattern beginning to emerge. Reason told her that science had explained the relationship between the sun, the moons and the planets, but instinct told her a different meaning, that life was one endless circle of life and death with only karma making sense in a world that had gone mad. The comet had been a portent of evil things to come and she let loose a dreadful curse on that very night. She had discussed this at length with Amita soon after the end of the epidemic that had stricken the world so soon after war had killed many millions of people. Now the stars whirled, the moon became dark with the blood of the slaughtered and a vision of terrible carnage once more visited her.

'Vicky, darling, please wake up, you're having a nightmare.' Nathan was holding her in his arms and gratefully she sank into his embrace.

'Why must you do this every night, it worries me so much, please sweetheart, can't you tell me what is troubling you?'

'I don't understand it myself, I only know that I need to try and make sense of the terrible things we have both seen over the years.' She said, drying her tears.

Nathan could understand part of this, after they had fought

side by side the death toll of the epidemic in India alone had been estimated at about 16 million, but both felt that short of the mark. Worldwide, the pandemic had taken ten times the lives of the war years and possibly many more. All he knew for now was that Vicky needed pleasant things around her and if she insisted on listening to different religions to ease her aching heart, then who was he to stop her?

I'm her husband, he thought, she should turn to me, but as fast as the thought came he pushed it away. 'Come back to bed and let me warm you up.'

Vicky laughed, for this night her heart was eased and if the future looked uncertain, then together as man and wife they would face it to the bitter end.

Early morning sunlight bathed the compound in a rosy glow, and once again Angela Frobisher felt that glow of contentment on arriving at the place she now thought of a second home. Eagerly she wanted to press on but just for a few minutes she decided to stop the wagons and drink in the sights.

Behind the wire, which was only used to keep the predatory animals outside were several long low white buildings arranged in a sort of rough semicircle with other, larger buildings dotted around at haphazard intervals. Inside the circle was a structure that could have been mistaken for a fountain in an English mansion, but was in fact, a deep well with a roof covering to keep out the heat of the long hot summers. The fanciful dolphin statue actually did gush water in the monsoon season, but it was more a torrent then than a fountain.

Angela knew the effort that gone into building this haven although many would never understand its complex nature. She had been one of the few nurses that had survived the pandemic although she had gone back to England for a brief spell after it was over in 1919. Finding English life stifling after the freedom of the war years, she had returned to India in time for the wedding of her friend Vicky to the handsome Nathan. That had been a strange affair as Vicky had always said she would never marry, but who could resist the dashing Major?

The wedding itself had been a fairly brief civil ceremony with an indifferent governor of some small state acting as the officer in charge.

The second ceremony had been far more colourful, with Vicky in a sari and Nathan in a plain suit. There had been many Indian people there and it was probably more of a blessing than a wedding, as some heathen priest conducted the ceremony. Still, she had learnt a great deal since that day. India was a strange and exotic mixture of people and religions. The land had a timeless beauty and one could easily imagine the impossible coming true.

Vicky's dream of starting an orphanage and hospital had struck Angela as an impossible, and maybe misguided idea, though she had proved it to be sincere with the ground already prepared and building underway by the time of the marriage in 1921.

Now, her musings done, she turned once again to the place called simply Maserat. The initial fight for the land and building permission had been resolved with a handsome bribe and the fictional story of becoming a mission. Indeed there was a very modest church run by none other than old Father Francis, though he did more drinking and dozing than actual prayer. Still, it kept the authorities happy.

Tin shanties had housed the growing number of children while Maserat was built, but as soon as the first building was completed Vicky opened this to young babies and toddlers, those either orphaned by the epidemic or whose parents were struggling to get back on their feet or working in the fields. It was a good solution as many babies were later returned to their parents or to distant relatives. Now the nursery was a much smaller building, with the majority of children between the ages of 3 and 12 years old, there were dormitories for the girls and ones for the boys.

Angela had been one of the first nurses to volunteer to aid with the clinic, as the hospital had proved more difficult to build and equip, but Vicky still had hopes for the future. Despite the sometimes cramped quarters and the primitive clinic, Angela had never been happier in her whole life.

Now she was returning from a long trip to the eastern side of the continent with essential medicines and a large store of food that couldn't be easily grown on these Western shores. She also had a wonderful surprise for both Vicky and Nathan in the form of a disillusioned doctor, who's every attempt to help the stricken population was frowned upon by the local governor, who had an eye to marrying him off to his plain daughter. Kevin Mc Cloud was an interesting man and a very experienced doctor; she was sure he would fit in and become, well, a diversion, at which thought she instantly blushed bright red.

Pulling her thoughts into line, she bade the convoy to resume their journey.

Vicky had risen at dawn, despite her nocturnal walk, with her energy levels depleted, but determined to start the day as always. Glancing at her husband still sprawled on the bed, she smiled as she made her way out of the door. Her first task was to visit the kitchens and make sure that Amita was not doing too much on her own. She had left the hiring of women to cook and clean in her big sister's hands, but Amita was soft-hearted and had sometimes been taken advantage of by distant kinsfolk. She still remembered the 'cousin', Meera, who had brought the chickens but then had disappeared only to re-appear when the building was done. Nathan had taken care of that problem by asking her to work with his 'boys' and pleading it was against her religion, she had soon left.

Sure enough Amita was lighting one of the big ovens in preparation for the midday meal, while Madhu and Sangita were nowhere to be seen. Amita said they were still in bed. Vicky, furious by now, stormed into the living quarters and dragged both complaining girls out of bed, saying this was their last chance and she could easily find more willing hands to do the work. Soon they were both hard at work, stirring the large pot of maize and raisins that made an unconventional but filling breakfast for the children.

From the small, but well populated Muslim quarters, she heard the call to prayers with an elder boy, Abdul leading the younger children in observance. Kneeling on mats spread out in the tiny courtyard, their bobbing heads and prostate figures always made Vicky feel humble, but she had much to do this day, so hurrying to the larger eating area she helped herself to a hasty breakfast and then took turns with another two girls in ladling out the makeshift porridge. Later she would cook Nathan a proper breakfast away from the eyes of the vegetarians. Although she had found it easier to give up meat, she had never tried to force this on Nathan, but the meal would be spare today with food stocks being so low.

That was the moment when she heard the rumble of wagons and knew that her best friend and head nurse had arrived back safely. Hitching up her sari, she dashed across the main courtyard and was in time to greet her friend as she alighted from the first wagon.

Nathan was there as well, and for a while there was much hugging and kissing, for the journey was still dangerous and she had feared for her friend. Angela made light of it as usual, nodding at the men who were still cradling their Enfield rifles as if they might turn back and fire on their owners. Barking out orders that would have frozen whole troops of men, she got the men to draw the wagons up to the storage area and under the watchful eyes of Vicky's two burly men they started to unload the precious cargo.

'I don't know why you bother,' Angela said as she watched them scurry two and fro.

'You know I can handle a rifle better than any man.'

Nathan laughed although he had no doubts as to her prowess, 'God spare us from rifle toting women,' he said.

'I can't even keep my own wife in line though I doubt I will ever see her wearing britches.'

Vicky cast him an evil glance, but couldn't help the bubbles of laughter that signified her relief. The supplies were much needed, and hopefully both the clinic and the food stores would now be restocked.

It was to the sounds of laughter that the man stepped down from the last of the wagons that held the lighter and more fragile supplies. He was a giant of a man, standing at least six feet four inches tall and maybe more. His face was weatherworn, while a shock of ginger hair stood up in bristles from his genial face.

'Kevin Mc Cloud at your service,' he introduced himself, first shaking Nathan's hand and then displaying an awkward but somehow endearing bow to Vicky.

'Doctor of medicine, sawbones for the army, fought the influenza and…Um, never found a reason to go back to Blighty.'

Angela interrupted hastily before he talked himself out of a much-needed job, 'don't you listen to his wittering; he's a damn fine doctor and an expert hunter to boot. Just a few days ago he shot a boar so I reckon on some feasting tonight. He's been travelling around the country offering his services for a bowl of rice and never complaining.' Here she stopped and gave a wry grin, 'except for my driving, of course, damn man hasn't the stomach for that.'

Nathan was delighted at finding a fellow Scotsman and led him away for a rare glass of whiskey and a few of his hoarded cigarettes.

Vicky and Angela went off arm in arm to discuss the merits of this fine new doctor and the problems of roasting a whole boar without offending the various staff and children.

The new doctor settled down quickly and became a popular man with both the children and the various staff. Angela blossomed under his attention and Nathan now had someone he could talk to. It was a relief to Vicky that her husband had another man with which to unload his sense of grief and failure, especially after the dash to England when Zara was dying. Now Vicky kept quiet about her second sight, afraid that Nathan would be further upset by the things she sometimes glimpsed. Her own feelings about Alex and Zara were overshadowed by the death of Nathan's mother and her own dear Aunt, although the actual relationship had been more of an adopted aunt than a true one, still she had been a Meverall in blood, if not in name and Vicky was still haunted by the deadly curse she had then released.

Amita was still with them, and now, freed from kitchen duties she spent more time with Vicky helping her to understand the Hindu way of life. Amita understood the Tiger spirit in Vicky and led her to see that her actions as a child were something that she couldn't have hoped to control at that time. Knowing that Alex had blamed her for the death of Zara was eating into her soul, but under the gentle guidance of her friend and sister she was slowly coming to the point when she felt she could write to Alex. Knowing little of the man except what she heard from Nathan, still she felt the gratitude of the kindness shown both to her dear brother Tim and to her beloved husband. For that alone she was in his debt so one day she sat down to write a long letter to him, knowing from the sight that his days were numbered and fearing for her own soul and the grief of her husband when poor Alex finally passed from his bitter life.

Dear Alex,

I hope you will stop at this point and not think of destroying this letter before I have a chance to make my peace with you. My heart and soul are in your hands right now and I beg for the sake of my dear brother Tim and the love you have for my husband that you will read this and judge me on my words alone, for there is no way I could ever return to England now after all the pain I have caused to you and poor Zara. Be assured that I have suffered on my own account for the deaths of my kin lie heavily on my shoulders. In one stroke of misfortune I condemned my whole family to die, that is my bitter pain and if I had the chance again I would gladly have sacrificed myself on the altar of the evil acolytes who sought to destroy not only our family but the whole of Brannon's Wood.

Much of that night is still a blur to me, but one thing I remember clearly that will go to the grave with me is this. Bound by my hands I was forced to the very place that held the spirit of all the goodness in the land. I saw deep steps leading down into the well and knew it for all that is pure and Holy. In that brief look it was if I saw the universe in its entirety with the sun and moon at its centre. That it was once a place where priests could hide from the wrath of the monarchy I beheld in seconds, though my experience seemed to last for an age. I have no doubt that he who laid the first stones had some knowledge of the future and prepared for that day.

However, it was the cup that held my whole attention and in that moment many thoughts assailed me. Its appearance was like to something more precious than any jewel in the land and it was within my very reach. Temptation held me in its thrall as I saw the wonders I could perform with the cup in my hands. Still I was but a child so the snake withdrew its fangs leaving me with a dilemma that was beyond my mortal span. I was but a child with a child's reasoning, though I think that God or some high force was with me that night, for I saw clearly that in the hands of evil people all its good would be unmade and the land fall into ruin and despair.

246

under the pretence of wishing to find important deeds, so my brother was lulled by greed, he paid for that with his life, peace be with him. All I saw were some mouldering papers, maybe letters left in hiding for some sweetheart.

A great anger built in my heart and I refused to do what I had been bidden, you know the result of that; rather than see me sacrificed my aunt laid down her life for me. It should have ended then but a fierce anger arose in me and the words were spoken before I had my wits again.

I can never change that night or take back that wretched curse but here in India I have learnt something that still holds hope for us all. From the words of one who is dear to me I have embraced the law of Karma. Now I fear no death for I know that this life is one small stage in the great wheel of the universe. My sins will follow me into the next life where I will have a chance to atone for my errors.

I cannot hope that you will understand, but I beg of you that you think on these matters, for I have been told that you are a man who enquires of the mysteries of life. May you and Zara be reunited in some other life where your kindness will be rewarded to the full.

Be assured by the love that my husband holds for you,

Peace be with you,

Victoria.

Angela sent the letter when she next went into Bombay. Vicky never expected a reply although she waited on the mail for a long time. Now she spent more time with Amita as the daily lessons were taught to the Hindu children. She heard the sacred stories with the same wonder as the young children laughing at the stories of the gods that took on human form and played their pranks on mankind.

Meanwhile she delighted in the progress that Nathan was making with the young boys given into his care. Her knowledge of the different races and religions had caused her much regret, as after the dreadful epidemic had ceased the differences between cultures had once more become an increasing problem with so few people of the right age to teach her young charges. The boys needed a man's guidance and Nathan had more than filled that role. Without his perseverance many of the boys would have either had given up or fallen into the hands of well meaning, but misguided missionaries.

This was not a land that welcomed change, but her heart was uplifted by the mingling of boys, mainly of the Hindu faith, but a few of the Muslim boys running and playing with no animosity between them.

Nathan took great care not to have favourites amongst the boys. He had nursed so many through the great sickness and after, when many families could barely sustain themselves, let alone the children that had suffered injuries trying to till the fields with no adult supervision. Her own little helper, the cheerful Kumar now came into his own as he settled disputes between the boys. Unlike the other boys, he had continued to assist her and showed great promise of becoming an exceptional scholar and maybe in time, a good doctor, but who would sponsor a child of India?

Many times she had despaired as the older boys left their care to go to the tea plantations or the cotton picking, in order to keep elderly relatives or to settle back into their own accustomed roles in life. Nathan often discussed this with her over their evening meal, but how could they go back on their own standards where they accepted the right of every child to follow their own religion and destinies?

Watching Nathan at play with the boys she saw what a good father he would make and wished with all her heart he could become a father, but that could never be. How could she carry his child and not forget the curse?

In deference to the different cultures she took the older girls under her wing and tried to teach them the basics of reading and writing and a sense of pride in their unique womanhood. Amita merely sighed, and said they would never find good husbands if they were taught this way. Still she tried and loved every minute of her classes when a young girl mastered her first word of English or sought to question her own role in life.

Some of the older girls became a pleasure to her when they started to apply their knowledge to assisting the doctor. By now many of the women who had survived the terrible illnesses attended the clinic but would not consent to being treated by a man or even an English nurse. Her 'girls' would translate the symptoms, either to Angela or to the doctor and would instruct the fearful women in the treatments needed for their ailments.

One day she hoped to have a proper hospital and trained staff to lift the burdens from her own shoulders. Perhaps she could even spend a little more time with Nathan, although he never complained of the long hours they both put in. Sometimes she felt as if she had no right to such happiness, but then she would watch as Nathan played football with his boys and knew that he, too, was content with the way their lives had turned out.

Her one worry was that he might want to return to England one day and take his place as master of Halleswell Hall. Much as she wanted to see the gentle rolling hills of Devon once again, she feared the curse would then claim them both.

For now she had her children, her friends and the wonderful garden that Nathan had lovingly planted for her, even fetching fragrant roses from the warmer, more sheltered south to adorn her own private garden.

Then came the day she had dreaded for the last few months, knowing that Alex was fading fast but loath to tell her dear husband that her visions were returning once more. Now each night she clung onto Nathan with the sure knowledge that soon he would be gone from her side. Their love-making became bittersweet as she counted the days until the letter would arrive. She knew that this would be the start of something which would eventually take her husband away for a very long time.

Midnight found her on the same grassy knoll where she had laid so many times before. The heat was almost unbearable, but she soon calmed her breathing and slipped once more into that trance-like state. Once more the stars whirled in the heavens, though this time the moon hung pregnant in the skies. Dizziness came over her and she surrendered herself into its strange embrace.

They found her the next morning, curled up like a baby in the mother's womb. Kevin checked her all over but could not find anything wrong bar a slight change in her heart rhythm, which was put down to a night spent out into in the open. Only Vicky knew the source of her brief illness, so when the letter arrived she was ready to tell Nathan that he must go to his uncle's side.

She insisted on being there when the ship sailed from Bombay, each moment a heartbeat away from begging him to stay. Now she felt the laws of Karma biting into her every thought and deed. Amita stayed with her, only she knew what this hour meant to her little sister.

Smiling cheerfully she attempted to take her husbands thoughts away from what he was leaving behind. At the last moment her resolve nearly failed her as Nathan clung to her, his body pressed so close to her she could feel the beating of his heart against hers.

'Go with God,' she said to him, although she knew his own beliefs were as nothing compared to her own.

'I leave my heart in your keeping,' he said just before he boarded the ship.

'And mine with yours,' she replied.

The baby died in her womb just as Nathan was reaching the shores of England. Angela held her one hand and Amita held the other as the tiny boy slithered from her body. She made it easy for Kevin as he tried to tell her that there would be no more children.

'I know already,' she said, 'but promise me that you will never tell Nathan of this?'

So the conspiracy was formed and never broken.

Little did they know that he looked on the moon that night and a shiver of sudden fear ran down both their spines.

ALEX AND NATHAN

Nathan sat at the table in the small room he had been living in since his return to India. He held a letter in his hands, staring at it, unseeing now. He had read the letter over and over and still his mind would not accept the contents.

Dear Mr Nathan,

I'm that worried about Mr Alex that I don't know what to do. He is desperately ill and yet will not write to you himself. I know that he would wish to see you before he passes from this life, and I fear that will be sooner than he thinks. Please say you will come with all speed, for I know how much he means to you and how much he longs to see you again.

Please excuse my writing, only there is no one else to tell you.

Florence Amiss

Halleswell Hall.

Finally Nathan scraped back his wooden chair and crossed the room to his window. That window looked out into the dusty yard behind the hospital building. There were few people about at this hour, but two children were throwing a ball to each other. One of the boys had an arm missing and was having great difficulty catching the ball with his remaining hand. Nathan smiled, he knew that boy well. He had been the one who had stemmed the blood from the terrible wound the boy had when he was brought to the hospital. He remembered it had been an accident on his parent's farm. They had not known what to do and hadn't wanted him to return to the farm afterwards. He wouldn't be able to work and would just be another mouth to feed. It had been Nathan who had sat all night with the boy as he clung to the edge of life. He had been the one who talked to the lad when he had come round and realised he had lost his arm. He had coached and encouraged and made the boy feel he still had worth. He had even taught him to write. It had been the boys own determination that had seen him through though. He wouldn't give up or fear for his future, Nathan had seen and encouraged the confidence in him that would see him through. Nathan watched for some time, his indecision beginning to give him a thumping headache.

His eyes turned to the other lad, he didn't live here but came every day without fail to play with his friend. It was a two mile walk from his home, but he made that trek every morning to be with his friend and every evening he made his weary way home. Nathan had arranged it so that he could attend the school room in the orphanage so that his support of his friend didn't cost him the chance of an education. He had felt that was the least he could do to reward such unflinching love for a friend.

He felt his heart was being pulled in so many directions, his work here was important and he was loath to leave, but he knew he had to see Alex before he died if he could. That was the least he could do for the man had been so kind and understanding to him in his hour of need at the end of the war.

A sound behind him made him turn; Vicky had come into the room and was looking at him. 'You are going back to England.' It was a statement rather than a question.

'I don't know, Vicky, this is tearing me in two. I would be with Alex before the end, but I don't want to leave you here on your own.'

'Hardly on my own,' she said with a glance at the boys in the yard. 'I think you must, I fear it will be the last time you will have the chance to see Alex and I know how close you have grown to him over the years. I think that you would regret it if you didn't go and I would not have that come between us.'

'Come with me Vicky; come back to your home.'

Nathan wished he had not said it as soon as the words left his lips. Vicky's face became hard and sorrowful. 'I can't Nathan, I just can't.'

I am sorry my love, I should not have suggested it, forgive me.'

'There is nothing to forgive, I wish I could see my home once more but that is not possible for me now and I don't think it ever will be. But you must go and go quickly. I don't know how much time Alex has and he is desperate to see you.'

He looked again at the boy in the courtyard. He made his decision. He could not abandon Alex now, there were people here who would look after Vicky until he returned. His place was at another bedside now.

The ship had been at sea for weeks now, and it seemed to Nathan that they were making very slow progress. He was impatient, needing to see the English coast, fearing he would be too late and that Alex would have died before he could reach him.

He loved the sea, something that was ingrained in the Meverall family. He thought of his recent trips and wondered if he would ever make a journey that wasn't filled with impatience and a need to make the trip as fast as possible. This brought thoughts of his last voyage to his mind, again a message from Halleswell Hall had made him jump on a ship to race half way around the world, and the return had been filled with impatience to be back at the hospital. It was the caring nature of the man to want to be where he was needed.

That last trip had been less than two years ago. It had been in February 1923 that he had got a letter from Alex imploring him to return. Zara was nearing the end of her life and as Nathan was the only other living Meverall, Alex wished for him to be at his side.

He had been too late on that occasion; Zara had passed from this life two weeks before he had arrived.

He could still remember the anguish on Alex's face when he had arrived. It seemed to him that Alex was suddenly a broken man. He had spent several years looking after his daughter and although she had been much improved after Nathan, 'had worked a piece of magic' as Alex had put it, she had still been hard work right to the end. According to Alex's letters she had been lucid for long periods, although much regressed, but she still had days where the madness seemed to get the better of her and the screaming and violence was still very much in evidence on those days.

Moving from the rail to a bench, he stretched out his legs. It was good to sit, his leg ached after he had been standing for long periods and he found himself rubbing his old wound, an action that was almost subconscious after all these years.

Closing his eyes, it was not long before sleep took him. His thoughts before drifting off crept into his dreams. He was once again at Halleswell hall. Alex was waiting at the door for him as his carriage passed through the grounds. Even at some distance he could see that Alex had aged since his last visit. The strain of looking after Zara and the pain of her death had taken their toll on him. His back was stooped and he leaned heavily on a cane. His hair was thinner than Nathan remembered and was now pure white.

The carriage came to a halt and Nathan had carefully stepped down. His wounded leg had become stiff on the journey and it took him a moment to get the circulation moving again. Eventually he made his way to the waiting Alex and greeted him. Both men were in sombre mood. Alex was clearly devastated by Zara's death and Nathan was mortified that he had not made it back before she had passed from this life.

'Alex, I am so sorry, you have my deepest sympathy for your loss.'

His words sounded formal and out of place in his head as he spoke, but he didn't know what else to say.

Alex didn't reply but stepped aside and with a gesture he invited Nathan in. As he turned to follow Nathan could see Alex was fighting back tears, he could find no words so he just followed Alex's lead.

Flo was waiting in the hall. When they entered she handed both men a drink and left as soon as they were both seated near the fire, squeezing Alex's shoulder as she passed him. Nathan saw the gesture and suddenly saw clearly that there was more affection in that gesture than was warranted from just a housekeeper. Alex was oblivious; in fact he didn't seem to notice anything at all. That worried Nathan more than anything. He suddenly wished Vicky was there with him. She knew how to handle things like this much better than he did. He felt awkward and at a loss to know what to say to the grieving man he sat with, even though he desperately wanted to help him.

'I am sorry I did not make it back in time, I wanted to be by your side but it took some time for your letter to reach me and I feared I would not be in time. How was she at the end?'

Alex didn't reply, didn't even seem to have heard him speak. Nathan had kept talking, finding it more and more difficult to think of things to say in this one sided conversation.

254

Flo eventually came to his rescue, asking for help in reaching something from a shelf for her. Nathan of course had known this for the spurious request that it was, but somewhat relieved rose to follow her from the room. Once they were out of earshot of the great hall, Flo turned to Nathan.

'If only you could have arrived before her passing, Nathan. It has been very hard on Alex and there was only us at the funeral.'

There were tears in her eyes as she spoke and once again he saw the affection she held for Alex.

'Zara was quite lucid at the end. She even said sorry to Alex for what she had become. I think that was the hardest thing for Alex to bear, but in some way I think it has brought him comfort too.'

Even in this most sombre moment Nathan had smiled inwardly at the way Flo spoke of the family, using their first names.

'I would like to visit her grave, Flo but know not if I should wait for Alex to invite me.'

'He will come round, I think your arrival has brought many things into focus to him and he is working through them in his head.'

Nathan was once more struck by just how insightful Flo was. She knew the family so well after all the years she had spent in service here, but it was more than that, he could not put his finger on it, but it was almost as though she could see their thoughts.

Flo had been right; Alex was somewhat more his old self that evening as Flo had served them dinner. He spoke of Zara and what had happened since Nathan had last been there. How she had seemed to be happier and more settled. How she had seemed to be improving, almost as though she was relearning how to live. She had even ventured out of her room for short periods.

Nathan found himself wishing that he had been here to see her, been here to add his encouragement and share her victories and successes.

'Would you like to visit her, Nathan? I would like you too and I am sure it is your wish to say goodbye.'

'Yes I would very much like to pay my respects to her.'

'In the morning then, I am tired Nathan, I think I shall retire. It is odd, for years I have been unable to sleep but now I feel tired most of the time and find that I am in need of more sleep than I have done since my childhood. Sleep brings a time when I don't have to think, although my dreams are not pleasant. Goodnight.'

255

Nathan sat by the fire for some time, He had feared that Alex would have taken Zara's death badly but had not realised just how much it would have affected him.

The sunny day seemed like an intrusion on the older man's grief, Nathan stood by Alex beside Zara's grave. Neither man had spoken; each was lost in their own thoughts. Finally Alex broke the silence.

'It was a waste of a life. For a time she had everything she wanted, I know she was spoilt by both myself and by the Tsar's children, but she deserved better than this end, a good marriage and children to love. I would have adored my grandchildren, Nathan, they would have wanted for nothing.'

Nathan looked at Alex, was there a touch of bitterness there? Did he blame Vicky for what had happened to Zara? He supposed he couldn't blame him.

'I had hoped Vicky would come with you. I would like to have seen her, but I understand why she did not.'

It was almost as though Alex had read his thoughts.

'There are many reasons why Vicky wouldn't come, not least of them being that she thought seeing her would upset you. She fears that you blame her for all that has happened and that she would receive scant welcome. I think she is scared to come back too, I think she fears for her sanity if she had to face what she has done. It haunts her Alex, I don't think she will ever forgive herself for what has happened and doesn't think that anyone else will forgive her either.'

'Forgive is a big word Nathan, but I don't blame Vicky for anything. What happened that night was appalling and maybe our family deserved everything we got. I don't know but for me at least it is in the past now. The passing of Zara is an ending, an ending of meaningful life for me. What else is there for me now? A lonely old man sitting in a house haunted by memories and waiting to die, that is my future, bleak as it is.'

Nathan could think of nothing to say, he had no answer for Alex. Briefly he thought of asking him to join them in India but decided against it. He knew Alex would never leave Halleswell hall, it was his home now and he would not leave Zara behind.

A commotion woke him and he sat up with a start. People were hurrying to the rail and chattering excitedly as they looked and pointed toward the horizon. Moving his eyes to follow where they were looking he could see land. England at last, a shiver ran down his spine, it had grown cold whilst he had slept but it was not cold enough to evoke that reaction. He didn't have time to ponder though as he was swept along with the crowd, all eager to get a first glimpse of England.

It wasn't long before the ship docked and he was on a train that would take him toward Devon. His impatience was growing and worry that he would be too late was starting to gnaw at him. He imagined the scene if he had arrived too late, he imagined arriving in time. Eventually he told himself to stop thinking about it at all. There was no way of speeding up his journey so there was no point in worrying. What would face him when he arrived would not be changed by him worrying at it.

As he came out of the railway station he looked around. Flo had said that Alex's car would be sent for him. Nathan was a bit nervous of that. He didn't have much experience with cars. They were not very common in India yet.

A voice hailed him from outside the station and it was not long before he was sitting in the back of the Rolls Royce as it purred along the country lanes. In other circumstances Nathan would have enjoyed the ride immensely but as it was he could only think of reaching Halleswell Hall as quickly as possible. He hadn't realised how tense he had been for the whole of the journey until the car pulled into the avenue that led up to the house. He let out an audible sigh and sat back in his seat as he waited for the car to pull to a halt.

Flo was waiting for him and opened the car door as soon as it stopped.

Nathan got out and was surprised as Flo flung her arms around his neck. 'Thank God you have made it in time Nathan. I have prayed that you would. Oh Nathan he is so sick, I think he has only held on to say goodbye to you.' Flo was crying now, desperate tears of someone driven beyond control, mixed in with a profound relief to see Nathan.

Nathan hesitantly returned her embrace. 'It's alright Flo I am here now.' He was amazed how calm his voice sounded because inside he felt anything but.

Flo pulled away, wiping her eyes and looking embarrassed.

'Come in Nathan, you will want to see him straight away of course.' She led the way into the house. Nathan followed, thinking how much she had aged in the two years since he had seen her last. Nathan knew she was about his age, but she looked older, that made him wonder what people thought about him, was he starting to age too?

He shook his head; there were far more important things for him to be thinking about right now. Nathan had expected Flo to lead him to one of the bedrooms and was surprised when she led him into the great hall. Alex was sitting by the fire. He was asleep, wrapped in a blanket. His breathing was ragged and he was coughing frequently. There was a small trickle of blood running down his chin from the corner of his mouth.

His eyes opened as they approached and the semblance of a smile crossed his features as he watched them.

Nathan hurried forward and took Alex's hand in his. 'Alex.' He said, not knowing what to add. He was shocked at how ill Alex looked. He didn't know what he had expected, but this was not it.

'It is nearly time for me to join my Zara.' He whispered in a rasping voice. 'Do not mourn for me Nathan; I go readily enough to rejoin my family. It is what I have wanted to do since my Zara died.' A racking cough interrupted him.

'I am glad I have had the chance to see you. I think it is right for me to hand over Halleswell while I still live. I know that you may not want to move in straightaway. I know you have responsibilities and so Flo has agreed to stay on and look after the place for you once I am gone.'

This long speech seemed to exhaust him and another bout of coughing had him leaning back in his chair gasping for air.

Flo stifled a sob and turned away, hiding her face from both men. Nathan realised in that moment just how hard it was going to be for Flo to be parted from Alex, and what a sacrifice she was going to make to carry out his wishes.

'I will take ownership of the Hall, Alex, and I will do my best to be a good master to it, but as you say I have responsibilities and don't know when I will be able to come here. Now I think you need some rest.'

'Rest, I will have plenty of time for that soon enough no doubt, but you are right I am so tired, tired to my very soul, tired of this life if truth be told. I don't go to my bed anymore, I can't manage the stairs and I refuse to lie up in my room so I do my sleeping here, such that it is. It is getting late though and you have had a long journey so you get some rest and I will see you in the morning.' With that he closed his eyes and leaned back. Nathan took that as his cue to leave. He rose, and with a glance at Flo, who nodded to him, he turned and led the way from the room.

'I have put you in your old room Nathan I hope that is ok.'

'That's fine Flo, here let me take that.' He said to Flo who was struggling to lift his heavy suitcase.

'Thank you, I am not as strong as I once was.' Her voice was strained; weariness was taking its toll on her.

'Are you sleeping Flo? You look exhausted.'

'I can't sleep, I catnap but I have to be on hand should Alex need me.'

'I will stay with him tonight; you get some rest while you can.'

'Thank you Nathan, I won't deny that I need sleep more than anything right now but please wake me should the need arise. Promise me.'

Nathan knew what she meant, although she didn't actually say the words. 'I promise Flo. I will wake you.'

'Good night then.' She said and turned to go up the stairs. Nathan returned to the great hall and sitting, prepared for a night of vigil with Alex.

Sitting there, he had a chance to think about the past, about the events that had linked himself to Alex. In many ways it was odd, they were so different, and Alex was used to mixing with royalty and being friends with rulers across the globe. Thinking about Alex, he realised what an amazing life he had lived. What would it have been like to be at a ball in the Russian palace as guests of the Tsar? He could only imagine from what Alex had told him. Yes Alex had seen some things in his life but he had lived through more than his fair share of hurt and torment too. He was a great man, a heart full of compassion for his fellow man, and he was going to have a very hard job indeed living up to the standards that Alex had set him. He thought how he would tell Vicky too. He didn't think she would exactly jump at the chance of moving back to England, no, she would refuse point blank if he even suggested it. He was still torn in two with no hope of bringing the two halves together.

He berated himself, here he was thinking of the future when his thoughts should be with the old man sitting across the room. Now he had settled, his breathing was somewhat easier and Nathan was pleased that the regular rhythm meant that Alex was properly asleep.

The following morning broke sunny and warm. The light of the first rays of the sun crept slowly across the room. Nathan woke with a start, and then rubbed at his neck that had become stiff after sleeping in an unnatural position in the chair. He glanced over at Alex. He was still asleep, restless now as the sun touched his face.

Flo hurried in, a look on her face that suggested concern at having spent so long away from Alex. Once she had seen that he was alright and still sleeping she went to prepare breakfast. Nathan went with her.

'Did he have a good night?' Asked Flo over her shoulder as she started cooking.

'Yes, he seemed settled once he fell asleep. He is very sick though isn't he?'

Flo stifled a sob in answer. 'I don't think he will be with us much longer, he weakens by the day. I don't know what I am going to do without him. I will keep my promise to him, but it will be hard living in this big old house with only my memories to keep me company. You get back to him and I will bring break-fast in a little while.'

Alex was stirring when Nathan re-entered the room, his waking accompanied by a fresh bout of coughing. Fresh blood appeared at the corner of his mouth which he wiped on a handkerchief.

He looked over at Nathan and said. 'I do not think that I have long left Nathan, and there are some things I need to tell you. Firstly the masters of this house across the centuries kept a journal, their memoirs if you like. They make a complete history of the Meverall family. Over the years I have translated the writing into modern English and condensed many volumes into one book. I thought that maybe it would become the legacy of our family'

He paused for breath, a rasping of his lungs spoke of his worsening condition, but he was strong minded enough to say his piece.

'I would have you read that work, Nathan, I think you will find it interesting and may help you understand the family. My version has omissions. There are things about my life that I would not have becoming public, things that are still too raw for me to share with just anyone.'

Nathan could understand Alex not being able to write about certain things that had happened in his life, and Tim had many issues that he had battled over within himself.

'Both Tim and myself did write our whole stories however, in a book that I have hidden with the rest of the originals. That version is for family eyes only. That one includes our stories in full but you know our history anyway don't you. If you get the chance you could add your words to my version, and the original if you would.' Alex needed a long pause before he continued. 'This is the important bit Nathan, I don't know if she told you but Vicky wrote to me some time ago. I didn't answer, I didn't know how.' He was wheezing heavily now but was determined to carry on.

Nathan had to listen very carefully to hear his words that were barely more than a rasping whisper.

'The letter is with my other papers, I would have you read it and maybe you will understand why I couldn't answer, and maybe it will help you understand your wife better too.'

Nathan still didn't answer, he knew Vicky had written to Alex, and knew that letter had caused her deep pain, but he didn't know its contents and wasn't sure that he should read it either. Alex made it very difficult for him to refuse however.

'I would also have you take a message to Vicky. Tell her that I forgive her any part in our misfortunes and ask that she does not torment herself any more over our fate. With my death that chapter is closed and she should take it as such.'

Nathan could do nothing but agree to do as he was asked. 'I will do as you ask; Alex and I think it will put Vicky's mind at rest to hear your words.

'Something else, I would like you to arrange an exhibition of Tim's work. There is his war work, but there are also earlier pieces, ask Flo to find them for you.'

'That is something I will happily do. Tim deserves to be remembered and his art is a fine way to honour him.'

Alex closed his eyes, the conversation had cost him more energy than he had left and by the time Flo came in with the breakfast Alex was coughing and gasping for breath. Nathan was kneeling in front of him, helping him sit and giving what comfort he could. The coughing had been going on for some minutes before coming to an abrupt halt. The silence was deafening until with a moan Flo dropped the breakfast tray with a loud clatter of silver and breaking crockery hitting the floor.

The funeral was three days later. It was a small affair. A few of the villagers were there to pay their respects along with Flo and Nathan of course. Nathan thought that it was somehow wrong. Alex should have had a fine ceremony and been buried with the honour he deserved but Flo had said that he had wanted it this way and so Nathan had to accept it as Alex's wish.

Nathan stared down at the coffin in its newly dug grave. He silently reaffirmed that he would do the things that he had been asked to do and that he would honour his memory as best he could.

That evening, Nathan was sat in Alex's chair looking through Tim's portfolio. There were hundreds of sketches and paintings in the thick folder. Once more he was astounded at the quality of the work. One piece in particular held his interest. It was a picture of a swan on the lake in front of this very house. There was something about it that Nathan could not quite put his finger on but he knew it was important. That picture would not go for sale but would have pride of place on the great hall wall along with the many other masterpieces. It would not look out of place thought Nathan. He was tired, it had been a long and stressful day and he was getting a headache.

He would be leaving tomorrow. He could not wait to see Vicky again, he had been away weeks already and it would be more before he saw her again. He thought of Flo, she had been deeply affected by Alex's passing but from what Nathan had seen she was determined to continue running the house.

She had understood Nathan too. 'You will not come back for many years will you Nathan?' She had asked.

'No Flo I don't think that will be possible. I will not be parted from Vicky anymore. My heart yearns for her every day that we are apart and I do not think I could bear to be parted from her again.'

Flo had nodded and left it at that.

Nathan knew an artist who would deal with Tim's exhibition. After he had seen the work he had been very impressed and said that the works would sell for large sums if the right buyers came to the gallery. Nathan was pleased, Tim should be recognised for his talent and this was the best way he could think of honouring him.

Everything was in place; he had carried out Alex's wishes in this country. It was time to go, time to face the second part of the tasks laid down for him. It was hard for Nathan to leave Flo, an affinity had grown between them but he was eager to get back as soon as possible.

The last thing he saw as the Rolls Royce drove slowly from the house was Flo, standing by the door waving a white handkerchief. He sighed, he was on his way. Every mile brought him closer to his Vicky.

He was on the boat before he remembered what Alex had said about the book of the history of the Meverall family. It was too late by then. There had been so much happening in such a short time that the book had slipped his mind. He would have liked to have read it. One day, he thought, one day.

SALLY INVESTIGATES

Sally Evans was exited, she was nervous too. The other girls in the back of the lorry were a bit older and seemed to know each other well from the way they were chatting and giggling as they bumped down the country lanes. Most of the girls came from London, but Sally was a local girl. She had lived in Devon all her life and she knew the country-side that they left in their wake like the back of her hand. She had been very happy to have got a posting so close to home, but at the same time she supposed she had wished for a posting somewhere foreign and exotic, yes she would have liked that. Palm trees and golden sands, her beloved Jim running through the soft blue surf to meet her, throwing their arms about each other as they kissed a kiss of long parting.

'Oi, Sally, you off in dreamland again?'

It took her a moment to realise one of the girls was talking to her. 'Oh sorry, guess I was dreaming.'

The other girl smiled at the younger. Looking at Sally she saw a pretty young lady, blonde with shoulder length hair showing beneath her blue cap and her slim build filling out her uniform in all the right places.

The girl doing the talking was a couple of years older than Sally, more than pretty and she knew it too. She had altered her skirt, making it at least three inches shorter than regulation and she wore more makeup than was strictly allowed.

Even though they had all gone through their training course together, Sally was still not completely comfortable with the rest of the girls. They were all town girls, loud and confident whereas she was a country girl who had led a completely different life to the rest of them. They were a good bunch though and they had taken Sally under their wing.

'Sorry Sarah, I was just thinking.'

'I bet you were. Which beach were you on this time?' asked Sarah with a grin.

Sally didn't answer, slightly embarrassed, but she did manage a smile.

'Do you know where we are Sally?' Asked Anne, she was a timid little thing, short and mousey with glasses. She should have looked plain but there was something about her that seemed to attract boys, not that she encouraged their advances but she didn't exactly push them away either.

'Oh yes, we are nearly there now. That last village we passed through was Braughton so we will be there soon. Halleswell Hall, who would have thought my first posting, would have been to that place.'

'You know it then, but you don't sound too keen on it, sounds rather grand to me. I've always wanted to live in a manor house.'

'There are stories about Halleswell Hall in these parts. The house is cursed or so I have heard, not sure why, but there have been stories about that house and the Meverall family that own it for years now. No one goes there unless they have to and then they want to leave as soon as possible. They say there is a spooky atmosphere about the place.'

All the girls were listening now; one or two of them were looking slightly alarmed.

Sally was starting to feel self conscious with all the attention focused on her, but at the same time was enjoying it. 'Well, the story goes that after the murder of one of the ladies of the house a young girl cursed the house and the family. It is said that they have all died horrible deaths over the years and that the curse is yet to be broken. They say the murdered lady haunts the grounds of the house and that it is not safe to go out at night as she can't rest until the curse is broken.'

Some of the girls were looking scared now and some of them plainly didn't believe a word of it.

There was much more that Sally could have told them about, the mad woman that had been locked in her room for years and the way in which the first lady had died, but she was not sure how much of it was true and how much had been tales that had grown with the telling over the years.

The road noise changed to gravel as they entered Halleswell Hall. Most of the girls pulled up the edges of the lorry flaps to get their first glimpse of their new home. For most of them it came as a bit of a culture shock, perhaps they had been imagining a fairy-tale mansion, but the brooding house they saw was certainly not what many of them had been expecting. Sally of course knew what the Hall looked like and couldn't hide a smile at the reaction of some of the other girls.

Flo was standing by the door together with Captain Reeves. Flo was to look after the girls during their stay at Halleswell and she was putting on a good show of being a stern task mistress. Captain Reeves looked like he would be no pushover either. He was a big man, in his forties but still well muscled. His moustache gave him a stern look, and he had that military air about him as though he wished he was seeing action somewhere rather than babysitting a bunch of girls. Some of the girls groaned at the sight of them, they had been hoping for an easy life out here in the country. It wasn't starting out too well for them.

When the lorry stopped the girls hopped down and formed up to salute the Captain. Returning the salute he invited the girls in and told them to wait in the great hall for instructions. Flo was silent but indicated with her arm that they should follow her.

None of the girls could resist staring around as they entered. Many of them had their mouths hanging open. They had never seen anything like this before. Sally had not seen the inside of the house before either, so she was just as overwhelmed as the rest of them. Even with the furniture removed to make way for the maps and charts that the girls would be using for their part of the war effort, the room was still an impressive sight. All the artworks had been left on the walls and the heavy velvet curtains gave the room the feeling of opulence that it deserved.

After a minute they formed up into a loose rank and waited for the Captain to give them instructions. When he did he was quite informal.

'Right girls, as you can see this is where we will be doing our part to scupper the plans of Jerry. When you are here you are in my charge. Normal military rules will apply while you are on duty, and at all other times you are in the charge of Flo.' He said, indicating with his arm to where she stood on the stairs. Standing a couple of steps up gave Flo an even more powerful presence and when she started speaking all the girls were listening carefully. Flo grinned inwardly; she would have no problems with this lot.

'Whilst you are in this house there are rules that will be obeyed. Some are at the request of Major Irvine-Meverall, who owns this house, and some of them are my rules. Both sets will be obeyed to the letter with no excuses, am I understood?'

There were a few hushed groans from the listening girls, but none raised a voice in dissent.

'Right listen up,' Flo was enjoying herself now; she was going to like her new role as chaperone she thought.

'First rule, the upstairs bedrooms are out of bounds except the ones I will show you. There is to be no smoking in those rooms either. You will use the bathroom that I will show you. The others are out of bounds. Downstairs you may go where you please, except the study, which will be locked. I would ask you to treat all Hall property with respect as it is only on loan to you. Blackout regulations are to be strictly obeyed for obvious reasons.'

Flo was really rising to her subject now and the girls were starting to go pale in front of this barrage of rules. 'Next we have some rules that are of my making. Firstly, you will not bring any boys into the house for any reason. You will all be indoors by ten o'clock at night and lights out will be at eleven o'clock.

I will wake you at seven in the morning, when you will bathe and then report to me in the kitchen to help prepare, both your breakfast and that of the officers who will be on duty in the great hall by then.'

Silence met the end of Flo's speech. She nodded as if satisfied and walked off to the kitchen. Once she was there she burst out laughing. The look on those young girls' faces had been a picture. She had made her point she thought. Those girls would be as good as gold and give her no trouble.

Back in the great hall Captain Reeves was continuing. 'Your duties will be assigned to you tomorrow. The rest of today you will be free to settle in and find your way around. Flo will be back in a moment and will show you where to take your bags.

It wasn't long before the girls were settling in to their rooms. Beds had been added to the originals in two bedrooms meaning that four shared in each. There were minor squabbles about who got to sleep in the ornate beds that had been in those rooms for many, many years, but eventually it was decided that they would swap on a weekly basis and everyone was happy. Sally was sharing with Anne, Sarah and another girl called Pauline. She was stick thin and wore a slightly sour expression on her face. Sally had been wary of her when they had first met, but had found that belying her expression, Pauline was a friendly girl with a quick sense of humour, although she did have a liking for practical jokes that had got her into trouble more than once.

They were left to their own devices that first evening after Flo had dished them up a meal. Sally and the others used the time to explore the house, or the bits that they were allowed to anyway. None of them wanted to get in trouble for going where they shouldn't.

Something happened to Sally as they were walking along one of the landings. They were just walking past a locked door when she suddenly went cold, none of the others seemed to notice anything but for some reason there was an echo of a scream in the back of her mind. She didn't think much of it, but it was odd that it had happened there, right outside one of the rooms they were forbidden to enter.

That night none of the girls slept particularly well. The old hall made night noises, that none of the girls was used to, and with the excitement of most of them being on their first posting none of them felt much like sleep.

It was a different story of course, at seven o'clock the next morning when Flo came to wake them. They all suddenly wanted nothing more but to be allowed to sleep. It wasn't going to happen however, and soon they were all at work in the kitchen helping to prepare breakfast.

After breakfast it was time for them to take up their assigned duties. Some of them were answering the telephone or telegraph. Some of them made up a small typing pool and a couple of them ended up as general dogsbodies who seemed to spend an awful lot of time making tea.

It didn't take any of them long to settle into the pattern of military life at Halleswell Hall and the routine soon became second nature to them. It was not all work however. Once they had all become proficient at their various tasks, a rota system was introduced to allow time off. It was this time that the girls looked forward to, the chance to go down to the village and have a drink or two at the Smugglers.

The locals were pleased to see the young ladies there too. Some nights became impromptu parties. Sarah especially, was popular with the men in the pub. Some of the farm workers paid her a lot of attention. Sally was known to most of the people in the pub, her family had lived in the village for generations, before her parents had moved a couple of villages away, so she didn't warrant the same attention the others received. Many of them knew she was devoted to Jim Cartwright anyway, so she did end up being a bit left out. She didn't mind though, she was quite happy to watch the young men making fools of themselves to impress her friends. Sally was counting down the days. Jim was due home on leave and she couldn't wait to see him.

Sally was working on the telegraph sending and receiving messages from the Asian theatre of war. She didn't take a lot of notice of much that passed through her hands. It was not for her to interpret the information that she handled, it was her job just to pass it on to others whose job it was.

She did come to look forward to messages from one Major in India. After they had been exchanging messages for some weeks he started adding a few words for her on the end of his missives. Sally just thought that they were friendly messages from a Major in India, and it wasn't until one day that he asked if she was happy living in his house that she realised who it was that she was receiving messages from. She vaguely remembered seeing Nathan Irvine- Meverall once; he had been sitting in the back of a Rolls Royce as it had driven through the village, although she hadn't known who he was at the time, the memory had stuck for some reason. She had thought at the time how handsome he had looked in his uniform. She had been a much younger girl then, so she guessed that he must be quite an old man now.

Sally was sitting reading in their bedroom one night when an exited Anne came in.

'Sally I need you to do something for me.'

'Oh?' Sally was wary, the last time Sarah had asked her to cover for her they had got caught by Flo and got a real lecture.

'Please Sally, tonight's the night.'

'Tonight's the night for what?'

'Oh Sally don't be dense, tonight is the night Dennis and me, well you know.'

'Oh I see,' said Sally, blushing.

'Well, will you do it?'

'Ok but you be careful. Have you thought this through Anne? It is not like you to jump into things like this.'

'Of course,' said Anne, not really listening. She was going through her clothes, holding dresses up in front of her and discarding one after another.

Sally was thinking about her Jim, so far away, she wasn't even quite sure where his unit was. The last she had heard from him he had been on a troop ship on the way to India. That had been over a month ago now; still the post wasn't exactly reliable at the moment so she wasn't too worried. She did miss him terribly though. She thought back to their first time and knew what Anne must be feeling. She had been a bag of nerves.

Life at Halleswell was good, if hard work for the girls. In the main they were enjoying themselves.

Sally was getting the breakfast as usual. It had become habit now and she did it almost automatically. That morning though she was not really awake having been down at the Smugglers the night before and she managed to knock a cup off the table, smashing it into a thousand pieces. After clearing up the mess she reached into the cupboard for a replacement. Captain Reeves liked his tea to be in a bone china cup and Sally had to search through the cups to find one that would be suitable. Her hand was in the back of the shelf when an odd feeling came over her. It was almost lethargy but more calming, a feeling of peace.

Anne came into the kitchen and sat at the table with her head in her hands. She didn't look at all well.

Sally withdrew her hand and forgot that odd feeling as she rushed to the table.

'Anne are you alright? You look awful.'

'I feel awful, don't know why, I didn't drink much last night and felt fine most of yesterday. It's odd I felt a bit sick yesterday morning too.'

Sally looked hard at her. 'Anne you're not.'

'No I can't be.' Anne looked shocked and scared at the same time.

She started to cry. 'Sally I can't be, me and Dennis only did it the once. I know I am a bit late, well a couple of weeks, but then I have never been regular.'

'I think we are going to have to get you to the doctor and do a test aren't we, to be sure of it.'

There was no way of doing it without involving Flo, and although both girls were petrified when they approached her they were surprised by the support they received from her. She got Anne in to see Dr Griffiths that very afternoon. Sally sat on her bed chewing her fingernails as she waited for Flo to bring Anne home.

Anne rushed into the room and flung herself on her bed crying hysterically. It didn't take much to know that the test had been a positive one.

'Oh Anne,' said Sally rushing over to put her arm round her friend.

It took Anne some time to calm down enough to speak coherently. 'I can't be pregnant, I can't. Its not fair.' The crying returned with renewed vigour.

Sally didn't know what to say. She tried with, 'everything will be fine, it will sort itself out.' But that didn't work.

'How can it be fine? I am having a baby.' She howled.

Sarah had chosen that moment to come into the room.

'Anne you're not are you?'

Sally nodded her head.

'Crikey, that's bad luck.'

A look from Sally told Sarah she was not helping and she left the room, undoubtedly to tell the other girls, thought Sally.

Three days later they were all standing on the drive in front of the house as they waved goodbye to Anne who waved back tearfully from the back seat of the car that was slowly driving away from the house.

Sarah, insensitive as ever said, 'Anyone coming down the smugglers tonight? I am meeting George Collins, says he has something special up his sleeve for tonight. I can't wait.'

Sally just shook her head. 'Don't you ever learn?' She said as she stalked off with a disgusted look on her face.

'What?' Said Sarah, spreading her arms wide.

Sally found herself outside the locked room on the landing with Sarah. Once again she felt that creepy sensation entering her soul. She shuddered and backed away. 'What's the matter with you?' Asked Sarah, watching Sally with an amused look on her face. She obviously felt nothing.

'You can't feel it?' Responded Sally, 'you can't feel the fear coming from that door?'

'What are you talking about Sally? It's a room, and a locked one at that.'

'Why is it locked though?'

Sarah laughed. 'Will you stop answering a question with a question? There you have got me doing it now.' She said with a grin.

'If you are so interested why don't you steal Flo's keys and have a look. No one would know would they?'

For an instant Sally actually contemplated doing just that. She immediately came to her senses and looked at Sarah with a look of terror even worse than the one she had given the locked door.

Sarah laughed again. 'Oh well there is probably nothing worth looking at in there anyway is there?'

'No probably not,' replied Sally, with a backward glance at the door they were walking away from. The room would not leave her mind, it was as though it was eating her from the inside, trying to make her find a way to enter.

Something happened a few days later. Maybe it was chance, maybe something else was to blame, but as Sally was washing up in the kitchen late one evening, Flo came in with another tray. As she had placed it on the table someone had shouted her name and she had turned and left the way she had come. Sally thought nothing of it until she looked down at the tray as she picked it up to take to the sink. To her astonishment there was a large bunch of keys sitting alongside the dirty plate.

Sally couldn't believe her eyes. Flo never let those keys out of her sight, not for an instant. It was a snap decision. This would probably be the only chance she would ever have.

Quickly she washed the last of the plates. No point in making it completely obvious what she was doing. Grabbing the keys and an oil lamp she walked to the door and peered into the corridor. Her heart was thumping against the wall of her chest. Flo was not in evidence, so she crept along the corridor, her ears alert for any sound of footsteps coming the other way. She saw no one and managed to slip across the great hall and up the stairs with no one seeing. The further she went on with this, the more terrified she was becoming; more terrified that Flo would catch her than anything else.

Passing the top of the stairs and heading for the back landing she headed into darkness. She didn't dare use the lights; someone would see them for sure. Climbing a second flight of stairs led her to the corridor she was looking for. The lantern she carried shed enough light for her to see by, but it cast shadows up the walls that were unnerving and somehow sinister. A little voice in the back of her mind was telling her to go back; this was not a great idea. She forced those thoughts back with an almost physical push. She was starting to feel a bit sick; her stomach was dancing along with the shadows on the wall.

It was not long before she came upon the door she was looking for. The feeling of fear that assailed her here overrode her fear of Flo. This was real fear, and it was coming from behind the door that she was attempting to unlock. The fourth key she tried did the trick and turned with a click that sounded very loud in the silence of the night. Her hand stopped moving as the key came to rest in its unlocked position. She noticed her hand was shaking slightly as she moved it to turn the knob that would open the way to what ever awaited her.

Slowly the door opened, surprisingly it didn't creak or scrape, making Sally's gritted teeth unnecessary.

Holding the lamp up in front of her, she was unprepared for what she saw. It was the fact that there was no ghoul or ghost waiting to strike her down, the fact that it was an ordinary room, or at least it looked as such on first inspection.

A more detailed inspection saw things come into the light of the slightly shaking lantern. It was a very feminine room. A large bed with a bright pink bedspread dominated the room. This stood on a plush ornately patterned carpet. Outside the carpet the floorboards were dark and covered in a layer of dust, showing that no one had been in here for years.

Carefully Sally took a long stride, almost jumping to land on the carpet so as to not leave any signs of her intrusion into the room's peace.

A large dark wardrobe stood across the far corner of the room. A matching dressing table stood against the wall at the foot of the bed. The mirror at the back of the dressing table was cracked from top to bottom, sending the light of Sally's lantern in all directions, and making her reflection become a surreal image.

There was nothing in the room to suggest why she was so terrified of it but she knew where she was. A glance at the window overlooking the dark woods confirmed it. The bars covering the glass were obviously to keep someone in rather than out. This was the mad woman's room. Rumours had being doing the rounds in the village for years about the young lady who had gone mad and needed to be locked up for her own, and the rest of the households safety. She tried to remember the woman's name but it was just beyond her grasp.

Slowly she walked across the room to the wardrobe. Hesitating only slightly, she opened the door. This one did creak. Very shrill it sounded to Sally's taut nerves. She was sure the rest of the house must have heard it, but as she listened carefully there was no sound of movement, so she opened it the rest of the way and held her lamp up to see what was inside. The rail contained women's dresses, rather old fashioned but rich in quality and Sally thought they must have been the height of fashion in their day. Underneath the dresses, almost hidden by the flowing skirts was a pile of books. Some of them looked ancient but some of them were newer. Inquisitiveness got the better of her and she lifted the first book off the pile. She rested her lantern on the dressing table and held the book close to read the title.

The diary and memoirs of Alex Stewart

Turning the pages slowly, she was amazed at what she was reading. Zara, that was the name she couldn't remember. Suddenly someone called her name and the sound of it echoed around the empty room. Sally nearly jumped out of her skin. She got to her feet quickly and without thinking stuffed the book she had been reading into the pocket of her apron. Grabbing the lantern she charged across the room, pausing only to lock the door and pocket the keys, she ran as fast as her legs would carry her. She flew down the stairs and then paused at the bottom to compose herself. It wouldn't do to let Flo see she was flustered or she would want to know why.

She came down the main stairs and Flo was waiting at the bottom. She didn't look angry, in fact she looked frightened as though she had just had a shock.

Sally decided to get in first.

'There you are Flo, I have been looking for you. I found your keys on the tray you left in the kitchen.'

'Oh thank you dear,' she said as she absently took them off her.

'Sally I think you had better come in here and sit down.'

Sally was suddenly afraid, what could make Flo suddenly so nice, she was usually so hard and assured. Something had happened while she had been upstairs, she knew it.

Once they were seated Flo said. 'Sally a letter arrived for you just now by special messenger. I am sorry.' There were tears in her eyes as she handed Sally a brown official envelope.

'No,' whispered Sally. She recognised the official ministry seal and knew what that letter contained. 'No,' she said again, she was crying now, wracking sobs of despair.

'Don't jump the gun Sally; it might not be what you think.' From the cracking of her voice, Flo didn't seem to agree with her own words.

Sally took the letter and slit the envelope. It didn't cross her mind as to why the letter had come to her and not to Jim's mother.

Inside was not the official piece of printed paper she had been expecting, but a hand written letter.

Dear Sally (Jim told me your name)
I apologise for the official envelope it must have given you quite a fright, but it was the only way I could get this letter to you quickly.

Jim Cartwright was brought to our hospital a few weeks ago. He was in a bad way. It seems he became separated from his unit in the jungles of Burma and through a wound and disease he wandered for weeks, avoiding all human contact for fear of capture by the Japanese. The good Lord knows how he managed to get this far.

He was unable to communicate for some weeks but he has been making good progress lately. We are fairly confident that by the time you receive this letter he will not be far off coming home.

He has spoken of his love for you and his wish that I should write to you after we had found that we all knew each other. Rest assured that Jim is on the mend and will make a full recovery.

Look for his return around the end of June. He will be coming to Halleswell.

In friendship
Major Nathan Irving- Meverall.

New tears were streaming down Sally's face when she lowered the letter, now though they were tears of relief. She turned to Flo and smiled through her tears.

'My Jim is ok, he's coming home.'

Flo threw her arms around Sally, her own relief very evident.

Sally showed her the letter and Flo said. 'Mister Nathan is a very kind man, Sally. I hope you meet him one day. I know you would like him. Now you get off to bed, it has been quite an evening for you hasn't it?'

Sally's head was a whirl of emotion; she just nodded to Flo and headed up the stairs.

It wasn't until she got to her room and started to undress that she felt the book in her apron pocket. Suddenly she felt very guilty. Both Flo and Major Nathan had been so kind to her and now she had stolen from them. There was no way she could get back into that room and put the book back and she couldn't let Flo find it, so she wrapped it in an old dress she no longer wore, and hid it in the bottom of her trunk where no one would find it.

June was warm and dry that year of 1944. The sun cast shadows across the parklands of Halleswell. Nightingales serenaded all who would hear them. For Sally the month couldn't pass quickly enough and as it drew to a close she began to feel more and more nervous and excited. Her Jim was coming home. She worried too, what had his experiences in the jungles of Burma done to him? Would he be the same young man she had loved since she was a little girl? She had no answers, and the longer the waiting went on the more those questions, and many others started to eat into her. She couldn't sleep, that only brought nightmares of her Jim crawling through thick jungle being set upon my every monster imaginable. She began to look ill herself, bags under her eyes and she was starting to look painfully thin. Flo was so worried about her that she was close to getting the doctor in to see her.

The end of the month came and went with no news, and no sign of Jim. Sally took to sitting in the window of her bedroom, staring down the drive hoping to see the figure of her man walking towards her. Hundreds of times she imagined that scene and on the sixth of July when her vision became reality she didn't believe it at first. A man in khaki uniform with a kit bag slung over his shoulder was walking down the path, exactly as she had imagined it hundreds of times. She rubbed her eyes and looked again. It was real. He was here. She flew out of the room, colliding with Sarah who was just entering.

'Hey what's the hurry?' Said Sarah, but Sally didn't answer, she was halfway down the landing before Sarah finished her sentence.

Out of the front door she raced and down the drive. Jim saw her, dropped his kitbag and started running. Both stopped when they met and their eyes drank in the sight of each other before Sally leapt into Jim's arms. Tears were flowing down Sally's cheeks as they embraced as if they never intended to let go again.

Sarah and the rest of the girls were watching now from the front door. Flo was with them and several were wiping a tear away as they watched the romantic scene on the drive.

Finally Jim let go of Sally and hand in hand they made their way toward the house.

Jim and Sally spent most of their time in each others' company over the next few days. Strolling through the sunny countryside with Jim's arm around her shoulders was something Sally could not get enough of. They talked, and although he was reluctant to start with Jim told of his experiences and how he had come to be rescued. When he had finished his tale he stopped walking and fell to one knee in front of Sally.

Holding her hand he said. 'I never want to be parted from you again Sally. Will you be my wife?'

Sally couldn't speak for a brief second that seemed to her to last an eternity.

'Yes, yes of course I will marry you,' she yelled. Jim stood up and Sally threw herself into his waiting arms, her lips met his and didn't part again for some time.

Eventually all good things come to an end.

Jim's convalescent leave was due to finish at the end of the summer. Sally began to brood as the time when they would be parted again started to loom on the horizon. She didn't think she could bear being parted from him again, not after he had come back to her once after she had thought she had lost him.

Flo came to the rescue and had a long talk with the pair of them. It was decided that their parting would be made easier if they were married before Jim had to go back to his unit.

Sally was delighted with this development, and her black mood lifted as her time was taken up with making arrangements for a rushed marriage.

Everyone chipped in, both sets of parents, delighted at the news, did their bit and the girls at Halleswell covered as many of Sally's duties as possible to give her more time to organise her big day.

The vicar at the small village church was only too pleased to agree to conduct the ceremony, and of course Flo ran the whole operation from behind the scenes.

The offer of use of the Hall and for Flo to cook the wedding breakfast was the icing on the cake for Sally. Who would have thought that a local country girl would be celebrating her marriage in a country mansion? Certainly not Sally.

Sarah and Pauline of course jumped at the chance to be bridesmaids and Flo said she would be proud to be her matron of honour. Sally had also sent a letter to Anne. She had been delighted to accept Sally's request and had promised to bring her baby for all the girls to see.

The morning of the wedding arrived. Late August did not disappoint with the weather. Warm sunshine and a clear deep blue sky greeted Sally as she woke. For a while she lay in bed smiling at the ceiling. 'I'm getting married today,' she told no one in particular.

Her peace didn't last long. There was an endless list of things for her to do before the service. A flurry of activity soon engulfed her. Washing, doing her hair and makeup were all attended to by her friends. Even as the moment arrived for her to put on her wedding dress final details being checked and rechecked.

Jim sat in his room above the Smugglers chewing on his finger nails. He was ready far too early of course. He had contemplated a trip downstairs for a pint or two to steady his nerves, but he was dissuaded by Keith, his best man and his father who were keeping him company.

It was time. Sally's father had arrived to accompany her on the short journey from the hall to the church. Nathan had given his blessing for the couple to have use of his Rolls Royce for the trips to and from the church.

Sally looked stunning in the white dress her mother had made as she walked, holding on to her father's arm. He looked like he was about the proudest man alive.

The service went by as a blur for Sally and Jim. Neither of them could dare to believe that it was happening. The drive back to Halleswell was the first time they were alone as a married couple and they made the most of it. Their lips didn't part until they arrived to cheers from their guests who waited for them by the lake.

For Sally this was the happiest day of her life. She danced well into the evening. Jim of course took most of her turns around the dance floor. It was quite late when the party finally wound down, allowing the happy couple to finish their celebrating in private.

Soon Flo was the only one left. She stood in the great hall and looked around at the remnants of the wedding party. For the first time in her life she said to herself. 'I will sort this out in the morning.'

The next morning Captain Reeve wasn't in the best of moods. 'Madam you are standing in the way of the war effort. I thought this lot would be out of the way by now. I need my equipment set up.'

'And you Sir are standing in the way of my broom. Now if you will let me get on with it I will have the room clear all the quicker won't I?'

'Humph.' was the only answer he could come up with. He did get out of the way though.

Mr and Mrs Cartwright were late rising that morning. When they did come down they were greeted with an assortment of smutty remarks, mostly from Sarah of course but Sally couldn't care less. She was the happiest she had ever been in her life.

The newlyweds had three weeks together before Jim had to return to his unit. It was an emotional goodbye, filled with promises to be careful and not to worry. The whole household came out to see Jim off. There were tears from one or two of the girls but Sally saved her tears until Jim was out of sight.

It was hard for Sally to get back into routine once Jim was gone back to war, but with the help of her friends and letters from Jim she coped and even managed to join in with the girl's jokes every now and again.

They had a few more months at Halleswell Hall. The nearing of the end of the war made their jobs redundant, and at the end of the summer of 1945 they received the news that they were to close up shop. Some of the girls went to other jobs but Sally decided to stay at her parent's house to wait for Jim to come home. While she was there she picked out a house for them to live in when Jim came home. It was in Exeter. They had agreed that they wanted to live in a bigger town when they finally got together properly and the fact that it near where Sarah was going to be living made up Sally's mind.

A New World Dawns

Plumes of thick black smoke drifted lazily on the evening breeze, making eyes water not just from sorrow. Tonight Amita was joining her ancestors, her soul ascending to heaven to be reborn at the right time. Vicky and Nathan stood hand in hand joined by their mourning but putting on a brave face as Kumar took the place of Amita's dead son, carrying the scared Kusha grass to the funeral pyre. All around them the prayers to Yama were intoned by the people who had loved this special woman, but Vicky could hardly breathe with the weight of her loss. Amita had been her first friend and her confidant. Her spiritual teacher and her guide to the mystery that was India. Now, in the English manner, Vicky had something to say but feared to break the ritual. Kumar caught her eye and nodded as if to say, 'it's alright to speak now.'

Hesitantly, Vicky stepped forward, her heart beating loud in her chest. Taking courage from Nathan's look of pure love, she knew exactly what to say.

'We are gathered together to celebrate the life of a remarkable woman and to aid her spirit to depart from the empty shell that once was her body. I know that many of you here this night may think it wrong for me to speak, but Amita was no ordinary woman and I know that she would wish this so. I know little of her family; indeed I feel that we became her family after the great sickness robbed her of home and her own kin. Despite her upbringing she believed in helping those less fortunate than herself, so when her entire family died she walked four miles on an empty stomach and with a heart full of love she came to the hospital to nurse the sick and dying.'

For a moment Vicky felt she couldn't go on, but then she remembered her everlasting debt to her friend and big sister. 'No job was beneath her, she gave all that she could in a time when many people fled from the brutal epidemic that robbed so many people of this land of everything they held dear.

She could have left after that, but instead she believed in my dream of starting a place where the children could start their lives anew. She fought alongside me and my husband when we took on the British authorities to open our clinic and our orphanage to people of every faith.'

A murmur from the crowd gave Vicky the strength to carry on. 'She lived and died as a true believer in the Hindu faith, but her vision was as great as that of Bapu Ghandi himself. Only in tolerance and the willingness to embrace each and every one of us as sisters and brothers in the sight of our gods could we ever hope to gain true enlightenment.'

A gasp ran through the mourners, surely now the English lady had gone too far. Would not Dr Kumar stop this nonsense now?

'My sister, yes, she became my sister, worked besides me every step of the way.' Now Vicky's voice held a hint of anger. 'She helped me with the children that no one else would shelter. She taught me about her beliefs and I came to believe that which she taught was right. But now I see that this country will remain divided until we all keep faith with our dear sister. Ours is a legacy of hope that one day all races and religions will stand together to ease the suffering caused by the evils of power-hungry men. Amita has earned her place amongst the enlightened ones. I pray that one day I may aspire to reach that place.'

With that she stepped down and head held high she followed, blinded by tears, in the wake of her husband and their adopted son.

Back at the compound she ran to her room and cried bitter tears. 'Would they ever understand?' She thought. It wasn't Nathan who came to comfort her then, it was Kumar.

Sitting quietly by her side he took her cool hand in his warm one. 'Do not grieve mother, you spoke well and some small good may come of this. It may never happen in our lifetime, but one day the gods will smile on us and then the earth will rejoice.'

Smiling through her tears she fell into his embrace.

It seems like yesterday, she thought, when she and Nathan had stood once again at a ship's rail, this time carrying their adopted son away across the ocean to England. He had been trained well by Dr McCloud, but knowing the difficulties he would have to face, they had sent him to finish his medical training in the top medical school in England. Five years later he had returned as a fully qualified doctor, and now he was second in command at their growing hospital. The unofficial adoption would never hold up in a court of law, but he was their son in all except name.

In the spring of 1936 Vicky became sick once again and this time even she knew that her punishing schedule would have to cease. Both Kumar and Kevin had advised a long break and so she had allowed Nathan to take her up into the mountains where the air was fresher and she could relax for a while. Nathan was restless, he had been like that since he had come back from Alex's funeral, but all he would say was that Alex had died peacefully. Somehow she had felt that maybe Nathan had hurried back too quickly and there was unfinished business left in England, but Nathan remained a closed book to her sight.

The bungalow was everything she could have wished for; set almost against the mountainside it was compact, but cosy, and had a real log fireplace. Somehow her husband had managed to hire some sturdy mountain ponies and every day they would ride out along the trails that led to the tea plantations.

In the afternoons she would take a short nap and allow Nathan to explore on his own. Invariably he would return with armfuls of Orchids to lie at her feet. Other times he would be gone for hours at a time but she was too contented to enquire about what he was doing.

In the evenings a local girl would come in and cook them a sumptuous meal, departing swiftly to allow them time together to lie in front of the fire and make love slowly and tenderly.

It was then that she decided to write her own memoirs to add to the long history of the Meverall family. There was so much she had experienced and a lot of it was unknown even to her dear husband. She knew there was another war coming in the near future and dreaded that Nathan would join it, even though his leg would keep him out of the action. To be parted from him even for a day was something she dreaded, yet her conscience could never let her stand in the way of anything he wanted to do, that was the depth of her love for him.

She did have some ideas about where he went on those long, lazy afternoons. The political climate in India was like a powder keg waiting to be ignited and reason told her that the movement for independence was firing the whole country. Nathan could never let his feelings cloud his judgement, but at heart he was British and would strive to keep the peace.

The day was sultry and she said she didn't feel like riding. He was full of concern for her but she reassured him that it was nothing more than a sick headache.

'Why don't you ride out on your own?' She said. 'Give yourself a chance to explore the mountains and maybe find one of those lovely roses? Sharmilla will be happy to keep me company.'

'You are sure you'll be alright?'

'Dearest, I survived a war, fought against an epidemic, raised countless children and put up with you... so an afternoon on my own will be a mere picnic.' She replied with all the guile she could use.

That afternoon she wrote frantically as if time was short, her memories flowing onto the pages like water burst from a dam. Once they returned to Maserat she would have little time and privacy to keep adding to her journal so now she must make the most of the time she had here. Besides, she hated keeping anything from Nathan and now, more than ever, she longed for his touch both night and day.

Three days later her resolve weakened and hastily she crammed the book into her sewing bag. She would finish it, but in her heart she knew that this time was precious and she should savour every moment.

The next day they went out riding and her thoughts turned to that night when they had galloped away on Hero's back. Giggling like a schoolgirl she reminded Nathan of that night.

'I swear I loved you from that very moment, your touch sent me into raptures of delight.'

'Wanton hussy, come here and I'll teach you about passion all over again.'

'Catch me first,' she laughed, spurring the little pony on. It was no contest of course; as he laid her down on the grass she was full of an urgent longing to have him inside of her.

Later on they ambled slowly back to the bungalow and repeated the earlier passion. Afterwards she fed him dainty morsels from the cold meal, and together they shared a rare bottle of wine, their featherlike kisses tasting of wine and spices.

'We have to go back soon,' she said.

'I know,' he replied, 'but I will never forget this time together as long as I live.'

'Neither will I,' she said and with that last note she dozed off in his arms.

Extract from the journal of Victoria Cavendish-Meverall.

It all seems so long and far away now, my entrance into the world of adults. Others have written of that night, but only Nathan and I can tell the story of our frantic flight to safety. I have no doubt at all that if we had not fled then my life would have ended that night. I recall little of that desperate ride, but I do remember my new home in France and how I felt so homesick for the sight of my brothers, especially Tim.

Madam F and family were kind to me in their own way, but if Nathan had not sought shelter and work nearby then I think I would never have recovered from that evil night.

Poor Nathan, how I begged him to take me back, or at least take me to his home in Scotland. Of course that was impossible, how could he when my own father had branded him as a kidnapper and a thief? Aunt Charlotte's death was covered up as a terrible accident; otherwise the scandal would have brought down the Meverall's long before the curse took hold of them. How then could Nathan regain his lost home? It didn't seem to bother him that much though; I have a feeling that he would have felt the responsibility like a noose around his neck. There was a cousin on his father's side who inherited the whole estate, this same cousin was only too eager to make a pact with Nathan when his name was finally cleared.

I hated every minute of the strict Catholic school I attended, but later on I was glad of the discipline they installed in me, for what nurse can turn away when a man screams for his mother as death grips him by the throat?

Later.

I was such a child when war broke out and Nathan left me to fight for Britain. My silly fists pummelled his chest in anger as he came to say au revoir. I remember screaming at him,

'Go on then, leave me as everyone else I love has left me,' I remember to his quiet voice soothing me,

'It was not from choice that your family have left you alone, rather that they value your life above all else. Don't you think it's just as hard for Tim and Rupert, knowing that you live but they dare not contact you? I will try to get a message to them but I dare not trust your father, not with the hold he keeps on Uncle Theo. Please Vicky, don't make this parting worse for me, and remember that I, too, have lost my family.'

Vicky read back the entry and surprised herself by the sudden tears. Yet she would not spare herself this outpouring of the past. Soon it would be time for her first class of the day but she still had time to read another entry before Nathan woke up.

I grew up quickly in the next year with the war coming to our very doorstep. If I had thought myself to be an adult before, now I saw just how naïve I had been. Nathan was true to his word with brief letters arriving by secret couriers from both Rupert and Tim. Oh God, how I worried then, for both my brothers were fighting in a war so terrible that none could see it and remain untouched.

The news from Halleswell Hall was bitter indeed as my father was accused of administering a fatal dose of opium to my uncle Theo. Did I love my father? To this day I am still unsure, but as I embrace the teachings of the holy men then I must forgive his part in that deed and hope that he will learn his lesson in another life.

The news from the war is beating us all down, how can we still respect ourselves when daily we hear news of dreadful defeat and carnage? When I am eighteen I will run away and join the nurses that treat our brave soldiers.

Closing the book Vicky made her way across the compound to the small classroom where she taught the older girls. With her health becoming daily more debilitating she had finally yielded to the pressure to stop the nursing side of her duties. Now she was training a new generation of young women to read, write and hopefully cast off their backgrounds to become anything that they wanted to be. As India campaigned for their independence from Britain, a new generation of people were taking their first steps towards that freedom. If she could help the younger generation towards fitting themselves to this new role, then she would count her job as a success. They still took in orphans and treated the sick, but increasingly the British Governors were sending pupils to her school.

It was so difficult to say that they only took on pupils who could not afford an education, when their premises were barely tolerated already for their stance towards freedom of religion and caste. I'm not going to give in, she thought, like Bapu Ghandi I will lead by example.

1938

The war that Vicky had foreseen was looming on the horizon and now Nathan made no secret of his trips to meet with the military advisors. Many thought that Hitler was just playing a power game, but others thought him as a tyrannical leader who would stop at nothing in a bid for world domination. Nathan would spend many days away and as Vicky's fears grew so her journal entries reflected that earlier war of which she had played her own part.

Extract dated 1938.
As I write this I fear that once again our world will be plunged into another devastating war. The sight is still with me though I have tried so hard to purge myself of this curse, for curse it is to see the future as a page in a book just waiting to be turned over. Once I turn that page there will be no peace for me as long as that book exists. Maybe by looking at my earlier entries I can push this demon away.

I celebrated my eighteenth birthday on 31st October 1915, if an extra slice of ham could be called a celebration. Food was scarce as the German troops started to advance and the brave French soldiers, aided by English troops, struggled to hold that advance at bay. It didn't take a General to see the inevitable outcome. Conditions in the trenches were horrendous, with soldiers barely trained and inadequately equipped to survive the chill weather. The women did what they could, knitting woollen socks and gloves to keep the troops from the scourge of frostbite, but by then we were suffering a similar fate.

Nathan's letter finally reached me in early November. My father had died in prison and worse was to come. Rupert had heroically wasted his life in a vain attempt to breach the German lines at Ypres. Tim had been posted to France as an ordinary soldier, although his status should have given him the rank of Captain. I started making my plans that day; if Tim were to die I would be alongside him, not as a soldier but as a nurse. I was tall for my age and my education would guarantee that few questions would be asked of me.

Patiently I sewed a lining into my sturdy serge skirt; I could not bear to leave the emeralds with my host family, for who could say if ever I would return to them?

I climbed out of the window on a raw December night, my few personal belongings tied around my waist. With my hair scrunched up into a bun I could easily pass for twenty-one, or so I hoped. I will not recount my journey on this page. Suffice it to say that I almost fell into the arms of a senior nurse some three weeks later. Half starved and flea-bitten I was first a patient before I even met a recruiting officer. Nathan once said I was the most stubborn woman he had ever met and I blessed that trait, for one month later I started my training as an intern.

Sighing heavily she put the journal away. The memories were just too painful to recall. Perhaps she could return to them later but for now she needed company and the presence of the little ones would lift her spirits.

Kumar met her just outside the ward, his face brightening up at the sight of his mother.

'I was about to do my rounds mother, it would please me if you joined me.'

Vicky looked at the tall handsome man she was privileged to call her son, 'it's just the tonic I need; I miss your father so much.'

Arm in arm they entered the ward that housed babies from as young as a few weeks to toddlers of three or four years old. Many came from families too poor to afford the medication and care so vital to their infant's survival. Others had been left outside the orphanage, a testament to the poverty that plagued the lives of the poorer castes.

One toddler hurled his tiny body at Vicky's knees demanding to be picked up. Laughing she lifted him into her arms and swung him around.

'You should have had many children mama; the little ones love you so much.'

'But I have had so many children my dear son and the best and brightest of them all is you.'

'You honour me with your love,' he replied and then joined her in laughter as one by one the little ones came forward for a cuddle.

Nathan came home on the weekend, his face bearing the strain of so many late nights. Still he swept her up into his arms with his usual greeting.

'How's my best girl?' He said as he kissed her soundly.

'Missing you each and every second of the day, why can't you tell them that you are retired now, I want you all to myself.'

'And so you shall when I get out of this damn uniform and into something more comfortable.'

'So I gather you won't be wanting any of my special goat curry?' She said joining in their usual banter.

'MMM I could eat a horse, curried, fried or even raw. '

'Nathan, how could you, just for that you'll get fried bananas and nothing else.'

Vicky crossed over the room and poured him a stiff gin and tonic.

'Right master, I order you to put your feet up and get that down your throat.'

She smiled in contentment as she ran his bath. Maybe he would fall asleep before he even got to the bath, but all she cared about was that he was home again. He was still awake so she eased the boots off his tired feet and started to undress him. Taking him by the hand she led him into the primitive bathroom and with a sigh of relief he eased himself into the tin bath.

Stripping down to her cotton shift she started to soap his body with an ease born of long familiarity and massaged his taught shoulder muscles. His body started to relax and his eyelids started to droop.

'Dearest I think we had better get to bed before you fall asleep in the bath.'

Wearily he climbed out and she helped him into their shared bed. Within seconds he was asleep, but she watched over him for

a while, tracing her fingers down the long lean body and marvel-
ling once again that this wonderful, thoughtful man belonged
body and soul to her alone. He turned over onto his side and she
cuddled into his body in the classic spoon position. Her last
thought before she succumbed to sleep was a feeling of deep and
everlasting love. 'He will live long after I am gone,' she thought,
but it didn't worry her.

Britain declared war on Germany on the 1st of September 1939.
The British Raj had discussed the possibility of war, but initially
they only had two hundred and five thousand Indian troops to aid
the allies. Nathan was asked to aid with the training and recruit-
ment of troops despite that fact that he was officially retired from
the army. He agreed on one condition only, that their hospital and
other services were to be left alone. His experience of WW1 had
taught him the bitter lesson; India would again become a source of
food supplies to soldiers and civilians in Britain. Now that they
were growing most of their own food, neither Nathan nor Vicky
could give up that small contribution to the food supplies.

Now Nathan was away all week as the number of volunteers
started to swell into a huge army. By the end of the war it would
be estimated that two and a half million Indian volunteers had
made up a fierce fighting unit that was revered across the world.
In the meantime all he knew was that he was rushed off his feet,
both day and night.

For Vicky the war passed as a blur of action, with Nathan
away so much she had started to nurse the sick again although
her heart problems were now accelerating month by month. The
worst blow came in 1941 when Kumar gently told his adopted
parents that he was going to join the army as a doctor.

Although Vicky pleaded with him it did no good, he knew
that his place was with his countrymen and the promise of
eventual independence only spurred him on.

'If the gods say it is my time to die then I would rather it be in
helping others, not here at home.' It was the fatalistic view shared
by many of his religion and others of different religions. They
could not plead shortage of trained doctors either. Kevin had
married Angela many years before and their children were
brought up as half British, half Indian.

Other doctors had joined the small, but efficient team and many of Vicky's orphans had trained as nurses. Others worked in the gardens, growing all kinds of vegetables and many of their grown-up children now sent a voluntary tithe of rice and other food that couldn't be grown. As an army officer Nathan was allowed a weekly ration of meat, which was eaten by those who could not take the step to become vegetarian.

Vicky kept up her journal, adding parts of her past to the passages from the present. One such entry was a remarkable tale of courage and self-sacrifice.

Even now I cannot bring myself to write about the aftermath of the Battle of the Somme. Although our unit was supposed to be well away from the front, we often found ourselves shifting position as a little land was lost and then regained. Every single type of vehicle was used to transport the wounded and dying, many never made it as far as our field hospital.

I felt Tim's death as a blow to my chest. I was helping an overworked surgeon and as the pain knifed through me I passed out. I was given a pass to recover in England, although there was no injury I was judged as suffering from fatigue.

The journey was long and I saw things that will haunt me for the rest of my life, but eventually I reached England and spent a few weeks as a patient in a crowded hospital. In vain I pleaded with the staff to allow me to help out, so in the end I was transferred to a London hospital. I planned my escape carefully and soon I was wandering the streets of London, my one goal to sell the Emerald necklace with a view to the future. My head reeled in shock at the sum of money placed in a safe account awaiting my return, that's if I ever did return.

My ignoble return to France in 1917 was carried out on a troop ship. Before I rejoined my post, I made a pilgrimage to the home of the de Castellans, a family connection that I had learnt about from Nathan. Little was left of the once grand castle, German guns had turned it into a pile of rubble, here and there an arch stood dark against the sky and I wondered if there was any family left at all. Had they been wiped out as distant relatives of the Meverall family?

I blundered back to my waiting transport and spent the rest of the war trying to atone for my sins; little did I know that my dear Nathan was attempting to do the same? When Germany finally surrendered I found myself at a loss. What to do next? My mind turned back to India and the medicine man that I thought could lift the curse. I paid for my passage with part of my money; the rest is really a short part of my life story.

Once I had finished my nursing in the pandemic I thought once again of how I could put the money to use. The money from the sale of Aunt Charlotte's emerald necklace became the rock I built my clinic and orphanage on. Somehow I feel that she would have approved.

At the end of the war Vicky had her first major heart attack. Confined to her bed, she watched the children playing and set about planning for her death. In this she was aided by her son, Kumar, who had distinguished himself in the war. It was hard keeping things from her husband, but Nathan fussed so and her time was getting short.

She rallied a little in 1947 when India was finally granted the independence they had fought so hard for. The same year she watched as Kumar married his childhood sweetheart, Janna, another of their many orphans.

Her relationship with Nathan entered a new phase of quiet contentment, no longer could she ride out with him and their love-making became a gentle act of mutual comfort.

Her second heart attack occurred in 1948 and now she knew her days were numbered. Kevin told her that with care she could live another ten years, but she was tired now of the struggle to live and only hung on for Nathan's sake.

One day she begged him to take her into the high ground she loved so much. Nathan never knew where she found the strength from, but once at the summit she rested in his arms. From here she could see across the land she had called home for so many years and a sudden wave of longing overcame her. With her head lying in his lap, she told him she wished to be laid at rest in the grounds of Halleswell Hall.

'You must return there when I am gone,' she told him.

'Hush my darling that will be many years in the future.'

'I cannot hang on much longer, we both know that, and I want to by your side into eternity.' Lovingly he stroked her hair, the dark red colour now shot through with grey, but to him she was still the same vibrant girl that he had adored from the first time he had set his eyes on her.

'Promise me you will plant roses for me, the scent will carry to the gates of heaven, if that is to be my hope and destination.'

'Together we will grow a field of roses if that's your wish,' he said, 'but stay with me until that time comes.'

Even as he said the words he knew she had slipped away. He continued to cradle her in his arms as he gazed unseeing into a lonely future.

According to her last Will and Testament she was cremated in a clinically clean new crematorium, Kumar performing the task of sending her soul on its long journey home. The funeral was attended by hundreds of people from many different religions, in that aspect Vicky had briefly united Hindu with Muslim, Christian with Catholic, even Nathan was staggered by the amount of respect shown to his beloved wife.

People came in droves, survivors of the pandemic along with their children and grandchildren. Elderly Indian soldiers from WW1 and many from the recent conflict lined up to pay their respects alongside British soldiers.

What money she had left was bestowed where it was needed most. Many poor families left that day enriched more in soul than by the money that would grant them respite from years of poverty. Small bequests were left to her large extended family but perhaps the greatest gift of all was the transfer of the deeds of ownership of the hospital to be held in perpetuity for the people of India.

Nathan was inconsolable; he looked much older than his age of sixty-seven. He walked around the empty rooms like a ghost that was about to disappear. A month after her death Kumar knew he had to do something before Nathan gave up on life, besides he had promised his mother that he would make sure his father would go to England as soon as possible, there were just too many memories here. He brought young Vicky with him, knowing that Nathan adored her. Nathan embraced him with some of the warmth he had always kept for his adopted son and granddaughter.

Vicky crawled onto his lap and searched his pockets for the usual sweeties. Nathan laughed and popped a small sweet into her adorable mouth.

'I think it is time we talked, my father,' Kumar spoke. 'I think it is better if Vicky is taken to play with the other children.'

Nathan nodded his assent and ringing a hand bell he summoned one of the older girls to take his granddaughter to play.

Although it was barely 2pm Nathan poured out a large whiskey and offered one to Kumar. To his surprise Kumar filled his own glass with a similar measure.

'I didn't think you drank very often, son,' he said.

'I am afraid it is bad habit I picked up in the war, sometimes a little alcohol is needed to loosen the tongue.'

'So you have come to lecture me,' Nathan replied.

'No father, I come with a heart full of both sorrow and joy. Sorrow for your empty life and joy for a task I was asked to perform at a time like this.'

In spite of himself Nathan felt a moment of intrigue. For the first time since his beloved wife had died he felt like talking.

'Go on, I'm listening,' he said.

'Mother knew that you would grieve forever if left on your own. She made me promise I would not allow this to happen for the love she bore for you. It was an easy promise to make for I too miss her and hate to see you this way.'

'Damn it son, I have very right to grieve as I see fit.' Tossing back the whiskey he poured himself another large glass.

'You have not filled my glass father?'

'I thought it was against your damn religion,' he said petulantly.

'If I am to join my father in his suffering then I must also share his method of coping with that sorrow.'

'Then let's get drunk together if that's what you want.'

'It is what you want and maybe what you need for this time, but I have something far more potent than the whiskey bottle.' Kumar rose and downed his drink in one long gulp.

'Read this and when you are ready we will talk again.' He said placing a sealed letter into Nathan's hands.

'Namaste, father.'

'Namaste , son'

The letter was written in Vicky's flowing script. Trembling with pain, he poured another glass before tearing the envelope open.

My darling husband,

If you are reading this then I have passed through the veil of life and gone to a better place. I know that you have always questioned my new beliefs but as I write this I am sure of one thing. Amita once said that we were soul mates and I have come to believe this is true, for without you by my side heaven would become hell. Maybe there is truth in every religion, for I cannot believe a love as strong as ours could cease with my passing.

The Hindu faith is similar to that of the Buddhists, we live our lives here on Earth and we have a second chance to live again in a different body to atone for the sins we have committed in our earthly life. Christians believe in an afterlife where we dwell in eternal bliss, I would wish to believe in that as well, for when we cast off the mortal body then we become pure light and love.

Imagine that my love, already we have shared some of this, for so often I feel your thoughts and desires in my mind and I know that you have felt mine too.

I am so afraid though, that you will despair and lose the will to live. This is a mortal sin in any religion and could keep us apart for many thousands of years. I don't ask you to believe in it, but I do so believe, and the very thought of us being parted once again is more than I can take.

For my sake please live on for me. As my illness progresses the things of this world seem so trivial compared to the adventure we face when we pass over.

Know this as truth, for you have shared in my visions and know that they always come to pass. I see you, my darling, you are back in England and are surrounded by children laughing and playing. In one vision I see you on a jet black stallion, his name is "Hero", you name him this in remembrance for the dear horse that

296

carried us to safety. You stand on a high place where the dark green slopes of Devon run down to the sea. I will be with you on that day and every time you ride with the wind in your hair, there, too, will I ride with you.

You will find me in the song of the sea, the rain that beats upon the windowpanes. Would I ever leave you, my darling? Look for me in the first buds of spring; listen as I sing with the soaring of the lark. Feel my presence beside you when snow falls gently; this is the blanket of my love.

I have no regrets for the hand that life has dealt me, without the pain I may never have met you and would never have known the joy of our physical union. You are, and always will be the gentlest loving soul to walk the face of this earth. What other couple could say they had a family of hundreds of children? Cry a few tears for me, as often I cried for you. But please, my darling, live for me and make that life something to be proud of.

Soon I must go, I hear them calling me, your mother is here by my side, she is very clear in my sight. Rupert is hovering in the background and Tim is smiling as he clings onto the hand of a young boy. It's our son, Nathan, the child I lost and could never bear to tell you about. He has your eyes and that little lock of hair falling across his eyes, so he must keep brushing it away, just as you always do. Another tall, very distinguished man is standing slightly apart; I think it must be Alex, although I never really knew him. A young woman places her hand on his shoulder, she is beautiful inside and out. There are others in the distance but I can't see them clearly.

Beloved, thank you for your constant love. Thank you for making my dreams a reality and thank you for just being you.

Your Dear wife and soul mate,

Vicky.XXXXXXXXXX

Inside the envelope lay a tiny silver locket that he had never seen before. His hands were shaking so badly that it took him minutes to open it. The twists of red and brown hair nearly fell to the floor before he recognised them. Somehow, sometime, Vicky had cut off a lock of his hair to twine with her own. Nestled inside were miniature pictures of them both.

Nathan cried then as he had never cried before. Out of the dark night of his soul a light glimmered strong and true. A scent of wild orchids and the heady aroma of newly opened roses wafted through the room and a light breeze ruffled his hair.

Once again the ship was in harbour, waiting to take him on his final journey. All his friends and family were there, their love washing in waves over his healed spirit. Clinging tightly to Kumar he made him promise to write as often as he could. In his heart he knew he would never see his son again in this life, but the sorrow was tinged with acceptance. Together he and Vicky had helped to make a fine man and if he could believe that Vicky was waiting for him, then he would see Kumar again one day.

The sun was just rising as the ship pulled way from the quayside. The tiny figures were now fading from sight, but India glowed with a special radiance of colours as the sun rose higher in the sky. It was a new dawn for India and the last of an era for the British Empire. Turning his back, Nathan faced towards the vast ocean and a new life waiting back in England.

Holding the casket in his hands he whispered, 'we made a difference Vicky, now let's go home.'

The Last Meverall

Nathan stood and slowly turned, his eyes taking in every detail of the great hall. It had been twenty- five years since he had last stood in this room. Not much had changed, apart from the dust covers that shrouded the furniture.

The silence was the thing that struck him; this was the first time he had been here when he was completely alone, always before other people had been in the house. Even if they had been quiet the quality of the silence was different to being here alone. He knew he would have to get used to it, this was his home now, the last of the Meverall family had come home to fulfil his promise to a dying Alex all those years ago.

He went over to the chair by the fireplace and pulled off the dustsheet. Running his hands along the polished wood, he thought of the man who had passed away in that chair.

'I told you I would come back, Alex. I have brought Vicky home with me too. She will be lying next to you and Zara very soon.' There was a catch in his voice; he had not really come to terms with the passing of his wife yet.

Moving round the chair, he sat as so many masters of this house had done over the generations. His mind slipped back to India, his home for so many years now.

It was amazing how the hospital and orphanage had evolved over the years. From humble beginnings when Vicky had struggled to keep the place going on little resources, few staff and a wing and a prayer, to the modern home, and well-equipped hospital it had become today.

Nathan smiled, somehow the early days had been the happiest, even though each day had been a struggle, it had felt so worthwhile, Vicky's dream had become reality, she had been so happy there, the ghosts that haunted her bearable, if not forgotten.

Pictures of his return from England came unbidden into his mind and he smiled to himself.

As the ship pulled in slowly to the dock he had rushed to the rail, searching for a glimpse of the woman that meant everything to him. She was there, their eyes met and locked together across the narrowing strip of water, that look had been electric, so much love and feeling was silently transferred between them in that one lingering look. It was a moment that Nathan would never forget, one of the happiest of his life. That night had been something to remember too, not just for the rejoining of their union, which had been wonderful, but the welcome he had received from the rest of the staff and the children. That had been truly special.

The years had passed quickly by as both he and Vicky, along with Amita worked hard to make the place a success. Much to the credit of them and the other staff, they had achieved much of what they had set out to do.

His thoughts were disturbed by the sound of a car pulling into the gravel drive. Curiosity made him cross the room to the window and glance outside; after all he had not been expecting a visitor, only the vicar knew he was here, or so he thought.

The man was a complete stranger, obviously well off by the look of his Saville Row suit and highly polished shoes. For a moment Nathan contemplated not answering, he was not really in the mood for visitors, especially ones he didn't know.

After a moment, he realised the man had seen him through the window, there was nothing for it, he would have to see what he wanted.' Probably wants to sell me something,' he thought as he made his way to the door.

'Yes,' said Nathan a touch sharper than he had intended.

The young man looked a bit taken aback, but he reached into his pocket and handed Nathan his business card, saying politely, 'good afternoon Sir, I am Stephen Drake, Art Editor at the Times newspaper. I am writing an article that I was hoping you might be able to help me with.'

'An article, about what?'

'This is where Timothy Cavendish- Meverall, the artist lived isn't it?'

'Yes it is. Are you writing an article about Tim then?'

'Yes Sir, I don't know if you are aware, but there is a big exhibition of his work in London at the moment and with the current amount of interest in his paintings my paper wants to run a story about his life.'

Nathan was not surprised, he knew that Tim's work had become very popular and had won high acclaim. He was suddenly interested and invited the young man in.

The reporter looked around at the grand surroundings. Even with the furniture still covered, there was no denying the grandeur of the great hall; it was more than enough to impress most people.

'You have a lovely house here Sir, are you moving in or out?'

'I have only arrived today, come back to take up my family home. Now you wanted to talk about Tim,' he replied, uncovering one of the shrouded chairs and indicating Stephen to take a seat.

Stephen sat and took a notebook from his pocket, nervously fiddling with it for a moment as Nathan took his chair and waited for him to continue.

'Timothy was in the army wasn't he?'

'Here we go,' thought Nathan, 'no messing about, straight in for the notoriety.'

'Yes Tim was in the army, a war artist as you will have seen through his work.' Nathan was determined not to make it easy for this young man to come up with any sensational headlines at Tim's expense.

He need not have worried. Stephen didn't seem interested in how Tim had died, at least not yet. Nathan determined to keep his guard up for any question that could be misleading.

'So the pictures he drew and painted were actually done at the front, in the midst of the action?'

'Yes as far as I know they were, most of his battle pictures were done in the trenches when there was a break in the action. I do know that some of them were done when he had leave from the front. I think those occasions were used for some of his more pastoral scenes that he painted at that time.'

'What type of man was he; his art seems to suggest that he was a sensitive sort of man with a keen eye that found a beauty in almost any situation. Even some of his most dramatic pieces seem to have an insight that sees right into his subject.'

Nathan was surprised, this young journalist seemed to know his art, and from his tone he sounded like he was an admirer of Tim's work. He paused for a moment before answering. 'Yes Tim was a very sensitive man; I think that is what allowed him to see beyond the surface of the things he was painting. I have one of his pictures here that I think you might be interested in.'

Nathan rose, and led the way to the painting of the swan that hung on the wall opposite the base of the stairs.

Stephen stopped by the stairs; he rested his hand on the carving of Eve and stared at the picture. There was something about it that went beyond art; he could not take his eyes off it, seeing something new in every part of the masterpiece before him. The main subject seemed to bore right into him. It made him feel odd inside; no other picture had ever evoked such feelings in him before now.

'That is an amazing picture' he said, not taking his eyes from it. I can see why you chose to keep that one, it is fantastic.'

Nathan turned and headed back to their chairs. 'Yes that is a fine picture, and one that says a lot about the man and other members of our family.'

'Oh why do you say that?'

With the loss of Vicky still so close to his heart, that was something he did not wish to discuss, so he just said' I was there the day that was painted and remember it vividly but I think that is a tale for some time in the future.'

Stephen saw the pain on his face and changed the subject.

'I suppose you have heard the news, Tim is to be posthumously pardoned and honoured for his work during the First World War.'

Nathan started, 'no I have not heard anything about that. I have only recently returned to this country, from India, and havn't even gone through the mountain of mail that was waiting when I arrived. Tell me more.'

'Well, after his work was first exhibited to great acclaim, there was a lot of public interest in his work. Now he is recognised for both the historical and artistic merit of his work. Many think him a modern genius and that his art should be hailed as such. What are your views on that?'

302

'I think that would be fantastic. Tim deserves to be recognised for his work, and I think that would be a wonderful way of doing it.' Flashes of that awful day crashed into his mind. It was something that he had managed not to think about for many years but this conversation was bringing it all back. His part in what had happened to Tim would never be exonerated in his own mind, but at least a pardon would free Tim in the eyes of the public and that was good enough for him. Stephen sensed that his visit was bringing up memories that were not pleasant for Nathan and he said. 'I have taken up enough of your time today, Sir and I thank you for your help.'

Nathan grunted, he had not really heard what Stephen had said, still deep in his own thoughts.

'I was wondering if it would be possible for me to photograph the swan, it is an undiscovered Meverall and I know the art world would fall in love with it as I have.'

Nathan thought carefully about that for long moments before giving his answer. That picture held so much that was personal to him, but would it be better to share those feelings with others, maybe so. 'Yes I think I would like this work to get public recognition, although the original will not go on public display while I live.'

'Thank you Sir, my piece will be much enhanced by this photo and I will do my best to do honour to the memory of Mr Cavendish-Meverall. Oh, one other thing, I wonder if you have any idea how much money that painting would be worth nowadays?' On that note the reporter took his leave. . Nathan stood long in front of the swan; it was getting dark when he finally moved. His thoughts were all over the place, so many memories running into one another. It had been some first day back at Halleswell Hall. He had planned to get the house opened up; all the dust covers removed and get it looking how he remembered it. That was not going to happen today, he realised, it was getting late and his mind was too full of other thoughts and feelings.

Three days later and Nathan was standing in his best suit by an open grave as Vicky was finally laid to rest.

The morning was bright and still, a slight mist rising off the lake. It was early, not long after dawn, the time of the day that Vicky had loved best. The dawn chorus was loud this morning, almost as though the birds were saying their own goodbye.

It was so peaceful in the spot that had been chosen for the resting place of the latter generation of Meverall's. A plot had been cleared in the midst of Brannon's Wood, near to the site of the old well. It seemed fitting that the place of Charlotte's sacrifice should be honoured in this way. Looking around Nathan saw that Vicky would have company. Not only Charlotte, but Alex and Zara together with Tim were buried in the little clearing. The family was nearly together again now. Only he remained to be added and then the Meverall line would come to a close. The family had first come to this place over 400 years ago. Much history there was to be told in that time and Nathan suddenly realised that he knew very little of it, and after he had gone it would all be consigned to the murky depths of unremembered history. In that moment, he resolved to do something about that so the family would be remembered.

The funeral had been as he had wanted, with just himself present to say goodbye to his beloved wife. There was a deep sadness in his heart as he stood there, but that was tempered by his cherished thoughts of the last days he had spent with his wife.

His mind drifted back to the high hills half a world away in India. It had been a morning such as this when he had helped Vicky to climb the last part of the hill from the rough track that led nearly to the summit. He had wondered at the time where she had found the strength to make that climb, as she had been so ill. He smiled at memories of Vicky's iron will. If she wanted to do something she was going to do it no matter what stood in her way. What she had achieved with the hospital was proof of that.

She had said that morning that she would look out at the Indian dawn. He had wondered at her request but had agreed reluctantly, fearing that it would be too much for her.

They had sat quietly as the warm sun rose over the flat valley in front of them; with Vicky leaning on Nathan's chest as he held her close.

'When I am gone, Nathan, I would like to be buried in England, I want to go home. I can't do it while I live, but I think I

304

would rest easier with the family that I destroyed around me. Maybe it will be my penance to spend eternity with them all around me. Will you do that for me my love; will you take me to England?'

Nathan was caught off guard by this but he answered calmly. 'You know I would do anything for you and I will do this. I will stay at Halleswell Hall too, both to be near you and to fulfil my promise to Alex.'

Vicky seemed satisfied with this answer and she snuggled closer into his body.

'We have had a good life here haven't we?' said Vicky.

'I would not have changed a thing, I could not have wished for a better life than the one I have had with you.'

Vicky smiled an unseen smile, she knew only too well how hard it had been for Nathan at times, but he had never complained, and had supported her through everything she had gone through. It was strange; she remembered the night Alex had died. She had felt it and knew that he had died. It was as if a great weight had been lifted from her. Knowing that in that moment the curse had been lifted and that she had been released from the terrible link she had to her family. She still did not know why Nathan had been unaffected by the curse, although perhaps he had been in some ways. She thought of his part in Tim's death and wondered if their love had helped to overcome that awful time?

Nathan failed to see the slight grimace of pain that passed over Vicky's face. He had continued talking to her long after she had stopped responding and then he just held her, as the sun rose higher in the sky.

That last morning together was a bitter sweet memory, one that he would cherish for the rest of his days. That morning had summed up their lives together and he found that he was content with that. They had been together more years than he could ever have dared hope for at one time, when it had seemed that they were never destined to be together. Although their lives had been tinged with much tragedy they had been happy and that was enough.

That was not to say that he didn't miss her terribly, he did, every moment of every day. He would find himself seeing

305

something and turning to comment on it to her only to find her not there. He would hear something funny but find that there was no one to share it with. The list went on and on. She had been such a huge part of his life it was like he was no longer whole and that hurt.

Long he stood there, unwilling to make that final step that would mean they were finally parted. Eventually he had to leave her and start the final stage of his life on his own.

Sitting in his chair in the great hall once more he thought about the hospital. It was run by a large staff of wonderful caring people now. They had not been needed for much of the hands on work for several years, but that did not lessen their welcome whenever they had gone to visit, which was most days. The place was part of both of them and neither could stay away for long.

Both had found plenty they could do to aid the staff, Vicky had spent most of her time with the children in the orphanage and continued to do that right up until the day she had passed from this life. She had found great comfort in the children, even though her heart would only let her make short visits; the children were always delighted to see her. She had tired very easily toward the end, but her presence was still of great benefit to the children, they loved to see her and always made a great fuss of her. Sometimes it was difficult to see who was looking after whom.

Nathan was happy with his decision to return to England, although he was very sad to leave the place that had been his home for over twenty years. It did not seem right to be there without Vicky somehow, the place held too many memories.

He had not forgotten the hospital though. He had set up a trust fund that was financed by a large proportion of the profits from Tim's art. He had more than enough money to keep him for the rest of his life, and he thought maybe Tim would have approved of the way Nathan was using the profits to bring aid to others. It was the sort of thing Tim would have done himself in the same circumstances he was sure.

The hospital was grateful too. Government funding was in short supply and Nathan found his money was going a long way toward keeping the place up and running.

The finance would continue for the foreseeable future too. Tim's art featured in many books now and royalties kept coming and would do for years to come.

It was a week later that something that Alex had said came back to him. He was in the study, clearing out old papers and looking through some of the ancient books in the halls extensive library. There were some beautiful books, some so old that they were hand written in Old English with fantastic artwork lovingly reproduced by the author. Each book that he opened brought more surprises and delights. It was these books that brought the Meverall journals to mind. Just before he had died Alex had told him of the work he had done, translating and copying the work of generations of Meverall memoirs into a single volume. Nathan had promised to read it but hadn't at the time, that was twenty five years ago, but suddenly there was a need deep inside him to do Alex's bidding. He searched for some time, but he couldn't find it amongst the rest of the Meverall book collection. Eventually, after some hours of fruitless search he came upon it in the study desk drawer. He felt that surge of relief that occurs at the fulfilment of a long search and soon he was seated in his chair with the volume opened on his lap. It was a red, leather bound book, thick and heavy, not really what he had been expecting to find. He was amazed at how many hours of work Alex must have put in, to not only rewrite but translate as well. His admiration for the man was renewed once again.

The first page was dated over four hundred years ago and spoke of the founding of Halleswell hall. From that very first page Nathan was engrossed

He had hoped it would contain the information he longed for about his ancestors. Things that he had thought of over the years but never really expected to find the answers to. There were many mysteries in the family's history. He had heard tantalising snippets, but he had never found out the whole story. He was not disappointed. Alex and his ancestors had done a remarkable job.

Over the next few days he sat next to the fire long into the night as he read and absorbed the history of the Meverall family. He was so engrossed that he didn't even notice the dawn catch up with him as he read the last few lines that Alex had written about his life. Finally he shut the cover, with a sigh.

The family had been through some rough times. There were a few things in that book that he was not sure he found quite believable, although knowing the talents his wife had used, he would not be surprised to find that other odd things had really happened in the depths of history.

The family's history had been so full of heartache and pain, but at the same time deep joy had found its way into several of the hands that had written their memoirs in this book. He resolved to finish the journal and tidy up the loose ends, after all he was the only living member of the family now and it would all die with him. If he could get the journal finished, it would be a legacy that would not let the family die and be consigned to unremembered history. He refused to see the Meverall's forgotten; after all they had been through over the centuries they deserved that.

As he reached the end he quickly realised that it felt unfinished. Alex had been right all those years ago, it would be down to him to finish it, to bring the history of the Meverall family to a close.

Nathan decided he needed time to think before he started to write the final chapter. There were so many other things that needed doing in the house that he decided to get some of them done out of the way before he started.

Looking around, most of the furniture was still covered in white sheets; in fact the whole place looked as unlived in as when he had arrived.

A crunching of tyres on gravel alerted him to company. Looking out of the window he saw a very elderly woman being helped out of a taxi. With a start of recognition Nathan hurried to the door.

'Flo,' he exclaimed both pleased and a little surprised to see her.

'Hello Nathan,' replied Flo smoothly. 'I am sorry I was not here when you arrived, I have been away for a few weeks and had not heard that you were coming back. I only found out when this kind gentleman informed me that the hall was occupied once more. I knew it could only be you.'

Nathan was a little taken aback. He had not given Flo a thought, maybe he had taken it for granted that she would be dead by now, or else moved away after Alex had passed away.

Flo grinned; maybe she could see what he was thinking from the expression on his face. 'Did you think I had abandoned the hall, Nathan?'

'No I...' Nathan was flustered and words let him down for a moment, he didn't want to admit that he had forgotten all about the woman who had looked after Halleswell for as long as he could remember.

'Never mind Nathan, are you going to invite me in or are we going to chat on the doorstep all day? I am not as young as I used to be you know.'

She was making fun of him he knew, but was so surprised to see her that he could think of no reply, so he just stood back and indicated for her to enter. The taxi driver, who had been patiently waiting by the open boot of the car, followed her in, carrying some of her cases. Nathan looked at the large trunks and he knew that Flo had returned to stay.

He had to grin to himself. Flo had been in charge so long that she saw the house as her domain and he realised that he couldn't stop her moving back even if he had wanted to.

Flo was standing in the great hall, taking in the room as if recommitting it to memory or, Nathan thought, seeing what needed doing and working out when she was going to do it.

Her expression was serious when she turned back to him. Dismissing the taxi driver she looked into Nathan's eyes. 'Vicky is gone then.' It was a statement rather than a question.

'Yes Flo, she has left me all alone. That is why I came back. I brought her with me; she is lying with the rest of the family by the well. It is what she wanted.' Nathan said this almost as if he wanted Flo's approval. In some ways he did.

'That is as it should be,' was Flo's reply.

'Now, I think it's about time we got rid of some of these dust sheets and made this place look like a home again, don't you?'

Swan Lake

The weeks turned into months, spring turned into a glorious summer as Nathan settled into life at Halleswell Hall.

As time passed he started to feel a peace settling in his soul. He still missed Vicky and not a day went by without him thinking of her, but that raw pain of bereavement was passing and his thoughts of her were now cherished memories rather than a heart wrenching feeling of loss.

The house was feeling more like home too, Flo had worked her magic, and together with the new staff that Nathan had hired to help her, she had everywhere clean and sumptuous meals once again arrived from the kitchen.

Outside, gardeners were restoring the lawns and flower beds to their former glory and a new groom was installed into the stables to look after the horses Nathan had bought. He loved to ride and found it easier to get round the estate on horseback. His wounded leg would not let him drive a car without pain and he felt being on horseback to be much more civilised anyway. Flo had lectured him about a man of his age charging about on horseback but he didn't think she had been that serious about it and he would have done it anyway. On horseback he found a feeling of freedom denied to him by his bad leg and he revelled in rediscovering the haunts of his youth, a tree that he had used to climb or the little hollow where he had seen his first badger. Passing a hayrick on one of the farms had him thinking of the young girl who had given him his first kiss so many years ago. He briefly wondered what had happened to her. He could see her smiling face but her name was just out of his grasp.

He often found himself on the hillside looking down on the sun drenched house; the lake glittering and shimmering as the gentle breeze moved its surface. Brannon's Wood cast its shadow over a green pasture but even the wood didn't look so dark on a glorious morning.

The hillside took his mind back to another high place, half a world away in India. He remembered the times he had spent there with Vicky. The love they had shared and their final goodbye.

Breasting the top of the hill, he dismounted and stretched out on the grass, idly chewing a stalk of grass his gaze took in the purple moors of Exmoor in the distance and the welcome glimpse of the sea in another direction.

He shed tears up there but there were smiles too. Part of the healing process, he realised so he welcomed both emotions. He missed her and knew that he always would but the emptiness in his heart was filling up with cherished memories that enabled him to go on with his life.

Urging his black stallion on, he descended the slope and headed toward the wood. There was a path now through the dark trunks. His many trips to his family's graveside had cleared a way through. The breeze in the trees was slightly hypnotic and had a calming effect on him. The peace in the wood now was in sharp contrast to its dark past. Many an evil act had occurred in here over the centuries.

He took to riding down to the village of an evening to share a drink or two in the Smugglers Arms. The locals were at first a little wary of the new Lord of the manor. Understandable as he owned a large number of their homes and several of them owed their livelihoods to him. It didn't take many visits to the pub for people to realise that Nathan was a down to earth character who was just as happy chatting to a labourer as a Lord. Of course the fact that he quite often stood a round of drinks did much to ingratiate him in the hearts of the locals.

Nathan enjoyed his trips to the Smugglers; they brought a hint of the camaraderie of India back to him. Here he could enjoy a laugh with the locals and this he did, his sharp sense of humour was appreciated and his tales of far off lands were always welcome to the less well travelled.

His interest in village life went much further than just going to the pub however and it was the children of the village who found themselves the recipients of much of his kindness. Although he wouldn't admit it even to himself, he missed the children of the orphanage and maybe helping out the youngsters of the village somehow filled the gap in his life that the orphans had left.

While out riding one day he came across a small boy sitting beside the track. He was crying and holding his knee. The lad had fallen and cut his leg on a sharp stone. Nathan dismounted and took a look at the injury. 'It's not as bad as it looks you know,' said Nathan as he carefully wiped some of the blood away so he could see the extent of the wound.

'But it hurts Mister,' said the boy through his tears.

'I know it does but we can make it better. Do you want to go for a ride on my friend here so we can get it fixed up properly?'

'You mean I can have a ride on your big horse, I would like that. Can we gallop?'

Nathan grinned. 'Yes we can go as fast as you like. Come on then up we go.'

He was soon holding on tightly to Hero's mane as Nathan galloped back to Halleswell where Flo administered first aid while Nathan gave Hero a quick rub down. The young lad's name was Tom and once his knee was cleaned and a bandage administered a grin appeared on his face when he found out he was to ride home with Nathan on Hero.

'Thanks Mister,' Tom said, when Nathan helped him down outside his parent's cottage and with a wave he ran into the house leaving Nathan grinning in the lane.

Nathan took to riding longer and longer, sometimes he was out all day and came back stiff and sore. Flo began to worry about him, but she came up with something to occupy his mind and stop him brooding. One day as she poured his coffee at breakfast she casually asked if he had added anything to Alex's book yet.

Nathan looked up; he'd put his promise to Alex to the back of his mind recently. His interest in the journals was immediately pricked again. They had slipped his mind since reading it. Flo left to find it with a grin; she could read Nathan like a book. She had thought it wouldn't take too much to get him interested again.

After breakfast Flo found Nathan in the Great hall looking at the swan. 'Have you ever noticed that looking at this picture brings peace to an aching heart? It goes further than art but however many times I look at it I can't work out why.'

'I think it's because of who painted it and what it represents isn't it. All that is dear to you is wrapped up in that picture. I think that's why it means so much to you.'

Nathan shook his head; he never ceased to be amazed at Flo's insight. His eyes travelled to the book in her hands and taking it from her with a word of thanks he headed for the study.

Flo brought him his lunch and was not surprised to see him sitting at the desk with a blank piece of paper in front of him.

He looked up as she entered. He was exasperated and his expression was slightly troubled. 'How did Alex ever do all this Flo? I've sat here all morning and found nothing to write, there is a lot that I could write but it is the knowing how to start and what to put in. I mean Alex omitted much of his life but a fair amount of mine overlaps his. Do I put it in as my thoughts or omit things because Alex did?'

'There are a lot of questions there, Nathan, and most of them, I think, you will have to find the solution to in your heart. I think I might be able to help though. Do you think it would help if you saw the original version? That way you could see what Alex wrote and maybe it would help you to decide perhaps.'

Almost as an afterthought she added, 'Why don't you get your journalist friend to help you, I am sure he would be only too pleased to discover more of the family history. He seemed interested last time he was here.'

'Yes I think I would like that very much and I think it would help too.'

He didn't answer the point about Stephen; he was unsure how much he wanted to tell the outside world.

'Come with me then, I've got to warn you though, Alex had me lock the whole lot in Zara's old room. I don't know why, but after he had finished his work he didn't want anything to do with it anymore.'

Nathan thought for a moment, he had not been in that room since his last visit to Zara all those years ago. He was being silly, he thought. It's just a room.

It was not long before they were standing outside Zara's old room. Flo looked at Nathan's face, was it paler than when they were downstairs? She unlocked the door. Nathan hesitated for an instant before entering and then, with a deep breath, stepped into the room that had been the scene of so much misery for the unfortunate inhabitant. Nothing had been moved since the last time Zara had been brought out of the room. The door had been locked and the only time anyone had been in since was when Flo had brought up the manuscripts.

Nathan stood in the centre of the room; it was all coming back to him as his eyes travelled around the room, the room that had known so much pain when Zara had been alive. He could almost see her sitting in front of the mirror combing her thinning hair, could almost hear the banshee scream that she had produced so often during her incarceration in her bedroom.

Flo was rummaging in a wardrobe, muttering to herself. Finally she straightened and came back to where Nathan stood. 'It's not there, I can't understand it, I am sure no one has been in here since I locked the door but the book Alex wrote in is missing. I am sorry, Nathan, I don't know how it happened unless Alex removed it without telling me.'

Flo sounded mortified as though she thought it was her fault that the book was not there.

'Don't worry, I expect Alex decided he didn't want anyone to see it and destroyed it.'

'Could be,' replied Flo, she still sounded unsure and less than happy.

They went back downstairs. 'Well I guess that settles it then. Alex didn't want his story recorded so I can't add anything about that part of my life but that leaves an awful lot that can be.'

Images from his life flashed through his mind as he spoke. He had done so much, seen so much throughout his life that he was suddenly sure that he could write a large amount without touching on the part that Alex had played in it. That was something he wasn't happy about. Alex had been such a good friend to him in hard times that it seemed a shame that history would claim him without the recognition that Nathan thought he deserved.

Sitting down behind the desk he began to run his thoughts over his past. Different countries, war, peace, poverty and splendour, he had known all of them in his life. Picking up his pen he started to write. The words seemed to flow now, faster than he could write. Three hours later, he sat back and was surprised by how much he had written. Enough for now he thought and stretched his aching muscles.

Over the following days he worked hard on his writing. He always threw himself wholeheartedly into anything he did, almost to the point of obsession. Smiling to himself, he pictured Vicky bringing him his usual gin and tonic and scolding him for overworking.

He reached the point when things started to get complicated, how much of the events that led to Charlotte's death and the curse that followed should he write down? He wouldn't write anything that would sully Vicky's reputation but as he thought about it, he realised that it had all been part of her and to try to miss it out would make his memories false and would indeed do injustice to the woman who had made his life complete.

A week later Nathan had a visitor, Stephen had become a frequent visitor to Halleswell Hall and an unlikely friendship had steadily grown between the two men.

'Come in dear boy,' he said, shaking the proffered hand, 'it's so good to see you again.'

Stephen loved coming here, he loved the atmosphere and the history of the old house and he often wandered about the house just 'soaking up the atmosphere', as he was wont to say.

Nathan had decided to tell Stephen about the book he was finishing and was correct when he thought that Stephen would be very interested.

He was amazed at the amount of history that book contained and he spent a long time flicking through it, picking out especially interesting bits that caught his eye. He came to where Nathan had started and the title stopped him.

'You are the last member of the Meverall family?'

'Yes unfortunately, we weren't blessed with children of our own, although I have an adopted son in India. Kumar, he runs our hospital there now. He's a fine boy, well man now, and all I could ever have wished for in a son. He wouldn't wish to be a Lord of the manor and apart from him there is no one else, when I die the family dies with me. That's why I thought it was important to get that journal finished because after my passing all that history would be lost unless I recorded it.'

'What will happen to the hall when you are gone?'

'I have no idea, I haven't thought about it to be honest.'

'It would be such a shame to see it sold and stripped of all its history and character wouldn't it?'

Nathan looked at the younger man before answering, trying to work out why he would be asking these things and where it was leading.

Stephen didn't wait for an answer but ploughed on, 'you've heard of the National Trust I presume?'

'Yes I have heard of them naturally, but what have they to do with this?'

'Well, I was wondering if you had ever thought of bequeathing the hall to the National Trust, if you did, this grand old place would stay as it is now for ever.'

Nathan thought about it, and as he did so, he realised it was a very good idea. The house should live on after its owners had left it behind and if they could make its future secure then he thought it would be a very good idea.

'Another thing, have you thought of getting these memoirs published, I think they would sell very well especially in the local area? If you were interested then I think I'd be in a good position to help you find a publisher and organise it all for you'

'I don't know, I don't think that I would have them published while I live but after I am gone, perhaps.'

Stephen finally noticed that maybe he had overstepped the mark. 'I am sorry Nathan, I think I've said more than it was my place to do I am sorry.'

'No that's quite alright, you'll have noticed that I'm not a young man, in fact I'm verging on ancient and its right that I should plan for the future of our ancestral home. When you get to my age death is a constant companion, whether my own, or the ones I love. The latter have already succumbed and it's only me that still puts up the fight against the inevitable. But I don't fear it because I shall be reunited with those I loved and once again I'll be in the arms of my Vicky. How could I not look forward to that happy day?'

Stephen looked slightly embarrassed at this frank speech and didn't know what to say.

'I'll think on what you have said this afternoon and I think I may well take up your first suggestion. It's the second I'm not sure of.'

There was silence for a moment before Nathan broke it.

'Now do you fancy a ride down to the Smugglers for a pint or two?'

That brought a smile to Stephen's face.

Winter came and although Flo tried her best to persuade him not to, Nathan still rode Hero across the frost covered parkland. Most days he either found himself at Vicky's graveside in the woods or high in the hills. A few times he even made his way to the top of Harland Point, looking out over the grey ocean as winter winds crashed the waves into the cliffs below him.

He was at the point one day when a thought struck him. This would be his second Christmas back at Halleswell Hall and the thought of spending the festive period with just Flo for company again didn't seem right somehow. Christmas was a time for children.

Where had that thought come from? As he stood there with the wind buffeting him it was almost as though it was bringing back to him the words of Vicky's last letter to him

I am so afraid though that you will despair and lose the will to live. This is a mortal sin in any religion and could keep us apart for many thousands of years. I don't ask you to believe in it, but I do so believe and the very thought of us being parted once again is more than I can take.

For my sake please live on for me. As my illness progresses the things of this world seem so trivial compared to the adventure we face when we pass over. Know this as truth, for you have shared in my visions and know that they always come to pass. I see you, my darling, you are back in England and are surrounded by children laughing and playing

He realised that had been just what he had been doing for the last year or so since his return from India. Wallowing and putting his life on hold. He had been going through the motions but not really living and certainly not enjoying the life he had left. Was it impatience to join Vicky? Maybe so, but what would she say to him when they were reunited

'You did just what I asked you not to do didn't you?' Nathan could hear it now and thought the last thing he wanted when he met Vicky again was to have her angry with him.

Vicky's words and memories of the parties in India gave him an idea. Turning Hero he raced down the hillside, kicking up clouds of glistening frost as he went. Arriving back at the hall he went in search of Flo, finding her in the kitchen he shared his idea with her. She loved it and her mind started to think of things she would need to prepare straight away. There was not much time and much to do. Flo was in her element, however much she complained, she loved doing this kind of thing.

Poor Flo ended up with most of the arrangements as Nathan had other things to occupy his time just before Christmas. He had contacted the National Trust and there were a series of meetings with both them and his solicitors to set up the transfer of ownership of the hall after his death.

The National Trust had been happy to take Nathan's offer, especially as Halleswell had been the home of Tim Meverall-Cavendish who was rapidly becoming a renowned artist.

A steady stream of delivery trucks wound there way up the drive to the hall. Produce of all sorts found its way into Flo's kitchen. Nathan did his part and he enlisted the aid of Bill and Ned from the Smugglers.

'I have something I'd like to ask you two,' he said to the two old men after he had pulled them aside in the pub.

'I am trying to arrange something and I need some help but it must remain top secret and go no further than us three.'

'You can rely on us Squire, we on't tell a soul will we Ned?'

'No, no not a soul, Bill.'

'Now what's it you want us t'do?'

Nathan grinned, 'it's going to be our little conspiracy and it will only work as long as it stays secret. Now you two gent's know everyone around here don't you?'

'Most everyone, Govna,' said Ned, 'And them as we don't

know by name we knows by sight.'

'Good that is what I wanted to hear. Now this is what we are going to do.'

The three old men were enjoying themselves; especially as the other regulars in the pub kept trying to find out what they were up to when they met in a corner of the pub with their heads together. They even dropped false hints to the eavesdroppers and soon rumours were flying around the village. All were wide of the mark and Nathan was delighted. He hadn't had so much fun in ages. Even Flo warning him that it all might backfire on him couldn't dampen his enthusiasm.

A week before Christmas and it was time to put the first part of his plan into action. He sent the Rolls to collect Ned and Bill, a touch they would appreciate, he thought, and give onlookers something else to wonder at.

When the car returned the two old men got out with huge grins on their faces. 'You should'a seen old Mrs Proudfoot's face when yer Roller pulled up outside ma house, it was a picture. I never seen anyone's jaw drop that far afore.'

Nathan laughed; he had not used the car since his return so it would not have been seen for many years. So far so good, he thought and invited his co-conspirators in.

'Right lads, I've written to everyone on the list we made up. Is there anyone you can think of that we have missed, it would be awful if someone got left out?'

'I think we got 'em all Squire, now you want us to take 'em round like?'

'No, I want you to take them to a young chap of my acquaintance. His name is Tom and he is expecting you. I have already asked him if he wanted a delivery job and he was pleased to do it for us, especially as I gave him a new bike to do it on. His legs are younger than yours and I have another job for you, one that is far more up your street. I want you to go to the Smugglers tonight and see what people are saying. They should all have their letters by then and I am hoping it will be the talk of the village. Be careful though you are bound to be asked questions and I don't want you giving the game away just yet.'

'Roight you are Squire. I am sure me un Ned can handle it can't we Ned.'

'Yeah, yeah that's roight that's summut we can do roight that is.'

Nathan was still grinning as he saw Bill and Ned off in the Rolls complete with a large sack of handwritten letters.

Flo was waiting when he turned into the house, still chuckling to himself. Flo didn't look pleased. 'Are you going senile in your old age? You're acting like it anyhow.'

'No Flo, I' m not going senile quite yet but I am having a lot of fun with this.'

'I'm sure you are and I am doing all the work.'

'Sorry Flo but it will be worth it, you will see,' said Nathan as he made his way into the study.

Flo smiled as she watched him go, she was pleased that he was having fun and she didn't mind the extra work, however much she complained about it. In some ways it was part of the game.

In the study Nathan sat down. He looked at the desk and saw one invitation left.

Dear Mr/Mrs_____

I should be pleased if you would accept my invitation to a night of celebration at Halleswell Hall on 24th December at 7.15pm. Please be assured that children are very welcome and will be provided for. No doubt you will excuse an old man's eccentric wishes, but I would like you bring a paper swan with you. (Instructions are on the back of the invitation).

With kind regards,

Nathan Irvine-Meverall.

Suitably vague thought Nathan. I wonder if you would approve of what I am doing my love. Somehow I think you would.

The last few days before Christmas went by in a blur for Nathan. There was so much to do. Flo had it even worse but eventually all was ready.

As darkness fell on Christmas Eve Nathan went upstairs to dress, a dinner suit was required for this occasion. Now the time was getting nearer he was becoming nervous, what if no one came, what if. Enough of the 'what ifs,' he said to himself, they will come.

Seven o'clock and time to reveal all, Nathan went to his bedroom window and looked out over the dark waters of the lake which glowed slightly under the moonlight. Someone threw a switch somewhere. Suddenly the whole area in front of the house was awash with a soft golden light rising from hundreds of lanterns arranged around the lake and the front of the hall. Strings of lanterns festooned the trees, lighting up the whole of the drive. Braziers were lit adding their own glow to the lanterns. It was a beautiful sight and one that Nathan drank in, it was all he had hoped it would be for this special night. Now he just needed his guests to come.

Flo was fussing with final details when he entered the great hall. She looked up as he came down the stairs. 'My word don't we look handsome tonight.'

Nathan gave her a small bow, 'why thank you madam.'

Flo smiled but after a moment she was serious. 'Have you really thought this through Nathan? This is the first time Halleswell has seen anything like this since that night.'

Nathan of course knew what that night was and he said, 'yes it is and its time for that night to be removed from history as the last great party at Halleswell Hall. You know the real reason for it though don't you?'

'Yes Nathan, I do and a fine tribute it will be. Are you going to tell your guests the real reason for the party?'

'I haven't decided yet but I think maybe I should. It is time for the end of secrets at Halleswell Hall I believe.

Bill came hurrying in from where he had been keeping watch on the drive. 'They're comin Squire, looks like the whole bloomin village marchin up together.'

'Thanks Bill.'

'Well Flo, the moment of truth, no time for second thoughts now.'

'No Nathan, that time has passed, I wish you well with tonight and may you find a peace through it.'

Nathan walked over to Flo and gave her a peck on the forehead, 'thank you Flo, for everything.'

Stopping by the front door, Nathan looked down the drive to see the whole village walking toward him. All of them had dressed in the best clothes and Nathan was touched by the effort they had all made. Every one of them carried a paper swan and several held torches. The village folk walked slower as they came up to the house, looking around at the lantern lit house and gardens, taking in the beauty of the scene. Smiles overtook the nervous looks that many a face had worn as they approached, the soft lighting relaxing their tension. Nathan waited until they had all gathered at the front of the hall, looking expectantly at him. The children were more interested in the sights and sounds of the evening and the smells of food in the offing had many a stomach growling, but when Nathan started talking even they hushed to listen.

'My friends welcome to this special Christmas Eve. Welcome to my home. I know we have maybe had a bit of fun over the past few weeks and have kept you all in suspense, and I know you are dying to know what is going to happen. Well that waiting is over. It is high time a party atmosphere came back to Halleswell Hall and who better to share it with than people who live and work so close to here, and yet, how few of you have been here before. I am hoping that will change after tonight and you will feel free to visit me here and to make use of the old public rights of way across the parklands and in Brannon's Wood.'

A cheer and enthusiastic applause met this speech and Nathan waited until it subsided with a smile on his face before continuing. When he did he was serious again. 'There is another reason for tonight which is personal to me but I would share with you. Some of you know that my darling wife passed away not so long ago. Her final wish was to have her ashes buried here at Halleswell. She lies at peace now with other members of the family in a grove in Brannon's Wood. That is one place I would ask you to respect if you are taking a walk in the woods.

'What of the swans? I am sure you are all curious as to their purpose. They are the personal part of the evening. The swan holds a very large part of my heart for several reasons and I thought it would be a fitting tribute to my Vicky if we set your swans free onto the lake tonight to celebrate her life and to honour Tim Cavendish-Meverall.'

There was respectful applause and a murmur of agreement.

Bill brought forward a large paper swan and handed it to Nathan, who said, 'if you would like to follow me I would greatly appreciate it, as would other members of my family that have left us.'

He made his way forward and the crowd parted to let him through, heads slightly bowed it became almost an honour guard as Nathan made his way through the crowd. Once he was through they turned and followed him in silence. Something told them that this was a special moment and they were all drawn into it.

Nathan stopped at the North end of the lake and kneeling on a specially built little wooden platform, he silently let his swan go. For a moment it floated in front of him before a light breeze caught it and it serenely floated down the lake. He rose and stepped back. The village folk took that as their cue and silently came forward in turn to release their swans. Soon dozens of the paper birds glided across the lake, driven by the breeze. Light from the lanterns made the swans look like they were floating across liquid gold. It was a special moment that none present would ever forget. There were tears on several faces, not least Nathan's as he softly said, 'farewell my darling, it won't be long before we are reunited.'

Nathan's swan floated on and was swallowed by the darkness out of reach of the lanterns glow. As soon as it had disappeared a real swan glided into the golden part of the lake. For a long moment it looked at Nathan before turning and leading the rest of the paper birds out of sight.

A hush settled over the crowd. They all knew they were present at something special, even though they did not know the significance.

Nathan stood with his head bowed and then there was a whoosh, and a single rocket exploded overhead, lighting up the sky with a myriad of golden sparks.

Nathan looked up and smiled through his tears. 'Come my friends it is time to celebrate.' Music started up and the joyful tune of a Christmas carol drifted out to the lake from the house.

Nathan led the way into the hall and there were gasps as the villagers caught sight of the beautifully decorated hall. A huge tree stood in the corner, white and gold lights sending a warm glow into the room. More lights strung along the walls added to the festive atmosphere, holly, its red berries reflecting the light, garlands and streamers all added to the party mood.

In the centre of the room the great table was groaning under the weight of all sorts of Christmas food. The centre piece of the table was a stunning display of white Christmas roses. Many of the gardeners from the village commented on its beauty. Another table had been set up as a bar with Ned, looking surprisingly dapper set up as barman.

'Come my friends eat, drink dance and enjoy this Christmas Eve,' shouted Nathan above the sound of the music.

The good folk of the village did not need telling twice. Soon the party was in full swing. The carols turned to dancing music and soon the floor was full of whirling couples, Children, more interested in food and exploring than dancing, found ample opportunity to do both. Nathan stood back and watched. He was delighted to see everyone having such a good time. Flo appeared, she had changed from her work clothes and the long dress she had chosen gave her a regal look. Nathan spotted her and crossed to the stairs to meet her. 'Welcome Flo you have worked wonders for me tonight and I am forever in your debt for that.' He stooped and kissed her hand before leading her onto the dance floor. She said not a word but danced with Nathan and then several of the men from the village. Nathan thought it was fitting that the woman who had looked after his family for so long should enjoy the evening she had helped make possible.

Nathan spotted several of the partygoers looking at Tim's painting of the swan and wondered what they were thinking, maybe they saw the significance, maybe not, but at least he thought he had given them all something to think about tonight.

Midnight came around and the chosen hour for the end of the party had arrived, Nathan had one more surprise for his guests. As they left a man in a red suit with a big white beard was waiting for them, sitting in the front porch.

As they filed passed him he handed out presents to all the children. They were delighted and for them it rounded off the perfect evening. Without exception the villagers thanked Nathan for a wonderful evening as they left and the happy chatter echoed back as they walked down the drive.

Nathan smiled, it had been a great night and he had thoroughly enjoyed himself.

Christmas morning and Nathan awoke late. He came down the stairs bleary eyed and made his way into the great hall. It seemed empty somehow after the crowds of last night. Flo had been busy and the room had been cleared of last nights leavings and the table had been laid for Christmas dinner. They were having guests. Bill and Ned, together with Tom and his parents would be arriving in a while for dinner, but first he had something else he had to do. Something he had been saving for three days since it had arrived. Sitting in his chair he pulled an envelope from his jacket pocket and looked at the envelope, savouring the anticipation of the news it would contain. He slit the envelope and took out the paper inside.

Honoured Father,

Greetings from your obedient son and family. I hope that you are in good health and this letter will reach you in time for the festival of Christmas. Does that sound strange to you, that we also celebrate Christmas here In India? Mother taught us to see that most religions shared a common background, that of a higher power which we see as Brahma, but many see as a one true God.

Lord Krishna himself was put on this earth as a baby so we do not find the birth of Jesus so hard to understand. Indeed we plan to bring a large tree into the orphanage for the children to decorate. The little ones become so excited to receive their presents and we love to see the smiles on their eager faces.

I have a present for you as well, but it may take some time to reach you. Janna is pregnant again and this time we hope for a boy. If we are blessed with a boy child we have chosen the name of Nandin, the nearest name we can find to Nathan. Little Vicky is so excited, although she is now old enough to ask about you and mother Victoria.

She misses you, dear father, as we miss you and we hope you are not alone on Christmas day. If wishes have wings then they fly from us to you so you do not feel alone.

I know that you find it hard to accept our belief that you will be reunited with mother some day, but try to believe as she did.

We are very busy at the hospital with wounded and malnourished people arriving every day. I fear that our people were not really ready for independence as daily refugees swamp us, but your generosity is richly rewarded with medical aid and places for people to sleep.

Mother would have been delighted to know that many of her children have gone on to higher education, returning to help us with nursing and teaching. Remember Waheed, the boy with one arm? He is now a minor official in the government and his intervention has helped us many times. You should feel proud, my father, for you taught him to live without fear.

Mother once said that you had the pride of a lion and the heart of an ocean. She was right, you know. Your love surrounds us every day and as the ocean sends its ripples to every shore, so your love touches everything you do and each person you meet.

Merry Christmas Father and kiss mother for me, as I know she is with you this day,

Your loving son, Kumar.

He read the letter several times before finally lowering it to his lap. What was he feeling? He didn't know, such a maelstrom of emotion battled within him, pride and satisfaction were winning. 'We did well Vicky my love, we did make a difference.'

ROSES OF REMEMBRANCE

After Christmas, winter slowly loosed its hold on the land and spring saw Nathan spending much of his time tending the roses he had planted in the glade where Vicky rested. The anticipation of their first flowering made him impatient, but he found just working on them, snipping a dead twig here, removing a leaf there and training the climbing varieties tempered that impatience. The hardest job he had was to build an archway at the entrance. That was the one job that he had to enlist help with. Bill had come to his rescue; he was a keen gardener himself and had been more than happy to help Nathan with that task. It was whilst he was helping that Bill mentioned the village summer fair. Many years ago it had always been held at the hall but the practice had been dropped for a long time now. Bill asked if there was any possibility of renewing the Halleswell Summer Fair. Nathan thought it was a great idea and readily agreed.

Nathan made sure the summer fair that year was something special, it didn't take long for the news that for the first time in many years it was to be held at Halleswell Hall and several people in the village offered help with the organisation.

Nathan had been delighted when he had been asked if the fair could be held in the Hall grounds. It was something Nathan looked forward to, and when the morning came he found himself to be excited by the prospect of having so many people of the village in the grounds of the Hall again.

There had been some misgivings amongst a few of the villagers. Not all the stories and rumours about happenings at the hall had been removed by Nathan's adaptation to village life, or by the events at the Christmas party.

Despite reservations, the good folk of the village streamed along the long drive toward the hall, to what had quickly come to be known as Halleswell Fair. The villagers saw it as a chance of a good day out plus there was the promise of treats that were still hard to come by, even though rationing was coming to an end.

Stalls and rides offering all sorts of goodies were set up in the paddock at the end of the drive. Coconut shies, a ducking stool and a tug of war were but few of the delights available for all to enjoy.

A large marquee held a flower display and fruits of many of the villagers labours were laid out on tables, ready to be judged in vegetable and jam competitions later in the day. The beer tent was well stocked and Nathan had even donated bottles of wine from the Halleswell cellars.

The villagers had formed their own band, with elderly farmers playing a merry tune on their fiddles. Some of the younger generations joined in with the guitars that were just becoming popular. Small children had paper combs to add to the noise.

'Come on Flo, let's show these youngsters how to do it,' said Nathan, as he indicated toward the dance floor, laughing at her look of surprise.

'Nathan, I'm too old for this,' she replied, but he could see the pleased smile on her face as she took his arm.

The day was a great success and Nathan was momentarily surprised by the warmth he felt from the villagers. They seemed to have accepted him with welcome arms now. One little girl had even begged him for a 'piggy-back' and despite his aching leg he was glad to oblige.

He had one last surprise for them as darkness started to cast its veil over the day's festivities. All eyes turned skyward as fireworks lit up the darkening sky. Many coloured lights cast a glow over the upturned faces and brought gasps from astounded locals, who were delighted by the climax to a great day.

Nathan would not have recognised himself in the way the people thought of him. The following night there were a good few of the local farmers discussing the previous day's events.

'He's a grand man, the Squire,' said one old gaffer.

'Aye, that he is,' replied another, 'I sees him riding about on that girt great horse of his, and himself must be all of seventy. But he sups his ale alongside o' us just like a regular labourer.'

'He don't hold with the fancy new ideas neither,' said

another, casting a belligerent look at the outsider sat in the corner.

Now there was a man to raise the hackles with his talk of opening gift shops and turning their beloved peaceful village into a mass of noisy, untidy visitors.

'He'm a fine looking man as well,' volunteered the barmaid. 'Still keeps that military air about him. They do say 'as how he was a great war hero, got that bad leg of his by fighting ten Jerries all on his own'

After the fair life returned to normal, it wasn't all tending roses and riding Hero however. Nathan found that running the estate took more time than he really wanted to spend on it. Mundane problems like a leaking gutter on one of the estate cottages, a dispute with rent with a tenant farmer or a hundred and one other problems meant that he had to set aside at least a couple of hours a day to deal with estate matters. The next winter he decided to make some radical changes. He spent many evenings running through the estate accounts. Several nights he ended up with severe headaches after staring at rows and rows of facts and figures. At the end of it he came to the conclusion that he didn't need the income from the outlying properties. Tim's paintings and books were bringing in far more money than he would ever need, so the rent he received was surplus to his requirements. He decided to offer the properties to the tenants to buy for a nominal fee. That would make his life easier and would also make his tenants futures secure.

Solicitors were contacted and the wheels set in motion. Most of the tenants were delighted to take him up on his offer and by the end of the spring it was all settled to everyone's satisfaction.

By the second summer the first real flowering of the roses he had so carefully nurtured became a reality. All his hard work had paid off, the glade was a beautiful sight with the roses in full bloom. The climbers had taken over the archway and the covering of white blossoms made a great show as he walked under it. The mass of flowers gave off a heady scent, and walking into the glade itself, was walking into a wonderland of colour. Although white was predominant, many other shades had their place. He was delighted with his labour and spent many an hour sitting on a bench he had brought in. Birds and insects had made their home in the glade now, adding their musical accompaniment to the visual display.

In the summer months he spent much of his time outside, either in the glade or riding on the estate or up to the point. Flo worried that he was spending too much time on his own, but he seemed content so she didn't push the matter. Most evenings he could be found at the Smugglers and she guessed he had more than enough interaction with other people there. That was not all of course, there were many visitors to the Hall now, either social or business. Tom became one of his favourite visitors, quite often he brought friends with him as well. Nathan didn't mind, it had been far too long since the halls had heard the laughter of happy children. Tom took great delight in exploring the house with his friends, giving them a guided tour. Nathan often told them stories of India, they were fascinated by the exotic tales he wove. He wasn't sure they believed half of them but that didn't matter at all.

Stephen was a regular visitor for both pleasure and business. He was now Nathan's business manager, looking after all things connected to Tim Cavendish-Meverall. It was a big job as Tim's legacy was growing over the passing years.

During the winter months Nathan worked on his part of the Meverall journal. He was writing two versions. Like Alex before him he wrote a toned down version in the one volume format but he also penned a full version to go with the original, to which he had also added Vicky's contribution. He had thought long and hard about doing that, but in the end decided that it would be hard to leave the work unfinished. Even though some of what he had to say he had misgivings about, he did it anyway. Stephen was involved in this too. Nathan had decided that he would like Alex's version published after his death and Stephen was the one who would be organising that.

The months and the years passed, and the villagers had gotten used to having the squire around, but many worried over his failing health. He seemed to be getting increasingly frail, although they would see him still riding his big black horse, Hero, but the spring seemed to have gone out of his step lately.

The next spring, his fifth since returning to the hall, saw Nathan spending a lot of his time in Brannon's Wood as usual. The roses had flowered wonderfully well over the years under his care and would flower again soon. He enjoyed his work there, even though it left him stiff and his back aching. That was one job he did on his own, a labour of love for him. He was cutting out some dead wood on a rose bush when he felt the first tightening in his chest, he didn't think that much of it, working too hard he thought to himself, but a few minutes later it was back and this time the pain was worse. He pitched forward landing on his face. He had fallen across Vicky's grave. He raised his eyes to her headstone and softly said. 'I'm coming my love,' the spring sunlight faded as his eyes closed for the last time.

Nathan's passing had come as a great shock to both members of the household and to the villagers, who learned of the tragedy as word quickly spread. Flo took it especially badly, but there were arrangements to make and she was determined to be the one to make them. The next few days passed in a blur for her as she spent every waking hour ordering flowers and visiting the Vicar and undertakers. She soon realised that it was going to be a large funeral, many visitors came to the Hall to express their condolences and everywhere she went in the village she met enquiries as to when the funeral would be held. She knew Nathan had wanted a quiet ceremony but that was not going to be possible now. It would not be right to deny the folk of the village the chance to say goodbye, and Flo did not think Nathan would have minded had he known the strength of feeling among the villagers. The hardest thing she had to do was speak to Kumar on the telephone and tell him what had happened. She thought long and hard about how she was going to tell him, but in the end decided that simplest was best.

The evening before the funeral saw Flo in the great hall with Stephen. He had arrived earlier in the day and had been helping Flo with the final arrangements.

Flo brought a file out of the study. Opening it had found a letter addressed to Stephen as well as one to her and one for Kumar, plus a copy of his will. The Will, Flo had seen before and knew of his wishes. He wanted to be buried with Vicky of course, and she knew he had wanted her to carry on looking after the house after he had gone, so she put the will to one side along with Kumar's letter and sat with hers in her hand. Stephen did the same; neither seemed willing to open their letters, but finally with a silent glance at each other they did so together.

Flo was in tears as she started to read hers. It spoke of her loyalty to the family and to Nathan in particular. It spoke of Nathan's wish that she not be sad at his passing but to be happy that he was with Vicky once more. He spoke of his life and all the joy he had felt, and how she had always been there to help him through the troubled times they had shared and finally he asked her to perform two last tasks for him once he was gone.

Stephen's letter was more business like. It contained instructions on how Nathan wanted his will carried out and it asked Stephen to be the one who made sure it was. There were also requests about the Meverall journals. Nathan had decided that he would like to have them published. There were stipulations however. He knew that Halleswell would be open to the public once the National Trust took over and was happy with that, but he wanted the journals to only be for sale at the house and profits to be split between the National Trust, for upkeep of Halleswell and the rest going to Kumar in India, for him to use in the hospital. There was also another request. The original journals Nathan wanted put in a protective container and then bricked up in a cavity in the wall of the wine cellar. *'They will be found by one who is meant to find them and they will know what to do with them.'*

It sounded like fortune telling to Stephen, but then nothing surprised him about Nathan. He had been a unique character.

When both of them had finished reading their letters they sat in silence. Both had a lot to think about.

Flo spoke first. 'Nathan has asked me to do some things for him and they involve you Stephen. Wait there please,' she said as she rose and left the Hall. When she returned she was carrying the red covered journal.

'I think Nathan wants you to get this published doesn't he? I think you should read his part; maybe it will help you to understand what he was thinking. As for the original I think he has expressed his wishes to you about what to do with them. I think we should do that soon and do it ourselves.'

'Yes I think we should, not tonight though. I would not feel right doing it before we have said goodbye.'

A car pulled to a halt on the drive outside. Flo smoothed the front of her dress and said 'They are here.' She sounded nervous and with a glance at Stephen went to open the door.

A tall, handsome Indian gentleman was walking toward the door with another who had one arm of his jacket pinned to his side. An older man was helping a lady from the back of the car. All four looked travel weary.

'You must be Kumar,' said Flo as she held out her hand to greet him. She was a little surprised when he ignored her hand and embraced her.

'You must be Flo, I have heard so much about the lady of Halleswell over the years. It is an honour to finally meet you,' said Kumar with a bow. 'This is Waheed, Dr McCloud and his wife Angela.'

Flo greeted each in turn and then invited them in, promising hot drinks and food.

Introductions were made to Stephen and Flo disappeared into the kitchen.

Kumar looked around the hall and said to Stephen. 'Many times my honoured father told me of this place, I did not ever expect to see it with my own eyes. I am glad that I have, it will make the memory of my father complete.'

When Flo returned, Kumar asked if he could visit his mother's resting place before the evening darkened. Long he stood there by her side, of his thoughts he told no one and no one asked.

After they had eaten, Flo gave Kumar the letter his father had written, and left him in the hall to read it in peace. The other three weary travellers went to bed early as did Stephen. It was going to be a long day tomorrow.

Once they were all settled Flo returned to Kumar. He was sitting in the chair by the hearth, his letter held loosely in his hand. He looked up when Flo entered.

'Nathan was a great man wasn't he. I have never known a person with as big a heart as my father.'

'He was indeed and he will be missed by far more people

than he would ever have thought, he touched so many lives in different ways. If you don't mind I must get to bed myself. Would you like me to show you to your room before I go?'

'Thank you, but I think I will sit here a while if that is ok.'

'Of course, good night then and thank you for coming, I know what it would have meant to your father.'

The following morning broke bright and warm. There was much preparation going on at Halleswell. Flo expected there would be quite a crowd coming back after the funeral.

By the time the cars arrived to take them all to the church all was ready, although Flo could not resist one final check. The little church was packed and the church yard held more people that could not fit in the church. Most of the village had turned out to pay their final respects. Those in the churchyard lined the path to provide an informal honour guard as Nathan was carried slowly into the church. Heads bowed they paid silent tribute.

After the service Nathan's coffin was brought out and laid in a carriage, pulled by Hero. The black stallion would have the honour of taking his master to his final resting place.

Hero pulled the carriage at a stately pace and was followed by a long line of mourners. When they arrived at Halleswell Ned led most of the people back to the hall. The laying to rest of Nathan would be a private affair. Flo and Stephen, along with the four from India and Bill would see him on his way. When they arrived at the edge of the wood Nathan's coffin was gently lifted from the carriage and a slow procession made its way through the wood to the sunlight glade.

As they started the sedate walk through the woods Kumar heard the sound of running feet and was a little surprised when a small hand caught hold of his. A young lad of about twelve had run after them and silently joined them. Kumar glanced at Flo who nodded and continued on toward the glade.

The Vicar said a few words as Nathan's body was gently lowered into the ground and they all stood with their own thoughts.

Kumar cut a single white rose and gently dropped it into the grave. For some time they all stood around the grave, each deep in their own thoughts. Finally they all felt a silent agreement and they walked toward the house. They took their time as they strolled across the pastures, silent as they set off but as they drew nearer to the house conversation started, memories of Nathan, the little things, the things that made them smile. By the time they reached the house their mood had lifted. The boy still held Kumar's hand until Flo spoke to him.

'You OK Tom?' She asked, putting her arm around his shoulders.

'Yes Flo, I am alright, going to miss Mister Nathan though.'

'I know Tom we all will, but we have our memories of him that they are something we will have forever.'

LIFTING THE VEIL – SEPTEMBER 1997

'Notice the intricately carved panelling,' Viv said as she led her final group of the day around the great hall. 'This is the only part of the original house that has been untouched since the early Elizabethan era. The style is Tudor in design, a remarkable achievement when other stately halls were partitioned off by later generations.' Gathering the group around her, she progressed towards the great fireplace with the enigmatic Swan painting displayed in splendour with only one modern spotlight to highlight its magnificence.

Some of the group showed only passing interest but others stopped in wonder, craning their heads to see above the enormous arched fireplace.

'If you look at your guidebooks you'll see that this is an early painting by the WW1 artist Timothy Cavendish-Meverall, a descendant of the family.'

Turning from the painting she resumed her tour, guiding the party up the great stairs to show off the minstrel's gallery before taking in the rest of the house.

Viv always felt a bit of disappointment when the group invariably 'oohed' and 'aahed' over the later additions to the house, the stately bedrooms with their four-poster beds and the grand drawing rooms with their crowded furniture and gilded ornamentation. These were of a much later era and somehow she felt them out of place in this grand old house. Still, it was her job to keep up the running commentary that she could now recite in her sleep.

The tour ended in the vast kitchens, although she would never show them the private study and the smaller, more compact kitchen where the last of the Meverall's had retreated into their privacy. Over the last two years she had come to love the old house and to cherish the memories of the last generations.

Of course she had read the story of the house and its occupants from the heavily edited version that was on sale, it was her job to know these things. Sometimes though, she felt as if there was something missing from the tales of adventures, smuggling and the exploits of a family throughout the centuries.

Sighing she lead the group through the doors to the grounds and allowed them to explore on their own for the last hour of the day.

It was then that she noticed the elderly lady, the one who had gazed on the painting with proper respect, hanging back from the group with a younger woman and a child of about eleven. She guessed the elder woman to be in her late seventies, although she kept an upright stance, only leaning on her walking stick when needed.

'The tea shop's still open for another half-hour,' she said, 'maybe you would like to rest awhile and let the little girl play in the gardens?'

Now why did she say that? Children were supposed to be supervised at all times.

'That would be lovely, perhaps you could join us, you look as if you need a rest,' the older woman smiled at her, a dazzling smile.

'Oh please do,' that was the younger woman, 'Becky's a good child, she'll be no bother.'

Viv found herself drawn to the family, grandmother, daughter and granddaughter, going by the uncanny family resemblance.

'Follow me,' she said, taking them behind the house to the tiny teashop.

Once settled down with a large pot of tea and some real Devon scones they soon got to chat about the house.

The elder woman introduced herself as Sally Cartwright and the daughter as Nicola Maitland.

'Actually I wanted to talk to you, my dear,' Sally addressed Viv.

'I was stationed here in the war and when Nicola suggested the trip I wanted to see the house again. I'm not quite as spry as in those days, but seeing the house has brought such memories back. Nicky wanted to come and Becky was so excited when we told her about it.' Once again that dazzling smile was back. Viv studied the woman and decided there was something about the woman that invited confidences, 'I'd love to hear more,' she said.

The teashop was about to close by the time Sally had outlined her story and still Viv wanted to hear more. She sensed that Sally was keeping something back from her, but the tour bus was about to leave and she wasn't sure what to do.

'Come on mum, you've got this far, now's the time to come clean,' Nicola said.

Sally reached inside her large bag and handed Viv a wrapped parcel.

'I think you should read this,' she said, 'after that I think I need to talk to you again, but for now I think it's time we left.'

'You'll need the phone number,' Nicky said, 'I've written it down for you, but I don't want you upsetting mum so could you ring me first. I'm staying with mum for a while so just ask for me if she answers.'

'Bossy boots,' Sally said, but there was love in her eyes for her daughter. 'Now where's Becky got to?'

'I'll go and look for her,' Viv needed time to think about this strange conversation.

She soon found Becky perched on the garden wall and talking to Graham as if she had known him all her young life.

'Your mum and gran are waiting for you,' Viv lifted her down and smiled at her husband.

The girl took Viv's hand and skipped along beside her, the blonde hair falling over her eyes.

'I think you've lost your pretty ribbon,' Viv had noticed the child's ponytail before.

'Mummy won't mind, she says I'm an awful tomboy, anyway that means I can come back and see the pretty lady.'

Viv was confused, she hadn't seen any 'pretty' ladies in the tour group that was made up of mostly pensioners, but children had vivid imaginations. Perhaps the child meant one of the many family portraits.

Watching Sally mount the stairs onto the bus Viv was struck by the grace of the woman. A jaunty red scarf and the matching red cardigan enlivened her neat navy trousers and crisp white blouse. 'She must have been a right stunner in her youth.' She thought. Becky waved from the back of the bus and as Viv walked away she thought of the strange parcel and what it might contain. For now though she had to check the house and then count the day's takings before locking them in the safe until Friday's trip to the bank.

Once that was done she would settle down with her husband and enjoy a leisurely meal while watching the evening news. It was a pattern they both settled into, only broken by the occasional meal out or a trip to the local pub. The villagers had finally accepted them and a few had even started to visit Brannon's Wood again. That was a strange place, with its roped-off clearing keeping strangers away from the family burial plot.

Martin Boyd had explained why most of the Meverall's had been buried in the ancient churchyard and why some were buried in the clearing. She wasn't sure it had been explained to her properly as merely a convenience, surely it must have been difficult to get the ground consecrated, but who was she to question it?

Later on as Graham dozed in front of the television Viv considered reading the journal that had been revealed on opening the parcel, but something told her it was better to read it by day. Tomorrow there was only one group booking for the morning and Jackie could easily cope with any casual visitors in the afternoon. Tonight she was restless and wanted to sit in the open air with a glass of wine.

September was a month for partings, she thought. The hasty packing for university and the tears she had quietly shed. Nick was her baby and although he was now doing his PHD she still felt that ache of separation as if it was yesterday. Jenny had married in early September and now lived in London, a career woman who would wait for the right time to make Viv a grandmother.

The evening sky had darkened to an indigo blue and the stars were beginning to appear as she sat and sipped her wine. Earlier on she had seen the swallows gathering for their annual pilgrimage to warmer climes. Somehow that always made her feel sad as if life was leaving her behind, but when winter came around she welcomed the cosy nights in front of the fire. She needed something to take her mind off the changing of the seasons, the journal would do that and comforted she went inside to the warmth awaiting her.

'Viv, did you hear me?' Graham said, his voice full of impatience.

Slowly she lifted her head up from the page she'd been reading.

'Sorry darling, what were you saying?'

'I've been trying to talk to you for the last ten minutes, its six o'clock and time to decide whether we stay in or go out for meal. Really, Viv, I'm starving, can't you get your head out of that damned book?'

She was startled, was it really that time; surely she couldn't have been reading for nearly five hours? Unconsciously she stroked the smooth red binding, taking care to shut it carefully as many of the pages were getting brittle. Reluctantly she set it aside, aware that her normally placid husband was getting very irate. It was time to take a break from the narrative anyway, the handwriting had gotten smaller and she was straining her eyes to read on.

'Give me a minute and we'll eat out. Only can we make it just the Smugglers for tonight, I don't fancy getting dressed up?'

That suited Graham just fine; the Smugglers did a cheap and cheerful meal with the added bonus of the best ale around.

Ten minutes later they were ready to set out, armed with a powerful torch, as the lanes were still unlit.

Graham put his knife and fork down on the empty plate. 'Nothing like a good old steak and kidney pie to hit the spot,' he enthused.

Viv looked up from her own plate where she was struggling to finish the large meal. 'I'm fit to burst,' she announced, laying down her own utensils.

'I could fit in another glass of wine though,' she responded waving her empty glass in the air.

'I'll get you a half bottle,' he replied, 'I think I'll treat myself to a large brandy.'

'Make that a full bottle,' she said, 'I think we need to talk.'

Graham looked surprised; Viv wasn't much of a drinker and normally was content to share a bottle of wine with him over their meal. Perhaps it was something to do with that mysterious book, he thought as he went to the bar to place their order.

A few of the locals nodded to him and some wished him a good evening. They liked to see the custodians of the Hall in the local pub. For some of them the success of the new couple running the Hall was welcome, the shops were benefiting from the tourist trade. Others were wary that it would mean the tourist board would offer an incentive to turn the village into a chocolate-box rendition of it's real self. The Edwards's had assured them this wouldn't happen and so far they had kept their word.

Graham topped Viv's glass up and sat back to savour his rare treat of a brandy.

'Okay darling, what gives? Something's bothering you apart from just the season.'

She stirred uneasily; loath to bring the subject up but knowing this was something that she had to share with her husband.

'You know the parcel that I was given the other day?'

He nodded.

'The elderly lady that gave it to me was stationed in the house during the war. She was very young and curious about the locked rooms; in fact there was one in particular she couldn't stay away from. One day she managed to get into the room and what she found there more or less killed her curiosity forever. A young woman died in that room, a member of the Meverall family, she went mad and had to be restrained for her own safety.' Viv took a gulp of her wine and then carried on, 'she also found a book, in this case a sort of journal. Before she had time to look at it the housekeeper nearly caught her. Terrified of being discovered she hid it away but never managed to put it back. The journal belonged to Alex, the girl's father. In it he recorded the family's deepest darkest secret. Don't you dare laugh,' she said as Graham started to splutter at the rather archaic manner of speech his wife was exhibiting.

'I've nearly read the entire journal and it sheds a lot of light on what happened to the family at that time. Remember how we have always speculated on the demise of the family? Well the journal is part of the family history, even if you don't want to believe what the contents say. I've only got a bit more to finish and after that I need to talk to Sally again.'

'Who's Sally?'

'Don't be so dim, Graham, you know who I mean. Anyway, there's always been a mystery about the house and I intend to solve it,' with that she sat back, her face flushed with a combination of acute embarrassment but also with the effort of actually putting her thoughts into words.

'This is important to you,' he answered, surprised by her vehemence.

She refilled her glass and he noticed her hands were trembling. Something in that damn book had got her upset and Graham didn't like to see his wife upset. She was gearing herself up to say something else and suddenly he wondered if he really wanted to hear it. Mentally shrugging his shoulders he bowed to the inevitable, when Viv wanted to speak he had no way of stopping her. The pub was noisy now and he had to lean forwards to catch her hesitant words.

'We never really solved the mystery around the house or in the woods, did we? Instead we became accustomed to it because we both knew we wanted to stay.'

He couldn't argue with that, he was fond of the house and loved his job of pottering around mending the small jobs and attending to the gardens. The occasional night noises had ceased to worry him and he thought that Viv had put it to the back of her mind.

'I think we have both ignored it, but it still troubles me and I think the journal may provide the answers I need. Please darling, say that you will help me, I can't do it alone?'

'Of course I will, now drink up and let's get home.'

Glancing at her watch she saw it was nearly eleven, had she really talked for that long?

Snuggling into her coat she was glad to be getting back, suddenly she felt as if she was truly going home.

October arrived with a spell of fine weather and the trees were putting on a grand display of green, brown, gold and red.

342

Halleswell Hall was closed until spring came around and for a short while Viv and Graham strolled in the woods kicking up the falling leaves like children at play. Viv knew she was putting off her detective work, but just for a short while she wanted to enjoy the season's beauty.

The idyllic time didn't last for long. Graham was busy pruning the roses around the graves in the clearing and Viv had wandered over to the old well. This was one place that the National Trust had wisely left alone. A team of experts had dated the original well back to the 6th century, although it was clear that it had undergone some renovation in the early 1900s. This had been upheld by the passages in the journal, but Viv wasn't yet ready to hand this over to the National Trust. Barbed wire kept the public away, but she had found a way around that and now sat near to the well whilst the trees whispered their secrets back and forth. Reading about the curse had both shocked and enthralled her, now she knew why her first instincts had led her to stay.

Help me, she cried out, I know why Alex took the cup, it was done in compassion for his daughter. He thought the cup would help her but now it's lost and peace will never reign here until it's back in the well. I know about the tiger-spirit, Alex wrote of that night and his sorrow over the Lady Charlotte, he was already half in love with her by that time. Vicky, you never meant any harm, speak to me, and guide me as you once guided so many on the path to grace.

Only the breeze sighed through the trees but suddenly a ray of sunlight peered through the gloom, alighting on the soft pink glow of the well, Viv's cry had been heard through the mists of time.

They found the bungalow with ease. It was in a complex on the outskirts of Exeter, the neat buildings painted white with mellow brown tiles. Winter pansies adorned the window boxes and the lawns were trimmed outside. Touches of individuality were present in the bright doors. Graham pulled up outside No 23 and Nicola hastened to greet them.

'Mother's so excited, I've had a hard time stopping her from baking enough scones to feed a small army,' she grinned to soften the hasty words.

'Actually it does her good, she's not been the same since her husband passed away some years ago. Oh, forgive me for twittering on, come in, welcome.'

Viv smiled, lucky Sally to have such a wonderful daughter, she thought and then felt guilty about Jenny who was only doing what she had been brought up to do.

Sally was waiting inside, her feet propped up on a recliner chair.

'Nicky's just fussing again, I'm fine, just a bit of arthritis,' she said. 'Would you like some tea and scones?' Graham and Viv said yes and Nicola bustled into the kitchen.

'She's such a lovely girl,' Sally said, 'a bit bossy, but then I can be a bit of a handful at times. I hope you don't mind but Becky will be along after school. Now let's get down to business.'

Viv laughed, this woman was definitely a force to be reckoned with. Seating themselves on the sofa neither knew where to start.

'You've read the journal so now you are wondering what to do about it,' Sally obviously decided on coming straight to the point.

'It's haunted me for years, you know, I was such a little mouse in those days, God only knows how I ever plucked up the courage to enter that room. That Flo was a right old dragon, but then she had served the family for most of her life. She didn't last long after Mr Nathan died. Jim and me had moved away from the village by then, but we heard she had a right grand funeral. That journalist fellow made sure of that. But that's not what you want to hear, of course.'

By now Nicola had brought the tea tray in and for a while they made polite small talk. With Nicola perched on the side of her mother's chair the conversation turned back to the days when Sally had been at Halleswell Hall.

'I read the journal, of course, it took me a while with running around for the bosses, but when it was done I was right scared. I'd heard the rumours, living so close to the village it was hard to miss them. My own ma was just a lass when it all started. She was courting my dad by then; Brannon's Wood was a good place for courting. That all stopped after the goings on at the big house, but a few people still went there. Mr Theo wasn't always a bad man; old Sidney always said he turned right queer after he got sick on that big old boat of his. He reckoned as how Mr Theo were brought up by his own dad to think he should be a sailor.'

Anyhow, after the party turned bad few folks went into the woods, except for the odd poacher and even them got scared when that big cat was loose.' she paused for a while and then went on, 'like as not you won't believe me, though plenty of folk had seen the big brute with their own two eyes. Ma said they had raised the devil that night, but when I read that book I believed every word. It all got hushed up as the matters of the big houses always do, though now I know the truth and so do you.' She looked directly at Viv as she said that.

'Now I've given the book back as Jim always said I should, remember though, I was still afraid and the time never seemed right. I knew when I saw you that the time had come.'

Now she looked directly at Viv.

'It's for you to put it right; you knew that from the start, didn't you?'

What could she say; Viv had known from the day she had spoken to the vicar, maybe even before that.

'Once I read the journal it all fell into place. I knew that the cup was special, I also knew that I'd seen it somewhere before. I've searched the house from top to bottom but I still can't find it. There's something else as well, I've read the history of the house, the one put out for the public, there's something missing though and I can't rest until I know what it is.'

Silence descended for a few minutes as people became wrapped up in their own thoughts.

'I think I may be able to help you look,' Sally spoke reluctantly.

All eyes turned to the old lady. Behind the surface of her white hair, the still trim figure, there was an aura of strength born of a strong and resolute personality.

'No mum, I can't let you do it,' Nicola was frantic with worry.

'Neither can I allow it,' Viv said. 'It's my problem and you've done enough already. '

Graham added his objections as well. They had reached an impasse; the clock struck 4 o'clock making them jump.

She burst into the room like a whirlwind, hair flying free from the confines of her ribbons.

'Oh goody,' Becky said, 'when do we leave?'

345

Viv hummed to herself as she made up the beds in the spare rooms, she was looking forward to having a child about the place again but the thought of chatting to Sally in confidence was an added bonus. It would also give Nicola time to spend with her husband, something that Viv felt they both needed. The decision to let both Sally and Becky stay for a week or two had been made fairly quickly once they had gotten over the shock of Becky's pronouncement.

Nicola had confided in her that the girl had always been prone to being a bit fey, there really wasn't any other thing they could call her sudden intuitions.

For once Graham was helping out by doing the cooking for the evening meal. The nights were starting to get a bit chilly so a good old-fashioned stew with chunky bread should set them up nicely. She was just putting the finishing touches to the rooms when Nicola's Volvo pulled up in front of the house.

Sally got out of the car a bit stiffly but was soon sitting in one of the large high-backed chairs that seemed to be a feature of the house. Becky was far too excited to sit still, so Graham took her outside for a while to let off some of her surplus energy.

Nicola sat in the kitchen with Viv, going over all the arrangements. She had produced a large hamper of delicacies and although Viv had protested at the extravagance, she was secretly pleased.

'Ma likes her little treats' she had explained, 'so I thought why not let you share them as well? Besides it will be a holiday for Richard and me. Not that he minds the time I spend with Ma, but well… we haven't had a lot of time on our own, what with him trying to get the business running and Becky being a bit of a handful at times.' She had run out of breath after this.

'Don't worry about a thing,' Viv reassured her, 'you should have seen my two when I was younger, right tearaways they were; now I miss them all the time.'

Eventually she had left after giving Viv strict instructions about her mother and daughter's bedtimes, what tablets Sally took and how to cope with Becky's moods.

Viv decided that apart from the tablets she would let things go at their own pace.

It was in this spirit of letting things unfold naturally that they all sat down to a latish supper at 8 o'clock. The stew was followed by one of Viv's own apple pies and the adults shared a bottle of white wine. Becky was yawning within an hour so needed no persuasion to settle down in her bed under the gables of the house.

'It's just like a ship,' she laughed, surprising Viv with a smacking kiss.

'I wonder if I'll see the pretty lady in my sleep.'

There it was again, that sudden mention of the woman. Tucking the child in, Viv kissed her back and then made her way downstairs.

Sally looked completely relaxed with a gin and tonic in one hand and the other resting lightly on the arm of the chair. Graham was playing the gracious host regaling her with stories of the various visitors they had shown around the Hall.

'She did what?' Sally grinned.

'Tried to get her fat husband on the four-poster bed with her.'

'You have to be joking?'

'Honest to God, you wouldn't believe what some people get up to.' Catching sight of Viv he smiled a bit sheepishly.

'Sorry honey, do you fancy a nightcap?'

'I'll have a G&T as well,' she replied.

'He's a good man,' Sally said when he went to the kitchen. 'I still miss my Jim although he's been gone a while now.' In a more sombre voice she suddenly said, 'my Jim would never have come home if it wasn't for Mr Nathan, the last master of Halleswell Hall. I never met him; of course, he lived in India in those days. There was quite a bit about him in that old journal, my Jim said he was a real gentleman, brave as well.'

'You don't have to talk about it tonight; I think it's been a long day for us all.' Viv was eager to know more, but not at the expense of her elderly guest.

'You're right; I do feel quite tired now. I want to talk to you some time tomorrow though. I always felt bad about taking that book, I'd like to help you find the cup and there's something else, something I've remembered since coming here.'

'It can wait until another day; now let me show you to your room.'

The next day dawned bright and crisp, just the sort of day for long walks and then a cosy fire. Becky was up and dressed by seven o'clock eager to start her explorations. Graham grumbled but in a good-natured way, 'it's the crack of dawn, what the hell have I let myself in for?'

'Go back to sleep then, misery guts; I don't intend to miss a lovely day like this.'

Viv washed and dressed quickly and soon was making scrambled eggs for her and Becky.

'Do you want to take your Nan a cup of tea?' she asked the child.

'Nan wouldn't like that; she says she wants to be independent.' Becky made the word sound like four words. 'She gets up early anyway; you have to give her a bit of time.'

Sure enough, Sally was making her way slowly into the kitchen.

'I smell scrambled eggs and toast, where's mine?' She hugged Becky.

'Too late, we've eaten them all up,' Becky giggled; this seemed to be a set routine Viv thought to herself.

'Better bring on the bacon then,' she said, poker-faced, sending the girl off into fits of laughter.

'Bacon? Did I hear that right?' Graham ambled into the kitchen.

'Don't speak to him until he's had his coffee, he's like a bear with a sore head.'

Becky thought that was hilarious and the kitchen rang with her laughter.

By ten they were ready to set off on what Becky called 'The Mighty Quest'. A look passed between Sally and Viv, the child already seemed to know this was no ordinary outing. But how could she know when they had not talked about it in front of her?

'Where shall we start?' Viv asked Sally, not sure about the older woman's stamina.

'I think it's best to go over the house while I'm fresh,' she answered, 'As tough as I think myself to be, even I know my limitations.'

'I'll take Becky around the woods,' Graham offered, 'leave you lovely ladies to have a girly chat.'

'I want a girly chat as well, Uncle Graham; I'm a big girl now.'

'Big enough to look for the tigers and the bears?' he quipped.

'Course I am, I thought you might be scared though,' whooping with delight she started to run along the path. With an exaggerated sigh he started to run after her.

They started in the great hall, prodding into the walls for hidden recesses. It seemed the appropriate place for something as valuable as the cup to be found. From there they started to work their way upwards along the South tower. Dusty, dishevelled and getting tired Viv called a temporary halt.

'It's no use, I've gone over the house so many times but all I get is a stuffy nose and aching feet. Let's take a breather and think about this logically.'

Sally agreed, she was getting tired and this seemed the right time to bring up the thing that had bothered her all along.

'This is the part of the house where I found the journal,' she confessed. 'I've been thinking about that night and there's something I now remember. When I picked up the journal I saw a large box besides it. It was half-hidden at the back of the cupboard. I was so scared, I was going to hide there until morning but I lost my nerve and started to panic. I don't know what made me look inside the box, maybe it was to take my mind off the fright, it was a very unpleasant room, full of bitter memories, I didn't need to be physic to know that. The corner lifted easily, as if it had been put away in haste. It was full of books, some red like the journal, others black and so worn that I got the impression they were very old. I took one and put it on the dressing table; I nearly jumped out of my skin when I saw the face. It was just my reflection in a shattered mirror but it gave me a nasty turn. It was another journal, but the writing was hard to follow. Now I am sure it was an old form of English, there was a date on the first page and I think it was 1705, but the light was poor.

When Nicola persuaded me to come back here I thought about those old books and imagined them to be locked up safely in a bank vault. I remember you saying that the man called Alex wrote about the history of the house and that started me thinking. You said yourself that the book seemed incomplete. What if the books were the old journals written by the generations of the Meverall's and what if they were then hidden away as Alex's journal had been?'

Viv looked at Sally with a deep respect; it couldn't have been easy telling that story. How many times had she thought the book to be incomplete? Surely the National Trust would have placed them in a museum or as Sally said, somewhere deep in a bank vault? Yet such books would bring in much needed money. She had seen other stately homes where such books were on display, secure behind a network of top security. Visitors would have come in droves to see such fragments of the past.

'Are you thinking the same as me?' she asked Sally.

'Yes, I am, I've had nearly a month to think it over. We know about the cup, but what if someone wanted to keep parts of the past hidden? They would be somewhere that nobody would think to look, unless that person cared enough about the past to look.'

'You are right, I never thought of it that way. But what do we do next, now we have two mysteries on our hands and no clues at all?'

'What about the journalist who drew up Nathan's will, I think I saw his name in the tourist book?'

'I spoke to his son when we decided to stay. I thought he might know about the cup, but he was genuinely puzzled. Christopher's a lawyer, he would have told me about any missing books. I'm afraid we've reached a dead end.'

Sally looked thoughtful; her face took on a look that Viv would have recognised if she had looked in a mirror.

'There must be clues somewhere; I'm not ready to give up before we've even started. Let's shake hands on it.'

The two women faced each other, one looking tired but obstinate, and the other younger but with that same determination. Hands clasped they swore a vow,

'Never give up, we will find both the books and the cup.'

The solemn moment was over, arms linked together they went home to food and a warm fire.

LIFTING THE VEIL – PART TWO

Graham was getting concerned about his wife and also their guests. This was the fifth day of their stay and Sally was looking tired and drawn. Even Becky's high spirits had dampened down in the last two days. He had become very fond of the girl as he took her on long walks around both the Hall and the woods. That first day he was enchanted by her vivid imagination as she spoke of the 'pretty lady'. She insisted that the lady was trying to talk to her but she could never hear her. One day she had apparently appeared before Becky with a large cat by her side. Her description of the cat sounded more like a Tiger, but he put that down to his joking about the Tigers and the Bears in the woods.

Some days they both joined Sally and Viv on the long searches around the house, though Becky seemed to find some parts of the house scary, as she put it. The only place she really felt comfortable in was the great hall and the large kitchens where once many cooks and maids prepared feasts for the grand ladies and gentlemen.

Often he would be the one to tuck her up in bed as he read her stories about the pirates, smugglers and the battles fought between the roundheads and the cavaliers. Some of it came from the tales about the Hall, but often he would just make them up on the spur of the moment.

In the meantime the women continued looking around the house or going back again and again to Alex's journal. He had been patient long enough and on the fifth day he decided that they all needed a break from the house or he would really lose his temper. He didn't much fancy going out for a meal or a drink on his own, but there was Becky to consider. Sunday lunch in the Smugglers would fit the bill nicely, he thought and arranged for a taxi to pick them up and drive them back afterwards.

It was another crisp autumn day and the pub was quite full. Sally's cheeks were flushed by the unexpected treat and even Viv was more relaxed than she had been for days. Becky thought it was a marvellous occasion and acted very much the grown-up young lady.

Once the puddings had been eaten, the adults lounged back with their gin and tonics while Becky pretended her glass of Cola was actually a tot of rum.

Graham had just got to the bar for a refill when he heard somebody call his name. Turning around he was pleased to see Tom Fletcher.

'How's things mate?' Tom asked.

'Quiet now with the season over but still plenty to keep me busy, but tell me about you. How long are you back for this time?'

'Probably a month this time, bookings have been down a lot, so I have a bit of time on my hands. But where's that lovely wife of yours?'

'Why don't you come and join us, we've got some guests staying.'

Tom was very much the gentleman, kissing Viv on the cheek and then instead of shaking Sally's hand he gave a little bow and then placed a light kiss on her hand. Becky giggled and solemnly he kissed her hand as well.

While Tom and Graham caught up on the latest news, Viv told Sally a bit about the debonair gentleman. Tom had been raised in Stratton but was younger than Sally so their different paths had never crossed. One of the son's of a poor family, he had risen above his background by first gaining a decent education at the grammar school in Barnstaple and then entering the navy. Now he was an officer on a cruise ship, but soon was due for retirement.

Sally looked thoughtful, 'he would have been a young child when Nathan came back to Halleswell Hall,' she remarked.

'Well, yes he was,' Viv replied.

'Then he could have known of Nathan?'

'What's that?' Tom said, catching part of the conversation.

'If you're talking about the squire then, yes, I knew him quite well when I was a lad.'

'You never told me this before.' Graham sounded surprised.

'You never asked,' Tom said, 'and to be honest I preferred to keep the memories of the Squire to myself. He'd been good to me as a child and I was barely in my teens when he died. It was Mister Nathan that made me knuckle down at school and when I passed my eleven plus to grammar school he was as proud as punch.'

Sally's old eyes glittered, 'I think we would all love to know what he was like, you see there's a mystery around him that we have been trying to solve.'

Tom looked guarded, 'I don't know as how I could be of help, Mr Nathan didn't like to talk about himself that much.' Without knowing it he had started to slip back into the local accent.

Becky had been quiet for too long, 'was he another of the pirates then?' she beamed at him. 'Uncle Graham says there were lots of pirates around the big house and I do love those stories. Perhaps that why the pretty lady always looks so sad, oh do tell us Mr Tom, sir?'

He looked confused as Becky spoke about the 'pretty lady', glancing at Graham he sought to take the lead from him.

'Becky is Sally's granddaughter; Sally was stationed at Halleswell Hall in the war. She found the journal that old Mr Alex wrote and brought it to us a few months back. Certain things in the journal have raised questions that we all want to find out about. Sally and Becky are staying with us for a while to help Viv with a project that we can't talk about here.'

'Tell him about the lady,' Becky was being forceful once more.

'Now just you shush young madam, we don't want to go telling anyone about her,' Graham was not to be sidetracked by what he thought was just an abundance of imagination.

'Why not come to the house for dinner tomorrow and then we can talk properly?'

'How can I turn down such an offer with three beautiful ladies,' Tom was full of charm.

'Will seven pm suit you, as this young madam needs little excuse to stay up way past her bedtime?'

'Fine by me,' Tom replied, and in an aside to Graham he whispered about his duty-free whiskey.

Viv and Sally were excited about the thought of a party; Sally had been charmed by Tom and was still up to a bit of flirting, after all, he may be younger than her but he was a fine figure of a man. They still had a joint of beef in the freezer from the hamper, Viv planned on having a choice of garlic mushrooms or fresh prawns as a starter. It was Becky that made the suggestion of having the meal at the big house.

'No, that's not possible, it would take ages to get the place clean,' Viv thought about all the work it would involve.

Graham surprised her by saying it was a good idea, 'we can use the smaller kitchen, it's fairly modern and it's near to that cosy dining room. Why not have it there, it'll be fun to play the Lord of the manor.'

'Right then, you make sure everything's in working order while Sally and I are out shopping.'

Becky was feeling very pleased with herself. She had been in the clearing early that morning and had seen the lady once again. She thought that maybe the lady had put it in her mind to ask about the party being held in the big house, even if she was wrong she thought that the sailor man would help them. Soon mummy would come and take them home so they had to find the cup and those books. Becky wasn't stupid; by being quiet she had heard a lot and thought she understood much more than the grown-ups thought they did.

She was glad to help Uncle Graham; he was cleaning the kitchen while she found all the fancy tablecloths and the cutlery. Now all she had left to do was to find some wine glasses and those little whiskey glasses. Spending time with her Nan she knew all about setting a table properly, also she had heard that whisper about a nice bottle of whiskey. Secretly she thought that all sailors, especially pirates, should drink rum, but that was a minor point.

The kitchen was still big, but not as big as the one where she had found the shiny silver cutlery and the lovely white tablecloth.

'Uncle Graham,' she called out, 'can you get me that little ladder, I need it to find some glasses.'

'Just you be careful,' he said as he brought in the little kitchen steps.

The glasses were on a shelf just above the plates. Carefully she took them down, two at a time. Graham came in then and helped her with the big bottle that he called a decanter.

'Hand me down those little glasses,' he said.

Becky had to reach far back to get to the tiny glasses.

'How many do you want?' She asked.

'Just four,' he replied, 'you're too young for whiskey.'

She passed down four of the little glasses and that was when she felt the tingle in her arm. There was something hidden at the back of the shelves, she felt a little shock, like the time she had twisted one of the Christmas lights on their tree. Her fingers reached back and touched something like a big goblet. It was like the brandy glasses they had at special occasions. Inch by inch she brought it into the light and very nearly fell off the stairs. Never had she felt the presence of the lady so close to her. Taking it carefully down the steps she put it onto the table and just stared at it.

Up close it looked like a plain pottery mug, the kind you saw in gift shops, but there was a line around the top that looked like silver.

'Look what I've found,' she told Graham. 'It looks sort of ordinary but when you hold it up to the light it's like it has been filled with water and see how it glows.'

He took it carefully from her hands; he could see that it was something far different from the other things in the house. Still, it came as a shock when he picked it up. Suddenly the ever-present pain in his back had vanished, leaving him feeling like a young man again.

Could it really be the cup that Viv and Sally were so sure belonged in the old well in Brannon's Wood? It seemed so plain with only the silver filigree pattern to suggest that it was more than just a piece of old pottery. Holding it up to the light he agreed with Becky, the inside seemed to shimmer.

'Let's keep it a secret for just a while,' he told the child.

The evening was a great success. Candlelight gleamed softly on the heavily laden table, whilst the kitchen was full of normal electric light. Viv and Graham took it in turns to dish up the various courses, enjoying the company and the chance to entertain properly again.

Sally looked a picture in her dark evening trousers with a

light beige twin set. Her white hair glowed like a halo around her head, the Sapphire brooch she wore winked in the light. Viv had dressed up as well, the long green velvet skirt and matching blouse a perfect foil to her chestnut hair.

Tom looked every inch the naval officer with his navy blazer and fawn slacks. Graham guessed he was probably in his late 50s or early sixties. He hadn't done so bad himself, with a white shirt and black trousers, although Becky had teased him that he looked like a high-class waiter with his jaunty red dickey-bow.

It was Becky though that had outdone them all. Granted permission to look through all the trunks of old clothes, she had settled on a jade green dress adorned with what looked like peacocks around the hem.

Eventually they all decided they could not eat another morsel, so Graham brought in the decanter of the finest Scotch.

Conversation flowed freely ranging from politics to local affairs. Becky shifted in her seat; she wanted to know about the pirates.

'I'll tell you in a little while,' Tom said, and Sally gave her permission for the child to play at billiards in the adjourning room.

With the child out of earshot Tom started to tell them all about Nathan. Though he had been so young at the time, his memory was still clear. With rising astonishment they heard about the man and to a lesser degree his lovely wife, who Nathan had spoken about so often. Once he had even shown Tom the miniature portraits in the locket. It was Sally that voiced the question on everyone's lips.

'I know this sounds daft, but there is a remarkable resemblance to Becky's 'pretty lady'.'

Graham took a long draught of the whiskey, 'I'm inclined to agree with the child, although I have never seen or heard of anything strange until this very day. Sorry Viv, I know that the early disturbances put us both on edge but we haven't seen or heard much since the early days.'

Tom chose his words carefully, 'my dad wouldn't go near the woods even when we didn't have a penny between us. He said that the woods were haunted and the house and family were damned.'

Sally nodded as if to say she agreed with him, it also fitted the events in the journal.

'My dad was a poacher, although the woods were said to be free to all. That came from Mr Theo's time, when he set traps for the unwary. After Mister Nathan come home he said we could take what we wanted from the woods, but people have long memories in these parts and it took a while before we felt easy again.'

Tom's revelations had loosened their tongues and before they knew it they were talking rapidly about Alex's journal and the missing cup. Graham thought it wise to stay silent at this point. He needed time to think although there was more to it than that.

The talk drifted back to the generations of the Meverall's and that was the moment when Becky re-joined them. Quick on the uptake she steered the conversation around to the pirates once again.

'I think it's time you went to bed young lady,' Sally said.

'Please Nan; let me stay up a bit longer, it's really important.'

'Let her stay,' Graham agreed.

'I keep asking about the pirates but nobody will tell me anything about them. I think it's important, honestly, it's all about those books you keep looking for.'

They were stunned into silence; none of then knew how the child had heard about that.

'I think she could well be right,' Tom stated. 'Just think about the history of the Meverall's, they were fond of the sea and we know that some smuggling went on both in the village and the Hall. If I had to make a guess I would say that there are cellars deep inside the ground and what better place to hide something as important as the family history?'

'There are cellars,' Viv said, 'though there's little more than mouse droppings and a few things scratched on the walls.'

'What sort of things?' Tim asked.

'Markings, some like circles, others crosses, wavy lines, I don't remember them all.'

Tom was clearly excited, 'there were many ways to mark a barrel. Brandy was normally three X's, Whiskey a circle; wine could be the wavy line. I'd have to look to see if I could recognise them...possibly there could be hidden recesses plastered over?'

'Why don't you drop in at about 11 o'clock,' Graham said as he topped up Tom's glass,

'We could look around the cellars for a few hours and then

pop back to the Smugglers for a few pints?'

'That's an excellent idea,' Viv was keen for Graham to have some male company. Even if it were a dead end once again, then at least he would be more relaxed.

They were just agreeing on the details when Becky reappeared, her hands holding a cloth-bound bundle. Acting in the manner of a conjurer she whipped off the cloth to reveal the pottery cup.

Seconds passed by, though it seemed like minutes. Eventually Viv stretched out her hand and a delightful shiver run down her spine. Wordlessly she nodded to Sally and the older woman stretched out her own hand, jerking back with an expression of surprise on her face.

'I felt like this once before,' she told them, 'we generally used the smaller kitchen to brew some tea and it was my turn to get the cups out. I couldn't quite reach the back of the shelf so I just felt around and the next thing I knew I was flat on my back with my fingers tingling.'

It was Tom's turn to touch the cup. He passed his hand lightly over the cup and his face lit up with a huge smile.

'It's just like riding on Hero,' he said, recalling that special day so long ago.

They couldn't take their eyes off it; to each it had given them a feeling of health and vitality, but also a vision of the past or the future.

'What shall we do with it for now?' Viv said quietly.

It was Becky that answered, 'put it back where I found it for now, it's been there for years, so a few more days won't matter.'

She sounded so grown up, Graham thought, but then she put her arms around his neck and told him she was tired.

Tucking her up in bed that night he realised why Viv longed so much for a grandchild, all the way back from the Hall he smelt her hair, the childish aroma he had had forgotten when he had first held his daughter in his arms. Whatever happened next he knew he would never forget this night.

'It's impossible,' Tom said as he gazed around the large cellar. 'We could search for years and never find anything.'

Graham was inclined to agree, the cellar stretched the full

length of the great hall. It had obviously been built with the founding of the house. In places some of the original foundations were showing through, in others there had been attempts to patch it up. Even with his own knowledge of building materials he couldn't say for sure which parts were ancient and which were more modern. There was so much debris that later generations could have used much of the old brickwork. In a house of this age, the cellars would have been fully stocked with kegs of many types of drinks. Small beer had been brewed for centuries, it was a staple part of many such houses, and even the women and children would have drunk it with their meals. Brandy would have been left to mature in kegs while all kinds of wine would have been imported, either legally or more often illegally. Bribes to the local magistrates were an expected part of the commerce of the early ages. With a large and important house as Halleswell had once been, who could tell, in later generations, which were which?

Now the cellars were empty and he couldn't envision any of the Meverall's finding a hiding-place in this vast room.

'Let's call it a day and go to the pub,' he told Tom.

As they supped their ale they had no idea what the women were up to back in the lodge.

'Just look at this passage,' Viv showed Sally.

In Alex's clear round hand they saw the parts of the history when George had first carried on the smuggling started by his ancestors.

'He talks about the villagers as if they were kin to him. What I'd like to know is how such a small village could hide such bounty from the Excise men?'

'They didn't,' Sally remarked, 'of course there's many a hidden cove around these parts, I played in some as a child. No,' she said thoughtfully, 'my guess is that there was a passage from the wood to the cellars. It would be common sense at that time. If the villagers were caught then the master of the house would be implicated in some way, it was almost a law then. Of course some slipped through the net, yet the master of the house would never allow them to stand on their own, at least if Alex's observations were right.'

Viv was starting to get excited, 'then we look for hidden

doors or passageways?'

'I don't think so, that would be far too obvious. The old routes would now be bricked up and yet my guess is that there were passages leading to the main kitchens, just imagine an excise man trying to get through a crowded kitchen? Women were much tougher then, they would never let such a source of income pass by their hands.'

'Bless you Sally; I do believe you are right. But how would the barrels get into the cellars?'

'Come with me and I'll show you.'

The passage leading from the kitchens was dank and cheerless, but Sally never gave it a second look. The two women stepped carefully down the winding stairs and emerged into a tiny room little larger than a walk in pantry.

'Look at the old wooden hampers,' Sally said.

Viv peered inside and a waft of decayed material assaulted her nostrils.

'These are the remnants of old washing,' she said cheerfully. 'They didn't go in for much washing in those days. Anything that couldn't be washed was dumped into the cellars ready for the tinkers. Now where's the door out of here?'

Viv slumped against the nearest wall; she was tired and dusty and fed up of the whole thing.

With a suddenness that made her yell she found herself slipping backwards as a great hole appeared in the wall. What had looked like solid brick was actually a thin layer of plaster over rotting wood. Peering forwards into the gloom she went feet first down a chute, landing in an ungainly heap in the depths of the cellar.

Sally laughed a clear ringing sound in that awful place.

'Hang on Viv, I'm coming down.'

'Lower yourself down gently, it's only a few feet and I'll catch you.'

When both women were safely down, and had stopped shaking from their fright, they shone the torch into the depths of the hole they had made. There, in a deep niche they found what they were looking for.

It took the whole of the next day to bring the journals up from the hidden room. Excited though they were, both Sally and Viv needed time to recover. Graham just took the one book so they could see if it was the real thing.

The next few days passed swiftly by as volume after volume gave up their secrets. By then they knew that they needed an expert in old languages to decipher the earlier books. Soon it would be time for Nicola to pick her mother and daughter up, but how could they leave Sally in such suspense?

It was Becky that put them all in their places.

'I don't think those dusty old books mean that much,' she announced, 'Cept for the fact that Nan found them for you. What is important is that the cup goes back to the well where it belongs and the lady can go home.'

'She's right,' Sally replied, 'I have loved being here but even the cup can't stop old age from creeping up on me. I want to be here at the end though, when you put the cup back in the well and I do hope that you will agree to have the journals put on display. From the bits that I have read it's a lovely story and will keep the visitors coming back year after year. There is also the question about who owns the woods, from the bit I have read I think the woods belong to the house and to the village. I, for one, would love to hear the sound of children laughing in the woods once again.'

Viv and Graham went to hug her. Tom stood in the background looking rather shy.

'I would like to meet the rest of your family,' he said, 'if they are as lovely as you and your grand-daughter then I would be honoured to meet them.'

Sally chuckled, 'I do believe that's an invitation to court me, but I warn you I'm very set in my ways. '

Tom blushed, he had never married but he was genuinely interested in this lovely woman.

'That's a date then,' he said, surprising himself.

They left a few days later, Sally beaming like a new bride. Graham and Viv felt quite lonely after they had left, though there was so much left to do. Should they bring in experts to decipher the book when Alex had done so much already?

The answer was found half way down the pile of books; it was a letter from Nathan, the last of the Meverall family.

To whom it may concern.

If you have read this far then you will know how much my family means to me. Only a very special person would have found these journals and I trust that person to make the correct decision whether or not these should be put on display. I was blessed with everything a man could wish for, a devoted and lovely wife. We never had children of our own but we had more children than anyone could have wished for and each of them was dear to our hearts.

Once my beloved wife passed away I returned to this place I now call home, yet part of my thoughts are still back in India where I learnt love, compassion and the belief that every person born to this earth is equal in their own right.

Few people know that Halleswell Hall is kept open by a trust fund that I set up when I knew that my days were getting shorter. Much of this goes to the hospital and orphanage that was set up by my wife and me in India.

Halleswell Hall has stood for many generations and with each generation there are both good and bad people, but it is my belief that we all have that spark of the Divine in our souls. If you believe in this you will know what it is you must do. I count my life as one of goodness and servitude to the people who have relied on me, my failure being the loss of the Holy Cup that belongs in the well near where my family lies in peace with me. My one wish is that if it is ever found that it be replaced where it belongs.

There comes a time when each man or woman will stand up for what they believe in, that day may be far away but each kind action, each reaching out to another in need brings that time much nearer.

Whatever you decide to do, I ask only this, that the document signed by King Charles 11 establishes the right for the villagers to have permanent access to Brannon's Wood.

May your God bless you and keep you in his heart forever,
Nathan Irving-Meverall.

Viv and Graham then knew what they must do, such courage, such love belonged to everyone. That night they slept a deep and fulfilling sleep.

EPILOGUE

Winter came early to Devon that year. A light drift of snow bathed Halleswell Hall in a carpet of white, decorating the great oak trees with a pristine pattern of white against brown. Branches sighed with the weight of the unaccustomed snow whilst the lake in front of the house glittered with jewel-bright frost. With two weeks left before Christmas the unofficial ceremony took on a special appeal. The great house stood as usual, the covering of winter's display could not change its gloomy visage, yet it, too, seemed to be holding it's breath with a strange foreboding.

The little group gathered around the clearing were well wrapped up against the chill of the early afternoon. Viv was concerned about Sally's health, yet the older woman seemed to radiate a calm warmth of her own making. Tom stood to one side of her, his face red with the cold. Becky looked a picture with her blonde hair tucked sensibly under a bright red bobble-hat. In her hands she held a bright bouquet of winter flowers. Graham fidgeted nervously, his whole being revolting against the ancient ceremony he was about to observe.

Yet it was the vicar, Martin Boyd, who seemed more out of place than the small group gathered there that day.

Vivien's hands trembled slightly as she bore the cloth-wrapped bundle to its true resting place. It had been her task to talk the vicar into this ceremony when all his instincts were to keep the Holy Relic for the church. He had read the manuscripts but doubts had assailed him until Viv had threatened to throw the cup into the well and damn the consequences.

Now they moved as one towards the well that was said to belong to all those of true faith.

Viv unwrapped the cup and in her hands it sprang to life with a fire of gold that put every sunrise and sunset to shame.

'Take it and conceal it where once it rested,' she said, looking into the face of the vicar. Hesitantly he stepped forward; suddenly he wondered if he was truly up to the task. Then he held the cup in his hands and knew what he should say.

'Many years ago a humble man of God came to these shores. His heart was true and his faith was pure. He built a community here of tolerance and respect. He knew that God had called him to guide the poor and the humble of heart. In our church we have revered him as a saint, but he was a man of the people and so we should never forget the lesson we have learnt. That all who came to him were never turned away, whatever sins they had made in life. Now this cup that was said to have wrought many miracles will be placed back in the well from whence it came. In the spirit of Brannon's faith I cannot do this deed. My faith faltered but one here has that purity of spirit.'

So it was Becky who, guided by Graham's hand nimbly climbed down and placed the cup into its alcove. That she knew exactly where to place it was no surprise to Viv or, indeed, to any of the party assembled there. If any had expected some miraculous happening, then they were to be disappointed, a slight waft of stale air drifted upwards, but that was all. In accordance with the instructions laid down by the National Trust, the well covering was screwed back into place. It was far too old and valuable to leave open to visitors who might damage the old brickwork.

It was a short step back to the clearing where the later generations of the Meverall family had been laid to rest. The vicar once again consecrated the ground where his predecessor had gone before. The ceremony was simple and yet it touched the hearts of all that were present that day.

'You can lay your flowers now,' Sally told her granddaughter.

Becky skipped ahead and laid her bouquet on the grave.

From somewhere a breeze blew, though the day had been cold and still. Dead leaves swirled around the grave and spiralled upwards.

'The pretty lady can go home now,' Becky said, 'the big cat's going home as well.'

The rest of the group started towards the gatehouse and the meal that awaited them. It was Viv that hung back and saw the bouquet resting on the small grave.

The headstone was very plain and simple.

'In Peace at Last', she read the inscription. 'Zara, beloved daughter of Alex.'

*

There is a certain kind of light that enhances the glow of a winter sunset on a snowy landscape. Painters have sought throughout the centuries to capture that hint of pink with the deeper touch of chill blue. None ever come close, for it's something that is glimpsed through the eyes yet held deep in the heart for all time.

Brannon's Wood lay calm and still under its burden of snow. For centuries it had stood there throughout the small lives of men. A traveller would catch a glimpse of the old house through the trees and wonder idly about the lives of the people who once had lived in that splendid mansion house. The traveller might buy a ticket and listen to the soft voice of the elderly woman that gave the guided tours. For some, imagination would people the Hall with all kinds of speculation, but who now could tell the truth of a family that had occupied it for nearly five hundred years?

To be sure there were the guidebooks that told of the history of both the building and the legends attached to the ancient woods. Others could buy a potted history of the Meverall family as taken from the journals of the inhabitants. Stirring stories of battles fought, lost or won, tales of the great people who lived there and made their mark on the annals of history.

Under the glass casing, visitors could glimpse a page of history in the old English writing that few could now read.

What they would never know would have startled some and led others into a profound state of enchantment. What they could never know is that life changes little down the centuries from the dawn of time. People are born into different states of life. Some are born to riches, others are destined to be poor and humble. Yet all share the same aspirations, the hopes and dreams of a better, brighter future. Children are born, grow up, marry, have children of their own and if they are very lucky they find love and contentment in their lives. For, in the end, it is always love that carries down through the ages, unchanged by any historical event.

Brannon's Wood may have been sacred to many and brought about miracles, but to the villagers it was a place to draw water, to bag a rabbit and occasionally a bird to fill the empty bellies of the poor. Children played beneath the ancient oaks, lovers met there to become, in turn parents of the children that picked the wild flowers growing amidst the forest glades. Who now could tell the difference between the child in her bonnet or the modern child with their noisy music and the same problems faced by any young person seeking to make their own way in life?

The trees kept their age-old secrets, the village people went about their own business and if sometimes the old rumours were gossiped about in the "Smuggler's Arms", why that was a country tradition and who could argue with that?

NOTES

Although we have tried to keep the different languages to a minimum, it has been necessary to use the languages of the times in certain parts of the narrative. We apologise in advance for the use of the various local accents. Over time accents change, therefore we have used an idealistic view of the Devon accent in particular. It is doubtful that the current Devon accent belonged in Olde Worlde English, but by staying fairly consistent throughout the narrative we have tried not to tread on too many toes.

1. Sir there are soldiers approaching the castle, a large number that outnumber us ten to one. They also have siege equipment. They must mean to take the castle.
2. Marcel, set the defences and send someone to fetch Captain Fletcher's guests. They will be leaving now

Some careful use is made of the Hindu religion as the heroine tries to balance her negative and positive attitudes to life. This is not a statement of the author's beliefs, but an answer to the problem posed by the Meverall Family 'Curse'. A Glossary of some of the terms used is shown here

Avatars – The embodiment of Gods in human form.
Bapu (Ghandi) – an honourary title of 'Father', used by the Indian people with respect.
dhoti – a peasant garment worn by many of the lower classes of the Indian People.
Krishna– an avatar of the gods mainly benign & mischievous.
Kusha (Grass) – Used in the cremation rituals for the Hindu religion. Usually the honour goes to the elder son.
Namaste – Traditional Hindu respectful greeting.
Yama – The god of death in many Indian religions, mostly the Hindu cremation ceremony.